BLOOD MEMORY

BOOKS BY GREG ILES

Featuring Penn Cage

Mississippi Blood
The Bone Tree
Natchez Burning
The Death Factory (a novella)
The Devil's Punchbowl
Turning Angel
The Quiet Game

Other Works

Third Degree
True Evil
Blood Memory
The Footprints of God
Sleep No More
Dead Sleep
24 Hours
Mortal Fear
Black Cross
Spandau Phoenix

TRUE EVIL

GREG ILES

POCKET BOOKS

NEW YORK   LONDON   TORONTO   SYDNEY   NEW DELHI

Pocket Books
An Imprint of Simon & Schuster, Inc.
1230 Avenue of the Americas
New York, NY 10020

This book is a work of fiction. Names, characters, places, and incidents either are products of the author's imagination or are used fictitiously. Any resemblance to actual events or locales or persons, living or dead, is entirely coincidental.

This Pocket Books mass market edition May 2022

POCKET and colophon are registered trademarks of Simon & Schuster, Inc.

For information regarding special discounts for bulk purchases, please contact Simon & Schuster Special Sales at 1-866-506-1949 or business@simonandschuster.com.

The Simon & Schuster Speakers Bureau can bring authors to your live event. For more information or to book an event, contact the Simon & Schuster Speakers Bureau at 1-866-248-3049 or visit our website at www.simonspeakers.com.

Cover design by Jae Song

Manufactured in the United States of America

10 9 8 7 6 5 4 3 2 1

ISBN 978-1-9821-8732-3
ISBN 978-1-4165-4533-0 (ebook)

IN MEMORY

Mike McGraw and Ryan Buttross

True evil has a face you know
and a voice you trust.

—Anonymous

TRUE
EVIL

CHAPTER

1

Alex Morse charged through the lobby of the new University Medical Center like a doctor to a code call, but she was no doctor. She was a hostage negotiator for the FBI. Twenty minutes earlier, Alex had deplaned from a flight from Charlotte, North Carolina, to Jackson, Mississippi, a flight prompted by her older sister's sudden collapse at a Little League baseball game. This year had been plagued by injury and death, and there was more to come—Alex could feel it.

Sighting the elevators, she checked the overhead display and saw that a car was descending. She hit the call button and started bouncing on her toes. *Hospitals,* she thought bitterly. She'd practically just gotten out of one herself. But the chain of tragedy had started with her father. Five months ago Jim Morse had died in this very hospital, after being shot during a robbery. Two months after that, Alex's mother had been diagnosed with advanced ovarian cancer. She had already outlived her prognosis, but wasn't expected to survive the week. Then came Alex's accident. And now Grace—

A bell dinged softly, and the elevator opened.

A young woman wearing a white coat over street clothes leaned against the rear wall in a posture of absolute exhaustion. *Intern,* Alex guessed. She'd met enough of them during the past month. The woman glanced up as Alex entered the car, then looked down. Then she looked up again. Alex had endured this double take so many times since the shooting that she no longer got angry. Just depressed.

"What floor?" asked the young woman, raising her hand to the panel and trying hard not to stare.

"Neuro ICU," said Alex, stabbing the 4 with her finger.

"I'm going down to the basement," said the intern, who looked maybe twenty-six—four years younger than Alex. "But it'll take you right up after that."

Alex nodded, then stood erect and watched the glowing numbers change above her head. After her mother's diagnosis, she'd begun commuting by plane from Washington, D.C.—where she was based then—to Mississippi to relieve Grace, who was struggling to teach full-time and also to care for their mother at night. Unlike J. Edgar Hoover's FBI, the modern Bureau tried to be understanding about family problems, but in Alex's case the deputy director had made his position clear: time off to attend a funeral was one thing, regularly commuting a thousand miles to be present for chemotherapy was another. But Alex had not listened. She'd bucked the system and learned to live without sleep. She told herself she could hack the pressure, and she did—right up until the moment she cracked. The problem was, she hadn't realized she'd cracked until she caught part of a shotgun blast in her right shoulder and face. Her vest had protected the shoulder, but her face was still an open question.

For a hostage negotiator, Alex had committed the ultimate sin, and she'd come close to paying the ultimate price. Because the shooter had fired through a plate-glass partition, what would have been a miraculous escape (being grazed by a couple of pellets that could have blown her brains out but hadn't) became a life-altering trauma. A blizzard of glass tore through her cheek, sinuses, and jaw, lacerating her skin and ripping away tissue and bone. The plastic surgeons had promised great things, but so far the results were less than stellar. They'd told her that in time the angry pink worms would whiten (they could do little to repair the "punctate" depressions in her cheek), and that laymen wouldn't even notice the damage. Alex wasn't convinced. But in the grand scheme of things, what did vanity matter? Five seconds after she was shot, someone else *had* paid the ultimate price for her mistake.

During the hellish days that followed the shooting, Grace had flown up to D.C. three times to be with Alex, despite being exhausted from taking care of their mother. Grace was the family martyr, a genuine candidate for sainthood. The irony was staggering: tonight it was Grace lying in an intensive care unit, fighting for her life.

And why? Certainly not karma. She'd been walking up the steps of a stadium to watch her ten-year-old son play baseball when she collapsed. Seconds after she hit the stairs, she voided her bladder and bowels. A CAT scan taken forty minutes later showed a blood clot near Grace's brain stem, the kind of clot that too often killed people. Alex had been swimming laps in Charlotte when she got word (having been transferred there as punishment duty after the shooting). Her mother was too upset to be coherent on the phone, but she'd communicated enough details to send Alex racing to the airport.

When the first leg of her flight touched down in Atlanta, Alex had used her Treo to call Grace's husband, whom she'd been unable to reach before boarding the plane. Bill Fennell explained that while the neurological damage had initially not looked too bad—some right-side paralysis, weakness, mild dysphasia—the stroke seemed to be worsening, which the doctors said was not uncommon. A neurologist had put Grace on TPA, a drug that could dissolve clots but also carried serious risks of its own. Bill Fennell was a commanding man, but his voice quavered as he related this, and he begged Alex to hurry.

When her plane landed in Jackson, Alex called Bill again. This time he sobbed as he related the events of the past hour. Though still breathing on her own, Grace had lapsed into a coma and might die before Alex could cover the fifteen miles from the airport. A panic unlike any she had known since childhood filled her chest. Though the plane had only begun its taxi to the terminal, Alex snatched her carry-on from beneath the seat and marched to the front of the 727. When a flight attendant challenged her, she flashed her FBI creds and quietly told the man to get her to the terminal ASAP. When she cleared the gate, she sprinted down the concourse and through baggage claim, then jumped the cab queue, flashed her creds again, and told the driver she'd give him $100 to drive a hundred miles an hour to the University Medical Center.

Now here she was, stepping out of the elevator on the fourth floor, sucking in astringent smells that hurled her four weeks back in time, when hot blood had poured from her face as though from a spigot. At the end of the corridor waited a huge wooden door marked NEUROL-

OGY ICU. She went through it like a first-time parachutist leaping from a plane, steeling herself for free fall, terrified of the words she was almost certain to hear: *I'm sorry, Alex, but you're too late.*

The ICU held a dozen glass-walled cubicles built in a U-shape around the nurses' station. Several cubicles were curtained off, but through the transparent wall of the fourth from the left, Alex saw Bill Fennell talking to a woman in a white coat. At six feet four, Bill towered over her, but his handsome face was furrowed with anxiety, and the woman seemed to be comforting him. Sensing Alex's presence, he looked up and froze in midsentence. Alex moved toward the cubicle. Bill rushed to the door and hugged her to his chest. She'd always felt awkward embracing her brother-in-law, but tonight there was no way to avoid it. And no reason, really. Tonight they both needed some kind of contact, an affirmation of family unity.

"You must have taken a helicopter," he said in his resonant bass voice. "I can't believe you made it that fast."

"Is she alive?"

"She's still with us," Bill said in a strangely formal tone. "She's actually regained consciousness a couple of times. She's been asking for you."

Alex's heart lifted, but with hope came fresh tears.

The woman in the white coat walked out of the cubicle. She looked about fifty, and her face was kind but grave.

"This is Grace's neurologist," Bill said.

"I'm Meredith Andrews," said the woman. "Are you the one Grace calls KK?"

Alex couldn't stop her tears. KK was a nickname

derived from her middle name, which was a family appellation: Karoli. "Yes. But please call me Alex. Alex Morse."

"Special Agent Morse," Bill said in an absurd interjection.

"Has Grace asked for me?" Alex asked, wiping her cheeks.

"You're all she can talk about."

"Is she conscious?"

"Not at this moment. We're doing everything we can, but you should prepare yourself for"—Dr. Andrews gave Alex a lightning-fast appraisal—"you should prepare for the worst. Grace had a serious thrombosis when she was brought in, but she was breathing on her own, and I was encouraged. But the stroke extended steadily, and I decided to start thrombolytic therapy. To try to dissolve the clot. This can sometimes produce miracles, but it can also cause hemorrhages elsewhere in the brain or body. I have a feeling that may be happening now. I don't want to risk moving Grace for an MRI. She's still breathing on her own, and that's the best hope we have. If she stops breathing, we're ready to intubate immediately. I probably should have done it already"—Dr. Andrews glanced at Bill—"but I knew she was desperate to talk to you, and once she's intubated, she won't be able to communicate with anyone. She's already lost her ability to write words."

Alex winced.

"Don't be shocked if she manages to speak to you. Her speech center has been affected, and she has significant impairment."

"I understand," Alex said impatiently. "We had an uncle who had a stroke. Can I just be with her? I don't care what her condition is. I have to be with her."

Dr. Andrews smiled and led Alex into the room.

As she reached the door, Alex turned back to Bill. "Where's Jamie?"

"With my sister in Ridgeland."

Ridgeland was a white-flight suburb ten miles away. "Did he see Grace fall?"

Bill shook his head somberly. "No, he was down on the field. He just knows his mother's sick, that's all."

"Don't you think he should be here?"

Alex had tried to keep all judgment out of her voice, but Bill's face darkened. He seemed about to snap at her, but then he drew a deep breath and said, "No, I don't."

When Alex kept staring at him, he lowered his voice and added, "I don't want Jamie to watch his mother die."

"Of course not. But he should have a chance to say good-bye."

"He'll get that," Bill said. "At the funeral."

Alex closed her eyes and gritted her teeth. "Bill, you can't—"

"We don't have time for this." He nodded into the room where Dr. Andrews stood waiting.

Alex walked slowly to the edge of Grace's bed. The pale face above the hospital blanket did not look familiar. And yet it did. It looked like her mother's face. Grace Morse Fennell was thirty-five years old, but tonight she looked seventy. *It's her skin,* Alex realized. *It's like wax. Drooping wax.* She had the sense that the muscles that controlled her sister's face had gone slack and would never contract again. Grace's eyes were closed, and to Alex's surprise, she felt this was a mercy. It gave her time to adjust to the new reality, however fleeting that reality might be.

"Are you all right?" Dr. Andrews asked from behind her.

"Yes."

"I'll leave you with her, then."

Alex glanced at the bank of CRTs monitoring Grace's life functions. Heartbeat, oxygen saturation, blood pressure, God knew what else. A single IV line disappeared beneath a bandage on her forearm; Alex's wrist ached at the sight. She wasn't sure what to do, and maybe it didn't matter. Maybe the important thing was just to be here.

"You know what this tragedy has taught me?" asked the familiar bass voice.

Alex jumped but tried to hide her discomfiture. She hadn't realized Bill was in the room, and she hated showing any sign of weakness. "What?" she said, though she didn't really care about the answer.

"Money isn't really worth anything. All the money in the world won't make that blood clot go away."

Alex nodded distantly.

"So, what the hell have I been working for?" Bill asked. "Why haven't I just kicked back and spent every second I could with Grace?"

Grace probably asked the same question a thousand times, Alex thought. But it was too late for regrets. A lot of people thought Bill was a cold fish. Alex had always thought he tended to be maudlin.

"Could I be alone with her for a while?" Alex asked, not taking her eyes from Grace's face.

She felt a strong hand close on her shoulder—the wounded shoulder—and then Bill said, "I'll be back in five minutes."

After he'd gone, Alex took Grace's clammy hand in

hers and bent to kiss her forehead. She had never seen her sister so helpless. In fact, she had never seen Grace close to helpless. Grace was a dynamo. Crises that brought others' lives to a standstill hardly caused her to break stride. But this was different. This was the end— Alex could tell. She knew it the way she had known when James Broadbent went down after she was shot. James had watched Alex charge into the bank just seconds ahead of the go-order for the Hostage Rescue Team, and he had gone in right behind her. He saw her take the shotgun blast, but instead of instantly returning fire at the shooter, he'd glanced down to see how badly Alex was hurt. For that concern he'd caught the second blast square in the chest. He wasn't wearing a vest (he'd taken it off upon learning that the HRT was going in), and the shotgun chopped his heart and lungs into something you saw behind a butcher's counter. *Why did he look down?* Alex wondered for the millionth time. *Why did he follow me in at all?* But she knew the answer. Broadbent had followed her because he loved her—from a distance, true, but the emotion was no less real for that. And that love had killed him. Alex saw tears falling on Grace's cheeks—her own tears, numberless these past months. She wiped her eyes, then took out her cell phone and called Bill Fennell, who was standing less than thirty feet away.

"What is it?" he asked frantically. "What's wrong?"

"Jamie should be here."

"Alex, I told you—"

"You get him, goddamn it. This is his *mother* lying here."

There was a long silence. Then Bill said, "I'll call my sister."

On impulse, Alex turned and saw him standing near the nurses' station. He'd been talking to Dr. Andrews. She saw him disengage from the neurologist and lift his cell phone to his cheek. Alex leaned down to Grace's ear and tried to think of something that would reach the bottom of the dark well where her sister now dwelled.

"Sue-Sue?" she whispered, simultaneously squeezing the cold hand. Sue-Sue was another nickname based on a middle name—a family tradition. "Sue-Sue, it's KK."

Grace's eyes remained shut.

"It's me, Sue-Sue. It's KK. I'm back from Sally's. Wake up, before Mama gets up. I want to go to the carnival."

Seconds dilated into some unknown measure of time. Memories swirled through Alex's mind, and her heart began to ache. Grace's eyes stayed shut.

"Come on, Sue-Sue. I know you're playing possum. Quit faking."

Alex felt a twitch in her hand. Adrenaline surged through her, but when she saw the frozen eyelids, she decided that the twitch must have come from her own hand.

"Kuh . . . kuh," someone coughed.

Alex turned, thinking it was Bill or Dr. Andrews, but then Grace clenched her hand and let out a sharp cry. When Alex whipped her head around, she saw Grace's green eyes wide-open. Then Grace blinked. Alex's heart soared. She leaned down over her sister, because though Grace was only thirty-five, her eyes were almost useless without glasses or contacts.

"KK?" Grace moaned. *"Iz zah wu?"*

"It's me, Gracie," Alex said, rubbing a strand of hair out of her sister's cloudy eyes.

"*Oh, Goth,*" Grace said in a guttural voice, and then she began to sob. "*Thang Godth.*"

Alex had to clench her jaw muscles to keep from sobbing. The right half of Grace's face was paralyzed, and drool ran down her chin whenever she struggled to speak. She sounded exactly like Uncle T.J., who'd died after a series of strokes left him without a shred of his old identity.

"*Wu . . . wu have tuh thave Jamie,*" Grace gargled.

"What? I missed that."

"*Havuh thave Jamie!*" Grace repeated, struggling to rise in the bed. She seemed to be trying to look behind Alex.

"Jamie's fine," Alex said in a comforting voice. "He's on his way here."

Grace shook her head violently. "*Wissen! Havuh wissen!*"

"I'm listening, Sue-Sue, I promise."

Grace stared into Alex's eyes with all the urgency in her soul. "*You—have—tuh—thave—Jamie . . . Gay-Gay. You thuh . . . onwe . . . one ooh can.*"

"Save Jamie from what?"

"*Biw.*"

"Bill?" Alex asked, sure she must be wrong in her translation.

With painful effort, Grace nodded.

Alex blinked in astonishment. "What are you talking about? Is Bill hurting Jamie in some way?"

A weak nod. "*Ee wiw . . . thoon ath I'm gone.*"

Alex struggled to understand the tortured words. "Hurt Jamie how? Are you talking about some sort of abuse?"

Grace shook her head. "*Biw—wiw—kiw—Jamie's—thole.*"

Alex squinted as though trying to decipher some coded text. "Bill . . . will . . . kill . . . Jamie's . . . soul?"

Grace's head sagged in exhaustion.

"Gracie . . . Bill isn't my favorite person. You've always known that. But he's been a good father, hasn't he? He seems like a basically decent man."

Grace gripped Alex's hand and shook her head. Then she hissed, *"Eeth a monther!"*

Alex felt a chill. "He's a *monster*? Is that what you said?"

A tear of relief slid down Grace's paralyzed cheek.

Alex looked at the anguished eyes, then turned and glanced over her shoulder. Bill Fennell was still speaking to Dr. Andrews, but his eyes were on Alex.

"Ith Biw coming?" Grace asked in a terrified voice, trying in vain to twist in the bed.

"No, no. He's talking to the doctor."

"Dogtor—duthend—know."

"Doesn't know what?"

"Whuh Biw did."

"What do you mean? What did Bill do?"

Grace suddenly raised her hand and gripped Alex's blouse, then pulled her head down to her lips. *"Ee kiwd me!"*

Alex felt as though ice water had been shunted into her veins. She drew back and looked into Grace's bloodshot eyes. "He *killed* you? Is that what you said?"

Grace nodded once, her eyes filled with conviction.

"Grace, you don't know what you're saying."

Even with a partially paralyzed face, Grace managed a smile that said, *Oh, yes, I do.*

"You can't mean that. Not literally."

Grace closed her eyes as though gathering herself for one last effort. *"You . . . onwe one . . . ooh can thop im. Too . . . wate . . . fuh me. I urd . . . dogtuh . . . out thide. Thave Jamie for me . . . Gay-Gay. Pleath."*

Alex looked back through the glass wall. Bill was still watching her, and his conversation looked as if it was winding down. Alex had always known Grace's marriage wasn't perfect, but what marriage was? Not that Alex was any authority. She had somehow reached the age of thirty without tying the knot. After years of badge groupies and badge bolters, she'd finally accepted a proposal, then terminated the engagement three months later, after discovering that her fiancé was cheating with her best friend. In matters amorous, she was a ridiculous cliché.

"Sue-Sue," she whispered, "why would Bill want to hurt you?"

"Thum-one else," Grace said. *"Wuh-man."*

"Another woman? Do you know that for a fact?"

Another half-paralyzed smile. *"Uh—wife—knowth."*

Alex believed her. During her engagement to Peter Hodges, a feeling very like a sixth sense had told her something was amiss in their relationship. Long before there was any tangible clue, she'd simply known there was betrayal. If she had possessed the same instinct about conventional crimes, she'd already be an SAC instead of a hostage negotiator. *Correction,* she thought, *I'm a common field agent now.*

"If Bill wants to be with another woman," she said, "why doesn't he just divorce you?"

"Muhn-ey . . . dum-me. Would coth Biw miw-yens . . . tuh do that. Five—miwyen . . . may-be."

Alex drew back in disbelief. She'd known that Bill had

been doing well for some years now, but she'd had no idea he was that wealthy. Why in God's name was Grace still teaching elementary school? *Because she loves it,* she answered herself. *Because she can't not work.*

Grace had closed her eyes, seemingly drained by her efforts. *"Tew . . . Mom . . . I tho-we,"* she said. *"Tew huh . . . I be waiting fuh hurh . . . in heaven."* The smile animated the living half of her face again. *"If— I—make it."*

"You made it, honey," Alex said, balling her free hand into a fist and holding it against her mouth.

"Well, look at this, Dr. Andrews!" boomed Bill Fennell. "She looks like she's ready to get up and out of that bed."

Grace's eyes snapped open, and she shrank away from her husband, obviously trying to use Alex as a shield. The terror in her eyes hurt Alex's heart, and it also thrust her into full-defense mode. She stood up and blocked Bill from coming to the bedside.

"I think it's better if you don't come in," she said, looking hard into her brother-in-law's eyes.

Bill's mouth dropped open. He looked past her to Grace, who was literally cowering in the bed. "What are you talking about?" he asked angrily. "What the hell's going on here? Have you said something about me to Grace?"

Alex glanced at Dr. Andrews, who looked confused. "No. Quite the reverse, I'm afraid."

Bill shook his head in apparent puzzlement. "I don't understand."

Alex probed his brown eyes, searching for some sign of guilt. Grace's fears and accusations were probably the product of a dying woman's hallucinations, but there was no doubt about the reality of her terror. "You're upsetting her, Bill. You can see that. You should go downstairs and wait for Jamie."

"There's no way I'm going to leave my wife's bedside. Not when she might—"

"What?" Alex asked, a note of challenge in her voice.

Bill lowered his voice. "When she might . . ."

Alex looked at Dr. Andrews.

The neurologist stepped toward Bill and said, "Perhaps we should give Grace and her sister some more time alone."

"Don't try to massage me like that," Bill said irritably. "I'm Grace's husband. I'm her husband, and I'll decide who—"

"She's my *blood*," Alex said with bone-deep conviction. "Your presence here is upsetting Grace, and that's all that matters. We need to keep her as calm as possible. Isn't that right, Dr. Andrews?"

"Absolutely." Meredith Andrews walked around Alex and looked down at her patient. "Grace, do you understand me?"

"*Yeth*."

"Do you want your husband in this room?"

Grace slowly shook her head. "*I wan . . . my bay . . . be. Wan Jamie.*"

Dr. Andrews looked up at Bill Fennell, who towered over her. "That's good enough for me. I want you to leave the unit, Mr. Fennell."

Bill stepped close to the neurologist, his eyes sheened with anger. "I don't know who you think you are, or who you think you're talking to, but I give a lot of money to this university. A *lot* of money. And I—"

"Don't make me call security," Dr. Andrews said quietly, lifting the phone beside Grace's bed.

Bill's face went white. Alex almost felt sorry for him. The power had clearly passed to Dr. Andrews, but Bill seemed unable to make the decision to leave. He looked, Alex thought, like an actor on a DVD movie after you hit PAUSE. Or that's what she was thinking when the alarm began to sing.

"She's coding!" Dr. Andrews shouted through the door, but the shout was unnecessary. Nurses were already running from the station to the cubicle. Alex jumped out of their way, and an instant later Bill did the same.

"Cardiac arrest," Dr. Andrews said, yanking open a drawer.

Because this was an ICU, there was no crash cart; everything was already here. The quiet cubicle suddenly became a whirlwind of motion, all directed toward a single purpose—to sustain the life fast ebbing from the body on the bed.

"You need to leave," said a tall male nurse standing behind Dr. Andrews. "Both of you."

Dr. Andrews glanced up long enough to give Alex a moment of eye contact, then returned to work. Alex backed slowly out of the ICU, watching the final act of her sister's life unfold without any hope of playing a part herself. Ridiculous regrets about choosing law school over medical school pierced her heart. But what if she had become a doctor? She would be practicing two thousand miles away from Mississippi, and the result would be the same. Grace's fate was in God's hands now, and Alex knew how indifferent those hands could be.

She turned away from the cubicle—away from Bill Fennell—and looked at the nurses' station, where banks of monitors chirped and blinked ceaselessly. *How can they focus on all those screens at once?* she wondered, recalling how difficult it was to watch multiple surveillance feeds when the Bureau had a TV rig set up on a static post. As she thought about that, she heard Dr. Andrews say, "I'm calling it, guys. Time of death, ten twenty-nine p.m."

Shock is a funny thing, Alex thought. Like the day she was shot. Two searing chunks of buckshot and a half pound of glass had blasted through the right side of her face, yet she'd felt nothing—just a wave of heat, as if someone had opened an oven beside her.

Time of death, ten twenty-nine p.m. . . .

Something started to let go in Alex's chest, but before the release, she heard a little boy say, "Hey! Is my mom in here?"

She turned toward the big wooden door that had brought her to this particular chamber of hell and saw before it a boy about four and a half feet tall. His face was red, as though he had run all the way from wherever he'd started. He was trying to look brave, but Alex saw fear in his wide green eyes.

"Aunt Alex?" said Jamie, finally picking her out of the uniformed crowd.

Bill's big voice sounded from behind Alex. "Hello, Son. Where's Aunt Jean?"

"She's too slow," Jamie said angrily.

"Come over here, boy."

Alex looked back at her brother-in-law's stern face, and the thing that had started to let go inside her suddenly ratcheted tight. Without thought she ran to Jamie, swept him into her arms and then out the door, away from this heartrending nightmare. Away from his dying mother.

Away from Bill Fennell.

Away . . .

CHAPTER

2

Five Weeks Later

Dr. Chris Shepard lifted a manila folder from the file caddy on the door of Exam Room 4 and quickly perused it. He didn't recognize the patient's name, and that was unusual. Chris had a large practice, but it was a small town, and that was the way he liked it.

This patient's name was Alexandra Morse, and her file held only a medical history, the long form that all new patients filled out on their first visit. Chris looked down the corridor and saw Holly, his nurse, crossing from her station to the X-ray room. He called out and waved her up the hall. Holly said something through the door to X-ray, then hurried toward him.

"Aren't you coming in with me?" he asked softly. "It's a female patient."

Holly shook her head. "She asked to speak to you alone."

"New patient?"

"Yes. I meant to say something before now, but we got so busy with Mr. Seward—"

Chris nodded at the door and lowered his voice to a whisper. "What's her story?"

Holly shrugged. "Beats me. Name's Alex. Thirty years old and in great shape, except for the scars on her face."

"Scars?"

"Right side. Cheek, ear, and orbit. Head through a window is my guess."

"There's nothing about a car accident in her history."

"Couple of months ago, by the color of the scars."

Chris moved away from the door, and Holly followed. "She didn't give you any complaint?"

The nurse shook her head. "No. And you know I asked."

"Oh, boy."

Holly nodded knowingly. A woman coming in alone and refusing to specify her complaint usually meant the problem was sexual—most often fear of a sexually transmitted disease. Natchez, Mississippi, was a small town, and its nurses gossiped as much as its other citizens. *Truth be told,* Chris thought, *most doctors here are worse gossips than their nurses.*

"Her chart says Charlotte, North Carolina," he noted. "Did Ms. Morse tell you what she's doing in Natchez?"

"She told me exactly nothing," Holly said with a bit of pique. "Do you want me to shoot that flat-and-erect series on Mr. Seward before he voids on the table?"

"Sorry. Go to it."

Holly winked and whispered, "Have fun with Ms. Scarface."

Chris shook his head, then summoned a serious expression and walked into the examining room.

A woman wearing a navy skirt and a cream-colored top stood beside the examining table. Her face almost caused him to stare, but he'd seen a lot of trauma during his medical training. This woman's scars weren't actually too bad. It was her youth and attractiveness that made them stand out so vividly. Almost fiercely, Chris thought. You figured a woman who looked and dressed this way would have had plastic surgery to take care of an injury like that. Not that she was a knockout or anything; she wasn't. It was just—

"Hello, Dr. Shepard," the woman said in a direct tone.

"Ms. Morse?" he said, remembering that the history said she was single.

She gave him a smile of acknowledgment but said nothing else.

"What can I do for you today?" he asked.

The woman remained silent, but he could feel her eyes probing him as deeply as a verbal question. *What's going on here?* Chris wondered. *Is it my birthday or something? Did the staff plan some kind of trick? Or does she want drugs?* He'd had that happen before: some female patients offered sex for drugs, usually narcotics. Chris studied the woman's face, trying to divine her real purpose. She had dark hair, green eyes, and an oval face not much different from those of the dozens of women he saw each day. A little better bone structure, maybe, especially the cheekbones. But the real difference was the scars—and a shock of gray hair above them that didn't look added by a colorist. Except for those things, Alex Morse might be any woman at the local health club. And yet . . . despite her usualness, if that was a word, there was something about her that Chris couldn't quite nail down, something that set her apart from other women. Something in the way she stood, maybe.

Laying the chart on the counter behind him, he said, "Maybe you should just tell me what the problem is. I promise, however frightening it might seem now, I've seen or heard it many times in this office, and together we can do something about it. People usually feel better once they verbalize these things."

"You've never heard what I'm about to tell you," Alex Morse said with utter certainty. "I promise you that, Doctor."

The conviction in her voice unsettled him, but he didn't have time for games. He looked pointedly at his watch. "Ms. Morse, if I'm going to help you at all, I have to know the nature of your problem."

"It's not my problem," the woman said finally. "It's yours."

As Chris frowned in confusion, the woman reached into a small handbag on the chair behind her and brought out a wallet. This she flipped open and held up for him to examine. He saw an ID card of some sort, one with a blue-and-white seal. He looked closer. Bold letters on the right side of the card read *FBI*. His stomach fluttered. To the left of the big acronym, smaller letters read *Special Agent Alexandra Morse*. Beside this was a photo of the woman standing before him. Special Agent Morse was smiling in the photo, but she wasn't smiling now.

"I need to tell you some things in confidence," she said. "It won't take much of your time. I pretended to be a patient because I don't want anyone in your life to know you've spoken to an FBI agent. Before I leave, I need you to write me a prescription for Levaquin and tell your nurse that I had a urinary-tract infection. Tell her that the symptoms were so obvious that you didn't need to do a urinalysis. Will you do that?"

Chris was too surprised to make a conscious decision. "Sure," he said. "But what's going on? Are you investigating something? Are you investigating me?"

"Not you."

"Someone I know?"

Agent Morse's eyes didn't waver. "Yes."

"Who?"

"I can't tell you that yet. I may tell you at the end of this conversation. Right now I'm going to tell you a story. A quick story. Will you sit down, Doctor?"

Chris sat on the short stool he used in the examining room. "Are you really from North Carolina? Or is that just a cover?"

"Why do you ask?"

"You talk like a Yankee, but I hear Mississippi underneath."

Agent Morse smiled, or gave him what passed for a smile with her—a slight widening of her taut lips. "You have good ears. I grew up in Jackson. But I'm based in Charlotte, North Carolina, now."

He was glad to have his intuition confirmed. "Please go on with your story."

She sat on the chair where her handbag had been, crossed her legs, and regarded him coolly. "Five weeks ago, my sister died of a brain hemorrhage. This happened at University Hospital in Jackson."

"I'm sorry."

Agent Morse nodded as though she were past it, but Chris saw held-in emotion behind her eyes. "Her death was sudden and unexpected, but before she died, she told me something that sounded crazy to me."

"What?"

"She told me she'd been murdered."

He wasn't sure he understood. "You mean she told you someone had murdered *her*?"

"Exactly. Her husband, to be specific."

Chris thought about this for a while. "What did the autopsy show?"

"A fatal blood clot on the left side of the brain, near the brain stem."

"Did she have any disease that made a stroke likely? Diabetes, for example?"

"No."

"Was your sister taking birth-control pills?"

"Yes."

"That might have caused or contributed. Did she smoke?"

"No. The point is, the autopsy showed no abnormal cause for the stroke. No strange drugs, no poisons, nothing like that."

"Did your sister's husband resist the autopsy?"

Agent Morse actually beamed with approval. "No. He didn't."

"But you still believed her? You really thought her husband might have killed her?"

"Not at first. I thought she must have been hallucinating. But then—" Agent Morse looked away from Chris for the first time, and he stole a glance at her scars. Definitely lacerations caused by broken glass. But the punctate scarring indicated something else. Small-caliber bullets, maybe?

"Agent Morse?" he prompted.

"I didn't leave town right away," she said, focusing on him again. "I stayed for the funeral. And over the course of those three days, I thought a lot about what Grace had told me. That's my sister's name, Grace. She told me she thought her husband was having an affair. He's a wealthy man—far wealthier than I realized—and Grace believed he was involved with another woman. She believed he'd murdered her rather than pay what it would have cost him to divorce her. And to get custody of their son, of course."

Chris considered this. "I'm sure women have been killed for that reason before. Men, too, I imagine."

"Absolutely. Even completely normal people admit to having homicidal impulses when going through a divorce. Anyway . . . after Grace's funeral, I told her husband I was going back to Charlotte."

"But you didn't."

"No."

"Was he having an affair?"

"He was. And Grace's death didn't slow him down in the least. Quite the reverse, in fact."

"Go on."

"Let's call Grace's husband Bill. After I discovered the affair, I didn't confront Bill. I engaged the resources of the Bureau to investigate him. His personal life, his business, everything. I now know almost everything there is to know about Bill—everything but the one thing I need to prove. I know far more than my sister knew, and I know a lot more than his mistress knows now. For example, when I was going through Bill's business records, I found that he had some rather complex connections to a local lawyer."

"A Natchez lawyer?" Chris asked, trying to anticipate the connection to himself. Unlike most local physicians, he had several friends in Natchez who were attorneys.

"No, this lawyer practices in Jackson."

"I see. Go on."

"Bill is a real estate developer. He's building the new ice hockey stadium up there. Naturally, most of the lawyers he deals with specialize in real estate transactions. But this lawyer was different."

"How?"

"Family law is his specialty."

"Divorce?" said Chris.

"Exactly. Though he also does some estate planning. Trusts, wills, et cetera."

"Had 'Bill' consulted this lawyer about divorcing your sister?"

Agent Morse shifted on her chair. Chris had the impression that she wanted to stand and pace, but there wasn't enough room here to pace—he knew from experience. He also sensed that she was trying to conceal nervousness.

"I can't prove that," she said. "Not yet. But I'm positive that he did. Still, there's no evidence of any relationship whatever between Bill and this divorce attorney prior to one week *after* my sister's death. That's when they went into business together."

Chris wanted to ask several questions, but he suddenly remembered that he had patients waiting. "This story is very intriguing, Agent Morse, but I can't see how it has anything to do with me."

"You will."

"You'd better make it fast, or we'll have to postpone this. I have patients waiting."

She gave him a look that seemed to say, *Don't assume you're in control here.* "After I found the connection between Bill and this divorce lawyer," she continued, "I broadened the investigation. What I found was a web of business relationships that boggled my mind. I know something about dummy corporations, Dr. Shepard. I started my FBI career in South Florida, and I worked a lot of money-laundering cases there."

Chris silently thanked his stars for being too afraid to say yes to the various friends who had offered to "put him into some investments" in the Cayman Islands.

"This divorce attorney has interests in just about every business you can think of," Morse went on. "Mostly partnerships with various wealthy individuals in Mississippi."

This didn't surprise Chris. "Is it strange that a rich lawyer—I'm assuming he's rich—would be into a lot of different businesses?"

"Not in and of itself. But all this activity started about five years ago. And after looking closely at these deals, I couldn't see any reason that the lawyer was put into them. They're brother-in-law deals, you might say. Only the lawyer isn't related to the parties in question. Not by blood or marriage. In some cases he acted as counsel, but in most, not."

Chris nodded and stole another glance at his watch. "I'm following you. But what does all this add up to?"

Agent Morse looked intently at him, so intently that her gaze made him uncomfortable. "Nine of the individuals that this divorce lawyer is in business with share a common characteristic."

"What? Are they all patients of mine?"

Morse shook her head. "Each of them had a spouse who died unexpectedly in the past five years. In several cases, a relatively young spouse."

As Chris digested this, he felt a strange thrill, an alloy of excitement and dread. He said nothing though, but rather tried to get his mind fully around what she was saying.

"Also," Agent Morse added, "they actually all died within two and a half years of each other."

"Is that unusual?"

"Let me finish. All these spouses were white, previously healthy, and all were married to wealthy people. I can show you actuarial tables, if you like. It's way off the charts."

Chris was intrigued by Morse's single-minded intensity. "So, what you're saying . . . you think this divorce lawyer is helping potential clients to murder their spouses rather than pay them a financial settlement?"

The FBI agent brought her hands together and nodded. "Or to gain sole custody of their children. That's exactly what I'm saying."

"Okay. But why are you saying it to me?"

For the first time, Agent Morse looked uncomfortable. "Because," she said deliberately, "one week ago, your wife drove to Jackson and spent two hours inside that lawyer's office."

Chris's mouth fell open. A wave of numbness moved slowly through his body, as though he'd been shot with a massive dose of lidocaine.

Agent Morse's eyes had become slits. "You had no idea, did you?"

He was too stunned to respond.

"Have you been having problems in your marriage, Doctor?"

"No," he said finally, grateful to be certain of something at last. "Not that it's any of your business. But look . . . if my wife went to see this lawyer, she must have had some reason other than divorce. We're not having *any* kind of marital trouble."

Morse leaned back in her chair. "You don't think Thora could be having an affair?"

His face went red at the use of his wife's first name. "Are you about to tell me that she is?"

"What if I did?"

Chris stood suddenly and flexed his shoulders. "I'd say you're crazy. Nuts. And I'd throw you out of here. In fact, I want to know where you get off coming in here like this and saying these things."

"Calm down, Dr. Shepard. You may not believe it at this moment, but I'm here to help you. I realize we're talking about personal matters. Intimate matters, even. But you're forced to do the same thing in your job, aren't you? When human life is at stake, privacy goes by the board."

She was right, of course. Many of the questions on his medical-history form were intrusive. *How many sexual partners have you had in the last five years? Are you satisfied with your sexual life?* Chris looked away from her and tried to pace the room, a circuit of exactly two and a half steps. "What are you telling me, Agent Morse? No more games. Spell it out."

"Your life may be in danger."

Chris stopped. "From my wife? Is that what you're saying?"

"I'm afraid so."

"Jesus Christ! You're out of your mind. I'm going to call Thora right now and get to the bottom of this." He reached for the phone on the wall.

Agent Morse got to her feet. "Please don't do that, Dr. Shepard."

"Why shouldn't I?"

"Because you may be the only person in a position to stop whoever is behind these murders."

Chris let his hand fall. "How's that?"

She took a deep breath, then spoke in a voice of eminent reasonableness. "If you *are* a target—that is, if you've become one in the last week—your wife and this attorney have no idea that you're aware of their activities."

"So?"

"That puts you in a unique position to help us trap them."

Awareness dawned quickly. "You want me to try to trap my wife? To get her jailed for attempted murder?"

Morse turned up her palms. "Would you rather pretend none of this happened and die at thirty-six?"

He closed his eyes for a moment, trying to restrain his temper. "You're missing the forest for the trees here. Your whole thesis is illogical."

"Why?"

"Those men you think murdered their wives . . . they did it to keep from splitting their assets and paying out a ton of alimony, right?"

"In most cases, yes. But not all the victims were women."

Chris momentarily lost his train of thought.

"In at least one case," said Morse, "and probably two, the murder was about custody of the children, not money."

"Again, you're miles off base. Thora and I have no children."

"Your wife has a child. A nine-year-old son."

He smiled. "Sure, but she had Ben even before she married Red Simmons. Thora would automatically get custody."

"You've legally adopted Ben. But that brings up another important point, Dr. Shepard."

"What?"

"How your wife got her money."

Chris sat back down and looked at Agent Morse. How much did she know about his wife? Did she know that Thora was the daughter of a renowned Vanderbilt surgeon who'd left his family when his daughter was eight years old? Did she know that Thora's mother was an alcoholic? That Thora had fought like a wildcat just to get through adolescence, and that making it through nursing school was a pretty amazing achievement given her background?

Probably not.

Morse probably knew only the local legend: how Thora Rayner had been working in St. Catherine's Hospital when Red Simmons, a local oilman nineteen years her senior, had been carried into the ER with a myocardial infarction; how she'd become close to Red during his hospital stay, then married him six months later. Chris knew this story well because he'd treated Red Simmons during the last three years of his life. Chris had known Thora as a nurse, of course, but he came to know her much better during Red's years in heart failure. And what he learned was that Red truly loved "his little Viking"—a reference to Thora's Danish ancestry—and that Thora had been a brave and loyal wife, a woman worthy of deep respect. When Red died two and a half years ago, he left Thora an estate valued at $6.5 million. That was big money in Natchez, but it meant little to Chris. He had some money of his own, and he was young enough to earn plenty more.

"Agent Morse," he said in a neutral tone, "I'm not

going to discuss my wife with you. But I will tell you this. Thora doesn't stand to gain or lose anything if we get divorced."

"Why not? She's very wealthy."

"She has money, yes. But so do I. I started saving the day I began moonlighting in emergency rooms, and I've made some lucky investments. But the real issue here is legal. We both signed a prenuptial agreement before we married. If we were to get divorced, each person would leave the marriage with exactly what he or she brought into it."

Agent Morse studied Chris in silence. "I didn't know that."

He smiled. "Sorry to punch a hole in your theory."

Morse seemed suddenly lost in thought, and Chris sensed that for her, in that moment, he was not even there. Her face was more angular than he'd thought at first; it had its own odd shadows.

"Tell me this," she said suddenly. "What happens if either of you dies?"

As Chris thought about this, he felt a hollowness high in his stomach. "Well . . . I believe our wills kick in at that point. And those override the prenup. At least I think they do."

"What does your will say? Who gets those lucky investments you made?"

Chris looked at the floor, his face growing hot. "My parents get a nice chunk."

"That's good. And the rest?"

He looked up at her. "Thora gets it all."

Morse's eyes flashed with triumph.

"But . . . ," Chris protested.

"I'm listening."

"Thora is worth millions of dollars. What would be the point? Kill me to get an extra two million?"

Morse rubbed her chin for a few moments, then looked up at the narrow window set in the top of the wall. "People have been killed for less, Dr. Shepard. A *lot* less."

"By millionaires?"

"I wouldn't doubt it. And people are murdered every day for reasons other than money. How well do you know your wife? Psychologically, I mean?"

"Pretty damn well."

"Good. That's good."

Chris was starting to dislike Agent Morse intensely. "You think my wife murdered her first husband, don't you?"

Morse shrugged. "I didn't say that."

"You might as well have. But Red Simmons had a long history of heart disease."

"Yes, he did."

Morse's inside knowledge of events was pissing him off.

"But no autopsy was done," she pointed out.

"I'm aware of that. You're not suggesting that one should be done now, are you?"

Agent Morse dismissed this idea with a flick of her hand. "We wouldn't find anything. Whoever's behind these murders is too good for that."

Chris snorted. "Who's that good, Agent Morse? A professional assassin? A forensic pathologist?"

"There was a mob enforcer some years ago who prided himself on this kind of work. He was a very reserved man with a massive ego. He had no formal medical training, but he was an enthusiastic amateur.

He's nominally retired now. We've had some people following him, just to make sure."

Chris couldn't sit any longer. He rose and said, "This is nuts. I mean, what the hell do you expect me to do now?"

"Help us."

"*Us?* That's only about the third time you've said *us* in this whole conversation."

Agent Morse smiled more fully this time. "I'm the lead agent. We're spread pretty thin on these kinds of cases since 9/11. Everybody's working counterterrorism."

Chris looked deep into her eyes. There was sincerity there, and passion. But he saw something else, too—something not so different from what he read in the eyes of those patients who tried to con him out of drugs every week.

"Murder's a state crime, isn't it?" he said slowly. "Not a federal one."

"Yes. But when you kill someone, you also deprive him of his civil rights."

Chris knew this was true. Several decades-old race murders in Mississippi had been dragged back into the courtroom by trying previously acquitted Ku Klux Klan killers for violating their victims' civil rights. But still . . . something seemed wrong about Alexandra Morse's story.

"The first victim you told me about—if these *are* murder victims—was your sister, right? Doesn't that create some sort of conflict? I'm not supposed to treat family members for anything serious. Should you be investigating your own sister's death?"

"To be perfectly frank, no. But there's no one else I trust to do it right." Agent Morse looked at her watch for the first time. "We don't have time to get deep into this, Dr. Shepard. I'll speak to you again soon, but I don't want you to deviate from your normal routine. Not in any way that your wife or anyone else would notice."

"Who else would notice?"

"The person planning to kill you."

Chris went still. "Are you saying someone might be following me?"

"Yes. You and I cannot be seen together in public."

"Wait a minute. You can't tell me something like this and just walk out of here. Are you giving me protection? Are there going to be FBI agents covering me when I walk out?"

"It's not like that. Nobody's trying to assassinate you with a rifle. If the past is any guide—and it almost always is, since criminals tend to stick to patterns that have been successful in the past—then your death will have to look natural. You should be careful in traffic, and you shouldn't walk or jog or bicycle anywhere that there's traffic. No one can protect you from that kind of hit. But most important is the question of food and drink. You shouldn't eat or drink at home for a while. Not even bottled water. Nothing bought or prepared by your wife."

"You're kidding, right?"

"I realize that might be difficult, but we'll work it out. To tell you the truth, I think we have some working room, as far as time is concerned. Your wife just consulted this lawyer, and this kind of murder takes meticulous planning."

Chris heard a note of hysteria in his laughter. "That's a huge comfort, Agent Morse. Seriously. I feel so much better now."

"Does your wife have plans to be out of town any-time soon?"

He shook his head.

"Good. That's a good sign." Morse picked up her handbag. "You'd better write me that prescription now."

"What?"

"The Levaquin."

"Oh, right." He took a pad from his pocket and scribbled a prescription for a dozen antibiotic pills. "You think of everything, don't you?"

"No one thinks of everything. And be glad for it. That's the way we catch most criminals. Stupid mistakes. Even the best of us make them."

"You haven't given me a card or anything," Chris said. "No references I can check. All you did was show me an ID that I wouldn't know was fake or not. I want a phone number. Something."

Agent Morse shook her head. "You can't call any-one at the Bureau, Doctor. You can't do anything that could possibly tip off your killer. Your phones may be tapped, and that includes your cell phone. That's the easiest one to monitor."

Chris stared at her for a long time. He wanted to ask about the scars. "You said everybody makes mistakes, Agent Morse. What's the worst you ever made?"

The woman's hand rose slowly to her right cheek, as though of its own volition. "I didn't look before I leaped," she said softly. "And somebody died because of it."

"I'm sorry. Who was it?"

She hitched her handbag over her shoulder. "Not your problem, Doctor. But you *do* have a problem. I'm sorry to be the one to turn your life upside down. I really am. But if I hadn't, you might have gone to sleep one night thinking you were happy and never woken up."

Morse took the prescription from Chris's hand, then gave him her taut smile. "I'll contact you again soon. Try not to freak out. And whatever you do, don't ask your wife if she's trying to kill you."

Chris gaped after Morse as she walked down the corridor toward the waiting-room door. Her stride was measured and assured, the walk of an athlete.

"So?" Holly said from behind him, startling him. "What's her story?"

"Cystitis," he mumbled. "Honeymoon syndrome."

"Too much bumping monkey, huh? I didn't see no wedding ring on her finger."

Chris shook his head at Holly's wiseass tone, then walked down the hall to his private office and closed the door.

He had a waiting room filled with patients, but as sick as some of them were, they seemed secondary now. He shoved aside a stack of charts and looked at Thora's picture on his desk. Thora was the antithesis of Agent Alex Morse. She was blond—naturally blond, unlike 98 percent of the golden-haired women you saw on the street—and of Danish descent, which was unusual in the South. Her eyes were grayish blue—sea blue, if you wanted to get poetic about it, which he had, on occasion. But though she might be mistaken for a Viking princess on the basis of appearance, Thora had no pretensions of superiority. She had spent four years married to Red Simmons, a down-to-earth country boy who'd made good by trusting his instincts and who'd treated people well after he made his pile. Chris believed Red's instincts about women were as good as his hunches about oil. Yes, Thora had become rich when Red died, but where was the fault in that? When a rich man died, someone always profited. That was the way of the world. And Red Simmons wasn't the type to demand a prenuptial agreement. He'd had a loving young wife who'd shared his life for better or worse—with quite a bit of worse in that last year—and she deserved everything he had, come hell or high water. That's the way Red would have put it. And the more Chris reflected on what Agent Morse had said in Exam Room 4, the angrier he got.

He picked up the phone and called his front desk.

"Yes?" drawled Jane Henry, his peppery reception-ist. The *yes* finally terminated after two long sylla-bles—maybe two and a half.

"Jane, I had a fraternity brother in college named Darryl Foster. That's D-A-R-R-Y-L."

"Uh-huh. And?"

"I think he's an FBI agent now. I don't know where. He was originally from Memphis, but the last I heard, he was working in the Chicago field office."

"And?"

"I need you to find him for me. His phone number, I mean. My old fraternity is trying to add on to the house up at Ole Miss, and they want to hit up every-body for contributions."

"And just how do you suggest I find this supercop?"

"Get on the Internet, I guess. You spend enough time on there playing poker and shopping eBay. The least you can do is locate one old classmate for me."

Jane harrumphed loudly. "I'll give it a try, I guess."

"Don't strain yourself."

She hung up without a word, but Chris knew she would have the number in less than an hour.

Don't change your routine, Agent Morse had said. *Don't do anything that might tip off your killer. . . .*

"My killer," Chris said aloud. "This has got to be bullshit."

He picked up his stethoscope and walked to the door, but Jane's buzz brought him back to his desk. He grabbed his phone. "You found Foster already?"

"Not yet. Your wife's on the phone."

Chris felt another wave of numbness. Thora rarely called his office; she knew he was too busy to spend time on the phone. He looked down at her picture, waiting for a spark of instinct about what to do. But what he saw before him wasn't his wife, but Special Agent Alex Morse, regarding him coolly from behind her scars.

Stupid mistakes, Morse had said. *Even the best of us make them.*

"Tell Thora I'm with a patient, Jane."

"What?" asked the receptionist, clearly surprised.

"I'm way behind already. Just do it. I'll call her back in a little while."

"Whatever you say. You sign my checks."

Chris started to hang up, but at the last second he said, "Find Foster's number for me, okay? Stat."

The playfulness went out of Jane's voice; she knew when her boss meant business.

"You got it, Doc."

CHAPTER

3

Andrew Rusk was afraid.

He stood at the window of his law office and gazed out over the jigsaw skyline of Jackson, Mississippi. Not an impressive vista as cityscapes went, but Rusk did have the corner office on the sixteenth floor. Looking north, he could see all the way to the forested plains where white flight was expanding once-sleepy counties into bustling enclaves for twenty-first-century yuppies. Farther on, the new Nissan plant was bringing relative wealth to the state's struggling blue-collar workers. They commuted up to a hundred miles a day, both ways, from the tiny towns surrounding the state capital.

Behind him—out of sight to the west—lived the uneducated blacks who had been dragging the city down for the past twenty years. Rusk and a few trusted friends referred to them as "untouchables." The untouchables killed each other at an alarming rate and preyed upon others with enough regularity to breed deep anxiety in the white citizens of Jackson. But they weren't the source of his fear. They were invisible from his office, and he worked hard to keep them that way in all areas of his life. To that end, he had built his home in an oak forest north of the city, near Annandale, a golf club that occupied the self-assured niche between the old money of the Jackson Country Club and the young optimists at Reunion.

Every afternoon at four thirty, Rusk took the elevator down to the garage, climbed into his black Porsche Cayenne Turbo, and roared northward to his stone-and-glass sanctuary among the oak and pine trees. His second wife was invariably lying by their infinity pool when he arrived. Lisa was still young enough for a string bikini, but she rarely wore swimwear in the summer. After a poolside kiss—or more often, lately, a session of listening to her bitch about nothing—he went inside for a stiff drink. His black cook always had supper waiting on the table, and Andrew looked forward to it every day.

But now the taste of fear overrode that of food. Rusk had not felt real fear for twenty-five years, but he'd never forgotten it. Fear tasted like junior high school: like being backed into a corner by a tenth grader who wanted to beat your face into red pulp, your friends watching but too petrified to help, your bladder threatening to send an ocean of piss down your leg. Rusk lifted a tumbler of bourbon to his lips and took a long pull. Whiskey at work was an indulgence, one he'd allowed himself more and more in the past weeks, a balm against the fear.

He refilled the tumbler with Woodford Reserve, then lifted a five-by-seven photograph from his desktop. The photo showed a dark-haired woman with an angular face and deep-set eyes—the kind of eyes that looked alive even on a piece of paper. Rusk knew that the woman in that picture would never fall for his sweetest pickup line. Maybe if he'd caught her young—a freshman in college when he was a senior, drunk at a frat party, like that—but even then he doubted it. This girl had what most women didn't—self-confidence—and she had it in spades. The apple of her daddy's eye, you could tell. That was probably what had led her to the FBI.

"Special Agent Alex," he murmured. "Nosy *bitch*."

Rusk's phone rang, and his secretary answered it. They still had secretaries at his little firm—not goddamn *personal assistants*—and they were old-school girls, all the way. They gave and received generous perks, and everybody stayed happy. Rusk had read that there was a rule at the Google headquarters in Mountain View: no worker should ever be more than fifty feet away from food. To that end, snack stations had been set up throughout the Googleplex. The Rusk rule—established by Andrew's father at his much more venerable firm—predated the Google edict by five decades, and it went thus: no partner should ever be more than fifty feet from a good and willing piece of ass. Andrew junior had imported this tradition into his own firm, with most gratifying results.

He gulped the last slug from the tumbler and walked to his desk, where his flat-panel monitor glowed insistently. Flickering on the screen was the portal graphic of a Dutch Web site called EX NIHILO—a black hole with a shimmering event horizon. Rusk remembered a little Latin from his days in prep school: *ex nihilo* meant "out of nothing." For a considerable fee, EX NIHILO provided absolute anonymity in the digital domain.

The company also provided other services requiring discretion, and it was one of those services that Rusk had contracted for today. He suspected that kiddie-porn addicts made up the lion's share of EX NIHILO's clients, but he didn't care. All that mattered was that the company could protect him.

Partners, he thought, recalling his father's cynical voice. *All partnerships fail in the end, just like marriages. The only life after death any human being will ever know is staying in a marriage or a partnership after it's over. And that's not life—it's living death.* Rusk hated most things about his father, but one thing he could not deny: the man had been right about most things in life. Rusk moved his cursor into a blank box and typed 3.141592653—pi to the ninth decimal place. As a boy, he'd memorized pi to the fortieth decimal place to impress his father. Immediately after his proud dinner recitation, dear old Dad had told him about an Indian boy who'd memorized pi to the six-hundredth place. Typical paternal response in the Rusk home. Nothing was ever good enough for Andrew Jackson Rusk Sr.

Rusk retyped his password, then clicked CONFIRM. With this act, he armed a digital mechanism that might well become his sole means of survival during the next few weeks. He had no illusions about that. His partner would tolerate zero risk; he had made that clear at the outset. In fact, the man was so obsessive about security that he had not only created a code name—Glykon—for Andrew to use in their conversations, which were few (Rusk had googled *Glykon,* but all he'd discovered was a Greek snake god that had protected his believers in AD 160 by dispelling a plague cloud with a magical spell),

Rusk's Glykon had rather absurdly insisted that Andrew *think* of him by the code name on any occasion where thought about their business was required. "Security is based on rigorous habits," Glykon insisted, and the funny thing was, he'd turned out to be right. They'd experienced five years of steady and staggering profits, without a hitch. But if Glykon perceived risk, Rusk knew, he would instantly move to eliminate it. And that meant only one thing: death.

The glue that had held their partnership together thus far was a Cold War strategy called MAD: Mutually Assured Destruction. Only when each party knew that his partner held the key to his destruction could trust be guaranteed. (Rusk had once observed an analogy to adulterers who were both married.) But now the situation had changed, and Rusk no longer felt safe. For the first time in their association, true danger had reared its head. There were two threats, and they had arisen almost simultaneously. One was internal, the other external. In the shadow of these threats, Rusk had come to the conclusion that for MAD to act as a true deterrent, each party had to *know* that a sword of Damocles hung above his head. Tacit understanding was no longer sufficient. EX NIHILO would provide that sword.

If Rusk did not log in to the Dutch Web site every day and authenticate his identity, then EX NIHILO would forward the contents of a large digital file to the FBI and the Mississippi State Police. That file contained a detailed record of the partnership's activities for the past five years, with accompanying photos and business records—enough legal dynamite to blast both men into Parchman Farm for life, where the worst of the untouchables lived out their miserable and violent days. There was a built-in grace period, of course. Without one, a random car accident causing a week-long coma might result in Andrew awakening miraculously only to be arrested for murder. But the delay wasn't much longer than a week. Ten days, in fact. After that, Glykon would be arrested, jailed, and sentenced to death.

The prospect of relating this information to Glykon was what had Rusk's sphincter quivering. The moment that he unsheathed this "sword," the ground would shift beneath his feet. He and Glykon would become adversaries, even if they continued working together, which was by no means certain. Intellectual genius and ruthless efficiency had made Glykon the perfect collaborator, but those same qualities would also make him the most formidable adversary imaginable.

Rusk's fear disgusted him. The walls of his office were lined with photographs that testified to his virility: brilliant snapshots of a blond ex–fraternity president wearing every type of survival suit known to man. Rusk owned all the best toys, and he'd honed the skills to use them. Extreme skiing. Monster-wave surfing in Hawaii. He had a stunt plane that he flew like a barnstormer. He'd even climbed Everest last year, and during one hell of a storm (albeit with oxygen). All this he'd done before the age of forty, yet he still felt like a boy in the presence of Glykon. It wasn't just the age difference, because Rusk felt superior to most sixty-year-old men he met. It was something else. A set of factors, probably, damn few of which he could put a name to, but that was the state of things.

Rusk knew he'd made a mistake taking the Fennell

case. The target's sister was an FBI agent, and her father had been a homicide cop. Rusk had planned to refuse the job, but he'd mentioned it to Glykon anyway, assuming that his paranoid partner would reject it out of hand. To his surprise, Glykon had taken the FBI connection as a challenge. By then Bill Fennell had offered a 50 percent bonus—*50 percent*—so Rusk caved. What else was he going to do? As Oscar Wilde once said, the only sure way to get rid of a temptation was to yield to it. But now Rusk had Special Agent Alex Morse crawling all over his life. Somehow she had latched onto him, like a fucking remora to a shark. He'd expected her to give up after a while, but she hadn't. She was tenacious. And that kind of tenacity only led one place.

Rusk was sure that Morse had broken into his office. He hadn't reported this, of course, not to the police and certainly not to Glykon. He'd merely made sure that she would never get in again. But that was closing the proverbial barn door after the horse had bolted. What had Morse discovered while she was here? There was no obvious evidence to find. The case-related data on Rusk's hard drives was encrypted (even encrypted, it was a violation of Glykon's rules), but Rusk had a feeling that Morse knew her way around computers. Probably around business records, too. His discreet inquiries into her CV had revealed a law degree from Tulane and a year working in South Florida with an FBI/DEA task force. Perfect preparation for unraveling one side of his operation. Morse had also spent five years as an FBI hostage negotiator. This had surprised him, until his source explained that there were more female hostage negotiators in the Bureau than males. It seemed that women were better at peaceful resolution of conflict than men. *That* was a surprise. An experienced divorce attorney, Rusk had met women with the predatory instincts of velociraptors—females malicious and manipulative enough to give Machiavelli remedial classes in the provocation of wars.

Despite a promising start, Alex Morse had proved unequal to the job of hostage negotiator. Her father's death and her mother's cancer had evidently pushed her into a zone where her judgment abandoned her, and she'd gotten somebody killed. She'd almost died herself, Rusk thought wistfully, and her butchered face bore the evidence of her brush with death. But the bottom line was, her emotions had short-circuited her professional restraint. She'd acted wholly on instinct, without regard for the consequences, and this disturbing precedent could not be ignored.

Glykon had to know about Alex Morse.

And Morse wasn't their only problem. Internal threats were always more dangerous than those from without, and right now a nuclear bomb was ticking beneath their partnership. "A *client,*" Rusk muttered in disbelief, swigging from his tumbler. "A goddamn *rogue client.*"

He started at the sound of his door, which had opened just enough for his secretary to lean inside. It was only mid-May, but Janice was already deeply tanned, making her look closer to thirty than thirty-five, her true age. She met Rusk's eyes with utter openness, the look of an intimate confidante.

"Almost everybody's gone," she said. "You want to do it before I go home?"

Rusk weighed her offer. Janice was older than his wife, and while not as beautiful as Lisa, she was much more accomplished and enthusiastic in bed. It was a perfect arrangement. Janice's husband was a cost accountant who bored her silly but was a good father, and Janice did not aspire to a higher social station. Moreover, Rusk paid her almost three times what other secretaries earned in the capital city.

"Are you all right?" Janice asked, stepping fully into the office. She was wearing a khaki skirt and white linen top that her bra showed through. Her calves and forearms rippled with muscle acquired from tournament tennis and obsessive workouts at the gym.

Rusk nodded, but he knew she could read him in all weathers.

"Is it your father?" she asked tentatively, knowing this was a chronic sore spot.

"No. There's just a lot going on right now."

Her gaze remained on him, but she didn't push. "Do you want me to just use my mouth?"

Rusk studied her eyes, which held only concern, and estimated the chances that his wife would want sex tonight. *What the hell?* he thought. *I could die in a car crash on the way home.* He summoned a smile for Janice.

She walked over, knelt before his chair, and unzipped his trousers. She could usually bring him off quickly when she wanted to, but today he sensed that it might take a while. He looked down at the photo of Alex Morse and let his mind wander. It was the timing that he couldn't believe. He was forty years old, and if business continued at its present pace, he would surpass his father's net worth within the year. Andrew Jackson Rusk Sr.—known as A.J. to his friends (among these, a list of governors stretching back fifty years)— was seventy-five years old and still practicing as a plaintiff's attorney. A.J. had earned millions in three recent cases that had garnered national media attention—two of them in Jefferson County, where the all-black juries handed out fortunes like party favors. It was tough to keep up with that kind of racket when you handled divorce cases—even the big ones—but Andrew had managed it. Which was good, because his father never let him forget that they were competing.

"Careful with your teeth," he said.

Janice mumbled something and kept working at him.

A.J. senior had labored to grind every trace of softness, idealism, and compassion out of his son, and for the most part he'd succeeded. When Andrew junior saw the father-son basketball game in *The Great Santini* for the first time—Robert Duvall bouncing the ball off his son's head—he'd found himself unable to breathe. And because his own personal Bull Meechum had not died in a fiery plane crash, the competition had not ended when Andrew reached adulthood. It intensified. Instead of joining his father's law firm, Andrew had joined that of his first wife's father—a mistake it had taken him several years to acknowledge to himself. His divorce from the senior partner's daughter had ended his tenure with that firm, but A.J. had not offered him a job after he was cut loose. Rather than join a lesser firm, Andrew had formed his own, taking every potential money case that walked in the door. Most of those had turned out to be divorces. And in that milieu he had discovered his gift. In subsequent years, he had often faced lawyers from his father's firm in court, and he'd triumphed in every battle. Those victories had been sweet, but it wasn't quite the same as licking his old man. But *this* year, he'd been telling himself, this year he was finally going to cut Big A.J. down to size.

"Will you rub my nipples?" Janice asked.

Rusk looked down. Her free hand had disappeared beneath her skirt. He reached down and absently pinched her. She moaned, then gripped him with her hand and went at him with renewed fervor. He looked at the top of her head, where the dark roots showed beneath the blond color job. Every solitary gray hair frizzed out in a direction of its own—

"Stop," he said.

"Wha . . . ?" she gurgled.

"I can't do it."

Her head came up, and she smiled with almost maternal encouragement. "Yes, you can. You need it. Just relax." She lowered her head again.

"I said *stop*."

He shoved her shoulders back hard enough to disengage from her mouth, but Janice would not be put off so easily—not when she was aroused. She stood and stepped quickly out of some blue panties, then hiked up her skirt and sat down on him. He didn't help her, but neither did he push her off, despite a rush of nausea. He let her do what she needed to do, focusing on her muscular thighs as she worked up and down. Janice's grunts grew steadily louder, but it didn't matter. He'd had the walls professionally soundproofed. He took his eyes off the wet tangle where he disappeared into her and focused on Alexandra Morse's picture. He imagined the FBI agent sweating over him like this. Then he inverted the image in his mind: now he was doing Special Agent Alex in a very painful way—making her pay dearly for all the inconvenience she had caused—

"*Oh,*" Janice groaned. "Now it's hard."

An image of Glykon suddenly filled his mind.

"Come on," urged Janice, a hint of panic in her voice. "Keep it up, baby. Think about whatever you have to."

He focused on Morse's eyes and gripped the breasts in front of him. They were good-sized but flabby; Janice's two kids had taken their toll, and surgery never quite brought boobs back to their prematernal state, no matter what the surgeons promised. Alex Morse had no children. Her tits would be firm and high, like Lisa's. And her IQ would be 50 percent higher, at least. Rusk closed his hands with savage force. Janice screamed in pain, but the scream drew out to a long moan as she broke through and peaked, gritting her teeth against his neck to keep from biting him, which she always wanted to do. Rusk was amazed to find himself climaxing after all; he shut his eyes and forced the leering visage of Glykon from his mind.

"I told you," Janice said. She stood up and looked down at him, still panting from her exertions. She obviously considered his climax a small victory in their ongoing sex play. "I told you you could do it."

Rusk gave her a perfunctory nod, thinking he might need to take half a Viagra on the way home, in case Lisa wanted servicing.

"Who's that?" asked Janice, pointing at Alex Morse.

"Nobody."

Janice fished her panties off the floor and worked them back up her legs. "She's obviously somebody."

He glanced at Morse again, then shook his head.

"Do you think she's hot?" Janice asked in a girlish voice.

"No," he said, meaning it.

"You're lying. You thought about her while you were inside me, didn't you?"

"I did. You know me, Janice."

She gave him a pouting glance.

"You don't have to be jealous of her," Rusk said.

"Why not?"

"She's dead."

"Oh." Janice smiled with satisfaction.

After Janice flattened her skirt and carried her shoes back to her desk, Rusk walked over to a credenza and removed a box of Reynolds Wrap from a drawer. It had lain there for five years, but he'd never had to use it. Opening the long box, he tore off two squares of aluminum foil, then laid them on a table by the northeast window of his office. There was packaging tape in the bottom drawer of his desk. He cut off several short lengths and stuck a line of dangling pieces to the edge of the credenza. With these he taped the foil to the eastward-facing window, shiny side out. In sunlight, the squares would be visible from Interstate 55, which was elevated for most of its length where it passed through the city.

The aluminum foil was another of Glykon's ideas. Those two goddamn squares of Reynolds Wrap would bring about a meeting that Rusk dreaded like no other in his life, one that would require all his powers of persuasion to survive. His hand shook as he drained another tumbler of bourbon.

He felt as though he had carried out a ritual to summon the devil.

CHAPTER

4

Chris Shepard dropped a baseball in midair and swung the bat in a fast arc, smacking a ground ball at his four-foot-tall shortstop. The shortstop scooped up the ball and hummed it to the first baseman, Chris's adopted son, Ben. The throw went wide, but Ben stretched out and sucked the ball into his glove as though by magic.

"Great catch!" Chris shouted. "Throw at his chest, Mike! He's wearing a glove, he can catch it."

The shortstop nodded and crouched for the next ball. Ben's eyes glowed with pride, but he maintained as stern a countenance as a nine-year-old could muster.

Chris pretended to aim another ball at the shortstop, then popped a fly over Ben to his daydreaming right fielder. The kid woke up just in time to dart out of the ball's path, but it took him several seconds to start chasing it toward the back of the lot.

Chris glanced covertly to his right as he waited for the throw. Two minutes ago, Thora's silver Mercedes had pulled onto the grassy bank behind the vacant lot where they practiced. She didn't get out, but sat watching from behind the smoky windshield. *Maybe she's talking on her cell phone,* he thought. It struck him how rarely Thora came to practice anymore. Last year, she had been one of the team's biggest supporters, always bringing the watercooler or even an ice chest filled with POWERade for every kid. But this year she was the rarest visitor. Curiosity had brought her out today, he knew. Instead of making his evening hospital rounds early, as was his habit during the season, Chris had picked Ben up from home right after his office closed. Thora had been out running, of course, so they'd missed each other. As a result, they hadn't spoken since his visit from Alex Morse.

Chris waved at the Mercedes, then started working ground balls around the infield. He'd avoided talking to Thora because he needed time to process what Agent Morse had told him, and a busy medical office was no place to reflect on personal problems. Running a baseball practice for nine- and ten-year-olds wasn't exactly Zen meditation, but he could steal a little time to work through the few factual details Morse had given him during their meeting.

He wished he had asked more questions. About the supposed murders, for example. Had the cause of death been stroke in every case? He doubted that Morse had forensic evidence to back up her extraordinary theory. If she did, she wouldn't need him to try to set up a trap; she would already have arrested the murderer. And yet . . . if he was completely honest with himself, he couldn't deny that in the past few hours he'd been turning over certain realities that had been bothering him on a deep level for some time.

Foremost was the baby issue. During their courtship,

he and Thora had agreed that they wanted to start having children of their own as soon as they married. At least one, and maybe two. Chris was thirty-six, Thora thirty. The sooner they started having babies, the healthier those children would be, and the better they would know their adopted brother. But after the wedding, Thora had seemed reluctant to get off the pill. Twice she'd claimed that she'd started taking the next month's pack by mistake. When he remarked on this rare absent-mindedness, she admitted that she'd been wondering whether they should move so quickly. Chris had tried to hide his disappointment, but it obviously showed through, because Thora had stopped taking the pill, and they'd begun waiting the obligatory three months required before conception could safely occur. Their sex remained good, but the frequency dropped precipitously. Thora complained that having to use other forms of birth control was a drag after the convenience of the pill. Before long, Chris felt lucky if they made love once a week. After the three months passed, they had abandoned all forms of birth control, but so far, Thora had not conceived. Not even a missed period. Whenever Chris brought up the subject, she subtly suggested that he should get himself checked out, since Ben's existence proved that she could bear children. Chris never responded verbally to these hints, but he had gotten himself "checked out," using his own office's laboratory-service provider. And the answer was unequivocal: high sperm count, high motility.

He wished Thora would get out of her Mercedes. Several other parents were sitting on blankets or lawn chairs on the hill beside the field; only Thora remained in her vehicle. It was this kind of behavior that earned you the reputation of snob in a small town: *uppity doctor's wife*. Last year, Chris couldn't have imagined Thora remaining aloof like this. She would have visited each parent in turn, all the while shouting encouragement to the boys from the sidelines. But maybe he was making a big deal out of nothing. If she felt like sitting in her car, where was the harm? The sun was burning down with unusual ferocity for May, and she might just be enjoying the air-conditioning. He couldn't tell whether her engine was running; the rumble of the generator in the batting cage was too loud.

"Alex Morse is nuts," he muttered, cracking a ball toward third base. His marriage might not be in a perfect state—if any such marriage existed on earth—but the idea that his wife was planning to murder him was so ludicrous that Chris hadn't even known how to respond. It was almost like someone telling you that your mother was planning to kill you. And yet . . . it wasn't, quite. There was no blood tie between husbands and wives—not without biological children. And for some reason, Chris couldn't get Morse's deadly earnest eyes out of his mind.

She clearly wasn't the kind of person who would waste time playing games with people's lives. The answer had to be something else. Like emotional instability. Maybe Morse believed absolutely in the absurd scenario she had outlined today. Given the recent death of her sister, that wasn't hard to imagine. Chris had seen many extreme grief reactions during his medical career.

But what should he *do* about it? Call the FBI field office in Jackson and report Morse's visit? Call his lawyer? Call FBI headquarters in Washington? Or discreetly try to get more information on his own? His receptionist had finally found a phone number for Darryl Foster, and Chris had tried to call his old fraternity brother, but he'd only reached an answering machine. He'd hoped that Foster—an active FBI field agent—would shed some light on the mysterious Agent Morse before he had to face Thora, but the cell phone in Chris's pocket had not rung. Until he knew more, he wasn't going to let Thora know anything was amiss. It wasn't that he believed anything Morse had told him, but if he related the afternoon's events to Thora, her first question would be *Who did you report her to?* And what would he say then? Why *hadn't* he reported her?

"You gonna hit the ball or what, Coach?"

Chris blinked himself back to reality. His catcher was staring up at him with confusion. Chris laughed to cover, then hit a high fly ball to center field. As he watched its arc, he caught a movement to his right. Thora was standing in the open door of her Mercedes now, her blond hair flashing in the afternoon sun. She was staring directly at him. Had she noticed his little zone-out at home plate?

She gave him a small wave and smiled beneath her sunglasses, dark avian things that gave her the look of an art deco hawk on the side of a skyscraper. She was wearing running clothes, her lithe, muscular body on display for all. *Maybe that's why she didn't get out,* he thought. But that was wishful thinking. For the past eight months—since running marathons had become fashionable among the young married women of the town—Thora had run between two and ten miles a day. She'd bought $200 shoes, the wrist GPS unit, and all the other gear of the modern distance runner. The thing was, with Thora it wasn't just for show. She actually had talent. After just three months' training, she'd started beating the times of women who had been running for two and three years. But Thora's running garb typified another point of tension between them.

When she was married to Red Simmons, Thora had dressed conservatively. Fashionably, yes, but never pushing the envelope of taste. After a suitable period of mourning, though—about the time she'd started seeing Chris—she had subtly begun changing her style. In the beginning, Chris had approved. The new look revealed more of her beauty and signaled an engagement with life that she'd sorely needed. But lately Thora had begun wearing things he would never have imagined she would buy, much less wear in public: ultrashort shorts; transparent tops meant to be worn with an outer garment, but worn alone; and push-up bras (when she wore bras at all). Chris had kidded her about this, hoping she'd get the hint, but Thora had continued to wear the stuff, so he'd shut up. He didn't feel he had the right to control the way she dressed. Maybe he was getting old, losing touch with the times. And until today, it hadn't seemed that big a deal. Nothing had, really. Only the issue of Thora getting pregnant had been disturbing enough to rob him of sleep.

"Coach Grant," he called to his assistant, another team father. "Let's run some bases and then call it a day."

The boys cheered, and their parents started rising from blankets and chairs, packing up ice chests and babies for the trek home. Chris ran the boys for five minutes, then circled them and led them in a team shout that reverberated off a thick stand of oak trees to the west. The boys packed the gear—a team tradition—and then everyone headed for his family car.

Ben walked beside Chris as they tromped toward the Mercedes. Chris tried to blank his mind but couldn't. Too many things were surfacing after a period of unconscious repression. Like the Mercedes. Last Christmas, Thora had bought herself an SL55 AMG. Hardly anyone in town knew how expensive this car really was. Several local doctors owned Benzes, but most were in the $50,000 to $80,000 range. Thora's SL had cost $145,000. Chris didn't begrudge her the car—it was her money, after all—but while she was married to Red Simmons, she had driven a Toyota Avalon: forty grand, fully loaded. She'd also worn a Timex watch. Chris had sometimes joked with her about it while she was on nursing duty. But a month ago, a Patek Philippe had quietly appeared on her wrist. He had no idea how much the watch cost, but the jewels on its bezel told him it was probably something north of $20,000—more than several fathers watching this practice earned in a year.

"Big Ben!" cried Thora, moving out from behind the SL's door with a grin and bending to hug her sweaty son. "You didn't miss a catch the whole time I was here!"

Ben shrugged. "I play first base, Mom. You can't play first if you miss balls."

Chris wished he could see Thora's eyes, but the sunglasses hid them completely. She gave Ben a quick squeeze, then straightened and gave Chris her thousand-watt smile. His gaze went to the Patek Philippe. *Stop it,* he said silently.

"You picked up Ben early today," she said.

"Yeah. I knew rounds were going to take a while, so I decided to do them after practice."

She nodded but said nothing.

He wasn't sure where to go next, but Ben saved him by asking, "Can we go to La Fiesta, Mom?"

Thora glanced at Chris over the top of her sunglasses, but he couldn't read her meaning. La Fiesta was a family-oriented Mexican restaurant with low prices and fast service; thus it was always loud and crowded.

"I really need to get to the hospital," Chris said. "You guys go, though."

Thora shook her head. "We've got plenty of food at home, and it's a lot healthier than Mexican. I made chicken salad this afternoon."

Ben rolled his eyes and wrinkled his nose.

Chris almost said, *I'll pick up something on the way home,* but that would only result in Ben begging for takeout and Thora getting irritated. "Help me load the gear, Son."

Chris and Ben tossed the two bulging canvas bags into his pickup. Then Chris gave Ben a high five, hugged Thora lightly to his side, and climbed into the truck. "I won't be too late," he said through the open window.

As though in answer, Thora took off her sunglasses. Her sea-blue eyes cut right through his feigned nonchalance. Her gaze had always caused a physical reaction in his chest, something between a fluttering and radiant warmth. (It caused a reaction lower down, as well.) Now that gaze held an unspoken question, but he broke eye contact, lifted his hand in a wave, then backed onto the road and drove north toward town.

CHAPTER

5

Alex Morse drove her rented Corolla into the parking lot of the Days Inn, pulled up to the door of room 125, and shut off the engine. When she opened the door of her room, her sister's calico cat mewed and dropped soundlessly from the bathroom counter to the carpet. Alex paid five extra dollars per night so that Meggie could stay in the hotel room. She only had Grace's cat because Jamie had begged her to take it after the funeral. Jamie loved Meggie, but his father did not, and the boy had been afraid that his dad would take her to the pound as soon as Alex flew back to Charlotte. Since Alex knew that Bill Fennell was quite capable of this small act of brutality, she'd accepted the burden. To her surprise, the bright-eyed calico had helped to ease the loneliness of the past five weeks. Alex took off her shoulder holster, massaged the wet place where it had lain against her ribs, then knelt and rubbed Meggie's chin with a bent knuckle. When she poured some food into the plastic dish by the bathroom door, the cat began eating voraciously.

Alex had checked into the Days Inn five days ago,

and she'd done what she could to make a home of her room. Her notebook computer sat humming on the desk, its screen saver an ever-changing montage of photos shot on the cruise she'd taken with Grace to celebrate Grace's thirtieth birthday. Beside the computer stood a photo of Jamie wearing his Jackson Academy basketball uniform—a gangly ten-year-old with auburn hair, a freckled, unfinished face, and deep-set eyes that projected heartbreaking uncertainty.

Looking at this picture, she remembered how frantic Jamie had been the morning after his mother died, when Alex told him she had to take him back to his father. Running off with him after Grace's death had been an act of desperation, and in the eyes of the law, kidnapping. If Alex had kept Jamie, Bill wouldn't have hesitated to have her arrested, and he would probably have done so the previous night had he been able to locate her. Many times since that day Alex had regretted returning Jamie, but she had enough experience to know that a successful custody kidnapping required careful planning and preparation. In the five weeks since that day, she had actually taken several steps in that direction. And if her efforts to prove Bill's complicity in Grace's murder should fail—which without Dr. Shepard's help was likely—then she would be ready to take drastic action.

On a low dresser beside the motel desk lay several neat stacks of paper, all relating to her mother's medical care. There were lists of oral medications and chemotherapy drugs; treatment schedules; bills to be paid by the insurance company; bills from private physicians for the fees the insurance company didn't cover; test results from the University Medical Center and from the lab of the private oncologist; and of course the correspondence between Grace and various cancer specialists around the world. Grace had dealt with their mother's cancer the way she'd dealt with every other crisis: she'd declared war on it. And she'd carried on that war with the implacable persistence of Sherman burning his way across the South. Woe betide the insurance clerk who made an error on a bill addressed to Margaret Morse; Grace's retribution was swift and sure. But now the running of that campaign had passed to Alex, and by Grace's standard she was doing a piss-poor job.

Her cardinal sin? She was not at her mother's bedside. Instead, she was camped out a hundred miles southeast, in Natchez, Mississippi, while paid nurses—*strangers!*—tended her mother in Jackson. And what was she doing in Natchez? Only burning through her life savings and risking her career in an almost certainly vain quest to punish her sister's murderer. Grace would have had plenty to say about that. But on the other hand, it was Grace who had charged Alex with "saving" Jamie from his father. And since Bill Fennell had legal custody of his son, the only way Alex could see to save Jamie was to prove that his father had murdered his mother.

Alex walked to the oversize card table she'd bought at Wal-Mart to arrange her case materials. This table was the nerve center of her investigation. It was fairly primitive stuff—jotted notes, surveillance records, digital snapshots, minicassettes—but her father had told her countless times that there was no substitute for putting your heels on the pavement or your ass behind the wheel of your car. All the computers in the world couldn't nail a killer if you never left your office. Alex kept a framed picture of her dad propped on the card table—her patron saint of cold cases. It wasn't actually a photograph, but a newspaper story that included two snapshots of Jim Morse: one as a fresh-faced patrolman in 1968, the other as a weary but determined-looking homicide detective who'd solved a high-profile race murder in Jackson in 1980.

Her father had gone into police work straight out of the army, returning to Mississippi after two tours in Vietnam. He'd seen action, but he'd never talked about it, and he never had any lasting problems that Alex knew about. But working as an MP in Saigon, Jim Morse had somehow wound up involved in a couple of murder cases. The work had left an impression on him, so when he'd found himself at loose ends on his twenty-first birthday, he'd registered at the police academy in Jackson. He did well as a patrolman, making sergeant before anyone else in his academy class. He passed the detective's exam when he was twenty-seven and quickly made a name for two things: brilliant detective work; and speaking his mind, no matter whom he happened to be talking to. The first trait would have assured rapid promotion, had he not possessed the second in equal measure. Alex had fought all her life to control the same tendency, and she'd mostly succeeded. But her father had watched men with much less talent and dedication climb past him on the promotional ladder for most of his career.

After retirement, Jim Morse had opened a detective agency with a former partner who'd served as his rabbi early in his career—a wise old redneck named Will Kilmer. The freedom of a private agency had suited both men, and they got all the referral business they could handle. Alex was certain that it was her teenage exposure to their livelier cases that had caused her to spurn all offers after law school and enroll in the FBI academy instead. Her father had applauded her career choice, but her mother . . . well, Margaret had reacted as she always did when Alex departed from the path of conventional Southern womanhood. Silent reproach.

A stab of guilt hit Alex high in the chest, followed by a wave of grief. To avoid the guilt, she looked down at a jumble of snapshots of Chris and Thora Shepard. In some shots they were together, but in most not. Alex had been following them long enough to form an impression of a classic upper-middle-class couple, harried by the demands of daily life and never quite catching up. Chris spent a remarkable amount of time working, while Thora alternated vigorous exercise with personal pampering. Alex wasn't yet sure how far that pampering extended, but she had suspicions. She also had some notes and photographs that Dr. Shepard might like to see, once he got over the initial shock of today's meeting. But not just yet.

Alex felt a vague resentment as she looked down at Thora; the woman looked better after a six-mile run than most women did after two hours of prepping themselves for a party. You had to hate her a little for that. Chris, on the other hand, was much more down-to-earth, a dark-haired Henry Fonda type rather than a pretty boy. A little more muscular than Fonda, maybe, but with that same gravitas. In that way Dr. Shepard reminded her of her father, another quiet man who had lived for his work.

Mixed in with the images of Thora and Chris were a

few of Chris and Ben, all shot at the vacant lot where Chris coached Ben's Little League team. Ben Shepard was only a year younger than Jamie, and his eyes held some of the same tentativeness that Jamie's did. *Maybe it's just their age,* she thought. *Or maybe children sense when there's something wrong at the heart of their families.*

Dwelling on Jamie's plight usually made Alex too upset to function, so she switched on the TV to make the room seem less empty. She turned on the water as hot as she could stand it, then soaked a washcloth, lay on the bed, and began to scrub her face. The heat spread through her scalp and neck, sending blessed relief down the length of her body. As some of the day's stress faded, her mind returned to Chris Shepard. The meeting had gone a lot better than it might have. Of course, for all she knew, Dr. Shepard had already called the Jackson field office and reported her visit.

How many people could react with equanimity to the kind of accusation she had made today? Reduced to its essentials, her message was *I think your wife is planning to kill you.* If Shepard *had* reported her, she would soon be getting a call from Washington. Like any successful field agent, Alex had made enemies as well as friends in the Bureau. But unlike most of those agents, she had both in high places. One of those enemies had almost gotten her fired after James Broadbent's death, but he'd been forced to settle for her banishment to Charlotte. If he suspected dereliction of duty there, the mildest response she could expect would be immediate recall to headquarters for an "interview" with the Office of Professional Responsibility, the Bureau's equivalent of Internal Affairs. Even a cursory investigation in Charlotte would prove their case, and then . . . a squalid end to her once-stellar career.

But Alex had a good feeling about Chris Shepard. He was quick on the uptake, and she liked that. He was a good listener—which was rare in men and seemed even rarer in male physicians, at least in Alex's experience. Shepard *had* married a witch—and a blond one at that—but then a lot of decent guys did that. He'd waited until he was thirty-five to get remarried, which made Alex wonder about his first wife. Shepard had married his college sweetheart during his first year of medical school, but two years after graduation—just as he was finishing up a commitment to practice in the dirt-poor Mississippi Delta to pay off his school loans—there had been a quick divorce. No kids, no muss, no fuss: nothing but "irreconcilable differences" in the court records. But there had to be more to it than that. Otherwise, how had a single doctor who wasn't hard to look at evaded marriage for almost five years after his divorce?

That first wife did a number on him, Alex thought. *He was damaged goods for a while. That's why he went for Thora, the ice queen. There's a lot of damage in that girl, too, and I don't think Dr. Chris knows much about it. . . .*

Alex reluctantly turned her mind to more mundane matters, like finances. A kindly accountant might tell her that the outlook was discouraging, but her own view was more succinct: she was broke. It cost real money to run a murder investigation, even when you were doing a lot of the legwork yourself. She was paying two private detective agencies regularly, and various others for small contract jobs. Most of the work was being done by her father's old agency, but even with Will Kilmer giving her all the breaks he could, the fees were eating her alive. Surveillance was the main drain. "Uncle" Will couldn't send out operatives on goodwill alone. Time spent working Alex's case was time stolen from others—man-hours piling upon man-hours, each day's accumulation taking a hefty bite out of her hemorrhaging retirement fund. On top of that, she was paying for gasoline, airfare between Jackson and Charlotte, private nurses for her mother . . . there was no end to it.

The Charlotte apartment was her most urgent problem. For the last three years, she'd leased a condo in Washington, D.C. If she had bought it instead, she could have sold it tomorrow for double her money. But that was a pipe dream. A prudent agent would have dumped the condo after getting transfer orders, but Alex had kept it, knowing that her superiors would learn that she had and would see this as a tangible symbol of her belief in her eventual redemption. But now on top of the condo she had a six-month lease on a place in Charlotte, an apartment she'd slept in fewer than a dozen nights. She'd paid her second month's rent to maintain the fiction that she was diligently working at her punishment duty, but she simply couldn't afford to continue. Yet if she broke the lease, her superiors would eventually find out. She thought of possible explanations, but none that would mollify the Office of Professional Responsibility.

"Shit," she muttered, tossing the cold washcloth onto the other bed.

Meggie leaped into the air, startled by the wet rag. Alex hadn't seen her curl up on the bed, and now she had an indignant cat on her hands. "I'd be pissed, too," she said, getting up and going to her computer.

She logged on to MSN and checked her Contacts list to see whether Jamie was online, but the icon beside his screen name—Ironman QB—was red, not green. This didn't worry her. Their nightly webcam ritual normally occurred later, after Bill had gone to bed. Though only ten years old, Jamie was quite talented with computers. And since one of the few things Bill was generous with was allowance—guilt money, she knew—Jamie had been able to purchase a webcam that allowed him to open a video link with Alex anytime that both of them were logged on to MSN. Secret communication with a ten-year-old boy might fall on the questionable side of the ethical spectrum, but Alex figured it paled in comparison to premeditated murder. And since Grace had charged her with protecting Jamie, Alex felt justified in maintaining contact any way she could.

Leaving her MSN screen name active, she got up from the desk, took her cell phone from her purse, and dialed her mother's house. A nurse answered.

"It's Alex. Is she awake?"

"No, she's sleeping. She's on the morphine pump again."

Oh, God. "How's she doing apart from the pain?"

"No change, really. Not physically. Emotionally . . ." The nurse trailed off.

"What is it?"

"She seems down."

Of course she is. She's dying. And she's doing it alone. "Tell her I'll call back later," Alex whispered.

"She's been saying you might be coming back to Mississippi soon."

I'm already in Mississippi. Alex shut her eyes against the guilt of the necessary lie. "I may be, but I'm stuck in Charlotte for now. Are the doctors checking on her regularly?"

"Yes, ma'am."

"Please call me if there's any change."

"I'll make sure someone does."

"Thank you. Good-bye."

Alex shoved her Glock into her waistband at the small of her back, flipped her shirttail over its butt, then picked up Meggie and walked outside to the parking lot. Room 125 faced the pool, which was empty at this hour. She felt like swimming some laps, but she hadn't packed a bathing suit, nor had she thought to buy one when she was at Wal-Mart. The lobby building of the Days Inn was styled after an antebellum mansion, in imitation of Natchez's primary tourist attractions. Beyond the lobby and a one-story line of rooms, an ancient tennis court lay beneath a rectangle of oak trees. Alex scratched Meggie's ears and walked toward it.

She had planned to register at the Eola Hotel downtown, which she remembered from a childhood visit to Natchez, but she'd found she couldn't hack the rate. The Days Inn was fifty-nine bucks a night, Meggie's fee included. Its parking lot led right onto Highway 61. Turn left and you were headed to New Orleans; turn right, Chicago. *I'm losing it,* Alex thought. *Get a grip.*

She stepped onto the cracked green surface of the tennis court and sniffed the air. She smelled a heavy potpourri of verdant foliage: forest leaves, kudzu, and pine needles laced with honeysuckle, azalea, and sweet olive. She smelled water, too, real running water, not the sterile pool behind her. Somewhere nearby, a creek was winding its way through the forested city toward the mighty river that rolled only a mile to the west.

Alex had only been to Natchez three times in her life, but she knew one thing: it was different from everywhere else. Most Americans considered Mississippi unique in their experience, but Natchez was unique in Mississippi. An arrogant city, to her way of thinking, though a certain amount of arrogance could be justified, especially about the past. The oldest city on the Mississippi River, Natchez had grown fantastically wealthy before the rich Delta upriver had even been cleared. Governed by England, France, and Spain in turn, the city had absorbed the style, manners, and architecture of those European powers and thus quite naturally saw herself as superior to the rest of the state of which she was nominally a part. This won Natchez few supporters outside her borders, but her cotton-rich leaders cared so little that they surrendered the magnificent city without firing a shot. It was for this reason that Alex, growing up in Jackson, had occasionally heard hisses when Natchez was mentioned in conversation. Yet that bloodless surrender had allowed the city to survive the terrible war intact, much like Charleston and Savannah, and Natchez remained a world unto itself, seemingly immune to history, outside of time.

As the fertile soil surrounding Natchez was depleted, the cotton business moved north to the Delta, yet Natchez did not die. Decades later, travelers from around the world began making pilgrimages to the pristine jewel of the Old South, to see decadent opulence preserved as though by divine intervention (though in fact its beauty was maintained by the free labor of countless society ladies). Even the hard-shell Baptists in rural Mississippi had a grudging fascination with the river city whose bars stayed open all night and whose black-owned whorehouse was known by name in Paris. The discovery of oil beneath the old cotton fields resurrected the city's vital spirit for another forty years, and some of its celebrated wealth returned. As a young girl visiting to take part in the Confederate Pageant, Alex had briefly been sucked into a social tornado that only old blood, new money, and simmering racial tension could generate. But by the time she visited again—during college with a sorority sister—the city had seemed a faded image of itself, everything smaller in scale, less vivid in color.

During the past five days, Alex had read the *Natchez Examiner* from front to back every morning while following Thora Shepard on her runs. What she saw in those pages was a city still wrestling with the demons of its past. Half-black and half-white, this former capital of the plantation South could not seem to find its place in the modern world. Alex wondered what had brought a man like Chris Shepard back here after a topflight performance in medical school. Maybe the city sang a siren song that only its natives could hear.

She walked back to the pool and set Meggie down at the shallow end. As the cat perched gracefully on the edge and lapped up the placid water, Alex thought of Chris Shepard in his white coat. After five weeks of frenetic investigation, her fate—and Jamie's—lay in the doctor's hands. She planned to give Shepard some time to think about today's meeting, but not too much. During their next visit, she'd feed him more facts—just enough to set the hook. He'd been intrigued by that first nibble, she could tell. Who wouldn't have been? She'd presented him with a classic murder mystery: Alfred Hitchcock brought to life. The problem was, it was Chris Shepard's life. And Shepard's wife. In the end, of course, the doctor's decision about whether to help her would be based upon factors Alex could never know: the secret realities of his marriage, unfathomable currents of emotion that no investigator could ever plumb. But she was betting that he would help.

She'd been following Thora for five days now, and she was certain that Thora was leading a secret life. On some level, her husband had to know that. But would he consciously acknowledge it? People saw only what they wanted to see, and only when they were ready to see it. Reality might be painfully obvious to others, but in love, everything was veiled. By hope, by fear, and most of all by trust. Alex's father had struggled to teach her this, but it had taken personal experience to etch the truth into the marrow of her bones.

Trust only your blood.

She picked up Meggie and walked back toward her room. A few miles to the south, Chris Shepard was probably lying wide-awake in bed, wondering if he knew the woman beside him at all. Alex was sorry for pulling his world inside out, but she didn't regret it. Left to the mercy of his wife, Shepard probably wouldn't have survived the month. As she reached for the doorknob, she realized that she had made her decision about the Charlotte apartment.

"Sayonara," she said softly.

She bolted the door behind her and sat down at her computer. Jamie still wasn't online. Her watch read 11:25 p.m. Alex's chest and throat began to tighten, as though she were breathing noxious fumes. She badly needed sleep, but she would wait until Jamie's icon turned green, no matter how long it took. She rubbed her eyes, fished a pink Tab Energy drink from her ice chest, sat back down, and drank half the can in a few seconds. By the time she burped, she could already feel the rush of caffeine absorbed through her tongue.

"Come on, baby," she murmured. "Come on. Talk to Aunt Alex."

Jamie's icon remained red.

Chris had never been a good liar. His father hadn't either. Buddy Shepard never earned much money, but he had earned respect wherever he worked, and he'd passed his integrity on to his son. Integrity wasn't an easy thing to maintain, Chris had found, in a world that ran according to the laws of human nature.

Walking down the dark path between his house and the remodeled barn behind it, he wasn't even sure what the right thing was. His tread was heavy, and he took no joy in his surroundings, which had always been a source of pride. After moving to Natchez, he had used a chunk of his savings to buy a large house sited on twenty acres of the former Elgin plantation, an estate south of town that predated the Civil War. Despite its isolation, the house was only five minutes from Ben's school and less than ten minutes from both Natchez hospitals. Chris couldn't see how this situation could be improved upon, but Thora had long wanted to move to Avalon, a trendy new subdivision springing up farther south. Red Simmons had always resisted this desire, but after several months of discussion Chris had finally given in, conceding that in the new neighborhood Ben would have more friends living nearby.

Their house in Avalon—he privately called it the McMansion—was three-fifths finished. Thora was personally overseeing construction, but Chris rarely visited the site. He had been raised in a series of rural towns (his father had worked for International Paper, and they were transferred every couple of years), and he believed that growing up in the country had played a large part in forging his self-reliance. He knew that Ben would benefit from a similar environment, and for this reason he had privately decided not to sell this land when they moved to Avalon.

A large building appeared before him in the darkness, but its rustic exterior belied its real purpose. Chris had remodeled this barn himself, converting it into a video production studio to house the technology of his avocation—his "camera hobby" as Thora called it, which bothered him more than he admitted. He unlocked the door and walked into his main production room, a haven of blond maple and glass, spotlessly clean and kept at sixty-five degrees for the health of the cameras, computers, and other equipment. Simply entering this room elevated his mood. Booting up his Apple G5 did even more. In this room he could leave the thousand importunities of daily life behind. Here, he actually had control over what he was doing. And deep down, he felt that he was doing something great.

Chris had gotten into filmmaking during college, where he'd worked on several documentaries, two of which had won national awards. During medical school, he produced a documentary called *A Day in the*

Life of a Resident. Shot with a hidden camera, this digital video had almost ended his medical career before it began. But after a fellow student sent the tape to a national news network, it had ultimately contributed to the limiting of work hours for medical residents. Once Chris began practicing medicine for real, though, he'd found that he had little time for filming anything. Medicine offered many rewards, but spare time wasn't one of them.

But last year, after associating with Dr. Tom Cage, an old-time general practitioner in Natchez, Chris had discovered a way to combine his vocation with his avocation. After close observation of his new partner, Chris began work on a documentary about the decline of traditional primary-care medicine. And Mississippi, which was ten years behind the rest of the country in most things, was the perfect place to do that.

Tom Cage was one of those doctors who would spend a full hour listening to a patient, if a sympathetic ear was what that patient needed most. Seventy-three years old, Tom suffered from several serious chronic diseases; and as he often admitted, he was sicker than many of his patients. But he still worked eighty-hour weeks, and when he wasn't working, he was reading journals to stay up on the latest standards of care. Dr. Cage frequently touched patients during his exams, and he paid close attention to what he felt. Most important, he questioned patients deeply about not only their specific symptoms, but also other areas of their lives that might yield clues to their general health. He thought about his fees in terms of trying to save his patients money (and thus he was not rich), and he never thought about the dozens of patients—many of them walk-ins—waiting to see him. Tom Cage stayed at his office until the last patient was seen, and only then did he declare his workday done.

For Chris, who had begun his private-practice career in a group of internists his own age, Dr. Cage's methods had come as a profound shock. To physicians of Chris's generation, a good practice meant high pay, short working hours, and an abundance of partners to take call, so that one night a week was the most you had to worry about phone calls from patients. Chris's former partners practiced defensive medicine, ordering every lab test remotely relevant to every patient's symptoms, but spending as little time as possible with those patients, all in the hallowed name of gross income. This kind of practice was anathema to Tom Cage. A system geared toward the convenience and gain of the physician was the tail wagging the dog. Dr. Cage saw medicine as a life of service: a noble calling, perhaps, but still a life of service. And that, Chris believed, was worth documenting for posterity.

Deep down, he shared a lot of Tom's feelings about modern medicine. His own ideas of service had cost him his first wife, and he had been cautious in love after that. Only after Thora Rayner entered his life had Chris felt emboldened to take such a risk again. For this reason, Agent Morse's visit had disturbed him more than it might have another man. Chris had fundamentally misjudged his first wife, and to admit that he might have done the same thing a second time would be hard. In fact, he reflected, the niggling worries that had surfaced during baseball practice were just that—inconsequential peeves. Every adult went through personality changes, and the first year of a marriage was always a time of adjustment. That Thora had started spending more money than she used to, or wearing tighter clothes, meant nothing in the grand scheme of things.

Chris opened the studio's refrigerator, poured a nearly freezing shot of Grey Goose, and drank it off. Then he sat down before his G5, opened Final Cut Pro, and began reviewing some scenes he'd filmed last week. Shooting directly to hard drives from his Canon XL2S meant that he wasted no time dumping footage from tape to his computer. Unfolding before him now was an interview with Tom Cage and a black woman who had been his patient since 1963. That woman now had a great-great-granddaughter, and that little girl was playing at her feet. Tom preferred not to treat children anymore, but this woman had refused to take her "grandchild" to any other doctor. Chris had more recent experience with pediatrics than Tom did, and he'd been proud to help in evaluating the child's high fever (which Tom had feared might be meningitis).

As the old woman spoke about Dr. Cage traveling to her home one night during the blizzard of 1963, Chris felt a strange tide of emotion moving through him. Until this morning, when Agent Morse had subversively entered his life, he'd felt more content than he had since childhood. His father had been a good man, but he'd rarely pondered life's deeper mysteries. In Tom Cage, Chris had found a mentor with a wealth of knowledge to pass on, but who did so without pretense or didacticism, almost like a Zen master. A trenchant question here, a small gesture while a patient's attention was elsewhere—in this unassuming way, Tom had been turning Chris into more than a first-class internist: he was turning him into a healer.

But a career isn't enough to sustain a man, Chris thought, feeling the vodka cross his blood-brain barrier. *Not even if it's a passionate calling. A man needs someone to engage his deepest emotions, to relieve his drives, to soften his obsessions, to accept the gifts he feels compelled to give, and maybe most important, to simply be with him during the thousands of small moments that in aggregate compose a life.*

For almost two years, Chris had believed that Thora was that person. Along with Ben, she had closed some magic circle in his life. Before he married Thora, Chris had not understood how acting as a father to Ben would affect him. But in less than a year, with Chris's patient attention, the boy had blossomed into a young man who amazed his teachers with his attitude and schoolwork. He was no slouch on the athletic field, either. The pride Chris felt in Ben had stunned him, and he'd felt it a solemn duty—even a privilege—to adopt the boy. Given what he felt for Ben, Chris could hardly imagine what having his own biological child might do to him. He almost felt guilty for asking more of life than he already had. Every week he watched men die without the things he now possessed, either because they had never found them or because they had foolishly cast them away. Yet now . . . everything had changed somehow. Alexandra Morse had released a serpent of doubt into his personal Eden, forcing him to wonder if he truly possessed any of the gifts he had believed to be his.

"Goddamn it," he murmured. "God*damn* woman."

"Did I mess something up?" asked a worried voice.

Chris looked over his shoulder and saw Thora standing behind him. She wore a diaphanous blue nightgown and white slippers with wet blades of grass on them. He'd been so absorbed in the footage and his thoughts that he hadn't heard her enter the studio.

"You were pretty late getting home from the hospital," she said diffidently.

"I know."

"You have a lot of admissions?"

"Yeah. Most of them are routine stuff, but there's one case nobody can figure out. Don Allen consulted Tom about it, and Tom asked for my opinion."

A look of surprise widened Thora's eyes. "I can't believe Don Allen consulted with anybody."

Chris smiled faintly. "The patient's family pressured him into it. It killed Don to do it, I could tell. But if somebody doesn't figure out what this guy has, he could die."

"Why not ship him up to Jackson?"

"Don already talked to all the specialists at UMC. They've seen the test results, and they don't know what to think either. I think the family figured Tom has seen almost everything in almost fifty years of practicing medicine, so they wanted him consulted. But Tom is stumped, too. For now, anyway."

"My money's on you," Thora said, smiling. "I know you'll figure it out. You always do."

"I don't know, this time."

Thora moved closer, then leaned down and kissed Chris's forehead. "Turn back around," she said softly. "Toward the monitor."

It seemed an odd request, but after a moment he turned and faced the screen.

Thora began to rub his shoulders. She had surprisingly strong hands for a lithe woman, and the release of tension in his neck was so sudden that he felt a mild nausea.

"How does that feel?"

"I almost can't take it."

Her hands worked up the sides of his neck and began to knead the bunched muscles at the base of his skull. Then she slipped her fingertips into his ears and began to massage the shells, working steadily inward with increasing pressure. Before long he felt like sliding out of the chair and onto the floor. One of Thora's hands vanished, but her other moved down into his polo shirt, the palm circling his pectoral muscles with surprising force.

"You know what I was thinking?" she said.

"What?"

"We haven't tried to get me pregnant in a while."

No remark could have surprised him more. "You're right."

"Well . . . ?"

She slowly spun his chair until he found himself facing her bare breasts. Normally, they were porcelain pale—her Danish blood—but like her friends, Thora had recently become an addict of the tanning salon, and her skin glowed an uncharacteristic burnished gold, with nary a line in sight.

"Kiss them," she whispered.

He did.

She a made a purling sound deep in her throat, a nearly feline expression of pleasure, and he felt her shift position. While her fingers played in the hair at the back of his neck, he worked delicately but steadily at her nipples. They were infallible sources of arousal, and soon Thora was breathing in shallow rasps. She bent her knees and reached down to see if he was ready. Finding him hard, she unsnapped his pants, then knelt and tried to pull them down. He raised his hips for her, then sat back down.

Without delay Thora lifted her gown and sat, wrapping her strong legs around his waist and the chair back. Chris groaned, nearly overcome by her urgency, which he had not experienced in some time. But tonight Thora was the woman he had fallen in love with two years ago, and the power of this incarnation pushed him quickly toward climax. She gazed into his eyes as she rode him, silently urging him on, but at the last moment she planted both feet on the floor and thrust herself up and off him.

"What?" he cried.

"That's not exactly the ideal position for bringing a new generation into the world," she said, her eyes teasing him with mock reproach.

"Oh."

Taking hold of his penis, she pulled him over to the leather sofa, then lay down on her back and motioned for him to mount her. After staring at her long enough to engrave the image in his mind, he did. As Thora whispered lewd encouragements in his ear, the interview with Alex Morse rose inexplicably into his mind. Their conversation had a surreal quality now. Could such a thing be possible? Had someone pretending to be a patient actually lied her way into his office and then accused his wife of murder? And *before* the fact? It was crazy—

"Now," Thora told him. *"Now, now, now . . ."*

Chris thrust deep and held the contact, letting Thora take herself over the threshold. When she cried out, her nails raking his shoulder blades, he let himself go, and a white glare burned away all ambiguity.

As he came slowly back to the present, Thora strained upward to kiss his lips, then fell back, sweating despite the steady flow of air-conditioning. Chris drew out and lay beside her on the cold leather.

"You can get up if you want to," she said. "I'm going to stay here a few minutes. Let things take their natural course."

He laughed. "I'm fine right here."

"Good answer."

They lay in silence for a while. Then Thora said, "Is everything all right, Chris?"

"Why do you ask?"

"You seemed distant today. Did something happen at work?"

God, did something happen. "Just the usual."

"Is the new house bothering you again?"

"I haven't even thought about it."

She looked disappointed. "I don't know if that's good either."

He forced a smile. "The house is fine. It just takes a while to turn a country boy into a city boy."

"If it's possible at all."

"We'll soon find out."

Thora pulled damp hair out of her eyes. "Oh, I forgot. I wanted to ask you something."

"What?"

"Laura Canning is going up to the Alluvian this week. She asked me to go with her."

"The Alluvian?"

"You know, that hotel in Greenwood. Up in the Delta. The one the Viking Range people remodeled. It's supposed to be stunning. You practiced up in the Delta for a while, didn't you?"

He laughed. "My patient base couldn't afford that kind of place."

"They supposedly have a terrific spa up there. People fly down from New York to stay there. Morgan Freeman has that blues club in the Delta, you know, and he's stayed at the Alluvian."

Chris nodded. He liked Morgan Freeman's work, but he wasn't into picking spas based on where Hollywood actors went. He wasn't into spas at all, to be honest. He broke all the sweat he needed to while maintaining the twenty acres of land around his house.

"If you don't want me to go, I won't," Thora said, seemingly without rancor. "But this is Ben's last week of school, and he always asks you for help with his homework anyway. I don't have the patience."

Chris couldn't argue this point. "When are we talking about?"

"A couple of days from now, probably. We'd just be gone three nights. Then right back home. Mud packs and champagne, a little blues music, then home."

Chris nodded and forced another smile, but this one took more effort. It wasn't that he didn't want Thora to have fun. It was Alex Morse's voice whispering in his head: *Is your wife planning to be out of town anytime soon?*

"Chris?" Thora asked. "Tell the truth. Do you want me to stay home?"

He recalled her face as she made love to him, the unalloyed pleasure in her blue-gray eyes. Now she was lying on her back on chilly leather so that his sperm would have the maximum probability of impregnating her. What the hell was he worried about? "I think I'm just worn-out," he said. "Between work and rounds and working on my project—"

"And baseball practice," Thora added. "Ninety minutes a day in eighty-five-degree heat with a bunch of wild Indians."

"You go up to the Delta and chill out," he said, though he had never associated the words *Delta* and *chill* in his mind before. "Ben and I will be fine."

Thora gave him an elfin smile, then kissed him again. "You stay right here."

He stared as she jumped up and ran to the studio door, then disappeared through it. She reappeared a moment later, holding both hands behind her back.

"What are you doing?" he asked, feeling strangely anxious.

"I've got a surprise for you. Two surprises."

He sat up on the couch. "What? I don't need anything."

She laughed and moved closer. "Are you sure?"

"Yes."

She brought her right hand from behind her back. In it was a plate of chocolate chip cookies. His mouth watered at the scent of them—until Alex Morse's warnings sounded in his head. Before he had to make a choice about eating the cookies, Thora held out a cardboard tube like the ones she used to carry blueprints for the new house. Chris forced a smile, but the prospect of discussing the Avalon house did not please him in the least.

"I see that frown," Thora said, setting the cookies beside him, then perching her perfect derriere on his knees. "You just wait and see."

She removed a sheet of paper from the tube, un-
rolled it, and spread it across her nude thighs. Chris
saw what appeared to be plans for a new building
behind the seven-thousand-square-foot house that was
now nearing completion. A rather large building.

"What's that?" he asked, groaning internally. "A
private gym?"

Thora laughed. "No. That's your new studio."

His face flushed. "What?"

She smiled and kissed his cheek. "That's my house-
warming present to you. I had our architect consult
with an expert in New York. You're looking at a state-
of-the-art video production studio. All you have to do
is select your equipment."

"Thora . . . you can't be serious."

Her smile broadened. "Oh, I'm serious. They've
already poured the foundation and run the high-tech
cabling. *Very* expensive."

This was almost too much to absorb after what
Chris had endured today. He wanted to get up and
pace the room, but Thora had him pinned to the couch.
Suddenly, she tossed the plans and the tube onto the
couch and hugged him tight.

"I'm not letting you slip back here every time you
want to edit your videos. You're stuck with me, understand?"

He didn't. He felt as though he had swallowed some
sort of hallucinogen. But then, if Alex Morse had not
visited his office this morning, none of this would seem
anything but a wonderful surprise.

"I finally surprised you," Thora said in an awestruck
voice. "I did, didn't I?"

He nodded in a daze.

She took a cookie from the plate and held it to his lips. "Here. You need your strength."

"No, thanks."

Her disappointment was plain. "I actually made these from scratch."

"I'm sorry. I'm really not hungry. I'll eat some later."

She shrugged, then popped the cookie into her mouth. "Your loss," she said, her eyes twinkling as she chewed. "Mmm . . . almost better than sex."

Chris smelled the melting chocolate in her mouth, watched her swallow with exaggerated pleasure. *Alex Morse is batshit,* he told himself.

Thora looked into his eyes, then took his hand and cupped her breast with it. "You up for a second round? We can raise the odds by two hundred million or so."

He felt like an astronaut cut loose from his spacecraft, drifting steadily away from everything familiar. *Who could live like this?* he wondered. *Second-guessing every move in my own house?*

He closed his eyes and kissed Thora with desperate fervor.

CHAPTER

7

Alex's heart leaped when she saw the little red icon turn green, indicating that Jamie had logged on to MSN. She'd been checking for the past three hours, playing Spider Solitaire and waiting for Jamie's icon to light up.

A new screen like a small TV appeared within her main screen, but the TV was blank. Then an image of Jamie sitting at his desk in his room at Bill Fennell's house flashed up. The immediacy of the webcam was overwhelming at first. It truly was like being in the same room with the person you were talking to. You could see every emotion in their eyes, every movement of their face. Tonight Jamie was wearing an Atlanta Braves T-shirt and the yellow baseball cap of his Dixie Youth team. His eyes weren't looking at her, but at his monitor, so that he could watch her image projected from his screen. She knew that she looked the same to him, since she was staring at his image and not the camera mounted atop her screen.

"Hey, Aunt Alex," he said. "Sorry I'm late."

She smiled genuinely for the first time all day. "It's

okay. You know I'll be here whenever you log on. What you been doing, bub?"

Jamie smiled. "I had a baseball game."

"How did it go?"

"They killed us."

"I'm sorry. How did *you* do?"

"I got a double."

Alex yelped and applauded. "That's great!"

Jamie's smile vanished. "But I struck out twice."

"That's okay. Even the pros strike out."

"Twice in one game?"

"Sure they do. I once saw Hank Aaron strike out three times in one game." This was a lie, but a harmless one. Hank Aaron was about the only player whose name she knew, and him only because of her father.

"Who's Hank Aaron?" Jamie asked.

"He hit more home runs than Babe Ruth."

"Oh. I thought that was Barry Bonds."

Alex shrugged. "It doesn't matter. You got a double, that's what matters. What else has been going on?"

Jamie sighed like a fifty-year-old man. "I don't know."

"Yes, you do. Come on."

"I think she's over here right now."

"Missy?" Missy Hammond was Bill's mistress.

Jamie nodded.

Anger flooded through Alex; she tasted copper in her mouth. "Why do you think that? Did you see her?"

"No." Jamie glanced behind him, at his bedroom door. "Dad thinks I'm asleep now. He came in to check, and I had the lights off. After a few minutes, I heard the back door. I thought he might be leaving, so I sneaked out to the rail. I didn't see anything, but after a while I heard somebody laughing. It sounded exactly like her."

Alex didn't know what to say. "I'm sorry, Jamie. Let's talk about something else."

The boy hung his head. "That's easy for you to say. Why don't you just come get me? Dad wants to be with her, not me. I'm not sleepy at all."

"I can't just come get you. We talked about that. But your father wants you, Jamie." Alex wasn't sure whether this was true. "He wants both of you."

The boy shook his head. "After the game, all Dad talked about was my strikeouts. And what else I did wrong. Nothing about my double."

Alex put on a smile and nodded as though she understood. "I think a lot of dads are like that. Your granddad did that when I played softball."

Jamie looked surprised. "Really?"

"Oh, yeah. He didn't hesitate to tell me what I did wrong."

This wasn't quite true. Jim Morse could give constructive criticism, but he knew how to do it without making you feel bad. And most of what Alex remembered from being ten years old was unconditional praise.

"Your dad's just trying to help you improve," she added.

"I guess. I don't like it, though." Jamie reached down, then lifted a heavy book onto his desk. "I was supposed to do my homework earlier, but I didn't feel like it. Can I do it now?"

"Sure."

"Will you stay on while I do it?"

Alex smiled. "You know I will."

Now Jamie was grinning. They had done this many times since Grace's death. While Jamie read his assignment, Alex sat watching him, her mind roving back through the past. For some reason her father was in her mind tonight. Jim Morse had loved his grandson more than anything else in the world, and that might have included his own daughters. When Grace and Alex were young, Jim had been building a business, and despite putting real effort into being a father, he had seen them mostly in passing. But with Jamie, he'd had endless hours to spend with the boy. Jim had taught him to hunt and fish, to water-ski, to fly kites, and not just to throw a baseball but to pitch one for real. Jamie Fennell could throw a curveball when he was eight years old. Jim had spent all this time with Jamie despite the fact that Jim and Bill Fennell did not get along. In Alex's eyes, her father had proved his manhood for all time by compromising as much as was required to keep close contact with his grandson.

One thing Alex knew in her bones, though: if her father had been alive to hear Grace's deathbed accusation of murder, the events of the past weeks would have unfolded differently. That very night, Bill Fennell would have been hauled into an empty room, slammed against a wall, and made to cough up all the sediment at the bottom of his soul. Had that treatment not proved sufficient to dredge up the truth, Bill would have been taken on an involuntary boat ride with Jim Morse, Will Kilmer, and some of the other ex-cops who worked for their detective agency. One way or another, Bill would have spilled all he knew about Grace's death. And Jamie would not be living in Bill's ugly mansion on the edge of the Ross Barnett Reservoir in Jackson. If the courts didn't save

Jamie, his grandfather would have taken him somewhere safe to be raised by people who loved him. And Alex would have gone with them. She wouldn't have thought twice about it.

None of that had happened, of course. Because like his daughter Grace, Jim Morse was dead. Alex had studied all the eyewitness accounts, but none of them ever dovetailed exactly—unlike the accounts of her own act of lunacy at the bank, when Broadbent was killed. Everybody had seen exactly the same thing on that day. But with her father's death it was different. At age sixty, Jim had walked into a dry cleaner's late on a Friday afternoon. He normally used the drive-through window, but that day he chose to go inside. Two female clerks stood behind the counter. A young black man wearing a three-piece suit was waiting in the store, but he was no customer. The real customers were lying flat on their stomachs behind the counter, beside a grocery bag filled with cash from the register.

Jim didn't know that when he walked in, but Alex figured it had taken him about six seconds to realize something was wrong. No one was going to bluff Jim Morse out of a robbery in progress, no matter how old he was. The girls behind the counter were so scared they could hardly speak when Jim walked up to the counter and started a monologue about the weather: how warm the fall had been, and how it used to snow once or twice a year in Mississippi, but nowadays almost never. One clerk saw Jim glance behind the counter without moving his head, but the other didn't. What she did see was Jim take his wife's clothes from the hanging rod and turn to leave the store. As he passed the waiting "customer," Jim flattened him with a savage blow to the throat. The clerk was shocked that "an old gray-haired dude" had attacked a muscular man in his early twenties. No one who knew Jim Morse was surprised. He'd often carried a gun after retirement, but he hadn't on that day, not for a short run to the cleaner's. Jim was digging in the fallen robber's jacket when the plate-glass window of the store exploded. One clerk screamed, then fell silent as a bullet punctured her left cheek. The other dived behind the counter. After that, few facts were known.

The medical examiner believed that the shot that killed Alex's father had been fired from behind the counter, not from the getaway car parked out front. Not that it mattered. After a lifetime spent courting danger, Jim Morse had simply run out of luck. And despite relentless efforts by the police department, by his old partner, and even a large reward offered by the Police Benevolent Association, his killers were never caught. Alex knew that her father had not wanted to die that day, but she knew something else, too: he would rather have died like that than the way his wife was dying now—in agony and by inches.

The sound of Jamie closing his book startled her from her reverie.

"I'm done," he said, his green eyes still on the screen. "It's way easier when you're with me."

"I like being here with you. It helps me work, too."

Jamie smiled. "You weren't working. I saw you. You were just sitting there."

"I was working in my head. A lot of my work is like that."

Jamie's smile vanished, and he looked away from the screen.

"Jamie? Are you all right? Look at me, honey. Look into the camera."

At length, he did, and his sad eyes pierced her to the core.

"Aunt Alex?"

"Yes?"

"I miss my mom."

Alex forced herself to repress her grief. Tears were pooling in her eyes, but they would not help Jamie. One thing she had learned the hard way: when adults started crying, kids lost all their composure.

"I know you do, baby," she said softly. "I miss her, too."

"She used to say what you said. That she was working in her head."

Alex tilted back her head and wiped her eyes, unable to shut out the memory of the night Grace died, when she'd snatched up Jamie and raced out of the hospital. She hadn't gone far, just to a nearby Pizza Hut, where she'd broken the news of Grace's death and comforted Jamie as best she could. Her own father had died only six months before, and his death had hit Jamie as hard as it had her. But Grace's death was a tragedy of such magnitude that the boy simply could not process it. Alex had buried his head between her breasts, silently praying for the power to revoke death, and hoping that Grace had been out of her mind when she accused her husband of murder.

Alex held an opened hand up to the eye of the camera. "You be strong, little man. You do that for me, okay? Things are going to get better."

Jamie put up his hand, too. "Are they?"

"You bet. I'm working on it right now."

"Good." Jamie looked back at the door. "I guess I better go now."

Alex blinked back more tears. "Same time tomorrow?"

Jamie smiled faintly. "Same time."

Then he was gone.

Alex got up from the desk with tears streaming down her cheeks. She spat curses and stomped around the motel room like a confined mental patient, but she knew she hadn't lost her mind yet. She looked down at the newspaper photo of her father. He would understand why she was living in this claustrophobic motel instead of keeping a deathwatch over her mother's bed. Right or wrong, Jim would be doing the same thing: trying to save his grandson. And no matter what it took, Alex was going to fulfill her promise to Grace. If the Bureau wanted to fire her for doing the job it should have been doing, then the Bureau could go to hell. There was law, and there was justice. And no Morse she was related to had ever had any trouble recognizing the difference.

Alex stripped off her pants and shirt, walked out to the empty pool, and started swimming laps in her underwear. It was too late for anyone decent to complain, and if a Bill Fennell type wanted to sit on the plastic furniture and ogle her ass while she worked out her frustration, then he was welcome to it. If he was still there when she got out, she'd kick his butt across the parking lot.

CHAPTER

8

Dr. Eldon Tarver walked slowly along the park path, his big head down, his eyes in a practiced state of general focus, searching for feathers in the tall grass. In one hand he carried a Nike duffel bag, in the other an aluminum Reach-Arm device, used by most people for picking up soda cans and litter from the ground. But Dr. Tarver was not like most people. He was using the Reach-Arm to pick up dead birds, which he then sealed inside Ziploc bags and dropped into the Nike duffel. He'd been out since before dawn, and he'd bagged four specimens already, three sparrows and a martin. Two seemed quite fresh, and this boded well for the work he would do later in the morning.

Dr. Tarver had seen only two other humans so far, both runners. Not many people ventured into this corner of the park, where branches hung low to the ground and the path was overgrown in many places. The doctor had startled both runners, partly by his simple presence at this place and time, but also because of his appearance. Eldon Tarver would never be mistaken for a runner.

He was not dressed in shorts or warm-ups, but in cheap slacks and a pullover from the Casual Male Big & Tall shop on County Line Road. Dr. Tarver stood six feet three inches tall, with a barrel chest and ropy arms covered with black hair. He had been bald since the age of forty, but he wore a full gray beard that gave him the look of a Mennonite preacher. He had preacher's eyes, too—not *parson's* eyes, but the burning orbs of a revealed prophet—bright blue irises that shimmered in the center of their dark sockets like coins at the bottom of a well. When he was angry, those eyes could burn like the eyes of a demon, but few people had ever seen this. More often, his eyes radiated a glacial coldness. Some women at the medical center thought him handsome, but others called him downright ugly, this impression being bolstered by what most people thought was a wine-stain birthmark on his left cheek. The disfiguring mark was actually a severe arteriovenous anomaly, a horror that had begun mildly during childhood but which during puberty had flamed to the surface like the sign of a guilty conscience. All these qualities had combined to make even the large male runner jig five steps to the right as he passed, for it took five steps to get clear of the bearded giant ambling along the path with his aluminum stick and duffel bag.

As the first yellow rays of sunlight spilled through the oak limbs to the east, another runner appeared—a girl this time, a vision in tight blue Under Armour with white wires trailing from her golden hair. The wires disappeared into an iPod strapped to her upper arm. Dr. Tarver wanted to watch her approach, but just then he noticed another bird off the path, this one twitching in its death throes. It might have fallen only seconds ago.

The girl's shoes swished through the dewy grass as she left the asphalt path on the side opposite the doctor. She tried to make it appear as though she'd done this out of courtesy, but she could not deceive him. He divided his attention between the girl and the bird, one filled with life, the other dying fast. She tried not to look at him as she sprinted past, but she couldn't manage it. Twice her pupils flicked toward him, gauging the distance, making sure he hadn't moved closer. Threat assessment was such a finely tuned gift, one of the blessings of evolution. He smiled as the girl passed, then turned and regarded her flexing glutes as they receded from view, appreciating their shape with the cool regard of an expert anatomist.

After she'd vanished around a bend, he stood still, breathing the wake of her perfume—an ill-advised accessory for morning jogs if one wanted to avoid unwelcome attention. After the fragrance had dissipated beyond detection, he knelt, donned surgical gloves, and withdrew a scalpel, a syringe, and a culture dish from his pocket. Then he tied on a surgical mask and laid open the sparrow's breast with a single incision. With a long finger he exposed the bird's liver. Inserting the tip of the hypodermic into the nearly black organ, he exerted a gentle back-pressure and probed with the needle until he was rewarded with a slow spurt of blood. He needed only a single cc—less, actually— but he took the full amount possible, then snapped the sparrow's neck with a quick twist and tossed its carcass into the underbrush.

Opening the petri dish, Dr. Tarver squirted some

blood onto the layer of minced chick embryo inside and rubbed it around with a sterile swab taken from his pocket. Then he closed the dish and slipped it into the duffel with the Ziploc bags. His gloves came off with a snap—those went into the bag, as well—and then he cleaned his hands with a dab of Purell. A good morning's work. When he got back to the lab, he'd test the last bird first. He felt confident that it was a carrier.

A slow shiver in the grass where he'd tossed the sparrow raised the hair on his arms. The accompanying sound was faint, but the sounds of childhood never faded. Dr. Tarver set down the Nike bag and walked lightly—very lightly, considering his size—toward the closing groove in the grass. As soon as he saw the rotting log, he knew. He closed his eyes for a moment, stilling himself at the center. Then he reached down with his left hand and lifted the log. What he saw beneath fluttered his heart: no crotalid, but a beautiful coil of red, yellow, and black shimmering in the sun.

"*Micrurus fulvius fulvius,*" he whispered.

He had uncovered an eastern coral snake, one of the shiest serpents in America, and undoubtedly the deadliest. With a fluid motion like that of a father stroking his child's hair, Tarver took hold of the stirring elapid behind its head and lifted it into the air. The brightly banded body coiled around his forearm—a full twenty inches of him—but this was not a strong snake. A cottonmouth or rattler would have struggled, using its strong muscles to try to whip away from him and strike. But the coral snake was no brutish pit viper, injecting prey with crude hemotoxin that caused terrible pain and swelling as it ate away the walls of blood vessels, bringing gangrene and infection to its human victims. No, the coral was a refined killer. Like its relative the cobra, it injected pure neurotoxin, which brought only numbness before shutting down the central nervous system of its prey, quickly bringing on paralysis and death.

Dr. Tarver was a pathologist, not a herpetologist, but he had a long history with snakes. It had begun in childhood, this education, and not by choice. For Dr. Tarver, serpents were inevitably bound up with the idea of God. Not the way his adoptive parents had seen this relationship—because only fools tempted death as a test of faith—but bound up with God nonetheless. As a boy Eldon had watched dozens of frightened rattlesnakes held high by chanting hillbillies who believed that God had anointed them against the lethal compounds in the bulging poison sacs behind the slitted eyes. He knew better. He had seen many of those hillbillies bitten on their hands, arms, necks, and faces, and every blessed one had suffered fleshly torments beyond their imagination. Some had lost digits, others limbs, and two had lost their lives. Eldon knew their fates because he had been one of those hillbillies once, not by choice or even by birth but by the authority of the State of Tennessee. He also knew that the skeptics who accused his adoptive father of keeping the snakes in refrigerators to make them sluggish, or of milking their venom before the services, had no idea whom they were talking about. The faith of those hillbillies was as genuine as the rocks they plowed from the brick-hard earth of the Appalachian foothills every day but Sunday. They *wanted* death in the church with them when they witnessed to the Lord. Eldon had personally gathered many of the vipers for Sunday and Wednesday services. The church elders had quickly seen that the big, birthmarked boy taken from the Presbyterian Children's Home in Knoxville had the gift—so much so that his adoptive father had begged him to take up the cloth himself. But that was another story. . . .

Eldon watched the sunlight play upon the coral's overlapping scales, each scale part of a perfect minuet of indescribable beauty. There had been no corals in Tennessee. You had to go east to North Carolina or south to Mississippi to find them. But during his long walks in the wilderness around Jackson, he had seen three or four in the past few years. It was one of the hidden pleasures of this much-maligned state.

The serpent's body curled around his arm in a fluid figure eight, a perfect symbol of infinity. His adoptive father's congregation had believed snakes to be incarnations of Satan, but the twin serpents on the caduceus that Eldon wore on a chain around his neck were far more representative of the reptile's true nature, at least in the symbolic realm. Serpents symbolized healing because the ancient Greeks had seen their skin-shedding as a process of healing and rebirth. Had the Greeks understood microbiology, they would have observed much deeper links between serpents and the secret machinery of life. But even the ancients had understood that snakes personified the fundamental paradox of all medicinal drugs: in small doses they cured, while in large ones they killed. He held the coral snake up to his face and laughed richly, then opened the Nike bag, slid the snake inside, and zipped it shut.

Turning toward the distant clearing where he'd parked his car, Dr. Tarver experienced a sense of fulfillment that far exceeded that which he had felt upon finding the dead birds. Indeed, he felt blessed. Americans lived in constant fear, yet they never really knew how close they were to death at all hours of the day and night. If you wanted to find death, you hardly had to go looking for it.

Stay in one place long enough, and it would find you.

Dr. Tarver's journey to his laboratory took him north along Interstate 55, east of the main cluster of office buildings that surrounded Jackson's great capitol dome. To his left, the AmSouth tower jutted up from the low skyline of the capital city. His gaze moved along the sixteenth floor, to the blue-black windows of the corner office. Eldon had driven along this interstate and checked those windows almost every day for the past five years. But today was the first time that sunlight had ever flashed back from the office like a silver beacon, reflecting off the aluminum foil that he had named as an emergency signal all those years ago.

The muscles of his big chest tightened, and his breathing shallowed. There had been bumps in the road before—small matters of planning, or miscommunication. But never had anything justified the use of this signal. The foil meant real trouble. Eldon had chosen this primitive method for precisely the same reason that intelligence agencies did. If you were truly in danger, possibly even blown, the worst thing you could do was contact your associates by any traceable method. Unlike a telephone or a computer or a pager, the foil was nonspecific. No one could ever prove it was a signal. Not even the NSA could train cameras on every square inch of land from which that square of foil could be seen. No, the foil had been a good idea.

So had the prearranged meeting. Andrew Rusk knew where to go; the question was, could he get there without being followed?

What could the emergency signal imply other than unwanted interest on the part of someone? But who? The police? The FBI? At the most fundamental level, it didn't matter. Dr. Tarver's first instinct was to eliminate the source of the danger. Only Andrew Rusk knew his identity, or anything about his recent activities. And Rusk could not be trusted to keep silent under pressure.

The lawyer thought he was strong, and by the standards of the early-twenty-first-century yuppie he might be. But that particular subspecies of *Homo sapiens* had no clue to the true nature of strength or hardship. No idea of self-reliance. Seconds after seeing the aluminum foil, Eldon was thinking of finding a comfortable perch overlooking one of the streets Rusk drove every day and putting a large-caliber bullet through the lawyer's cerebral cortex. Only by doing this could he insure his own safety. Of course, if he killed Rusk, he would never know the nature of the threat. Killing Rusk would also mean activating his escape plan, and Dr. Tarver wasn't ready to leave the country yet. He still had important work to do.

He glanced down at the Nike bag on the front seat beside him. The prearranged meeting place was thirty miles away. Did he have time to run the birds out to his lab? Should he risk meeting Rusk at all? *Yes,* answered his instinct. *Not one death has yet been called murder by the police. Not publicly anyway.* Even logic dictated that he should risk the meeting. No one could trap him in the place he had designated.

A new possibility arced through Eldon's mind. What if Rusk had put up the aluminum foil as *bait*? What if he'd somehow been caught and, in exchange for leniency, was offering up his accomplice on a platter? There might be cops waiting at the lab right now. Eldon could afford to lose the birds. West Nile was an unpredictable virus, highly variable in patient populations, depending on preexisting immunities, cross-immunities, other factors. The possibility of capture outweighed any possible gain in research. Dr. Tarver gripped the wheel tighter, exited I-55 at Northside Drive, then got back onto the elevated freeway, heading south.

What about the coral snake, though? He hated the idea of ditching it with the birds. Perhaps it should attend the emergency meeting. Or should he do as he'd once done after his briefcase was stolen from his car at the mall? Park his unlocked car in a remote section of the lot with an expensive bag on the seat. In the chaotic free-for-all of crime that was Jackson, a thief had stolen the bag in less than thirty minutes. Dr. Tarver had always imagined the look on the felon's face when he expectantly opened the bag and found not plunder but a coiled whip of muscle and deadly fangs. *Instant karma, shitbird . . .*

A wicked smile glittered in his beard. It was funny how seemingly unrelated events revealed hidden significance as time passed. The foil on the building and the coral snake might well be connected in some Jungian web of synchronicity. Maybe the snake was somehow the resolution of the problem signaled by the foil.

He unzipped the bag and waited for the yellow-banded head to emerge. Ten miles melted beneath his tires before it did. When the first red band slid out of the bag, Dr. Tarver took the coral's head between his thumb and forefinger and drew its body out of the bag. Children were sometimes bitten by corals because the snakes were so beautiful that kids couldn't resist picking them up. Were corals not naturally so secretive, there would be a lot more dead children in the American South.

The serpent hung suspended for a moment, then coiled itself around the doctor's big forearm for the second time. A euphoric rush dilated his blood vessels. Unlike chemically induced highs, the reaction caused by the sliding of scales against his bare skin never lost its potency. He felt the thrill of a young boy holding a gun for the first time: the intoxicating power of holding death in your hand. The death of others, the ability to bring about your own . . .

As he drove southward, Dr. Tarver reveled in the proximity of eternity.

CHAPTER

9

Even after three shots of vodka, Chris found himself unable to sleep. At 5 a.m. he finally gave up. He slid silently out of bed and dressed in the closet, then walked out to the garage, loaded his bike onto the rack on his pickup, and drove twenty minutes to the north side of town. There, under a violet sky, he topped off his high-pressure tires, mounted his carbon fiber Trek, and started pedaling north on the lonely gray strip of the Natchez Trace.

The windless air had felt warm and close while he was filling his tires, but now his forward motion cooled him to the point of a chill. This far south, most of the two-lane Trace was a tunnel created by the high, arching branches of the red oaks that lined the parkway. The effect was that of a natural cathedral that extended for miles. Through the few breaks in the canopy Chris saw a yellow half-moon, still high despite the slowly rising sun. He pumped his legs with a metronomic rhythm, breathing with almost musical regularity. Small animals skittered away as he passed, and every half mile or so, groups of startled deer leapt into the shelter of the trees.

A warm, steady rain began to fall. Landmarks rolled by like a film without a sound track: Loess Bluff, with its steadily eroding face of rare soil; the split-rail fence that marked the ranger station at Mount Locust; the high bridge over Cole's Creek, from which you could see Low Water Bridge, the site of some of Chris's happiest childhood memories. After he crossed the high bridge he got serious, pumping his thighs like a Tour de France rider, trying to work out the accumulated anxiety of the past eighteen hours. The thing was, you couldn't work out anxiety arising from circumstances that remained outside your control, and Special Agent Alex Morse was definitely not under his control. He jammed it all the way to the end of this stretch of the Trace, then made a 180-degree turn and headed back southwest.

Out of the whisper of tires on wet pavement came a faint chirping. It took him fifty feet to recognize the sound of his cell phone. Half the time he had no reception out here; that was one reason he chose the Trace to ride. Reaching carefully backward, he dug his cell phone from the Gore-Tex pouch hanging beneath his seat. The LCD said UNKNOWN CALLER. Chris started to ignore the call, but the early hour made him wonder if one of his hospital patients was in trouble. It might even be Tom Cage, calling about the mystery case on 4-North.

"Dr. Shepard," he said in his professional voice.

"Hello, Doctor," said a strangely familiar voice.

"Darryl?" he asked, almost sure that he recognized his old fraternity brother's voice. "Foster?"

"Hell, yeah!"

"You finally got my message, huh?"

"Just now. I know it's early, but I figured you hadn't changed much since college. Always the first one awake, even with a hangover."

"I appreciate you calling, man."

"Well, that name you mentioned really woke me up. Why in the world are you asking me about Alex Morse? Did you meet her or something?"

Chris debated about how much to reveal. "If you don't mind, I'd rather not say yet."

"Woo-woo-woo," Foster said mockingly. "So what do you want to know about her?"

"Anything you can tell me. Is she really an FBI agent?"

"Sure. Or she used to be, anyway. The truth is, I'm not sure about her official status now."

"Why not?"

"I don't know the lady, Chris, so take all this with a grain of salt. But Alex Morse was a bona fide star in the Bureau. She started out as what we call a blue flamer. Kind of like you in college—A's on everything, always doing more than you had to. She made quite a name for herself as a hostage negotiator. Word was, she was the best. Anything high-profile or hush-hush, the director flew her in to handle it."

"You're speaking in the past tense."

"Absolutely. I don't know the whole scoop, but a couple of months ago, Morse lost her shit and got somebody killed."

Chris's legs stopped pumping. "Who got killed?" he asked, coasting along the pavement. "A hostage?"

"No. A fellow agent."

"How did that happen?"

"Word is, it was a super-tense hostage scene, and Morse flipped out. The Hostage Rescue Team—basically our SWAT guys—was given the order to go in, and Morse couldn't deal with it. She charged back into the scene—apparently to try to keep negotiating—and everybody started shooting. An agent named James Broadbent got his heart blown out by a shotgun. I *did* know Jim personally. He was your all-American guy with a wife and two kids. There was some talk that he was having an affair with Morse at the time, but you never know what's true in those situations."

Chris was trying to absorb this fast enough to ask intelligent questions. "So you don't know if Morse is legit or not," he temporized.

"No. You want me to find out?"

"Can you do it without setting off any alarms in Washington?"

"Maybe. But you need to tell me what this is about."

"Darryl, is there any chance that Morse could be involved in a murder investigation?"

Foster said nothing for a while. "I don't think so. We don't handle murder cases, you know? Not unless there are special circumstances. Civil rights murders, stuff like that."

"On TV it's always FBI agents chasing the serial killers."

"That's Hollywood bullshit. One very small branch of the Bureau *advises* local and state cops on murder cases—if they request it—but they never make arrests or anything like that."

Chris couldn't think of any brilliant questions, and he didn't want Foster to get aggressive with his own. "I really appreciate you calling back, Darryl. Thank you."

"You can't give me any more details than you already have?"

Chris searched his mind for some plausible explanation. "Morse was originally from Mississippi, okay? That's all I can say right now. If anything strange happens, I'll call you back."

"Guess that'll have to do," Foster said, sounding far from satisfied. "Hey, how's that new wife of yours?"

"Fine, she's good."

"Sorry I missed the wedding. But Jake Preston told me she's hot. Like *really* hot."

Chris managed a laugh. "She looks good, yeah."

"Goddamn doctors. They always get the hot ones."

Chris laughed genuinely this time, hearing some of his old friend's personality come through. "Thanks again, Darryl. I mean it."

"I'll call you back when I get the story on Morse. Could be today. Probably tomorrow, though."

"Any time is fine. Hey, where are you living now?"

"Still the Windy City. It's nice this time of year, but I froze my ass off last winter. I'm ready for Miami or L.A."

"Good luck."

"Yeah. Talk to you soon."

Chris stuffed his phone back into the seat pouch and dug in hard. There were cars and trucks moving along the Trace now, most carrying workers who lived beyond the borders of the long but narrow strip of federal land. The speed limit on the Trace was fifty—great for bikers if the commuters had observed it, but none did. Checking his watch, he realized that he probably wouldn't make it home in time to take Ben to school. That would make Thora wonder, but he'd had to do something to dissipate the tension that Morse's visit had caused.

Now Foster's call had canceled out any relief he'd felt from the exercise. He had more information now, but no real answers. Alex Morse was a star FBI agent who'd screwed up and gotten someone killed. Fine. She'd admitted the screw-up herself. But what was she *now*? A field agent working a legitimate case? Or a rogue agent working her sister's murder without permission? In one respect it didn't matter, because Chris was convinced that in her views of *his* situation, she was out of her goddamn mind.

He wrenched his handlebars to the right as a car blasted by from behind, its horn blaring, its tires spraying water. He almost took a spill on the shoulder, then made a last-second recovery and edged back onto the wet pavement. The driver was too far gone to see now, but Chris flipped him off anyway. He wouldn't normally have done that, but then he wouldn't normally have allowed a vehicle to catch him unawares on a seldom-traveled road.

As his tires thrummed along the pavement's edge, he saw another biker in the distance, approaching on the opposite side of the Trace. As the distance closed, Chris saw that the rider was female. He raised his hand in greeting, then hit his brakes.

The rider was Alexandra Morse.

CHAPTER

10

Agent Morse wasn't wearing a biking helmet, but her dark hair was drawn back into a soaking-wet ponytail, making her facial scars all the more prominent. It was the scars that allowed Chris to recognize her. He could hardly believe her presence, and he was about ready to sprint right past her when she crossed the road and hissed to a stop a yard away from him.

"Good morning, Doctor."

"What the hell are you doing?" he asked.

"I needed to talk to you. This seemed like a good way to do it."

"How did you know I was here?"

Morse only smiled.

Chris looked her over from head to toe, taking in the soaked clothes stuck to her body and her dripping ponytail. She had chill bumps on her arms and legs, and the cotton TULANE LAW shirt she was wearing would take forever to dry, even if the rain stopped.

"And the bike?" he asked. "You a big cyclist?"

"No. I bought it four days ago, when I found out that you were a biker and your wife was a runner."

"You've been following Thora, too?"

Morse's smile faded. "I've shadowed a couple of her runs. She's fast."

"Jesus." Chris shook his head and started to ride away.

"Wait!" Morse cried. "I'm not a threat, Dr. Shepard!"

He stopped and looked back. "I'm not so sure of that."

"Why not?"

He thought of Darryl Foster's words. "Call it instinct."

"You have good instincts about sources of danger?"

"In the past I have."

"Even when those sources are human?"

A red pickup truck whizzed past, its rider staring at them.

"Why don't we keep riding?" Morse suggested. "We'll be less noticeable talking that way."

"I don't intend to continue yesterday's conversation."

She looked incredulous. "Surely you must have some questions for me."

Chris looked off into the trees, then turned and let some of his anger through his eyes. "Yes, I do. My first question is, did you personally see my wife go into this divorce lawyer's office?"

Morse took a small step backward. "Not personally, no, but—"

"Who did?"

"Another agent."

"How did he identify Thora?"

"He followed her down to her car, then took down her license plate."

"Her license plate. No chance of a mistake? No chance he got one number wrong, and it could have been someone else?"

Morse shook her head. "He shot a picture of her."

"Do you have that picture?"

"Not on me. But she was wearing a very distinctive outfit. A black silk dress with a white scarf and an Audrey Hepburn hat. Not many women can pull that kind of thing off anymore."

Chris gritted his teeth. Thora had worn that same outfit to a party only a month ago. "Do you have any recordings of her conversation with the lawyer? Copies of any memos or files? Anything that proves what they talked about?"

Morse reluctantly shook her head.

"So you admit that it's possible that they talked about wills and estates, or investments, or something else legitimate."

Agent Morse looked down at her wet shoes. After a while, she looked back up and said, "It's possible, yes."

"But you don't believe it."

She bit her bottom lip but said nothing.

"Agent Morse, I happen to know from my wife's recent behavior that what you suggested yesterday is impossible."

The FBI agent looked intrigued, but instead of asking what he was talking about, she said, "It's ten miles back to your truck. Why don't we ride back together? I promise not to piss you off, if I can help it."

Chris knew he could leave Morse behind in seconds. But for some reason—maybe just the manners he'd been raised with—he decided not to. He shrugged, engaged his cleats with his Look pedals, and started southward at an easy pace. Morse fell in beside him and immediately started talking.

"Have you called anybody about me?"

He decided to leave Darryl Foster out of the conversation. "I figured you'd already know the answer to that. Aren't you tapping my phones?"

She ignored this. "I'm sure you have some questions for me, after all I said yesterday."

Chris shook the rain out of his eyes. "I'll admit I've done some thinking about what you told me, especially about the medical side."

"Good. Go on."

"I want to know more about these unexplained deaths, as you called them."

"What do you want to know?"

"How the people died. Was it a stroke in every case?"

"No. Only my sister's."

"Really. What were the other causes of death?"

"Pulmonary embolism in one. Myocardial infarction in another."

"What else?"

A hundred feet of road passed beneath them before Morse answered. "The rest were cancer."

Chris looked sharply over at her, but Morse kept watching the road. *"Cancer?"*

She nodded over her handlebars, and water dripped off her nose. "Fatal malignancies."

"You're kidding, right?"

"No."

"You're telling me this cluster of suspicious deaths that has you so worked up involves people who've died of cancer?"

"Yes."

He thought about this for a while. "How many victims were there? Total?"

"Nine deaths tied to the divorce lawyer I told you about. Six cancers that I've traced so far."

"Same kind of tumor in every person?"

"That depends on how picky you are. They were all blood cancers."

"Call me picky. Blood cancer encompasses a whole constellation of diseases, Agent Morse. There are over thirty different types of non-Hodgkin's lymphomas alone. At least a dozen different leukemias. Were all the deaths from one type of blood cancer, at least?"

"No. Three leukemias, two lymphomas, one multiple myeloma."

Chris shook his head. "You're out of your mind. You really believe someone is murdering people by giving them different kinds of cancer?"

Morse looked over at him, and her eyes were as grim as any he'd ever seen.

"I know it."

"That's impossible."

"Are you so sure? You're not an oncologist."

Chris snorted. "It doesn't take an oncologist to realize that would be a stupid way to murder someone— even if it were possible. Even if you could somehow induce cancer in your victim, it could take years for that person to die, if they died at all. A lot of people survive leukemia now. Lymphomas, too. And people live well over five years with myeloma after bone marrow transplants. Some patients have two transplants and live ten years or more."

"All these patients died in eighteen months or less."

This brought him up short. "Eighteen months from diagnosis to death? All of them?"

"All but one. The myeloma patient lived twenty-three months after an autologous bone marrow transplant."

"Aggressive cancers, then. Very aggressive."

"Obviously."

Morse wanted him to work this out for himself. "These people who died . . . they were all married to wealthy people?"

"All of them. To *very* wealthy people."

"And all the surviving spouses were clients of the same divorce lawyer?"

Morse shook her head. "I never said that. I said all the surviving spouses wound up *in business* with the same divorce lawyer—and only *after* the deaths of their spouses. Big deals, mostly, one-offs that had nothing to do with the lawyer's area of expertise."

Chris nodded, but his mind was still on Morse's cancer theory. "I don't want to get into a technical argument, but even if all these patients died from leukemias, you're talking about several different disease etiologies. And the actual carcinogenesis isn't understood in a majority of types. Include the lymphomas, and you're dealing with entirely different cell groups—the erythroid and B-cell malignancies—and the causes of those cancers are also unknown. The fact that your 'blood cancers' killed in less than eighteen months is probably their only similarity. In every other way they're probably as different from each other as pancreatic cancer and a sarcoma. And if the best oncologists in the world don't know what causes those cancers, who do you think could intentionally cause them to commit murder?"

"Radiation causes leukemia," Morse said assertively. "You don't have to be a genius to give someone cancer."

She's right, Chris realized. Many initial survivors of Hiroshima died of leukemia in the aftermath of the atomic bomb, as did many "survivors" of the Chernobyl disaster. Marie Curie died of leukemia caused by her radium experiments. You could cause sophisticated genetic damage with a metaphorically blunt instrument. His mind instantly jumped to the issue of access to gamma radiation. You'd have to consider physicians, dentists, veterinarians—hell, even some medical technologists had access to X-ray machines or the radioactive isotopes used for radiotherapy. Agent Morse's theory was based on more than wild speculation. Yet the basic premise still seemed ludicrous to him.

"It's been done before, you know," Morse said.

"What has?"

"During the late 1930s, the Nazis experimented with ways of sterilizing large numbers of Jews without their knowledge. They asked subjects to sit at a desk and fill out some forms that would take about fifteen minutes. During that time, high-energy gamma rays were fired at their genitals from three sides. The experiment worked."

"My God."

"Why couldn't someone do the same thing to an unsuspecting victim in a lawyer's office?" Morse asked. "Or a dentist's office?"

Chris pedaled harder but said nothing.

"You know that researchers purposely cause cancer in lab animals all the time, right?"

"Of course. They do it by injecting carcinogenic chemicals into the animals. And chemicals like that are traceable, Agent Morse. Forensically, I mean."

She gave him a skeptical look. "In an ideal world. But you said yourself, it takes time to die from cancer. After eighteen months, all traces of the offending carcinogen could be gone. Benzene is a good example."

Chris knit his brow in thought. "Benzene causes lung cancer, doesn't it?"

"Also leukemia and multiple myeloma," she informed him. "They proved that by testing factory workers with minor benzene exposure in Ohio and in China."

She's done her homework, he thought. *Or someone has.* "Have you done extensive toxicological studies in all these deaths?"

"Almost none of them."

This stunned him. "Why not?"

"Several of the bodies were cremated before we became suspicious."

"That's convenient."

"And in the other cases, we couldn't get permission to exhume the bodies."

"Again, why not?"

"It's complicated."

Chris sensed that he was being played. "I don't buy that, Agent Morse. If the FBI wanted forensic studies, they'd get them. What about the families of these alleged victims? Did they suspect foul play? Is that how you got into this case? Or was it your sister's accusation that started it all?"

Two big touring motorcycles swept around a long curve ahead, their lights illuminating the rain.

"The families of several victims suspected foul play from the beginning."

"Even though their relatives died of cancer?"

"Yes. Most of the husbands we're talking about are real bastards."

Big surprise. "Had all of these alleged victims filed for divorce?"

"None had."

"None? Did the husbands file, then?"

Morse looked over at him again. "Nobody filed."

"Then what the hell happened? People consulted this lawyer but didn't file?"

"Exactly. We think there's probably a single consultation—maybe two visits, at most. The lawyer waits for a really wealthy client who stands to lose an enormous amount of money in his divorce. Or maybe the client stands to lose custody of his kids. But when the lawyer senses that he has a truly desperate client—a client with intense hatred for his spouse—he makes his pitch."

"That's an interesting scenario. Can you prove any of it?"

"Not yet. This lawyer is very savvy. Paranoid, in fact."

Chris gazed at her in disbelief. "You can't even prove that any murders have occurred, much less that anyone specific is involved. You've got nothing but speculation."

"I have my sister's word, Doctor."

"Spoken on her deathbed, after a severe stroke."

Morse's face became a mask of defiant determination.

"I'm not trying to upset you," Chris said. "I'm very sorry for your loss. I see that kind of tragedy week in and week out, and I know what it does to families."

She said nothing.

"But you have to admit, it's a pretty elaborate theory you've developed. It's Hollywood stuff, in fact," he said, recalling Foster's words. "Not real life."

Morse did not look angry; in fact, she looked mildly amused. "Dr. Shepard, in 1995, a forty-four-year-old neurologist was arrested at the Vanderbilt Medical Center with a six-inch syringe and a four-inch needle in his pocket. The syringe was filled with boric acid and salt water. I'm sure you know that solution would have been lethal if injected into a human heart."

"That's about the only thing a four-inch needle's good for," Chris thought aloud.

"The neurologist was planning to murder a physician who'd been his supervisor when he was a resident there. When police searched a storage unit he owned, they found books on assassination and the production of toxic biological agents. They also found a jar containing ricin, one of the deadliest poisons in the world. The neurologist had planned to soak the pages of a book with a solvent mixture that would promote the absorption of ricin through the skin." Morse looked over at Chris with a raised eyebrow. "Is that elaborate enough for you?"

Chris shifted down two gears and pedaled ahead.

Morse quickly rode alongside him again. "In 1999, a woman in San Jose, California, was admitted to the hospital with nausea and blinding headaches. They gave her a CAT scan and found nothing. But a technician had laid the woman's earrings down next to a stack of unexposed X-ray film. When they were developed, the tech saw an apparent defect on each of the films. It was very distinctive. He finally figured out that one of the woman's earrings had exposed the films."

"The earrings were radioactive?"

"One of them was. The woman's husband was a radiation oncologist. The police called in the Bureau, and we discovered that her cell phone was as hot as a piece of debris from Chernobyl. Turned out her husband had hidden a small pellet of cesium inside the phone. Of course, by that time he'd put the pellet back into its lead-lined case at his office. But the traces were still there."

"Did she develop cancer?"

"She hasn't yet, but she may. She absorbed hundreds of times the permissible exposure."

"What happened to the radiation oncologist?"

"He's in San Quentin now. My point is, doctors aren't immune to homicidal impulses. And they're capable of very elaborate plans to carry them out. I could cite dozens of similar cases for you."

Chris waved his right hand. "Save your breath. I know some stone-crazy doctors myself." Despite his casual retort, he was sobered by Morse's revelations.

"There are four and a half thousand doctors in Mississippi," she said. "Add to that about five thousand dentists. Then you have veterinarians, med techs, university researchers, nurses—a massive suspect pool, even if you assume the killer is from Mississippi. And I've only been onto this theory for seven days."

As Morse spoke, Chris realized that the apparent enormity of the task was illusory; it only existed because of a lack of baseline information. "You've got to find the cause of death in these people—or rather the cause of the cause, the etiology of these blood cancers. If it is radiation, you could start narrowing your suspect pool pretty quickly."

Her voice took on an excited edge. "An expert I talked to says radiation is the surest and simplest method."

"But you don't have forensic evidence? No radiation burns, or strange symptoms noted long before the cancer was diagnosed?"

"No. Again, because local law enforcement authorities don't believe these deaths were murder, there's a problem of access to the bodies."

"What about the medical records of the alleged victims?"

"I managed to get the records of two victims from angry family members. But experts have been over both of them in microscopic detail, and they haven't turned up anything suspicious."

Chris blinked against stinging sweat that the rain had washed into his eyes.

"But I'm told that radiation could explain the variation in the cancers," Morse went on. "You expose somebody to radiation, there's no way to predict how their cells will react."

Chris nodded, but something about this idea bothered him. "Your expert is right. But then, why are blood cancers the only result? Why no solid tumors? Why no melanomas? And why only superaggressive blood cancers? You couldn't predict something like that with radiation."

"Maybe you could," Morse suggested. "If you were a radiation oncologist."

"Maybe," Chris conceded. "If you managed to expose the bone marrow primarily, you might get more blood cancers than other types. But if that's true, you just shrank your suspect pool by about ten thousand people."

Morse smiled. "Believe me, every radiation oncologist in Mississippi is under investigation at this moment."

"How many are there?"

"Nineteen. But it's not a simple matter of alibis. I can't ask some doctor where he was on a given day at a given time, because we have no way to know when the victims were dosed. You see?"

"Yeah. *Dragnet* methods are out the window. But it's not just a doctor you're looking for, right? It's the lawyer, too. If you're right, he functions almost like the killer's agent."

"Exactly. Only he handles an assassin instead of a quarterback or a singer."

Chris laughed softly. "How would a relationship like that get started? You can't go scouting for promising young assassins. There's no national draft. Does your greedy lawyer put an ad on the Internet to recruit someone who can kill people without a trace? Does he hire a medical headhunter?"

"I know it sounds ridiculous when you put it like that, but we're talking about a lot of money here."

"How much?"

"Millions in every case. So the lawyer has a pretty big carrot to hold out in front of someone who probably makes a hundred grand or less at his legitimate job."

To break the monotony of the ride, Chris gently steered left and right. Morse gave him room to ride his serpentine course.

"Lawyers get to know a lot of professional criminals in the course of their work," she pointed out. "And necessity is the mother of invention, right? I think this guy simply saw a demand for a service and then found a way to provide it."

Chris pedaled out in front of her so that a large truck could pass. Illegally, since big trucks weren't allowed on the Trace. "A lot of what you say makes sense," he called over the sound of the receding truck, "but I still say your theory doesn't add up."

"Why not?" Morse asked, pulling alongside again.

"The time factor. If I want to kill someone, it's because I *really* hate them, or because I stand to gain a hell of a lot if they die. Or maybe I stand to lose millions of dollars if my wife goes on living, like you said yesterday. What if she wants to take my children away forever? I'm not going to wait months or years for her to croak. I want immediate action."

"Even if that's the case," said Morse, "the most likely result of any conventional murder—especially in a divorce situation—is the killer going to jail. And if you're not going to try the murder yourself, who do you hire? You're a multimillionaire. You don't have a gangsta posse to turn to. Imagine how someone that desperate might react to a slick lawyer offering him a risk-free road out of his problems. A perfect murder is worth waiting for."

She has a point, Chris thought. "I can see that. But no matter how you slice it, there's an element of urgency in a divorce situation. People go *crazy.* They'll do anything to get out of their marriage. There's a frantic desire to move on, to marry their lover, whatever."

"You're right, of course," Morse agreed. "But you've already waited years for your freedom. Maybe decades. Any divorce lawyer can tell you that obtaining a divorce—the whole process from beginning to end—can take a very long time. If the divorce is contested, we're talking nightmare delays. Even filing under irreconcilable differences, spouses often argue back and forth for a year or more. People are hurting, they stonewall, negotiations break down. You can wind up in court even if it's the last thing you wanted. Years can go by." Morse was suddenly puffing hard. "If your lawyer told you that in the same amount of time that your divorce would take, he could save you millions of dollars, guarantee you full custody of your children, and prevent them from hating you—you'd have to at least *consider* what he had to say, wouldn't you?"

They were crossing the high bridge over Cole's Creek. Chris braked to a stop, climbed off, and leaned the Trek against the concrete rail.

"You've got me," he said. "If you remove urgency from the equation, then a delayed-action weapon becomes viable. You *could* use something like cancer as a weapon. If it's technically possible."

"Thank you," Alex said softly. She leaned her bike against the concrete and gazed at the brown water drifting lazily over the sand fifty feet below.

Chris watched a burst of tiny drops pepper the surface of the water, then vanish. The rain was slacking off. "Didn't you tell me that some of the victims were men?"

"Yes. In two cases, the surviving spouses were female."

"So there's a precedent for women murdering the husbands in this thing."

Morse took a deep breath, then looked up at him and said, "That's why I'm here with you, Doctor."

Chris tried to imagine Thora secretly driving up to Jackson for a clandestine meeting with a divorce lawyer. He simply couldn't do it. "I buy your logic, okay? But in my case it's irrelevant, and for lots of reasons. The main one is that if Thora asked me for a divorce, I'd give her one. Simple as that. And I think she knows that."

Morse shrugged. "I don't know the lady."

"You're right. You don't." The concrete rail was not even waist high to Chris. He sometimes urinated off it during his rides. He suppressed the urge to do so now.

"It's beautiful down there," Morse said, gazing down the winding course of the creek. "It's looks like virgin wilderness."

"It's as close as you'll find. It hasn't been logged since the 1930s, and it's federal land. I spent a lot of time walking that creek as a boy. I found dozens of arrowheads and spear points in it. The Natchez Indians hunted along that creek for a thousand years before the French came."

She smiled. "You're lucky to have had a childhood like that."

Chris knew she was right. "We only lived in Natchez for a few years—IP moved my dad around a lot, between mills, you know?—but Dad showed me a lot of things out in these woods. After heavy rains, we'd each take one bank of the creek and work our way along it. After one mudslide, I found three huge bones. They turned out to be from a woolly mammoth. Fifteen thousand years old."

"Wow. I had no idea that kind of stuff was around here."

Chris nodded. "We're walking in footsteps everywhere we go."

"The footsteps of the dead."

He looked up at the sound of an approaching engine. It was a park ranger's cruiser. He lifted his hand, recalling a female ranger who'd patrolled this stretch of the Trace for a couple of years. After she moved on, he'd seen her face on the back of a bestselling mystery novel set on the Trace. The place seemed to touch everyone who spent time here.

"What are you thinking, Doctor?"

He was thinking about Darryl Foster, and what Foster had told him about Alexandra Morse. Chris didn't want to bluntly challenge her, but he did want to know how honest she was being with him.

"From the moment we met," he said, looking into her green eyes, "you've been digging into my personal life. I want to dig into yours for a minute."

He could almost see the walls going up. But at length she nodded assent. What choice did she have?

"Your scars," he said. "I can tell they're recent. I want to know how you got them."

She turned away and stared down at the rippling sand beneath the surface of the water. When she finally spoke, it was in a voice that had surrendered something. Gone was the professional authority, yet in its place was a raw sincerity that told him he was hearing something very like the truth.

"There was a man," she said. "A man I worked with at the Bureau. His name was James Broadbent. People called him Jim, but he preferred James. They often assigned him to protect me at hostage scenes. He . . . he was in love with me. I really cared for him, too, but he was married. Two kids. We were never intimate, but even if we had been, he would never have left his family. Never. You understand?"

Chris nodded.

She looked back down at the water. "I was a good hostage negotiator, Doctor. Some said the best ever. In five years I never lost a hostage. That's rare. But last December . . ." Morse faltered, then found the thread again. "My father was killed trying to stop a robbery. Two months later, my mother was diagnosed with ovarian cancer. Very advanced, and you know what that means."

"I'm sorry."

Morse shrugged. "I sort of lost it after that. Only I didn't know it, see? My dad had raised me to be tough, so that's what I tried to be. 'Never quit,' that's the Morse motto. From Winston Churchill to my father and right down to me."

Chris nodded with as much empathy as he could.

"I'm getting to the scars, I promise," she said. "Nine weeks ago, I was called to a hostage scene at a bank. Not a normal bank. A Federal Reserve bank in D.C. Sixteen hostages inside, most of them employees. A lot of suits at the Bureau had the idea this was a terrorist attack. Others thought it was about money. It could have been both—a sophisticated robbery raising capital for terrorist operations. But my gut told me it was something else. The leader spoke with an Arabic accent, but it didn't sound real to me. He was angry, maybe schizophrenic. He had a lot of rage toward the government. I could tell he'd experienced loss in the recent past, like a lot of people who try something extreme." Morse gave Chris a tight smile. "Like me, you're thinking? Anyway, an associate deputy director named Dodson had overall command, and he didn't give me enough time to do my job. I had a real chance to talk the leader down without anyone firing a shot. All my experience and instinct told me that. And there were sixteen lives at stake, you know? But there was a lot of pressure from above, this being Washington in its post-9/11 mind-set. So Dodson jerked me out of there and ordered in the HRT."

Chris saw that she was reliving the memory as she

recounted the events. She'd probably been over it a million times in the privacy of her head, but how many times had she spoken of it to someone else?

"There was no way to resolve the situation with snipers. It had to be an explosive entry, which meant extreme risk to the hostages. I couldn't accept that. So I marched right back through the cordon and into the bank. My people were screaming at me, but I barely heard them. Some HRT guys didn't get the word in time, and they blew the doors and windows just as I reached the lobby. Flash-bang-crash grenades, the works." Morse touched her scarred cheek as though feeling the injury for the first time. "One of the robbers shot me from behind a plate-glass partition. I caught shards mostly, but what I didn't know was that James had followed me into the bank. When I was hit, he looked down at me instead of up for the shooter, which was what he should have done. His feelings for me were stronger than his training. And they train us *hard*, you know?" Morse wiped her face as though to brush away cobwebs, but Chris saw the glint of tears.

"Hey," he said, reaching out and squeezing her arm. "It's okay."

She shook her head with surprising violence. "No, it's not. Maybe someday it will be, but right now it's not."

"I know one thing," Chris said. "In the shape you're in, you don't need to be working a murder case. You need a medical leave."

Morse laughed strangely. "I'm on medical leave *now*."

As he looked down at her, everything suddenly came clear. Her deep fatigue, her obsessiveness, the thousand-yard stare of a shell-shocked soldier . . . "You're on your own, aren't you?"

She shook her head again, but her chin was quivering.

"You say *I* a lot more than you say *we*."

Morse bit her bottom lip, then squinted as though against bright sunlight.

"Is that how it is?" he asked gently. "Are you alone?"

When she looked up at him, her eyes were wet with more than rain. "Pretty much. The truth is, almost everything I've done beginning five weeks ago was unauthorized. They'd fire me if they knew."

Chris whistled long and low. "Jesus Christ."

She took him by the wrists and spoke with fierce conviction. "You're my last shot, Dr. Shepard. My no-shit last shot."

"Last shot at *what*?"

"Stopping these people. Proving what they've done."

"Look," he said awkwardly, "if everything you've told me is true, why *isn't* the FBI involved?"

Frustration hardened her face. "A dozen reasons, none of them good. Murder's a state crime, not a federal one, unless it's a RICO case. A lot of what I have is inference and supposition, not objective evidence. But how the hell am I supposed to get evidence without any resources? The FBI is the most hidebound bureaucracy you can imagine. Everything is done by the book—unless it involves counterterrorism, of course, in which case they throw the book right out the window. But nobody's going to nail the guys I'm after by using the Marquess of Queensberry rules."

Chris didn't know what to say. Yesterday morning

his life had been ticking along as usual; now he was standing on a bridge in the rain, watching a woman he barely knew fall apart.

"If you're acting alone, who saw Thora go into the lawyer's office?"

"A private detective. He used to work for my father."

"Jesus. What does the FBI think you're doing right now?"

"They think I'm in Charlotte, working a prostitution case involving illegal aliens. When they transferred me there after I was shot, I got lucky. I found an old classmate from the Academy there. He's done a lot to cover for me. But it can't go on much longer."

"Holy shit."

"I know I'm not making perfect sense about everything. I haven't slept more than three hours a night in five weeks. It took me two weeks just to find the connection between my brother-in-law and the divorce lawyer. Then another week to come up with the names of all his business partners. I only came up with my list of victims a week ago. There could be a dozen more, for all I know. But then your wife walked into Rusk's office, and that brought me to Natchez. I've been splitting my time between here and Jackson, where my mother is dying, and—"

"Who's Rusk?" Chris cut in. "The divorce lawyer?"

"Yes. Andrew Rusk Jr. His father's a big plaintiff's attorney in Jackson." More tears joined the raindrops on her cheeks. "*Fuck,* it's a mess! I need your help, Doctor. I need your medical knowledge, but most of all I need you, because you're the next victim." Morse's eyes locked onto his with eerie intensity. "Do you get that?"

Chris closed his eyes. "Nothing you've said today even remotely proves that."

Her frustration finally boiled over. "Listen to me! I know you don't like hearing it, but your wife drove two hours to Jackson to meet with Andrew Rusk, and she lied to you by not telling you about it. What do you think that adds up to?"

"Not murder," Chris said stubbornly. "I don't believe that. I can't."

Morse touched his arm. "That's because you're a doctor, not a lawyer. Every district attorney in this country has a list of people who come in on a weekly basis to plead with them to open a murder case on their loved one. The deaths are recorded as accidents, suicides, fires, a hundred things. But the parents or the children or the wives of the victims . . . they know the truth. It was murder. So they work their way through the system, begging for someone to take notice, to at least classify what happened as a crime. They hire detectives and spend their life savings trying to find the truth, to find justice. But they almost never do. Eventually they turn into something like ghosts. Some of them stay ghosts for the rest of their lives." Morse looked at Chris with the furious eyes of a hardened combat soldier. "I'm no ghost, Doctor. I will not stand by and let my sister be erased for someone's convenience—for his *profit*." Her voice took on a dangerous edge. "As God is my witness, I will not do that."

Out of respect, Chris waited a few moments to respond. "I support what you're doing, okay? I even admire you for it. But the difference is, you have a personal stake in this. I don't."

Her eyes narrowed. "Yes, you do. You just haven't accepted it yet."

"Please don't start again."

"Doctor, I would do anything to get you to help me. Do you understand? I'd go over there in the bushes and pull my shorts down for you, if that's what it would take." Her eyes gleamed with cold fire. "But I don't have to do that."

Chris didn't like the look that had come into her face. "Why not?"

"Because your wife is cheating on you."

He tried to keep the shock out of his face, but nothing could slow his pounding heart.

"Thora's screwing a surgeon right here in town," Morse went on. "His name is Shane Lansing."

"Bullshit," Chris said in a hoarse whisper.

Morse's eyes didn't waver.

"Do you have proof?"

"Circumstantial evidence."

"Circumstantial . . . ? I don't want to hear it."

"Denial is always the first response."

"Shut up, goddamn it!"

Morse's face softened. "I know how it hurts, okay? I was engaged once, until I found out my fiancé was doing my best friend. But pride is your enemy now, Chris. You have to see things *straight*."

"*I* should see things straight? You're the one spinning out Byzantine theories of mass murder. Cancer as a weapon, a newlywed planning to murder her husband . . . no wonder you're out on your own!"

Morse's level gaze was unrelenting. "If I'm crazy, then tell me one thing. Why didn't you call the FBI to report me yesterday?"

He stared down at the concrete rail.

"Why, Chris?"

He felt the words come to him as if of their own accord. "Thora's leaving town this week. She told me last night."

Morse's mouth dropped open. "Where's she going?"

"Up to the Delta. A spa up in Greenwood. A famous hotel."

"The Alluvian?"

He nodded.

"I know it. When's she leaving?"

"Maybe tomorrow. This week, for sure."

"Returning when?"

"Three nights, then home."

Morse made a fist and brought it to her mouth. "This is it, Chris. My God . . . they're moving fast. You have to deal with this now. You're in extreme danger. *Right now.*"

He took her by the shoulders and shook her. "Do you hear yourself? Everything you told me is circumstantial. There wasn't one fact in the whole goddamn pile!"

"I know it seems that way. I know you don't want to believe any of it. But . . . look, do you want to know everything I know?"

He stared at her for a long time. "I don't think so." He looked at his watch. "I'm really late. I need to get back to my truck. I can't wait for you now."

He climbed onto his bike and started to leave, but Morse grabbed his elbow with surprising strength. With her other hand she removed something from her shorts. A cell phone.

"Take this," she said. "My cell number is programmed into it. You can speak frankly on it. It's the only safe link we'll have."

He pushed the phone away. "I don't want it."

"Don't be a sap, Chris. *Please*."

He looked at the phone like a tribesman suspicious of some miraculous technology. "How would I explain it to Thora?"

"Thora's leaving town. You can hide it for a day or two, can't you?"

He angrily expelled air from his cheeks, but he took the phone.

Morse's eyes fairly shone with urgency. "You have to drop the nice-guy routine, Chris. You're in *mortal fucking peril*."

A strange laugh escaped his mouth. "I'm sorry, I just don't believe that."

"Time will take care of that. One way or another."

He wanted to race away, but again his Southern upbringing stopped him. "Will you be okay out here?"

Morse turned and lifted the tail of her shirt, revealing the molded butt of a semiautomatic pistol. It looked huge against her tiny waist. As he stared, she climbed onto her bike and gripped her handlebars. "Call me soon. We don't have much time to prepare."

"What if I call the FBI instead?"

She shrugged as though genuinely unconcerned. "Then my career is over. But I won't stop. And I'll still try to save you."

Chris mounted his pedals and rode quickly away.

CHAPTER

11

Andrew Rusk gunned his Porsche Cayenne, shot across two lanes of traffic, then checked his rearview mirror. For the past week, he'd had the feeling that someone was following him. Not only on the road, either. He usually ate lunch in the finer local restaurants, and on more than one occasion he'd had the sense that someone was watching him, turning away just before he looked around to catch them. But he felt it most on the highway. Yet if someone was tailing him, they were good. Probably using multiple vehicles—which was a bad sign. Multiple vehicles meant official interest, and he didn't want to have to say anything to Glykon about official interest. And he hadn't had to, so long as he remained unsure.

Today was different. Today a dark blue Crown Victoria had been pacing him ever since he climbed onto I-55. He had made several extreme changes in speed, and the Crown Vic had stayed with him. When Rusk pretended to exit the freeway, then shot back onto the interstate at the last second, his pursuer had finally betrayed himself. The good news was that a law enforcement entity using multiple vehicles would be extremely unlikely to make a bush-league mistake like that. The bad news was that Rusk had a meeting to make, and no time to waste losing a tail.

As he drove southward, a possible solution came to him. Exiting onto Meadowbrook Drive, he drove under the interstate and headed east. The Crown Vic stayed ten car lengths behind. Soon he was rolling through Old Eastover, one of the most exclusive neighborhoods in the capital city. Rusk wondered if the Ford might be a government car. The FBI sometimes used Crown Vics. Underpowered American crap . . .

He kept to the main street, which was slowly but steadily dropping in elevation. He wondered whether his tail knew that this gradual drop was caused by their increasing proximity to the Pearl River. A few years ago, the area ahead of them had been a flood plain, unsuitable for building. It was still a flood plain, but in the interim money had spoken, and now the low-lying land was a spanking new housing development.

A few years back, Rusk had done some kayaking on the Pearl with a friend who was getting in shape for a float trip in Canada. At that time, the woods near the edge of the river had been honeycombed with dirt roads, most of them kept open by crazy kids on four-wheelers. If Rusk was right, some of those rutted roads would still be there, in spite of the new houses. . . .

He turned right and parked the Cayenne in front of a large ranch house. Would the Crown Vic pull up behind him? Or would it try to preserve some illusion of unconcern? He watched the dark blue silhouette slow as it passed the opening to the street, then drive on. Rusk shot forward, following the residential street through its long U-shape and back to the main road of the subdivision. When he emerged, the road in front of him was empty.

He checked his rearview mirror: the Crown Vic was idling about a hundred yards behind him. Rusk floored the accelerator, and the Turbo roared, pressing him into the seat like an astronaut in the boost phase of a launch. In seconds he was hurtling toward a wall of trees and chest-high weeds.

As the dead-end barrier expanded to nightmare proportions, Rusk spied a dirt road to the left of it. The opening was scarcely wide enough to accommodate the Porsche, but he didn't hesitate. With a rush of adrenaline, he wrenched his wheel left, gunned the Turbo, and blew right through the opening in the trees, praying that he wouldn't meet some kid on a four-wheeler and crush him like a bug on his grille.

The Cayenne jounced up and down like a dune buggy in Baja, but Rusk kept his foot jammed nearly to the floor. The ass of the Cayenne flew into the air, and its nose slammed down into a deep hole, spraying water in all directions. Before all momentum died, Rusk jiggered the steering wheel and applied power, letting the four-wheel drive do its work. After a few tense moments, the rear tires found traction and he scrambled up out of the hole, his front wheels spinning with a high whine. Rusk howled with delight when his front wheels grabbed the sandy ground and hurled him down the rutted track, his engine growling like an angry grizzly bear.

No cheap-ass Crown Victoria could follow him through *that* hole. The only remaining trick was to find his way back to a paved road before his pursuer figured out where he might emerge. He kept bearing toward the river—or where he thought the river was—keeping his eyes open for a wider track. His instinct didn't fail him. In less than a minute, he saw the broad brown stream of the Pearl cutting through a wide ravine thirty yards below. He whipped the wheel to the right and started following the river's course.

Where was the Crown Vic? Was its driver a Jackson native? Would he guess that Rusk was trying to work his way south and back onto paved roads? The mystery man in the Crown Vic could easily call for backup: another car, or maybe even a chopper. A chopper would be tough to evade, unless Rusk abandoned the Cayenne and went to ground in the woods. But what would that accomplish? They already knew who he was. He'd long had an escape plan in place—one that would put him out of reach of all American authorities—but it would be tough to implement if they were already sending choppers after him.

They're not, he told himself. *It's not even a* they, *as far as I know. It's one guy.*

"Yeah, but who?" he said aloud.

That fucking girl.

Rusk gritted his teeth against the juddering of the Porsche. All he could do was play the hand he was dealt.

A beautiful wooden canoe rounded the river bend ahead of him, piloted by two college-age girls with bright red backpacks stowed between them. Rusk wondered if they'd started out on the Strong River, then entered the Pearl not far away. He'd floated that trip back in high school, with some fellow Boy Scouts. As Rusk watched the girls, that memory brought strange baggage with it. He was a long way from the

Boy Scouts now—good old Pack 8. And their motto . . .
holy Christ. There was a reason people called babes in
the woods Boy Scouts—

Rusk mashed his brake pedal. Just beyond a cluster
of thick bamboo stalks on his right, a dark tunnel
opened in the trees. Deep wheel ruts led into it, and at
the opening lay a pile of half-burned logs and about a
hundred empty beer cans. Rusk nodded with satisfaction. That road led back to civilization. He gave the
Porsche some gas, ramped over a sand berm, and raced
toward the tunnel. Ten seconds later the shadows swallowed him. He was still laughing when he bounced
onto clean asphalt and drove unmolested toward the
I-55 overpass towering in the distance.

CHAPTER

12

The sun was fully up now, and Chris was pushing his pickup well over the speed limit. The rain had finally petered out, but his left front wheel threw up a wall of glistening spray as he swung onto the bypass that would take him to Highway 61 South.

Alex Morse's final revelation had left him hollow inside. He couldn't really think about it yet. But at least he'd solved the mystery that Darryl Foster had been unable to explain. Special Agent Morse was a rogue agent conducting a murder investigation that the FBI knew nothing about. And not just an investigation, but a quest, a single-minded mission to punish those she believed had murdered her sister. She had been on that mission for five weeks, yet all she had produced were some fascinating theories and circumstantial evidence. *And yet,* he thought with something like shame, *when she finally offered to reveal real evidence, I cut her off.* As he passed the Super Wal-Mart, he picked up the cell phone Morse had given him and dialed the only number in the SIMM memory.

"It's Alex," Morse answered. "Are you okay? I

know I hit you pretty hard back there about Thora."

"What evidence do you have tying my wife to Shane Lansing?"

Morse took an audible breath. "Twice this week, Dr. Lansing has stopped at your new house while Thora was there."

Chris felt a wave of relief. "So what? Shane lives in that neighborhood."

"The first time he stayed inside for twenty-eight minutes."

"And the second?"

"Fifty-two minutes."

Fifty-two minutes. Long enough to— "Thora was probably showing off the place to him. She designed the house herself. And there were workmen there, right?"

Morse's reply was as blunt as a hammer. "No workmen."

"Neither time?"

"Neither time. I'm sorry, Chris."

He grimaced. "That could still be innocent contact, you know?"

"Is that how you think of Shane Lansing? A choirboy?"

Chris didn't think of Lansing in those terms at all.

"No matter who I ask about him," Morse said, "I hear three things: he's a gifted surgeon, he's an arrogant asshole who treats nurses like shit, and he's a pussy hound."

Chris flinched.

"I also hear he likes them pretty," Morse added. "Thora definitely meets that requirement."

"Is that everything?"

"No. I've talked to a few nurses in the last five days."

"And?"

"They say Thora had an affair with a married doctor when she first got to town. Seven years ago. That was before you knew her, right? The guy was an ER doctor. Did she ever tell you about that?"

"Who was the guy supposed to be?"

"His name was Dennis Stephens."

A faint memory of a young, bearded face went through Chris's mind. "Never heard of him."

"Apparently the affair started getting out of hand, so Stephens took a job in another state."

"The hospital is always buzzing with gossip like that."

Morse said nothing.

"Thora would have been single at that time, anyway."

"There's also a story about her and an ophthalmic surgeon who was here for a while. This would have been just before she married Red Simmons."

"A lot of nurses hate my wife, Agent Morse. They think she's arrogant."

"Is she?"

"That's hard to answer. Thora's smarter than half the doctors here, in terms of raw intelligence. You can imagine the effect that has on them. Most of them are men."

"I can relate to that." The cellular connection crackled with static. "I'm your friend, Chris, even though you don't know me. Friends tell the truth, even when it's tough."

"Are you my friend? Or is it just that you need me?"

"Give me a chance to show you. Then make up your own mind."

I'll bet she was a good hostage negotiator, he thought as he hit END. *She's manipulating me already.*

CHAPTER

13

Four hours after bicycling the last mile to her car, Alex Morse sat on a bench in the shadow of a Catholic cathedral in downtown Natchez and watched Thora Shepard walk out of the Mainstream Fitness center, her blond hair flying from beneath a blue silk scarf. She turned right and started walking west on Main Street. A quarter mile in this direction would carry her to the two-hundred-foot bluff that overlooked the Mississippi River. Thora often ran along the edge of that bluff, which stretched for miles with only chain-link fencing or a few scrub bushes separating her from eternity. Alex had jogged along behind her once, amazed by the vastness of the Mississippi River. The muddy flood was a full mile across at Natchez, and beyond it the Louisiana Delta stretched flat beyond the limits of human vision.

But Thora would not be jogging today. She was wearing Mosquito sunglasses and a tailored pantsuit that cost more than Alex earned in a month. As Thora strode gracefully down the street, she looked fit for a magazine cover shoot. Alex could see the double-takes as Thora passed people on the sidewalk. The thing was, it wasn't only men who stared—women stared, too. She was that kind of woman. And maybe that was the root of Alex's antipathy. Alex had never been able to like blondes. She didn't want to stereotype anyone, but in the case of blondes, it was hard not to. They had a certain way of walking, of talking, of flipping their goddamn hair, that just plain got to her. That helpless lilt in their voices—the pathetic little-girl sound—even the smallest trace of it made Alex want to hit somebody. And that was leaving out the whole "dumb" issue. She knew that blondes weren't all dumb by genetic command, but on the other hand, she hadn't known many—if any—who were rigorously intellectual. And *that* was the core of her problem with them. Most blondes had simply never had to work hard to get what they wanted in life; therefore, they had developed few skills—beyond flirting and inserting knives between female shoulder blades—that would prove useful in any practical situation.

Of course hardly any "blondes" nowadays were true blondes. She had to give Thora that. Few human beings—even those who were blond as children—made it far through adulthood without their hair darkening naturally. But Thora had Danish blood, and her Viking blond hair was almost the same shade of straw as that of her father, who at fifty-eight still had a shockingly full head of hair. For this reason, Thora Shepard—unlike the frosted, streaked, bottled, frizzed, teased, and dark-rooted blondes Alex saw and despised every day—radiated a kind of predatory confidence, an avian watchfulness that signaled you would not get far trying to pull something over on her. It also made men and women turn and stare after her as she walked by them on the street. And finally, it had made a smart and fairly good-looking young doctor named Chris Shepard propose marriage to her—not to mention legally adopt a fatherless baby born nine years before. Not bad for a woman with her past.

Alex hurried across Main Street and began walking behind Thora, who was a block ahead now. She felt a pang of irritation as a young man wearing a business suit turned 180 degrees to watch Thora walk away from him. Then an older man stopped Thora and engaged her in conversation. Thora spoke animatedly, using her hands often to make her point. Alex turned and looked into a shop window.

She had instinctively disliked Thora from the beginning, but she wasn't sure why. No one could argue that Thora had had an easy childhood. She had begun life with a silver spoon in her mouth, but that spoon had quickly been snatched away. The daughter of a renowned Vanderbilt surgeon, Thora Rayner had spent the first eight years of her life in the elite social world of Nashville, Tennessee. A tony school, the right country club, the riding academy, the works. But when Thora was eight, her mother's alcoholism had reached a crisis point. After several attempts at drying out, Anna Rayner slipped into an alcoholic daze that showed no sign of abating. With the help of some friends, Lars Rayner committed his wife to a state hospital, then filed divorce papers. Six months later he was free of her, but the price of keeping his fortune had been his daughter. Signing away his rights to Thora had little effect on Dr. Rayner, but this act profoundly altered the little girl's future.

Thora's life became an odyssey from one small East Tennessee town to another. She attended public schools, private academies being far out of economic reach, as her court-mandated child-support payments were squandered on alcohol. Her mother's drinking waxed and waned by no particular rule, but on several occasions Thora had to be taken in by her paternal grandmother. Her high school grades were middling to poor until her junior year, when she apparently decided to show her father what she could do when she put her mind to it. When Thora blew the top out of both the ACT and SAT, Lars Rayner finally took notice. He offered to pull strings to get Thora into Vanderbilt, and also to foot the bills. Thora refused. Instead, she applied on her own and won an academic scholarship to her father's alma mater.

Sadly, her luck did not last long. Her maternal genes and conditioning were against her. After a perfect first semester, her grades steadily worsened until the second half of her sophomore year, which she did not complete. When she took a job as a waitress in a dive in the Printers Alley district, the reason soon became apparent: Thora was pregnant. The boyfriend vanished, but Thora chose to have the baby in spite of this. With financial and babysitting help from her grandmother, she entered nursing school and after two years graduated with honors. She began work at the VA hospital in Murfreesboro, Tennessee, but quit after only nine months, suddenly and inexplicably relocating to Natchez, Mississippi. Alex suspected that a messy affair lay behind this move, but she had no proof (though she did have a detective working to find it). Thora had been hired by St. Catherine's Hospital, and it was there that she'd met Red Simmons, the oilman who would become her first husband and soon after make her a widow. A very rich widow.

Alex glanced to her left. Thora spoke for another twenty seconds, then hugged the older man and continued down Main Street. Alex took a small camera from her purse and shot a picture of the man as he passed. He looked sixty, probably too old to be a paramour.

Alex had long prided herself on her physical conditioning, but simply following Thora through her daily routine was exhausting. Up at dawn for a morning run—four miles, minimum, and sometimes ten—then a quick shower at home, followed by a trip to the Shepards' building site in Avalon. Thora would argue with the contractors for a half hour or so, then drive her Mercedes convertible to the country club for a swim or a couple of sets of tennis (Alex usually watched from the parking lot). Afterward, she alternated touch-ups on her hair and nails with serious weight work at Mainstream Fitness. Another shower, and then lunch with at least one girlfriend. She favored Thai food, from an excellent restaurant not far from Mainstream, and that was probably her present destination. After her meal (very little nourishment, Alex had noted from a nearby table), Thora often made a second trip to the building site.

The only absolutely required stop of her day was St. Stephen's Prep, to pick up Ben. While most mothers waited in line for up to twenty minutes—in case their children came charging out of school right after the bell—Thora always showed up twenty minutes late. That way she avoided the boring wait and usually found Ben shooting baskets alone on the playground.

After taking him home to the maid, she would spend the remainder of the afternoon running errands or shopping, then stop by the Avalon site one final time before going home to the Elgin house.

It was during these end-of-the-day stops that Dr. Shane Lansing had twice stopped by for an informal visit. Alex had never entered the house while Lansing was inside, but if the surgeon showed up again, she planned to try. After her two meetings with Dr. Shepard (whom she hadn't expected to be so staunch in defense of his wife's morals) she regretted not bringing Will Kilmer to Natchez with her. Her father's old partner routinely worked marital cases, and he owned equipment that could listen in on and decode digital cell calls in real time. But Will was already going beyond the call of duty in his surveillance of Andrew Rusk, and Alex couldn't afford to pay one of his operatives to come to Natchez. She was working on hacking into Thora's e-mail account, though. Thora carried a Treo 650 everywhere she went and frequently logged on to the Internet with the device. Alex felt sure that if she could obtain a single e-mail proving that Thora and Lansing were lovers, Dr. Shepard would realize the danger he was in and get on board with her plan.

Thora stopped again, this time to speak to a man about her age. As Alex cautiously moved closer, trying to catch the conversation, her private cell phone rang. When she moved away and answered, she heard the gravelly voice of Will Kilmer.

"Hey, Uncle Will," she whispered, though the honorific was purely one of affection.

"Got some news for you," said the old man.

"Good or bad?"

"Bad, in the short run. A little while ago, Andrew Rusk made one of my guys and turned rabbit."

"Oh, shit. How did he lose one of your guys?"

"Bastard took that four-wheel-drive Porsche down to the Pearl River and drove slap *into* the mud. My guy was in a Crown Victoria—supercharged, but that don't do you much good in the mud. And I don't think Rusk was doing it for fun. I think he was headed somewhere important. Otherwise, why go to the trouble?"

"Damn it."

"I told you we needed more cars. But you said—"

"I know what I said," Alex snapped, furious that she lacked the money to pay for the kind of surveillance this case required. *Penny-wise, pound-foolish*, her father whispered from the grave. Now all the surveillance she'd paid for up to now was wasted. Rusk was gone, and she could do nothing about it until he chose to show up again.

Thirty yards away, Thora Shepard shook hands with the man she was talking to, then crossed Commerce Street and turned right. Alex followed.

"I'm sorry, Will. This is completely my fault. I hamstrung you."

Labored breathing came down the line. Kilmer was seventy, and he had more than a touch of emphysema. "What you want me to do now, hon?"

"Put someone out at Rusk's house, if you can. He has to come home eventually, right?"

"Sure. He'll be home tonight for sure."

"Unless we really spooked him."

Will said nothing.

"You think a guy like that would blow town because of this?"

"No, I don't. Rusk is dug in. He's got a high-dollar job, a wife, a big house, kids."

"His kids don't live with him," Alex pointed out.

"Take it easy. Rusk is a rich lawyer, not a CIA field agent. He'll be home."

She forced herself to calm down. Thora had almost reached the Thai restaurant.

"I'll send somebody out there," Will said. "And if I don't have anybody free, I'll go myself."

"You don't have to do—" Alex froze in midsentence. Thora had stopped dead on the sidewalk to answer a cell call. Now she was backing against the wall of a building with the phone held close to her ear.

"God, I wish you were here," Alex breathed.

"What's the matter?"

"Nothing. I've got to go. Call me."

As she hit END, Thora leaned out from the wall and looked obliquely through the window of the Thai restaurant. Apparently satisfied, she nodded, then put the phone back into her pocket and reversed direction, moving quickly back toward Main Street.

Straight toward Alex.

Alex darted into the nearest shop, an everything-but-the-kitchen-sink place, filled from wall to wall with antique furniture, framed mirrors, prints, woven baskets, and trays of pecan pralines for sale. When Thora passed the shop, her features were set in an expression of severe concentration. Alex counted to fifteen, then walked out of the shop and followed Thora toward her Mercedes.

Something was about to happen.

CHAPTER

14

Andrew Rusk checked the Porsche's odometer once more, then started searching the trees for the turn. He'd left I-55 forty minutes ago, and after twenty miles he'd turned onto a narrow gravel road. Somewhere along this road was the turn for the Chickamauga Hunting Camp. Rusk had been a member of the elite camp for fifteen years, buying his way in after his father-in-law opted out, and the membership had proved useful in many ways beyond providing recreation in the fall.

Rusk saw the turn at last, marked by a sign over the entrance road. He swung his wheel and stopped before the steel gate blocking his way, then punched a combination into the keypad on the post beside his vehicle. When the gate swung back, he drove slowly through. He still had a half mile of gravel to cover, and he did this slowly. Despite the vast wealth of the club's members, this road was poorly maintained. He wondered if they left it that way to preserve the illusion of primitive conditions. Because illusion was all it was.

Though the camp buildings appeared to be log cabins, they contained hotel-style rooms with private baths, central air and heat, and satellite TV in the common room. For serious hunters, the expense was justified. There were more whitetail deer per acre in this area than in any other part of the United States. And they were *big*. The largest trophy buck ever taken had been shot in Mississippi. Whitetail loved the deep underbrush of second-growth woods, and the virgin forests around this part of the state had been logged out almost 200 years ago. This was deer heaven, and hunters from around the country paid premium prices for hunting leases here. The prices were even higher to the southwest, right around Natchez. *That* was deer heaven.

As Rusk drove up to the main cabin and parked, he scanned the clearing for Eldon Tarver. He saw no one. Climbing out of the Cayenne, he checked the main cabin's door but found it locked. That made sense, because Eldon Tarver was not a member of the club and thus had no key. But Tarver did have the combination to the front gate, courtesy of Andrew Rusk. That was the arrangement they had made long ago, in case of emergency. They chose Chickamauga because they had planned their first joint venture here. Their acquaintance predated that meeting by two years, but there had been almost no physical contact in the interim. Any further meetings had been kept to less than two minutes, and at a place so public that no one would even call their contact a meeting.

Despite the emptiness of the clearing, Rusk was certain that Dr. Tarver was already here. He would have hidden his vehicle, in case any other members happened to be here—an unlikely event out of season, but you never knew. The question was, where would Tarver wait for him?

Rusk closed his eyes and listened to the sounds of the forest. He heard the wind first, the rustling dance of a billion spring leaves. Then the birds: sparrows, jays, martins. A lone bobwhite. The erratic *pop-pop-pop* of a woodpecker. Beneath all this, the low hum of distant trucks on Highway 28. But nothing in the varied symphony gave him a clue to the presence of another human.

Then he smelled fire.

Somewhere out to his left, wood was burning. He set off in that direction, moving with long, sure-footed strides through the trees. The farther he walked upwind, the more intense grew the smell of smoke. And *meat*. Someone was cooking out here! That made him doubt it was Tarver, but he had to make sure.

A moment later he found himself in a small clearing, at the center of which sat Eldon Tarver. The big pathologist was tending a cast-iron skillet over a small fire, and the sound of sizzling meat filled the clearing. Hanging on a wire beside Dr. Tarver was a dead fawn, freshly skinned but only partly butchered.

"Take a seat," Tarver said in his deep baritone. "I'm cooking the tenderloin. It's sinfully good, Andrew."

By killing the fawn, the pathologist had broken a sacred rule of the camp. By killing it out of season, he had broken several state and federal laws. But Rusk wasn't going to say anything about that. He had bigger problems to deal with, and whatever rules and laws Dr. Tarver had broken, he had done so with full knowledge and intent. Tarver speared a shaving of tenderloin with a pocketknife and held it out in the air. Rusk took the knife and ate the meat as a sign of their bond.

"It's good," he said. "Damn good."

"As fresh as it comes, this side of raw."

"Have you ever eaten it raw?"

A bemused look crossed the pathologist's face. "Oh my, yes. When I was a boy . . . but that's another story."

I'd like to hear that story sometime, Rusk thought. *When I have more time. I'd like to know what could turn a boy into a character like this.* He knew a little of Dr. Tarver's history, but not enough to explain the man's odd behavior and interests. But today was not the day to tease out that kind of thing.

"We have a problem," Rusk said bluntly.

"I'm here, am I not?"

"Two problems, really."

"Don't rush things," Tarver said. "Sit down. Have some more venison."

Rusk pretended to look down at the fire. He saw no rifle near Dr. Tarver, not even a handgun. There was a Nike duffel bag near his feet, which might contain a pistol, or even a submachine gun. He'd have to keep an eye on that. "I'm not really hungry," he said.

"You'd prefer to move straight to business?"

Rusk nodded.

"Then we should get the formalities out of the way first."

"Formalities?"

"Take off your clothes, Andrew."

Adrenaline blasted through Rusk's vascular system. *Would he tell me to strip if he wanted to kill me? To save himself the trouble of stripping my corpse? No. What would be the point out here?* "Do you think I'm wearing a wire, Doctor?"

Tarver smiled disarmingly. "You said we have an emergency. Stress makes people do things they might not ordinarily do."

"Are *you* going to strip?"

"I don't have to. You called this meeting."

That made sense. And if Rusk knew Tarver, nothing substantive was going to be said unless he complied with the doctor's order. Thanking God he had left his own pistol in the Porsche, he bent and untied his Cole Haans, then unsnapped his pants and stepped out of them. Next he removed his Ralph Lauren button-down, which left only his shorts and socks. Tarver seemed to be watching the campfire, not him.

"Is this far enough?" Rusk asked.

"Everything, please," Tarver said in a disinterested voice.

Rusk swallowed a curse and pulled off his shorts. He felt an odd and surprising shyness at this point, and it disturbed him. He had stripped in front of men hundreds of times at the health club, and he'd spent his whole youth doing the same in locker rooms around the state. He certainly had nothing to be ashamed of, not by the standard measure, and several women had commented that he was well-hung. But this was different. This was stripping naked in front of a guy with God only knew what sexual perversions, and a pathologist to boot—a man who had coldly stared at a thousand corpses, sizing up every anatomical flaw. It was creepy. And Dr. Tarver wasn't making it any easier. He was now staring at Rusk's body like an entomologist studying an insect mating.

"You've been working on those latissimi dorsi," Tarver observed.

It was true. Lisa had commented that age was taking a toll on his back, so Rusk had been putting in extra time on the Nautilus at the club to remedy the alleged deficiency. But how the hell Tarver knew that from a single glance—

"You should spend more time on your legs," the pathologist added. "Weight lifters are obsessed with their upper bodies, but underdeveloped legs ruin the whole effect. Symmetry is the thing, Andrew. Balance."

"I'll remember that," the lawyer said with a trace of bitterness. Rusk knew he had skinny legs, but they had been good enough in college. Besides, he had more to worry about every day than working out. And who the hell was Tarver to talk? The guy was big, sure, but what kind of tone did he have? Rusk suspected that underneath the unseasonable flannel shirt was a jellied wall of beer fat.

"Get dressed," Dr. Tarver said. "You look like a turtle without its shell."

Rusk pulled on his shorts and pants, then sat down to put on his shoes. "The last time we were here," he said, "you told me you hated the woods."

The doctor chuckled softly. "Sometimes I do."

"What does that mean?"

"You know so little about me, Andrew. Even if I told you . . . my experience is wholly outside your frame of reference."

Rusk tried to read this as arrogance, but it hadn't been intended that way. Tarver seemed to be saying, *You're from a different tribe than I am—perhaps even a different species*. And this was true. However Dr. Tarver felt about the woods, he was certainly no stranger to them. On that last trip—five years ago now—he had come to Chickamauga as the guest of an orthopedic surgeon from Jackson. For two days he had killed nothing, to the increasing amusement of the other members, who were killing record numbers of deer that year, albeit mostly does, and on the smallish side. But all anyone talked about that weekend was the Ghost, a wise and scarred old twelve-point buck who'd managed to evade the best hunters in the camp for almost ten years. After two seasons of invisibility, the Ghost had been sighted the previous week, and everyone was gunning for him, man and boy alike. Each night, Tarver had listened in silence as the members told Ghost stories by firelight—some true, others apocryphal—and each morning he'd vanished into the woods before dawn.

On the third day—a Sunday, Rusk recalled—Eldon Tarver had marched back into camp carrying the 220-pound carcass of the Ghost across his shoulders. He upset quite a few club members by killing their near-mythical beast, but what could they say? Tarver hadn't shot the Ghost from a tree stand, the way most of them hunted now, waiting in relative comfort for a deer to walk right under them—a tactic that regularly allowed eight-year-olds to bag a deer their first time out. Dr. Tarver had gone out and stalked the Ghost in the old way: the Indian way. He stalked the big buck for three days across the length and breadth of the camp, a damned tough slog through thick underbrush and rainy-autumn mud. Tarver had never revealed more than that (he seemed to cling to the ancient superstition that telling a thing lessened its power), but eventually the members had pieced together a legend. Those hunting from tree stands reported hearing odd sounds just after dawn on the day of the kill—mating calls, fighting grunts—sounds that could only have been mimicked by a master hunter. Then had come a single rifle blast, a perfect spine shot that would have dropped the Ghost right where he stood. It was as close to a painless death as the big buck could ever have hoped for—no running miles through the brush with half his heart blown out or his stomach filling up with blood—just instant paralysis and death.

Late that afternoon, Rusk had found himself gutting his own trophy buck outside. As though sent by fate, Eldon Tarver had walked up and offered to show him some time-saving tricks for dressing a deer. After Rusk gave over his skinning knife, he witnessed a demonstration of manual dexterity and anatomical knowledge that left him in wordless awe. He'd barely followed Tarver's words, so fascinated was he by the man's deft knife-work. And that part of his brain not wholly occupied with the bloody spectacle before his eyes was turning over an idea that had been born some years ago in the dark recesses of his soul, an idea born from need but unrealized due to moral scruple and a lack of opportunity. But the more years he practiced law, the more those scruples had eroded. And morality, Rusk had known even then, was not a component of Eldon Tarver's personality.

"Two problems," Tarver said, taking a slice of tenderloin from the skillet and dropping it into his mouth. "That's what you said."

"Yes. And they might be related."

Tarver chewed slowly, like a man accustomed to making his supplies last as long as possible. "Does anyone know who I am, Andrew?"

"No."

"Does anyone know that you and I are connected in any way?"

"No."

"Does anyone know what you are doing?"

"No."

"Does anyone suspect it?"

Rusk licked his lips and tried to appear calm. "I can't rule that out. Not with a hundred percent certainty."

"Who?"

"An FBI agent."

Tarver stuck out his bottom lip. "Who is he?"

"It's a girl. Grace Fennell's sister. Her name is Alexandra Morse."

A strange smile touched Tarver's lips. "Ahh. Well, we knew she was a risk. Why is this girl suspicious of you?"

"Bill Fennell thinks his wife may have said something to Morse just before she died. Morse was very upset by her sister's death, remember? She kidnapped Fennell's son."

"But she returned him before the funeral, yes?"

"Right. They'd had a lot of trauma in that family even before we stepped in. The father was shot during a robbery. The mother is dying now, ovarian cancer. Morse was almost terminated from the Bureau a couple of months after her father's death, for getting a fellow agent killed."

"Has she talked to you directly?"

"No."

Dr. Tarver's eyes bored into Rusk's with relentless intensity. "The question, Andrew, is how does she even know you exist?"

"I don't know that."

"Would Fennell have told her anything about you?"

"He could have . . . but would he? I don't think so. He's not stupid."

"Is he fucking her?"

"I don't think so," Rusk replied, asking himself this question for the first time, which was pretty sloppy in a divorce lawyer, he realized. "I mean, not that I know of."

This answer obviously did not satisfy Tarver.

"She'd never screw Bill Fennell," Rusk said more confidently. "She's too goody-goody for him. Too hot, too."

"She has a vagina, doesn't she?"

"Point taken."

"Why isn't she his type?"

"You remember the file on the Fennells, don't you? He's a snake, basically."

"You malign that creature by your comparison," Tarver said with strange severity.

Nonplussed, Rusk blinked a few times, then continued. "I checked Morse out before the operation, remember? She's a by-the-book agent, always plays by the rules. Or did, anyway. That's why she joined the FBI and not the CIA."

"But you know nothing about her deeper psychology."

"I guess not, when you put it that way."

"It could be the business connection," Tarver said thoughtfully. "The real estate deal between you and Fennell."

"Yes."

"You should have stuck to diamonds."

"This deal is better than diamonds, Eldon. *Way* better."

"Not if it kills you."

Rusk instantly noted two highly disturbing things: first, Dr. Tarver's use of the singular pronoun; second, he had not said anything about prison—he had gone straight to death. Do not pass go, do not collect two million dollars.

Tarver was watching Rusk with fresh interest. "What has Agent Morse done to upset you so? You're obviously worried."

"I think I might be being followed." *The understatement of the year. No mention of the Crown Vic or the chase along the Pearl River . . . nothing to trigger Eldon Tarver's overdeveloped instinct for self-preservation—*

Tarver had gone still. "You *might* be? Or you *are*?"

"It's possible. I'm not sure."

"Who do you think is following you? The FBI?"

"Honestly, I don't think so."

"Leave out the adverbs, Andrew. Give me facts."

Rusk resisted the urge to cuss the pathologist. "If Alex Morse is digging into her sister's death, she has to be doing it on her own time. Morse is already in deep shit with her superiors. Why would the FBI investigate Grace Fennell's death? It's a state crime."

"You're the lawyer. Look into it."

"I will."

"What else has Morse done?"

Here goes . . . "She may have broken into my office."

Tarver stared without blinking. "Are you certain of anything, Andrew? Or are you simply afraid to tell me the truth?"

"I'm not afraid," he said, which was the height of absurdity. "Even if she did break in, there's nothing in my office to find. Nothing incriminating, I mean."

"There's always something. I know your type, compulsive about writing things down. Come on . . ."

"If she got into my computer, she might be able to

trace some business relationships. Nothing illegal, though. Everything's aboveboard."

"But the *connections,*" Tarver said softly. "Connections to other corpses. *Spouses* of corpses."

"Only the earliest jobs," Rusk said. "The latest three years ago."

"If you discount Grace Fennell," Tarver reminded him.

"Right."

Tarver dropped several more slices of raw meat into the skillet. Rusk considered using this silence to tell Tarver about EX NIHILO, but somehow the time wasn't quite right.

"I've still only heard about one threat," murmured Dr. Tarver.

"The second is more direct, but also more manageable."

"Continue."

"It's one of our former clients. William Braid."

"The barge-company owner in Vicksburg?"

"That's the guy."

"What about him?"

"He's having a nervous breakdown. I kid you not, Eldon. It's from the guilt, from watching his wife die. He's hallucinating, seeing his dead wife in crowds, all kinds of crazy shit. It took her so long to die, you know? He just couldn't stand it. I'm afraid of what he might do. Who he might talk to. His pastor? A shrink? The police, even."

"Braid called you?"

"He stopped me at the goddamn golf course! He drove by my fucking house yesterday! Lisa just about freaked out."

Dr. Tarver's face drew taut. "Was he seen?"

"Only by Lisa, and I played that off."

"What did Braid tell you at the golf course?"

"He's thinking of killing himself."

"What's he waiting for?"

Rusk forced a laugh, but he was too worried about his own skin to indulge in levity.

"Why tell you that he's suicidal?" Dr. Tarver reasoned aloud. "Why not just go ahead and do it?"

"Exactly. I don't think he's the suicidal type. Too much self-regard. I think at the end of the day, he'll lay the blame on us and confess to the police."

Tarver stared at Rusk awhile, then shrugged philosophically. "This was bound to happen sooner or later. Inevitable, really."

"What should we do?"

"Braid has children?"

"Three."

"You think he forgot your warning? He forgot what happened to his wife?"

"I don't think he cares anymore, Eldon. He's that far gone."

"These people," Tarver said with almost tangible disgust. "So *weak*. They're like children themselves, really. No wonder women despise men nowadays."

Rusk said nothing.

"Where was Mr. Braid's precious conscience while he was paying us to murder the old frump?"

The lawyer shrugged. "He's a Southern Baptist."

Tarver looked puzzled for a moment. Then he laughed. "You mean Saturday night is a lot different from Sunday."

"Worlds apart, my man."

Tarver scooped the rest of the meat from the crackling skillet and laid it on one of the stones around the fire. "I used to know people like that."

"What do you think we should do?"

The doctor smiled. "We? Is there something you can do to get us out of this?"

Rusk almost blushed. "Well . . . I meant—"

"You meant, what am *I* going to do to save your ass."

This is going to cost me, Rusk suddenly realized. *Big-time.*

Dr. Tarver stood erect and stretched his long frame. Rusk could hear tendons popping. Tarver looked like that gray-bearded guy who was always shilling for starving children on late-night TV. Except for the birthmark. That fucking thing was hideous. *Get plastic surgery, for Christ's sake,* he thought. *It's the twenty-first century, and you are a fucking doctor.* Of course, he knew quite a few doctors with bad teeth, come to think of it.

"I'll take care of Mr. Braid," Tarver said in an offhand voice.

Rusk nodded cautiously. He wanted to know when the doctor meant to act, but he didn't want to anger him by asking.

"Will Braid be home tonight?" Tarver asked.

"Yes. I told him I might drive over to talk to him."

"Moron. What if he told his mistress that?"

"She left him ten days ago. Nobody talks to him now. His kids have been staying with their grandparents for the last two weeks."

"All right."

Rusk was breathing easier. No mention of money so far.

"Two hundred fifty thousand," Tarver said suddenly, as though reading his mind.

Rusk crumpled inside. "That seems like a lot," he ventured. "I mean, he's a threat to both of us, right?"

All humanity went out of Dr. Tarver's face. "Does Braid know my name?"

"No."

"Does he know my face?"

"Of course not."

"Then he's no threat to me. *You* are the only conceivable threat to me, Andrew. And I advise you not to make me dwell on that."

"How do you want the money?"

"The safe way. We'll make the transfer here, sometime next week."

Rusk nodded. *A quarter of a million dollars . . . just like that.* All to shut the mouth of one guilt-ridden client. He had to start screening better. But how? It was tough to predict who had the intestinal fortitude to watch someone they'd once loved reduced to a hollowed-out shell before they checked out. Shooting someone was a lot quicker, and loads easier to deal with. One trigger pull, and the source of your temporary madness was lying in the morgue. Three days later she was prettied up for her final appearance in the casket, and then *poof*—gone forever. That was fine in the old days, of course, the days of Perry fucking Mason. But this was the modern age. You couldn't shoot anyone you knew and get away with it. Nor could you strangle them, poison them, or push them off a hotel balcony. Just about any way you could kill somebody was traceable and provable in a court of law; and spouses and family members were automatically prime suspects in every murder. It was axiomatic: the first thing a homicide detective learned.

No, if you wanted to kill your spouse and get away with it, you had to do something truly ingenious: something that *wouldn't even be perceived as murder*. And that was the service that Andrew Rusk had found a way to provide. Like any quality product, it did not come cheap. Nor did it come quickly. And perhaps most important of all—as William Braid was proving—it was not for those with weak constitutions. Demand was high, of course, but few people were truly suitable clients. It took a deep-rooted hatred to watch your spouse die in agony, knowing that you had brought about that pain. But on the other hand, Rusk reflected, some people bore up remarkably well under the strain. Some people, in fact, seemed almost ideally suited for the role. They stretched their dramatic wings, donning a suit of martyrdom that they enjoyed all the more for its being unfamiliar. Rusk tried not to judge anybody. That was not his function. His job was to facilitate an outcome that a great number of people desired, but only an elite few could afford.

"If the money bothers you," Dr. Tarver said, "think about being gang-raped in Parchman prison for twenty-five years. Or think about sticking your hand inside that bag." Tarver gestured at the blue Nike bag at his feet. "Because I could make a strong argument for that. There's no risk to me, and it absolutely guarantees my safety."

"It would also deprive you of your future income," Rusk said bravely.

Tarver smiled. "I'm already rich, Andrew."

Rusk said nothing, but he was on surer ground here.

Dr. Tarver had earned millions from their association, but the pathologist had already spent much of his money. His private research work ate up capital at a staggering rate. Rusk wasn't sure what he was working on, but whatever it was, Rusk couldn't see the point—unless it had nothing to do with money. He knew that Tarver had once been fired by a pharmaceutical company for some sexual impropriety, and this had deprived him of the fruits of whatever research he had done for them. Maybe Tarver's goal was to prove to those people that they'd made the worst mistake of their lives. All this went through Rusk's mind in a matter of seconds, and only at a shallowest level of thought, for the core of his mind was focused on the question *What's in that Nike bag?* He had been watching the bag for twenty seconds now, and he was almost positive that it was moving.

"Do you want to see?" Tarver asked.

Rusk shook his head. With Eldon Tarver, there was no telling what was in the bag. A poisonous snake? A fucking Gila monster? God only knew. "We need to talk about something else."

"What's that, Andrew?"

"My safety."

A new watchfulness came into Tarver's eyes. "Yes?"

"I knew today would upset you. Especially the stuff about Morse."

"And?"

"Because of that, I felt I had to take steps to protect myself."

The doctor's eyelids dropped like those of some South American lizard sunning itself on a stucco wall. "What did you do, Andrew?"

"Take it easy, Eldon. All I did was make a simple and absolutely safe arrangement whereby if I don't do a certain thing every day, certain events will be set in motion." Rusk heard his voice quavering, but he had to go on. If he didn't, he'd never get it out. "Events which would insure you going to prison for multiple murder."

A strange light had come into the half-lidded eyes. "Don't tell me that you left some sort of confession with your attorney? Or put something in a safe-deposit box somewhere?"

"No, no, it's much more discreet than that! And much more reliable."

"What if you happen to die accidentally?"

"You'll have a couple of days to get out of the country. No more, though. And that's not so bad. We're already set up like kings. You'd just be leaving a little earlier, that's all. The bottom line is this: you can't kill me and stay in America. But why would you want to kill me? I'm making you more money than you could get any other way."

Tarver was breathing in long, rhythmic respirations. "That's not true. Your idea of wealth is very provincial, Andrew. The profits from my research will dwarf what we've earned. I consider our little operations piecework, like a student cutting lawns during medical school."

For some reason this irritated Rusk, who believed what they were doing to be a revolutionary business. But he didn't argue the point. He was still looking at the bag. There was definitely something alive in it.

"I need to get back to the city," he said.

Tarver reached down and unzipped the Nike bag. "Your idea of a city is provincial also. Jackson, Mississippi . . . my God."

As Rusk edged away from the fire, something black and yellow emerged from the opened zipper of the bag. It looked like a lizard's head. A black lizard with a yellow band across its head. *Too small for a Gila monster,* he thought, *unless it's a baby.*

"Before you go," said Dr. Tarver, "tell me about the woman."

"The woman?" Rusk echoed, for some reason thinking of Janice and her muscular thighs.

"Alex Morse."

"Oh. She was a hostage negotiator for the Bureau. The best they had, until she fucked up."

"What was the nature of her mistake?"

"She let her emotions override her logic."

"A common pitfall." With an almost balletic fluidity, Tarver reached behind the black and yellow head and lifted a brilliantly colored snake from the bag.

Oh, shit . . .

The narrow, brightly banded tail was twenty inches long, and it coiled around Tarver's arm as though around the trunk of some pale, hairy tree. Rusk stared at the alternating bands: *red, yellow, black; red, yellow, black—*

His blood pressure dropped so rapidly that he thought he might faint. It was a goddamned *coral snake.* A stone-fucking killer! Unless, unless . . . there was a king snake that looked almost exactly like the coral. *The scarlet king snake!* He remembered a story about some guys scaring the piss out of a pledge with one during Hell Week. He tried to remember the rhyme he'd learned as a Boy Scout: *Red over yellow . . . kill a fellow?* Was that it? *Red over black, friend to Jack?* If he was right, then Eldon Tarver was holding a goddamn coral snake in his hand as casually as Rusk would hold a kitten.

"Where did you get that fucking thing?" Rusk asked in a quavering voice.

"I found him this morning. He's a shy fellow, like all his kind."

"He came right on out of that bag when you opened it."

Tarver smiled. "I think he wanted to warm himself in the sun. He's cold-blooded, remember?"

Just like you, you crazy motherfucker.

"Is Agent Morse married?" Tarver asked.

"Never."

"Interesting. Children?"

"Just the nephew, Fennell's boy."

"Are they close?"

"Very."

Dr. Tarver seemed lost in thought.

He's a rough old cob, Rusk thought. Not freakishly ugly—except for the birthmark—but repulsive in small ways. He had big pores, for one thing. If you looked closely at his face, it was like looking onto a landscape of holes, like interior lining on the roof of an old Volkswagen. And he was pale the whole year round, as though the relentless Mississippi sun had no effect on him.

"Oh, one more thing," Rusk said. "I've got a potential client tomorrow. This guy is a total redneck, but there's nothing provincial about his bank account. And I know for a fact that he hates his wife. She might consult one of the local divorce sharks any day now, but Lisa tells me she hasn't yet. Any reason I shouldn't pitch him if he looks likely?"

"Greedy boy. What's the potential take?"

"We could each clear a million, I think."

Dr. Tarver held the snake's head mere inches from his eyes. "Really?"

"Hell, yes. It would cost him ten times that to get divorced."

"Then do it."

"No worries about Braid?"

Tarver shook his head. "Forget Braid. Focus on your sales presentation. That's your gift, Andrew. Sales."

Rusk laughed genuinely this time, partly because it was true, and partly because Tarver's last remark indicated that the doctor saw a future for him—one that did not include the coral snake coiled around his forearm. Rusk wondered absently if William Braid had a blind date with that snake, but the truth was, he didn't want to know. Snakes gave him the fucking willies, if he was honest about it. Even from a distance. "I really need to go."

Tarver smiled. "Say good-bye to my little friend."

Rusk shook his head. "No thanks."

"Take some tenderloin with you. For your ride back."

"Not hungry." Rusk had already backed fifteen yards away from the fire. "How will I know that Braid has been taken care of?"

Irritation flashed in Tarver's blue eyes. "Have I ever promised anything that did not become fact?"

"No. My mistake."

"Go away, Andrew. And remember—two hundred and fifty thousand dollars. I want uncut stones—white crystals, but not that flashy stash you use to seduce college girls."

"Uncut white crystals," Rusk acknowledged, finally in the trees now. "You'll have them next week."

Tarver was mostly a silhouette now, but Rusk saw him hold up the arm with the coral snake coiled around it. *"I will indeed,"* he called.

Rusk turned and started running.

CHAPTER

15

Chris had been working nonstop for hours. The last face he expected to see when he walked into his private office for a break was his wife's. Thora was sitting behind his desk, typing on the keypad of her Treo. She wore blue silk pants and a white silk top so fine that he could see through it. At the rustle of his white coat, she looked up and gave him a brilliant smile.

"Hey," he said. "What are you doing here?"

She started to answer, but then her eyes clouded. "Chris? Are you all right?"

"Sure. Why?"

"You look green, baby. What's the matter?"

He closed the door behind him. "I just diagnosed a fifty-five-year-old woman with advanced carcinoma of the lung. She was a friend of my mother's when we lived in Natchez."

Thora pulled off the pale blue scarf she was wearing in her hair and laid it on the desk. "I'm sorry. I know that kind of thing tears you up."

"I'm really glad to see you. I'm just surprised."

"Well, I happened to be driving past on the highway, so I turned in here to see your face and get a kiss." She got up and came around the desk, stood on tiptoe, and kissed him on the cheek. "Sit down."

He did. Thora moved behind him and began rubbing his shoulders. The soft scent of perfume reached him, and soon he was back in his studio, in the moments before she made love to him last night.

"Feel good?"

"This job really sucks sometimes."

"That's because you let it in. Doctors like my father shut it all out. They come in for the cutting, then take their check and move on."

Shane Lansing rose into Chris's mind: Lansing shared that trait with Lars Rayner.

"Relax," Thora said softly. "Just for a minute."

"I'm trying."

She kneaded the base of his neck, trying to ease his tension. He tried to go with it, but mostly to please her. A massage wasn't going to resolve any of his current problems.

"Oh, I ate lunch with Laura Canning at Planet Thailand," Thora said. "She told me the Alluvian had a cancellation this morning. They gave us reservations for the next three nights. The only catch is that we have to stay together—as in the *same room* together."

Chris leaned back and looked up at her inverted face. "You mean you're driving up there today?"

"No, no, tomorrow night. We won't leave until tomorrow morning."

He leaned forward again, absorbing this in silence.

"Don't worry, I'll still take Ben to school, and Mrs. Johnson can take him to Cameron's birthday party, if you can't get away."

Chris had completely forgotten the birthday party: a bowling party, like so many held by Ben's classmates.

Thora came around the chair and sat on the desk. His mood had deflated her excitement, but she looked more concerned than irritated.

"You're pretty quiet," she said, her eyes intense.

He wished he could do something about his mood, but after Alex Morse's accusations and a morning of dealing with terminal illness, it was tough to get excited about vacation plans. As he looked at Thora propped on the desk, something struck him with odd force. He'd actually noticed it last night, but his starved libido had relegated it to minor importance.

"How much weight have you lost?" he asked, staring at her concave belly beneath the silk top.

Thora looked flustered. "What?"

"Seriously. You look too thin."

A little laugh. "That's what running does to you."

"I know. And it can be unhealthy. Are you still menstruating normally?"

"I had a period two weeks ago."

Chris tried to remember any signs that this was true. "I want you to go in the hall and let Holly weigh you."

Thora reached down and squeezed his thigh. "You're being silly, Chris."

"No, I'm being serious. Come on," he said, standing, "I'll weigh you myself. I want to draw some blood, too."

"Blood?" Thora looked stunned. "No way."

"Look, you hardly ever come to the office. When was the last time you had a complete physical?"

She thought about it. "I can't remember. But Mike Kaufman checked me out during my last gyno visit."

"That was more of a focused exam. I'm worried

about your general health. Plus, you weren't running nearly as much when Mike looked at you. That could be interfering with your ability to conceive."

Thora looked sober but said nothing.

"What are you worried about?" he asked with genuine concern.

"Nothing. I just don't like needles. You know that."

"That's no reason to put it off. Come on." He took her by the arm and walked her out to Holly's nurse's station. Leaving her sandals on, Thora stepped up onto the medical scale. Chris shook his head and told her to take the sandals off. After she did, he worked the black iron balances until the bar settled into a level position.

"A hundred and eleven pounds," he said. "How much did you weigh when we got married?"

Thora shrugged. "I don't remember."

"I do. A hundred and twenty-six."

"I never weighed that in my life."

Chris chuckled. She was definitely lying about that, but there was nothing sinister in it. "You're five feet six, Thora. You don't need to lose fifteen pounds when your starting point is one twenty-six."

She sighed and stepped off the scale.

Chris knew he'd never get her down the hall to the lab, so he sat her down and fastened a blood-pressure cuff around her upper arm. After he'd pumped it up, he dug into Holly's bottom drawer and took out one of the syringes she used for injections.

"Hey!" Thora cried. "What do you think you're doing with that?"

"Just sit back and be calm. I'm very good with a needle."

"He is," said Holly from behind him. "He could find a vein on an overweight elephant."

"I'm not sure that's relevant here," Thora said. "What gauge needle is that?"

"A twenty-one," said Chris.

She grimaced. "Can't I have a twenty-three?"

"Stop being a baby. Most people get twenty-ones, you know."

"I'm not most people." She pulled her arm away at first, but after a few evasions she sat back and let him draw ten ccs of dark venous blood into the barrel of the syringe. If they were in the lab, he would have filled several tubes, but this was better than nothing. "God," Thora said, clenching her inner elbow to facilitate clotting. "I come in for a kiss and I get violated instead. No wonder I don't come here very much."

Chris laughed, but he was thinking that something he'd always suspected about Thora's attitude toward his office was true: it reminded her of her father in some way, and she didn't want to be around it. "I thought you liked me violating you," he said.

"Not today." She got up and walked back toward his office.

When Chris got there, she had put her scarf back on and was slipping her Treo into her purse. "I've got a lot to do to get ready for my trip," she said, coming to the door.

"Will you be home when I pick up Ben?" he asked. "We've got baseball practice today."

"Practice?" Thora's eyes narrowed. "Ben has a game tonight, Chris. You're playing last year's championship team."

"Jesus, you're right."

Thora laughed with real pleasure. "I can't believe you forgot and I remembered. The world must be rotating backwards today."

"After the morning I've had, it wouldn't surprise me. I hope the rest of the day is better."

She shook her head as though puzzled. "It's afternoon already, Chris."

He looked at his watch. She was right. "God. I'll bet the staff is ready to kick my ass."

"Have you eaten anything?"

"Not since this morning."

Thora walked into the corridor and looked back at him. "You need to shut this place down and run over to the hospital cafeteria."

"I think I will. Do you want to come?"

"No, I'm full of sushi."

"Somehow I doubt that. You probably took two or three bites, total."

She pushed him playfully, then called good-bye to Holly, who was down by the door to X-ray. "I'll see you at the house, okay?" Thora leaned close to him. "Maybe after Ben's game we can do a replay of last night."

He was about to answer when he felt her hand close around his testicles. She looked meaningfully at him and squeezed.

"Maybe so," he said, turning red.

Thora laughed softly, then turned and walked toward the private exit, her silk pants swishing gracefully around her ankles. After she'd gone, Chris walked down the hall and handed the full syringe to Holly.

"What tests do you want done?" she asked.

"A CBC and a standard Chem-20. But don't throw

any serum away. I may do some more tests, depending on what I find."

"Okay." Holly walked quickly toward the lab.

As Chris turned, he saw Jane, his receptionist, leaning through the window that opened onto the hall. "Are you okay, boss?" she asked.

"Yeah, why?"

"You don't seem like yourself today."

"I'm good to go."

Jane snorted. "Then maybe you should. It's time to tie on the feed bag, darlin'."

"Past time," said his lab tech from behind him. "Even Dr. Cage left out of here forty-five minutes ago."

Chris shook his head. If Tom was gone to lunch, he had definitely stayed too late.

"You've still got one patient," Holly reminded him, coming back up the hall. "Room four, Mr. Patel. Sounds like a hot gallbladder."

Chris walked back to his office and closed the door. He needed to examine Patel, but right now he couldn't summon the concentration. He walked around his desk and sat in his chair again. Without quite knowing why, he opened his drawer. As he did, he realized that he was checking to see if Thora had been through his things.

Why should I worry about that? he wondered.

Then he saw the answer. Lying on top of a prescription pad was the silver Motorola clamshell phone that Alex Morse had given him on the Trace that morning. If Thora had opened this drawer, she would have seen it instantly. *Maybe she did,* he thought. *No . . . if she'd seen a new cell phone, she would have asked me about it.*

As Chris turned the Motorola in his hand, he saw that its blue LCD window said 1 MISSED CALL. The phone's ringer was set to SILENT. He flipped open the phone and checked the time of the call. One minute ago. Strangely flustered, he speed-dialed the only number programmed into the memory. After only half a ring, a woman said, "It's Alex. Can you talk?"

"Yes."

"I'm right outside your office. Thora just left."

He felt a wave of disorientation. "Why are you here?"

"I followed your wife here."

"Crap, Alex. What are you doing?"

"Trying to save your life."

"Jesus. I told you—"

"I have something to show you, Chris. Something unequivocal."

Dread settled in his chest. "What is it?"

"I'll tell you when I see you."

"Goddamn it. You said Thora's gone?"

"Yes."

"Just come into my office then."

A hesitation. "That would be a mistake."

"You can use my private entrance."

"No. You come to me."

"I still have patients! I can't leave now. Besides, where would we go?"

"There's some kind of park at the end of this boulevard."

"That's not a park, it's a historical site. The Grand Village of the Natchez Indians."

"Fine, whatever. It's deserted, and it's only a quarter mile away."

"Agent Morse, I—"

"Is Thora leaving town today, Chris?"

"Tomorrow morning."

A quick expulsion of breath. "This won't take ten minutes. You owe it to yourself. To Ben, too."

Irrational anger flooded through him. He considered asking Morse to wait ten minutes and then slip into his office, but sometimes one or two staff members stayed through lunch and ate Lean Cuisines in the lounge. He couldn't be sure that wouldn't happen today. "I'll meet you there in five minutes."

"I'll be waiting on the big hill in the middle," Morse said.

The big hill? "That's a ceremonial mound, not a hill. An Indian mound."

"Great. Please hurry."

Fifteen minutes later, Chris was trotting under a thick stand of oak trees, heading for a vividly lit stretch of grass almost half a mile long. He jogged past a replica of an Indian hut and broke out into the sunlight. In the distance stood two steeply sloped mounds separated by eighty meters. The nearer was a ceremonial mound where the chief of the Natchez, the Great Sun, had once presided over the rituals of this unique tribe. Farther on stood the Temple mound. Both had been built by the sun-worshipping natives that settled this land a thousand years before the white man came. Like many old cities, Natchez had been founded upon murder, in this case the massacre of the Natchez Indians by French troops from New Orleans, in retaliation for a rebellion in the previous year—1729.

Chris shielded his eyes with the flat of his hand and

studied the crest of the nearer mound. A small silhouette appeared against the sky. He wasn't sure that the shadow figure was Alex Morse, but he walked in that direction anyway. He scanned the village grounds as he walked, sighting half a dozen tourists near the Temple mound, all moving in groups of two.

He breathed harder as he climbed the mound, but it was nothing compared to Emerald Mound north of the city. There the Natchez had constructed an earthen analog of the Mayan structures in the Yucatán, though anthropologists believed that no direct connection existed.

"It's been twenty minutes," said the silhouette above him.

When Chris reached the crest, he recognized Morse. She had exchanged her wet biking garb for khakis and a pale yellow top. He saw no sign of her gun. Maybe it was in the brown handbag that lay at her feet.

"What do you have to show me?"

"We're pretty exposed here," Morse said. "Can we move somewhere else?"

"Jesus. I guess so. St. Catherine's Creek runs through this site. There's a path under those trees over there that leads down to it."

"Fine."

She started in that direction without waiting for him. Chris shook his head in frustration, then followed.

Along the path, the trees changed from oak to elm and then to cottonwood. Thick stands of bamboo appeared on either side, and then they were walking on damp beige sand. The humid air smelled of dead fish. Only two years ago, Chris recalled, one of the most beautiful young girls in the city had been killed along this creek—not far away from here, in fact. Tom Cage's son had defended the prime suspect in the case—a Natchez internist, of all people—and only by exonerating the suspected physician had Penn Cage escaped the ill feeling that had attached to his client during the investigation. But escape he did, for less than two months later Penn had been voted into the mayor's office during a special election.

"How far away is this creek?" Morse asked, breathing hard and sweating harder.

"Fifty more yards."

"Should we just stop here?"

"No. We're in mosquito heaven."

The trees gave way to an empty sandbar, beyond which lay a wide, placid creek. The calm water was misleading. During thunderstorms, Chris had seen the creek reach a depth of twenty feet as it swept through town carrying massive tree trunks along like matchsticks. It had been that way on the day that poor girl was murdered—

"That's far enough," said Morse, stopping in the middle of the sand. "Put your game face on, Doctor."

Chris clenched his fists at his sides.

She opened her purse and handed him a sheet of printer paper still damp with ink. It was a photograph of Thora standing face-to-face with Shane Lansing. Behind them was a seamless sheet of black granite that Chris recognized as the face of the fireplace in the great room of their new house in Avalon. Thora's face was highly animated—seemingly by anger, but he couldn't be sure—and she was gesturing with both hands. Lansing was listening with a submissive expression Chris had never seen on his face before. It was difficult to read what was being discussed, but the two of them were standing very close together—definitely in each other's space, though not quite at an intimate distance.

"Where did you get this?" Chris asked.

"You know where."

"I mean *how* did you get it? And when?"

"I took that picture forty-five minutes ago. I printed it in my car on a portable Canon."

Chris felt unsteady on his feet. Thora was wearing the same silk top and blue scarf she had worn to his office only minutes ago, and she had said nothing about talking to Shane Lansing. "You sneaked into the house with them?"

"I shot it through a window. I was tired of you telling me I'm full of shit. That I have no proof of anything."

Chris looked downstream at a fifty-foot bluff covered with thick, green kudzu. "What do you think this picture proves?"

"That your wife is doing something besides giving Dr. Lansing the threepenny tour of your house. This is their third meeting this week."

"Did you hear what they said?"

"I couldn't get close enough without her seeing me."

Chris walked over to a large driftwood log and sat down heavily.

"Dr. Shepard?"

He didn't reply. He was thinking of last night, when he and Thora had made love on the couch in his studio. Of Thora's efforts to get pregnant . . . her surprise plans for his studio . . . "I know this looks bad," he said in a monotone, holding up the picture. "But it doesn't *prove*

they're having an affair. Maybe Lansing is having problems at home. Maybe he's confiding in Thora about
something."

Morse opened her mouth in astonishment. "You're
acting like a *wife*, Chris. A long-suffering wife defend-
ing her cheating husband to her family and friends."

"Goddamn it," he said in a low voice, "you don't
know Thora."

"Maybe you don't either."

He looked up. "You're saying she got it on with
Shane Lansing, then drove straight to my office to give
me a kiss?"

"You've got to wake up, Chris! Adulterers lie like
that all the time. My fiancé left my best friend's bed,
then came straight to my apartment and had sex with
me. He never even showered. But maybe that's just my
life. Did Thora tell you she came to your office to give
you a kiss?"

Chris looked away and dropped the photo on the
sand. "What else did she do today?"

"The usual. She ran, she showered, she swam at the
country club. Then she drove to Mainstream Fitness
for her weight lifting. She showered again there, then
started walking to Planet Thailand."

He nodded distantly.

"At the last minute, her cell phone rang. She took
the call, then suddenly turned around and went back to
her car. That's when she drove out to Avalon."

Chris looked up sharply. "Thora didn't eat at Planet
Thailand?"

"No. What did she tell you?"

*I ate with Laura Canning at Planet Thailand
today. . . . No, I'm full of sushi. . . .*

"Chris?"

He couldn't look at Morse. An equivocal photo was one thing, an outright lie was another.

"She lied to you, didn't she?" Morse said. "If you still have any doubts, check her cell phone bill. You can do it online. There'll be a call from Lansing at twelve twenty-eight p.m. today. You have the picture that proves she met him immediately afterward, and you know she lied to you about where she was during lunch. Once you put those things together—"

"I get it, okay!" Chris snapped, turning away. "Just give me a minute here!"

Alex walked down to the water's edge, leaving Dr. Shepard to absorb the new reality at his own pace. *It was the lie that did it,* she thought with satisfaction. She could have talked until she went hoarse and Shepard might have remained in denial. He was even prepared to make excuses explaining the photograph. But now that didn't matter. Thora had damned herself with a single lie.

It hadn't even been a necessary lie, Alex reflected. But that was human nature, as her father had explained many times. When people got into the habit of lying, they came to depend on it as a means of sliding easily through life. Thora probably hadn't even considered the risk of that little fib. After all, she had *planned* to eat lunch at the Thai restaurant. And Chris would never check on something so small. . . .

Alex looked down into the creek in search of fish, but all she saw was a cloud of tadpoles. The creek and the woods made her think of Jamie, and how her father had taught the boy to fish in the various waterways around Jackson. Bill Fennell had been glad for those fishing trips, she remembered, and now she knew why. Getting Jamie out of his hair had made it that much easier for Bill to meet his mistress for a quick screw. It left only Grace to get rid of, and Grace stayed so busy that she was easy to evade—especially after their mother's diagnosis.

Oh, God, Alex thought, *I need to check in with the nurses.*

She turned back to Chris, ready to call out, *That picture's not going to change, no matter how long you look at it*—but in the event she said nothing.

Chris Shepard was gone.

CHAPTER

16

The crowd roared at the clang of the aluminum bat, and two hundred eyes followed the arc of the hard-driven baseball beneath the lights. Coaching first base, Chris tensed and watched Ben race toward him from the batter's box. The boy had smacked the ball between the second baseman and the bag, but the center fielder had charged forward and was already scooping up the ball.

"Turn and look!" Chris shouted.

Ben pivoted off the bag with his right foot and sprinted a third of the way to second base. The throw would easily beat him to the bag.

He had to come back.

Chris heard Thora cheering from the bleachers, but he didn't look up. He'd been in a mild state of shock since seeing the photograph Alex Morse gave him on the bank of St. Catherine's Creek. His first instinct had been to drive home and confront Thora, but by the time he passed the hospital in his car, he had calmed down enough to turn around, go inside, and make rounds instead. After that, he'd returned to his office and finished out the afternoon. Most of Thora's blood tests had been completed by then, and the only abnormality he found was mild anemia, which he often saw in distance runners—

"Dad?" said Ben. "Do you want me to steal on a passed ball?"

Chris stared at Ben as though in a trance. This handsome young boy who called him Dad was the son of a man Chris had never met, the issue of a chapter of Thora's life that remained largely unknown to him. Before Alex Morse arrived in Natchez, the unknowns in Thora's life had not much bothered Chris. But now everything had changed. He hadn't spoken to Thora since she left his office that afternoon. After work, he'd called Ben and told him to be waiting outside the house. Thora had waved from the kitchen window when he drove up, signaling for him to wait, but Chris had left for the baseball field without a word.

"Dad!" Ben said again. "Do I steal or what?"

Chris tried to force his mind back to reality. He hadn't eaten lunch or dinner, and he'd been feeling dizzy since the game started. It was the bottom of the sixth inning, and the opposing team was up by one run. If his boys couldn't score and push the game into extra innings, it was over. He looked at the batter's box, and his heart sank. He'd reached the bottom of his batting order: three weak nine-year-olds in a row. They were good boys, but they couldn't hit a baseball if their lives depended on it. He had moved Ben deep in the order to keep some power late in the lineup, but Ben could only do so much. Chris knelt beside him, met his eyes, and whispered, "Steal no matter what."

Ben started to question this call, then thought better

of it. He understood the situation. The instant the next pitch crossed the plate, Ben bolted for second base. The catcher caught the ball cleanly, jumped to his feet, and fired the ball across the pitcher's mound. His throw was a little high—just high enough for Ben to slide safely under the second baseman's glove as it whipped down to tag him. Half the crowd went wild, and the other half groaned.

Chris gave Ben a thumbs-up and watched his left fielder walk nervously into the batter's box. The boy took his position at the plate, then looked worriedly at Chris. Chris hitched up his belt, giving the signal to bunt. While he waited for the pitch, he glanced over the chain-link fence to his left. As he did, he realized that his eye had been drawn by movement. A young woman was riding past the field on a bicycle. When she lifted her right hand in a subtle wave, Chris's heart thudded in his chest.

Alexandra Morse.

She'd probably panicked after he disappeared from the creek bank. She'd called his cell phone so many times since that meeting that he'd switched it off. She'd even tried calling his office, but his staff had refused to put her through. Chris didn't care. As Morse rode slowly away, his head whipped around at the ring of a baseball hitting aluminum. His left fielder had bunted the ball six feet in front of the plate and was now charging toward first base, his arms windmilling wildly in an effort to keep himself balanced.

Chris screamed encouragement, but in vain. The catcher drilled the ball into the first baseman's glove while the boy was still ten feet from first base. The first baseman tried to throw Ben out at third, but Chris knew before he looked that Ben had made it. He patted his left fielder on the shoulder and told him he'd made a good play. *Stay focused on the game,* he thought, fighting an urge to glance in Morse's direction again. *Ben is on third . . . we can tie it right here.*

There were two outs on the scoreboard. His next batter already had a strike against him. The opposing pitcher hadn't thrown many wild balls today; most of his pitches were straight down the pipe. A strikeout was a near certainty. To tie it up, Ben would have to steal home plate. He had the speed, but would he have the opportunity?

Chris looked across the field at his third-base coach, a local welder. The man was looking at him questioningly. Chris closed his eyes for a moment, then tugged on his right earlobe. If the catcher missed a ball, Ben would go for it.

"Swing hard, Ricky!" Chris shouted. In this league, a swinging bat increased the odds that the catcher would miss the ball, especially the way Ricky Ross swung the bat. He was as likely to hit the catcher's mitt as he was to hit the ball as it flew over the plate.

The pitcher unloaded a fastball. Ricky swung like Mark McGwire overdosing on steroids—and missed. The ball glanced off the catcher's mitt and caromed off the backstop behind him. Ben exploded off third base, reaching full speed in five steps, but the pitcher was already dashing to cover home plate. The catcher wouldn't beat Ben to the plate for a tag, but the pitcher might.

Ben sprinted as far as he dared before dropping into his slide, and then he was skidding down the baseline in a cloud of dust. Every voice in the bleachers fell silent, and Chris's heart rose into his throat. He thought Ben had it, but a flash of white at the center of the dust cloud made him clench his fists in fear.

"*Out!*" screamed the umpire.

The stands erupted in a schizophrenic roar of fury and joy. Chris ran toward the plate, but it was no use arguing the call. He hadn't seen the play. Instinct told him that no one had, including the umpire. There was so much dust that the final act of the game had been obscured. Ben got up, his face red, and stared at the umpire with tears in his eyes. He seemed on the verge of challenging the ump, so Chris caught him by the arm and pulled him into the dugout.

"It was a good try," Chris said, "but it's over. Time to be a man."

The two teams lined up, then filed past each other saying, "Good game, good game," and then it was over. Chris gathered his team behind the dugout, gave them an encouraging wrap-up talk in the gathering dusk, and dispersed them to their waiting parents. Four or five fathers told him he should file a protest about the final call, but Chris shook his head and told them to start thinking about the next game.

"Dad?" said Ben, tugging at his arm. "Can we stay and watch C.J.'s game?"

"No, honey," said a female voice from behind Chris. *Thora's voice.*

"Aw, come on, Mom! Dad didn't say no."

"All right, then," Thora said in a clipped voice. "Ask your dad and see what he says."

Ben grinned and looked up at Chris. "Can I, Dad? Can I?"

"Sure," said Chris. "Let's see how C.J. does against Webb Furniture."

Ben screeched in delight and ran off toward the bleachers.

"Why did you do that?" asked Thora, stepping in front of him with a betrayed look. "I thought we were going to spend some time together at home."

Chris choked back a half dozen replies. "He really wants to stay."

"But I'm leaving tomorrow."

"By your choice."

She looked at Chris as though he'd slapped her.

"You'll only be gone three days," he said. "Right?"

Thora nodded slowly but said nothing.

He walked past her toward the bleachers. He thought she might call after him, but she didn't. As he walked, he tried to get a handle on his emotions. After going back to his office, he had done as Morse suggested and checked the online billing records for Thora's cell phone. He'd found several numbers he didn't recognize, but none belonged to Shane Lansing. Chris knew this because he had called them all to check. Stranger still, there had been no call at 12:28 p.m. There wasn't even a call in the thirty-minute window surrounding 12:28. Either Agent Morse was mistaken, or Thora had a cell phone he knew nothing about.

CHAPTER

17

Eldon Tarver stood alone beneath a flaming sky, staring at a mansion built by slaves 150 years before he was born. One of the most splendid homes in Vicksburg, the Greek Revival palace stood on a hogback bluff overlooking a once-strategic bend of the Mississippi River. Not far away lay the big cannons that had held Ulysses Grant at bay for fifty siege days while the citizens of the town ate rat flesh and clung to their long-cherished beliefs. How many had died in that lost cause? Dr. Tarver wondered. Fifty thousand casualties at Gettysburg alone, and for what? To free the slaves who built this house? To preserve the Union? Had Stonewall Jackson died to create a nation of couch potatoes ignorant of their own history and incapable of simple mathematics? If those brave soldiers in blue and gray had seen what lay in the future, they would have laid down their muskets and walked home to their farms.

Dr. Tarver moved deeper into the shadow of an oak tree and watched a Lincoln Continental sail slowly up the long, curving driveway to the house. After it parked, a heavyset man in a soiled business suit staggered out of the driver's door, straightened up, and made his way toward the mansion's front door.

William Braid.

Dr. Tarver removed his backpack and laid it at his feet. He breathed in sweet honeysuckle, the scent of spring. It reminded him of his childhood home in Tennessee—a mixed memory.

Braid struggled for nearly a minute to fit his key into his front door. He hadn't shaved for days, and his suit was a wreck. After another thirty seconds, he took out a cell phone and called someone. He seemed to be ranting, but Eldon couldn't make out his words. As Braid walked farther from the house, probably to improve his reception, Eldon glanced at his watch and returned to his thoughts.

Like William Braid, America seemed hell-bent on self-destruction. She was squandering her power in half-fought wars and exporting her manufacturing base to future enemies—in short, practically begging for Darwinian retribution. Of all the great modern thinkers, Dr. Tarver believed, Charles Darwin had proved the most prescient. His laws worked at every level, governing the life cycles of microbes, men, and nations. Dr. Tarver tracked the elegant operations of those laws like a watchmaker observing a flawless timepiece. Like all scientific laws, Darwin's could be used not only to describe the past but also to predict the future. Not by chance had Eldon Tarver been one of the few scientists to predict the emergence of HIV in *Homo sapiens*. Darwin's laws had also revealed to him that the new paradigm of war so ballyhooed in the news media—war against terrorist groups rather than nations—was merely an illusion.

There was nothing preternatural about his insight. The future was barreling toward America with such momentum that nothing could stop it, and any child of the Cold War should have seen it five years ago. That future was China, an ancient empire reborn as industrial superpower, a single-minded engine of economic expansion that cared nothing for ethics, the environment, loss of life, or the destinies of other nations. This insured that in a very short time, China would be locked in mortal combat with the only other monolithic power on the planet. And the United States, Tarver knew, was woefully unprepared for this Darwinian battle for survival.

William Braid had been walking aimlessly as he talked on the phone, but now he took a sudden turn toward Dr. Tarver's hiding place. The doctor tensed until the fat man veered left and stopped beside a well-tended bed of roses, still ranting at full volume. From this distance Dr. Tarver could tell that Braid was stone drunk.

The battle between the United States and China would begin as a cold war, with leaders on both sides denying that a conflict even existed. But in a world of scarce resources, industrial giants could dissimulate for only so long. The first skirmishes would occur in the area of international trade, then escalate into the realm of international banking. Long before armies ever faced each other on land or sea, the targeting coordinates of nuclear missiles on opposite sides of the globe would be changed to reflect the new reality. And for the second time in history, the world's smaller wars would recede into the background as children grew up in the shadow of a polarizing conflict that brought with it a unique and almost comforting order.

William Braid barked something in Dr. Tarver's direction, then threw down his cell phone and reeled up to his front door like a boxer about to drop to the canvas. Bending over his key again, Braid uttered a startled cry of triumph and disappeared inside the house.

Dr. Tarver removed a pair of surgical gloves from his pocket, put them on, and studied his watch. He would give Braid a minute or two. The only future he would ever know.

Unlike the last cold war, this one would not drift along for decades, punctuated by self-limiting crises. Because the Chinese weren't the Russians. The *Russians,* as Tarver often told his colleagues, were basically just like us: white Europeans with a strong Judeo-Christian heritage, despite whatever lip service they'd paid to communist denials of God. But the Chinese were most assuredly *not* like us. When push came to shove, the Chinese were capable of destroying half of their population to wipe us off the face of the earth. As Mao once said, "If nuclear war kills half a billion of our people, we will still have half a billion left." And then he'd laughed.

But Mao had not been joking. War with China was inevitable, and Eldon Tarver knew it. But unlike the professional ostriches now running the country, he wasn't content to sit back and watch it happen. In 1945, Eldon's adoptive father had fought his way across four blood-drenched islands in the Pacific, and he'd learned a thing or two about the Asian mind. He might have been a bitter old bastard with iron-hard hands, but he had inculcated the lessons of that war into all his children—even the one he'd adopted solely to obtain an extra worker on his farm. Thus, unlike the dilettantes who reveled in anti-Chinese repartee on the cocktail party circuit, Eldon Tarver had a plan. He had studied his enemy for decades, preparing to wage what the Pentagon called *asymmetrical warfare*. But Dr. Tarver had a simpler phrase for it: *one-man war*.

A light clicked on in the master bedroom of the Braid house, spilling low-voltage halogen light onto the perfectly manicured lawn. Dr. Tarver knew about the halogen bulbs because he'd spent time in that bedroom nearly two years before. He lifted his backpack and moved swiftly around the house to the patio doors. Braid would not have switched on his security system yet; like most people, he was a creature of habit. And like most people—at least in relatively safe Mississippi—Braid did not feel the least bit threatened while the sun was still shining. That was why Dr. Tarver had come early.

He opened the French doors with his key—a key that Braid had given Andrew Rusk over two years ago—then slipped inside and moved toward a closet beneath the main stairwell. Dr. Tarver was halfway there when a brief ping echoed through the house. He stepped into the closet and stood absolutely still, listening the way he had when he'd hunted for food as a boy.

He heard nothing.

He had planned to wait until Braid went to sleep to do his work, but now that he was here, he couldn't bear the thought of the wasted hours. It wasn't as if this operation were going to add a single line of data to his research notes. As he stood fuming in the closet, a possible solution struck him. If Braid was in the shower now, Eldon could do what he needed to do and be headed home before the moon was up. All it would take was a little audacity, which was not a scarce resource in the Tarver gene pool.

He removed his shoes, then opened the door and moved quickly along the carpet runner in the hall. At the end of this runner lay the master bedroom. He listened at the bedroom door with the same concentration he'd used in the closet. Nothing. Braid was almost certainly in the bathroom.

Dr. Tarver silently opened the door, confirmed that the room was empty, then moved straight to the closed bathroom door. Braid was either taking a shower or taking a crap. Eldon hoped it was the former. Looking down, he saw a faint trace of steam wafting up from beneath the door.

He moved to a highboy against the wall to his left. In the top drawer he found the weapons he had known would be there (man was a creature of habit): a dozen vials of insulin and two bags of syringes. There were two types of insulin: short-acting Humulin R and the longer-acting Humulin N.

Unsnapping his pack, he removed a 10 cc syringe and stripped off the packaging. This syringe could hold five times more liquid than the standard diabetic syringes in Braid's drawer—twenty times his usual dose. The doctor lined up ten vials from Braid's drawer, then quickly filled the syringe to capacity. To complete the charade that would later be played, he loaded two of Braid's syringes as well, then uncapped the needles on both. Held in one hand, they looked like the fangs of some cybernetic serpent.

As he reached for the doorknob, Eldon dimly heard the shower flowing. He had to move fast. If Braid emerged and saw him, there might be a struggle, despite the man's inebriated state. Even if Braid was suicidal, Eldon could not count on a passive victim. Facing the black maw of death, some would-be suicides would kill a dozen men to save themselves. Dr. Tarver turned the knob with his gloved hand and pushed.

He heard the hiss of wood against the nap of the carpet. The bathroom was large, but thick with steam. Braid had forgotten to switch on the exhaust fan. *He must have the water very hot. He's so drunk he can't feel it.*

Dr. Tarver felt intense satisfaction. This scenario was far better than his original plan. His sleeping gas left a traceable residue in the tissues for up to thirty-six hours (if you knew what to look for), and in some people it could cause allergic reactions. This method involved no forensic risk—only iron nerves.

He laid the two smaller syringes on the bathroom counter, then positioned himself to the left of the shower door. Behind the etched glass, a pale, flabby blur swayed in the steam. Eldon heard four wheezing breaths, then a groan that made him suspect Braid was either urinating or masturbating. A moment later, a strong odor confirmed the former. It took more than urine in the shower to disgust a pathologist, but Dr. Tarver was disgusted—not by the bodily function, but by Braid's essential weakness. The man had decided to change his life, then proved unequal to his desire. Braid's mental process eluded him. Why had the man broken down? Had he decided that it was all right to murder your wife quickly but a mortal sin if she suffered? That was the kind of contradictory thinking that afflicted the nation as a whole. Eager to be away, Eldon slid two gloved fingers behind the stainless steel pull on the shower door. Then he knelt, opened the door, and speared his needle into a prominent vein in Braid's lower leg.

There was no reaction.

He had injected almost the full barrel of insulin before Braid jerked away and gasped, "*Wha . . . ?*" It reminded Eldon of the time his adoptive brother stuck a penknife into a cow's side. At first, nothing. Then the cow shambled three steps away and looked back at him in dumb incomprehension. Had Braid even felt the needle? Or was it the draft he'd noticed?

It was the draft! He was reaching out blindly to close the door. Either Braid suffered from severe neuropathy, or he was blind drunk. Before the door closed, Dr. Tarver slipped one hand behind Braid's ankles and yanked his feet out from under him. The man went down hard, banging his head on a tiled seat and possibly breaking his hip. After more than a minute of groaning, Braid tried to get back to his feet, but his left leg refused his considerable weight.

Dr. Tarver crabwalked away from the shower door and sat on the commode behind a small partition. Whatever injury Braid had sustained, the pain was severe enough to burn through the anesthetic alcohol. His groans slowly escalated to bellows of rage, then screams of panic. A plump white hand emerged from the open door, clutched the tiled edge of the shower basin. Eldon worried for a moment that the fat man might extricate himself from the shower, but then the insulin began to take effect. The fingers of the hand stopped moving, the screams faded back to groans, and finally the groans to silence.

Coma would soon follow.

Dr. Tarver got up, tossed the two unused syringes into the shower, then the empty vials from the drawer. Now came the truly unpleasant part of tonight's work. Before he left this house, he would have to search it from top to bottom, including the computers. He could take no chance that Braid had left behind a confession in any form.

Walking back to the shower stall, Eldon bent and pulled up one of Braid's eyelids. The pupils were fixed and dilated. William Braid was well on his way to being a vegetable, if he didn't die of shock on the journey. For the first time in many years, Eldon reflected, the fat man's face was not lined with care. As he walked down the hall toward Braid's study, Dr. Tarver decided that it would be no stretch to say that this operation had been a mercy.

Amen.

CHAPTER
18

It was nearly dark in Natchez, but the stadium lights of three baseball fields had turned the surrounding park into an emerald island in the night. Chris had seen no further sign of Alex Morse, but he sensed that she was close. He had delayed going home to give himself time to think, but he wasn't going to get that time. After moping by the fence for a few minutes, Thora was now making her way up to him in the bleachers, two sweating bottles of Dasani in her hands. Chris had chosen a seat on the top bench, hoping to avoid endless recitations of medical symptoms. Thora spoke to every patient she passed, and they responded with the effusive welcome reserved for the wives of physicians on whom they depended.

"Are you going to tell me what's wrong?" Thora whispered, sitting beside him at last.

"Nothing," he said, staring straight ahead. "I just don't like to lose."

She set one of the bottles on the bench seat. "Seems like more than that."

"Nope."

Leaning toward him, Thora kept her eyes forward and spoke in a low voice. "I thought the prospect of sex would get you home early, win or lose."

He looked at her then. When she turned to him, Chris saw unfamiliar lines of tension around her eyes. "What did you do today?" he asked.

She drew back slightly. "That's a quick transition."

He shrugged.

"The usual things," Thora said, looking back toward the field. "I ran, I swam, I worked out at Mainstream. Then lunch. Then I argued with the contractors and bought a few things for my trip."

Chris almost said, "How did lunch go?" but instead he asked, "What's happening with the contractors?"

Thora shrugged, then clapped for a St. Stephens boy who'd hit a double. "Same old, same old. Delays on the woodwork, change orders. They want more money in advance."

Chris nodded but said nothing.

On the next pitch, Ben's friend C.J. cracked the ball out to the right-field fence, driving in the run and scoring a triple.

"*Dad!*" Ben cried from two rows down. "Did you see that? Are y'all even watching the game?"

"I saw it, all right. Next year maybe we can get you and C.J. on the same team."

"Oh, yeah." Ben high-fived one of his buddies, then climbed up to Chris's side.

Chris almost sighed with relief. He didn't want to talk to Thora. Not here. Not at home either, come to that. He wished she were leaving for the Delta tonight.

With Ben so close, Thora watched the game in silence. Chris couldn't help but notice that almost everything Ben said was directed toward him. As the game wore on, Chris scanned the fences and the other bleachers. He knew nearly every face he saw. That was how it was in small towns. Some families had four generations sitting at this field, the infants rolling around in the dirt while their great-grandparents sat against the fence in wheelchairs. Looking down toward home plate, he saw a man about his own age waving at him. A strange numbness came into his hands and face. The man was Shane Lansing.

Before he was even aware of it, Chris found himself reappraising the surgeon's sharp-jawed handsomeness and athletic build. For the first time it struck him that Lansing bore a marked resemblance to Lars Rayner, Thora's absentee father. Their hair color was different, but apart from that, the similarities were considerable. They were both lean and muscular, both arrogant and sometimes cruel, both surgeons with outsize egos. Lars Rayner, of course, was a topflight vascular surgeon and thus had reason for his arrogance. Shane Lansing, on the other hand, was a journeyman cutter who cared as much about golf as he did about medicine. He was grinning now, and Thora was waving back as though Lansing were a long-lost relation.

"*Wave,* Chris," she urged, nudging him in the side.

Fuck him, Chris thought, almost saying it aloud. He inclined his head slightly in Lansing's direction, then looked pointedly back at the game.

"What's gotten into you tonight?" Thora asked.

"Nothing, I told you."

"I thought you liked Shane."

"I thought he was waving at you."

She looked at him strangely. "What's going on with you? What's the matter?"

"Hey, Ben?" Chris said, taking out his wallet and handing the boy $2. "Run get me some popcorn."

"Aw, Dad, there's a line! A long one."

Chris handed him the money and gave him a push. Ben got up and walked dejectedly down the steps.

"You ever see Lansing out at Avalon?" Chris asked in a casual tone.

"I saw him today," Thora said without hesitation.

This admission brought Chris up short. "You did?"

"Yes. He stopped by the site on his way home for lunch."

"What for?"

"To look at the house, for one thing."

"What else?"

For the first time, Thora looked uncomfortable. "I've been meaning to talk to you about this. But you've been so busy lately—"

"About what?" Chris felt his face flushing. "You've been meaning to talk to me about what?"

"God, Chris. What's the matter? Shane asked me to come work for him, that's all."

Chris didn't know how to respond. Nothing could have surprised him more. "*Work* for him? Doing what?"

"You can't tell anybody this, but Shane is planning to build a large outpatient surgery center. It will compete with the local hospitals, so you can imagine the stink it will cause."

The idea that Shane Lansing wanted to build a surgical center didn't surprise Chris. Lansing was one of the new breed; they started building their empires the first year they could legally tack the letters *MD* after their names. But why Lansing would want Thora to work at his surgical center was beyond him.

"What does he want you to do?"

"Supervise the personnel. Nurses and technicians mostly."

"But . . ."

"But what?"

"You're a multimillionaire, for God's sake. Why would you go to work as a nursing supervisor?"

Thora laughed, her eyes twinkling. "I didn't say I was going to take it."

"Are you considering it?"

She looked down at the field. "I don't know. I get pretty bored sometimes playing the yuppie housewife."

Chris said nothing.

She looked at him again, and this time she let her real self shine through. "Are you going to tell me what you think? Or can I already tell?"

"Is that Lansing's only interest in you?"

Thora laughed louder this time, the sound like a handful of bells. "What do you mean?" she asked, but the flicker in her eyes told him she knew exactly what he meant.

"Don't be disingenuous."

Her smile faded. "Shane's married, baby."

"And if he wasn't?"

In the silence that followed this question, the give-and-take of their previous exchanges escalated to something more unsettling. "Come on now," Thora said. "You're not serious?"

"Shane's had three affairs that I know about in the last year."

"That's just gossip," she said dismissively. "You know this town."

"No, the gossip has him screwing six or seven nurses in the past year. The three affairs I mentioned are fact. He had to pay off two of the women to make them go away."

Two tall boys had joined Shane Lansing behind the backstop. The surgeon had four sons, all handsome, all good athletes.

"I hadn't heard that," Thora said thoughtfully.

"I can't believe I've actually heard some gossip that you haven't."

"I'm not in the hospital loop, you know that."

Chris turned his attention back to the game. Thora's revelation of a job offer had flabbergasted him. Could that be the explanation for their secret contact? If Lansing was putting together his own surgical center, he was right to keep it a secret. The two local hospitals would do all they could to stop him. After a silent inning, Chris said, "I've got to pee," and climbed down to the ground, choosing a route that took him behind the backstop. When he passed Lansing, he stopped and shook the surgeon's hand, fighting a juvenile urge to crush it in his grip.

"Heard you guys lost tonight," Lansing said.

Chris forced down a surprising amount of bile and nodded. "What about y'all?"

The surgeon laughed. "With four boys, you win some and lose some every night."

"Hey, Thora told me you came by the house today."

The remark seemed to take Lansing by surprise, but he recovered quickly. "Yeah, the place is really coming along. It's hard to believe Thora designed it all."

"Not if you know her. She can do pretty much anything she sets her mind to."

Lansing chuckled again. "Yeah, I heard she used to upset a lot of doctors by telling them how to do their jobs."

"Where did you hear that?"

Lansing shrugged. "Around. You know the hospital."

Chris forced a smile. "Been playing much golf lately?"

"When I can, you know me."

"I was thinking about playing this week. You going to be in town?"

Lansing's eyes locked onto his. "Yeah, sure."

"All week?"

"Yeah. You want to play a couple of rounds?"

Chris nodded. "I'll call you."

Lansing smiled, then turned back to the field at the sound of a hit.

Chris walked toward the restroom, his ears ringing as though he had tinnitus. Halfway there, he looked back at Thora. She was staring intently at Shane Lansing. Lansing was watching the game, though. After several moments, Thora turned toward the restroom and spied Chris watching her. He looked back at her long enough to let her know he'd seen her watching Lansing, then turned and walked on.

He was standing at the kid-size urinal when a female voice hissed, "Chris! Can you hear me?"

He almost pissed on his jeans as he whipped left to find the source of the voice. When it came again, he realized that the cinder-block wall dividing the men's and women's restrooms stopped six inches short of the tin roof. The voice was coming from the crack there.

"Agent Morse?"

"Who else?" she whispered. "What did you do this afternoon? You didn't show Thora the picture, did you?"

"No."

"Did you confront her about Lansing?"

"No. Not directly."

"What did you say?"

"Don't worry about it. It's not what you think, okay?"

"Christ, Chris. Are you kidding me?"

"Just leave me alone, damn it!"

"I wish I could. But I can't."

"I'm going back to my seat."

"Call me tomorrow," she said. "As soon as Thora leaves town."

Chris flushed the urinal.

"Will you call?" Morse asked as he washed his hands.

"Who the hell is talking?" drawled a deep male voice.

A man wearing grease-stained overalls had walked into the men's room behind Chris. Chris smelled alcohol, which was forbidden at the park but which always seemed to be a part of Little League games nevertheless.

"Some chick in the ladies' room," Chris said. "I think she's looking for some action."

The man in the overalls was trying to climb onto a lavatory to see through the crack by the roof when Chris walked out of the restroom.

Alex was late logging on to MSN. Discouraged by Dr. Shepard's response at the baseball field, she had stopped at a liquor store and bought a $12 bottle of pinot noir.

Before she reached the motel with it, one of her mother's nurses had called and informed her that the oncologist was moving her mother back to the critical care hospital because of worsening liver involvement. Alex had started packing and drinking at the same time, all the while checking her computer to see if Jamie had gotten online. She drank more than she'd intended to—a lot more—and as a result had passed out in her clothes, only to startle herself awake at 11:45 p.m. with a full bladder and a terror of having let both Jamie and her mother down.

A flood of relief went through her when she saw the little green man that signaled Jamie's presence on the network. Before she could type a word, an invitation for a videoconference popped up on-screen. She accepted, then watched the miniature video screen appear. When Jamie's face materialized, her voice caught in her throat. The boy's face was red, and there were tears on his cheeks. Bill must have told him that his grandmother was going back into the hospital.

"What's the matter, little man?" she asked, hoping it was only a lost baseball game. "What happened?"

"Missy's moving in with us."

Alex felt a thunderclap of shock. "*What?* Why do you say that?"

"She came over to eat with us tonight. She was acting all weird, like she's my new best friend or something. Then Dad said something about how great it would be for me to have a lady around again. They both watched me really close after he said it. I'm not stupid, Aunt Alex. I know what they're doing."

Alex almost got up and walked away from the webcam. She couldn't conceal her emotions in this situation. But maybe she shouldn't hide them. What the hell was Bill thinking? His wife hadn't been in the ground six weeks, and he was planning to move his mistress into the house with his bereaved son? The man had no shame!

"What should I do?" Jamie asked, and in that moment Alex felt the full weight of responsibility for his future.

"You hang tight, bub. That's what you do."

Jamie wiped his eyes. "Do I have to stay here if she moves in?"

Alex gritted her teeth and fought the temptation to give him false hope. "I'm afraid you do. According to the law, anyway."

He winced, but anger seemed to be getting the better of his sadness, now that Alex was online.

"Can you do anything to help?" he asked. "Is there any way I can come live with you?"

"Maybe. I'm working on that every day. But you can't say anything about it. Not to your dad, and not to Missy."

"I hate her," Jamie said with real venom. "Hate, hate, hate."

Missy's not the problem, Alex thought. *Bill is the fucking problem.*

"I didn't do my homework," Jamie said uneasily. "I told Dad I did, but I didn't. I couldn't think about it."

"Do you think you can do it now?"

Jamie shrugged. "Can you stay on while I do it?"

Alex needed to start for Jackson. She was already late, and it was a two-hour drive. But how could she turn away from the confusion and fear in Jamie's eyes? What choice would her mother make in this situation?

Alex forced herself to smile as though she had all the time in the world.

"Absolutely. Just let me run to the bathroom."

Jamie giggled. "Me, too! I was afraid I'd miss you, so I waited right here in this chair. I almost peed in my Coke can."

"See you in a minute."

Jamie held his opened hand up to the camera, their substitute for physical contact. Alex held up her hand in reply, but she had to turn away to hide her face. *That boy,* she thought proudly, *that boy is keeping me alive right now. And he's worth ten of his daddy.*

As she walked away from the computer, she spoke softly but with conviction, in a voice that could have come from her father. "That boy is a Morse, not a Fennell. And he's going to be raised by somebody who gives a damn."

Five miles from Alex Morse's hotel room, Chris lay in his adopted son's bed, listening to the slow, rhythmic sound of Ben's breathing. He was exhausted, and he'd about decided to sleep right where he was. Today had been one of the worst days of his life, and he had no wish to continue it by getting into further discussions with Thora before bed. His mind was spinning with Morse's accusations and Thora's explanations, and beneath that storm of words was an inchoate terror of having screwed up yet again. He had dated his first wife for five years before marrying her, and he'd thought he knew her well. But in a few short years, life had proved him wrong.

Kathryn Ledet had been a physical therapy student at UMC in Jackson when Chris married her. A native of

Covington, Louisiana, she'd attended Tulane as an undergrad, and thus was ecstatic when Chris was able to secure his residency at Tulane Medical Center in New Orleans. But when the time came for Chris to repay his school loans by practicing two years in the impoverished Mississippi Delta, Kathryn had been less than ecstatic. Still, she toughed it out, until Chris was informed that his replacement would be four months late. Chris was ready to leave the Delta, too; he had a plum job waiting with a premier internal medicine group in Jackson. But despite this, he did not feel that he could abandon the near-desperate patients he'd been treating for two years. Kathryn felt no such obligation. When Chris told her that he felt obliged to stay on until a replacement could be found, she packed up her things and drove back to New Orleans. After his replacement arrived, Chris went after her to try to save the marriage, but there was no point. He had already proved that he was not the man Kathryn wanted. By the time he'd worked three months in Jackson, he realized that neither Kathryn Ledet nor boutique medicine were for him. But lingering over him like a pall was the realization that, even after living with Kathryn for years, he had not seen through the beautiful facade to the true woman within.

He'd dated Thora less than a year before proposing to her. He'd known her longer than that, of course, mostly as the devoted wife of one of his patients. And in that time, he had come to respect and desire her more than any other woman he'd met in the seven years since his divorce. But now . . . even without Alex Morse whispering at his side, he sensed that the Thora he had come to know as Red Simmons's wife was only one facet of a much more complex character. How deeply could you know a woman, anyway? A sailor could sail around the world a couple of times and believe he knew the sea, when in fact all he knew was a set of waves and tides that had long since changed behind him.

And what about Ben? In a remarkably short time, the boy sleeping beside him had put all his trust and faith in Chris. Ben looked to him for answers, for friendship, for support and security. Not financial security—Thora could provide that on her own—but for the feeling that there was a man twice his size ready to stand between him and any danger that might come his way. And though some of the boy's admiration would fade during his teenage years, right now he looked up to Chris as though he were invincible. It was hard to believe that Thora would put that bond at risk to have an affair with a guy like Shane Lansing. Almost impossible, really. And yet . . . he had seen friends and patients cast off everything of value in a desperate grasp for something they believed they needed.

A vertical crack of yellow light appeared in the darkness. Then a shadow darkened the crack. Thora was at the door, looking in at them. Chris closed his eyes and lay still.

"Chris?" she whispered.

He didn't answer.

"Chris? Are you sleeping?"

No reply.

After several moments, Thora tiptoed in and kissed each of them on the forehead. "Good-bye, boys," she whispered. "I love you."

Then she slipped out and closed the door behind her.

CHAPTER

19

Alex blinked and stirred at a groan of pain. She had been hovering in some purgatory between sleep and wakefulness. Her butt was numb from sitting in the hospital chair, which she'd pushed up to the side of her mother's bed. Her back ached because she had been lying for hours with only her head on the mattress, beside her mother's shoulder. Now faint blue light was leaking around the window blinds.

Margaret Morse really belonged in intensive care, but one week ago she had signed a DNR form, which meant that no extraordinary measures would be taken to save her life, should she crash. The cancer that had begun in her ovaries and grown undetected for years had now, despite three surgeries, spread unchecked to her liver and kidneys and had also disseminated into various parts of her abdomen. Her liver was swollen to twice normal size, and severe jaundice had set in. She also was skirting the edge of renal failure, which was unusual in ovarian cancer. Yet still she clung to life, well past the time that Dr. Clarke had told Alex to prepare for the worst. Alex could have told the oncologist a thing or two about her mother's resilience, but she'd kept silent and let events teach the doctor about his patient.

Alex had almost run off the road twice during last night's drive up to Jackson. Jamie's "homework" had taken over an hour, and only images of Chris Shepard leaving the park with his wife at his side had brought Alex back to alertness. Yesterday afternoon at the creek, she'd felt sure that the incriminating photo and the shock of Thora's lie had convinced Chris of her guilt. Yet one of Alex's father's lessons had come back to her during the drive. If a cuckolded male did not actually catch his wife in bed with her lover—if all he heard was gossip and innuendo—then a period of denial was inevitable. Sometimes even obvious evidence would be ignored, and IQ had nothing to do with it. Just as with initial reactions to death or terrible disease, the survival instinct enforced a period of emotional resistance to the dawning truth, so that adaptation to the new reality could take place without radical—and possibly fatal— reactions. Chris Shepard was obviously living through that period right now. The question was, how long would it take him to progress to anger?

Margaret groaned again. Alex squeezed her hand. Her mother was now taking so much morphine that periods of consciousness were less frequent than periods of sleep, and lucidity was a forgotten state. Twice during the night, Margaret had begged Alex to bring her father and sister into the room, then railed at their callous absence during her illness. With death so close, Alex had not found it within her to remind her mother that both her husband and eldest daughter had died in the last seven months.

Alex jumped at the chirp of her cell phone, which was tucked in her purse on the floor. Without letting go of her mother's hand, she stretched out her other arm and retrieved the phone.

"Hello?" she said softly.

"It's Will, darlin'. How's she doing?" Will Kilmer had stayed with Margaret until Alex arrived from Natchez, a demonstration of true devotion to a partner's wife, who would never know the difference.

"No better, no worse."

"Did she keep sleeping after I left?"

"Not all night, but she slept more than I did."

The old detective sighed angrily. "Damn it, girl, I told you last week you need to take a break from this case. Take a horse pill and sleep for twenty hours straight. That damn Rusk isn't going anywhere. But you're too big to listen to me now."

Alex tried to chuckle for Will's sake, but she couldn't manage it.

"Anyhow, I've got some news that's going to wake you up," Kilmer said.

"What is it?"

"Remember William Braid?"

"Sure. The husband of victim number five."

"I told you last week that I'd gotten reports about him drinking heavily."

Margaret began to snore. "Uh-huh. And you said his mistress left him."

"Right."

"Well, what's he done now?"

"Looks like he tried to off himself."

A shiver of excitement brought Alex fully awake. "How? When?"

"Last night, at home in Vicksburg. That's what the Vicksburg police think, anyhow."

"Go on."

"Braid was diabetic. Last night, or sometime between last night and this morning when his maid found him, he shot himself full of enough insulin to put him into a coma. A permanent coma."

"Holy shit," Alex breathed. "Could it have been an accident?"

"Possible, but Braid's doctor said it's unlikely."

"Holy *shit*. This could be what we've been waiting for. This could be our break."

"Could be," Will said in the cautious tone of an old hunter who has watched a lot of game slip from his grasp.

"It was guilt," Alex thought aloud. "Braid couldn't handle the reality of what he'd done to his wife."

"She died hard. Worse than most of the others."

"We need to find out everything we can about Braid's last few days. Do you have any operatives in Vicksburg?"

"Know a guy over there who does matrimonial work. Owes me a couple of favors."

"Thanks, Uncle Will. I'd be dead in the water without you."

"One more thing," Kilmer said. "I've got a guy willing to spend two nights at the Alluvian Hotel for you. His wife has always wanted to go up there and see the place. If you'll pay the cost of their room, they'll pay the rest."

"How much is the room?"

"Four hundred."

"For two nights?"

Will chuckled softly. "One."

Alex summoned a mental image of her last surviving bank account, then shoved it out of her mind. She had to do whatever it took to get Chris Shepard on her side. "Do it. I'll pay."

"Are you going back to Natchez today?"

"I don't have a choice. Shepard's my only chance."

"You making any headway there?"

"He'll come around. Nobody likes to find out their whole life is a lie."

Will sighed in agreement. "Tell your mama I'll be by sometime today."

Alex looked at her mother's sagging face. Her mouth hung open, and drool ran steadily onto the pillow. Alex had the absurd impression that the fluid in the IV bag was being drooled out of her mother's mouth at exactly the same rate that gravity was pushing it into her veins. "I will."

"Hey, little girl . . . you okay?"

"Yeah. I just . . . I'm sitting here looking at Mom. And I can't believe someone would intentionally do this to another person. Much less a person they once loved."

She heard the raking sound of Will's emphysema. When he spoke again, it was in the voice of a cop who had put in twenty years with his eyes wide-open. "Believe it, darlin'. I've seen human beings do things God couldn't create a bad enough hell for. You look out for yourself, you hear? You're the last child your daddy left on this earth, and I don't want you throwing your life away trying to avenge the dead."

"I'm not doing that," Alex whispered. "I'm trying to save Jamie."

"We'll do that one way or another," Will said with certainty. "You just be careful. I got a feeling about this case. These are bad people we're messing with. And just because they've killed slow in the past don't mean they won't strike quickly if you threaten them. You hear me?"

"Yes."

"All right, then."

Alex hung up, her eyes on her mother's jaundiced face. What more could she do here? She stood and kissed a yellow cheek, then let go of her mother's hand.

Time to move.

CHAPTER

20

Andrew Rusk had finally hooked the big one. He knew it as surely as that time off Bimini when the big swordfish had hit his bait and run like a jet ski tearing across the waves. He had Carson G. Barnett himself sitting opposite his desk, a larger-than-life man of forty-six, a millionaire so many times over that he'd quit counting. A legend in the oil business, Barnett had made and lost three fortunes, but right now he was in an up cycle—*way* up.

For the past hour, Barnett had been describing his marital situation. Rusk was wearing his most concerned look and nodding at the appropriate places, but he wasn't really listening. He hadn't had to listen for quite a few years now. Because the stories were all the same: variations on a theme—a very tired one. The only time Rusk pricked up his ears was when Barnett slid into the business side of things. Then the lawyer made sure he recorded every syllable. But right now was the worst part . . . a melodramatic soliloquy on how misunderstood Barnett was.

Rusk knew where the oilman was going long

before he got there. Rusk could recite the lines of this movie without even thinking. *She hasn't grown at all since the day we got married. Not emotionally or psychologically or intellectually or sexually,* the softer ones would qualify. Quite a few would add, *Her ass, on the other hand, has grown like a goddamn baby elephant.* Another universal refrain was *She doesn't understand me.* And of course the grand-prize winner: *She doesn't even* know *me!*

In Rusk's experience, the opposite usually proved true. In most cases, the wife knew the husband *too* well—knew him more deeply than he wanted to be known, in fact—and understood him better than he did himself. Therefore she did not ooh and aah every time he bragged about his latest business triumph, and she complained long and loud when he disappointed her, which was often. She no longer thought he was brilliant (or even smart), or imaginative in bed, and he certainly wasn't funny anymore—not to someone who had long ago heard every pathetic joke he'd ever memorized, and most of them twice.

And then of course there was the mistress. Some clients came right out and admitted they were having an affair; others tried to hide it, to appear noble and self-sacrificing. Rusk had come to respect directness more than anything else. Men and women who were considering divorce were always walking time bombs of frustration, guilt, lust, and near-psychotic levels of rationalization. But no matter who sat in that chair opposite him—a brilliant physician or a redneck barely able to total up his investment portfolio—they finally figured out a couple of things. One, there was no pain-free choice. Whatever they decided to do, someone was going to suffer. The only real question was, would they endure the suffering themselves by giving up their paramour and staying in the marriage? Or would they pass the suffering on to their spouse and children by breaking up the family? Rich or poor, here was the essential agony of divorce.

Rusk had come to believe that once children entered the picture, women were less inclined to sacrifice family in the search for happiness than men. This didn't mean they wanted happiness less—only that they were less willing to buy it at the expense of others. But this was based on anecdotal evidence from a limited geographic area. Rusk had no interest in the dynamics of divorce in New York or Los Angeles—he didn't live in those places. Besides, he figured that the motives of a bunch of damn Yankees were about as neurotic and self-obsessed as a Woody Allen movie, only without the laughs.

Carson Barnett's marital problems had their own particular twist, and would not be without interest to an anthropologist or sociologist. But to a lawyer, they meant little. However, Carson Barnett was very rich, and in Rusk's view—as in his father's—the rich were entitled to a fuller hearing than people of more limited means. Mrs. Barnett—Luvy, Carson called her—had begun the marriage as a Baptist, but this had played no bigger part in her life than the fact that she was a Chi-Omega. But sometime after the kids were born, Luvy's interest and involvement in the church had increased exponentially. Around the same time, her interest in all matters sexual had decreased in direct proportion. Carson had suffered through this as best he could for a while, and then, like any red-blooded male, he had sought relief wherever he could find it.

"If there ain't no food in the freezer, you go to the store," he boomed. "Ain't that right, Andy?"

"Yes, it is," Rusk agreed.

"I mean, even a dog knows that. If there ain't no food in his dish, he goes on the prowl. Don't he?"

"He does indeed." Rusk gave an obligatory laugh.

He had seen this pattern many times. Men who sought sexual relief went through a period when they would screw anyone who'd drop their pants for them. And surprisingly, this didn't usually impact the family at all. In fact, things seemed to run more smoothly all around. The trouble started when the man—or woman—found someone who was "different" from the rest, a "soul mate" (this term could almost trigger spontaneous vomiting in Andrew Rusk), or a relationship that was "meant to be." When love reared its ugly head, divorce was soon to follow. Barnett was telling a similar story right now, and his "soul mate" had proved to be a sweet young thing who worked over at the barbecue place on Route 59, a restaurant where he'd done quite a few oil deals in the past—*big* deals, too—scribbling out a map of the prospect on a cocktail napkin and sealing the agreement with a handshake.

"Anyhow," Barnett said, as big drops of sweat rolled down his neck, "I love that little girl like nobody's business. And I aim to marry her, one way or another."

Rusk liked Barnett's choice of words. Because despite the man's crude way of expressing himself, Barnett was speaking in a kind of code—a code that Andrew Rusk was silently fitting into a particular system of moral calculus, one evolved over years of listening to frustrated people, most of them men. Everybody got angry during a divorce; it was axiomatic. Most people even got homicidally angry for a day or two. But the majority of those people soon got over their anger and resigned themselves to the fact that life from then on was going to be one long compromise.

But *some* people refused to compromise. Especially the very rich. It was probably a matter of habit as much as anything. Whatever the case, Carson Barnett had already fallen into line with a couple of essential laws of Rusk's system, and they were coming to the part of the conversation in which the lawyer could play a meaningful part.

"So you want to divorce your wife," he said in a somber tone.

"Yessir, I do. I never thought it would come to this, but by God she's drove me to it."

Rusk nodded sagely. "A lot of attorneys would discourage you, Mr. Barnett. They'd encourage you to seek counseling."

"Call me Carson, Andy. Please. And let me stop you right there. The only counseling Luvy would try was her pastor, and one visit was more than I could stomach. You never heard such hogwash in your life. I stood up and told him Jesus doesn't have a damn thing to do with our marriage, and the Lord was lucky for it."

Rusk smiled in appreciation of his client's rustic wit. "I'm not going to discourage you, Carson. Because I can see that you're in love. Truly in love."

"You got that right."

"True love is a wonderful thing. But I can tell from all you've told me, and from your manner, that you anticipate some trouble from Luvy with this idea of splitting up."

"Oh, hell, yes," Barnett said with a look of something like fear in his eyes.

Rusk had a feeling that Luvy Barnett was a formidable woman.

"Luvy don't even believe in divorce, Andy. Says it's a sin. Says it's the root of all the evil in this world."

"I thought money was the root of all evil."

Barnett snorted. "Luvy don't have nothing against money. No, sir. No problem with money *at all*."

"Isn't that convenient?"

"You said it, brother. I talked to her about filing under irreconcilable differences, like my buddy Jack Huston did. Jack's wife and Luvy was best friends a few years back. But, no, she wouldn't hear of it."

"What did Luvy say exactly?"

"She said I didn't have no grounds to divorce her, and she wasn't going to give me one. She says if I try to go to court, she'll deny me as much time as she can with the children, seeing how I'm a sinner and a terrible role model for them. Course if I stay with her and try again, I'm just an all-around great guy. How about that?"

"She wants you to martyr yourself for the children."

"You said it, brother! Jesus all over again. Only you can forget the kids. I'm supposed to give up everything for *her*."

"Has Luvy said anything about the financial side of things?"

Barnett gritted his teeth for some time before answering. "She claims she doesn't want any money for herself—beyond half of what I earned while I was married to her—but she wants everything she can legally get for the children, which means all future production from the wells I hit while we was married, or even prospects I mapped out while I was married to her."

Rusk shook his head as though rendered speechless by the enormity of Luvy's greed.

"She's also hired the meanest goddamn divorce lawyer in Jackson, too, from what I hear."

Rusk leaned forward at the news of this complication. "Who did she hire?"

"David Bliss."

"You're right, Carson. That's bad news, indeed. David Bliss has accountants on permanent retainer who specialize in various businesses. The hot new thing with lawyers like Bliss is medical practices. He gets all the doctors' wives. He has his Jews take their businesses apart piece by piece. By the time the ink is dry on the divorce, the poor medic will be working for his wife for the next twenty years."

"Well, I'm no doctor, thank God."

"I'm afraid your position is even worse, Carson. You own tangible assets with documented records of monthly production. You can consider half of those wells gone as of this moment."

Barnett swallowed audibly.

"And not only could a judge award Luvy half ownership in all your current wells, but he could also base an alimony figure on your current production numbers, while in fact those wells will be going steadily downhill year after year. Correct?"

Barnett had gone white.

"You'd have to go back to court every time the price per barrel dropped, or else you'd be paying too much. You'll spend half your time in court, Carson. Do you have time for that?"

Barnett got up and started pacing the office. "You

know what the price of oil's done lately? Even my old wells have tripled in value. For the past year, I been kicking off wells I capped five years ago. If a judge did projections based on my current production . . . holy Jesus, I'd owe her at least twenty million, and maybe more. Then there's the rigs, the houses, the boat, the goddamn restaurant . . ."

Rusk turned away to hide his excitement. This was the client he had been waiting for, the payday that would take him into retirement at forty. The timing couldn't be better, either. Being in business with Eldon Tarver would not be an option for that much longer.

"Please take a seat, Carson," he said softly. "You came to me for a reason, didn't you?"

Barnett stopped his flow, looking more than a little lost. Then he sat down and stared at Andrew Rusk like a penitent staring at a priest empowered to offer him a papal dispensation.

"A clever lawyer would tell you to forget about getting divorced."

"What?" An animal look of suspicion.

"You can't afford it."

"What do you mean? I'm worth fifty million bucks."

"Twenty-five, Carson. If you're lucky."

"That's still real money."

"Yes, it is." Rusk leaned back and folded his hands across his chest. "Let's talk about your kids. Don't you have a son playing football for Jackson Academy?"

A smile broke out across Barnett's face. "Sure do. Jake's damn good, too. Faster than I was, by a damn sight."

"How old is Jake?"

"Thirteen."

Rusk smiled like a proud uncle. "That's good. At

least he'll have some input into the custody issue. What about your other children?"

Barnett's smile vanished. "Got two little girls, twins."

"How old?"

"Six. Course, one is eighteen minutes older than her sister."

A sober nod. "Six years before they even get to express an opinion. You see what I'm getting at, Carson?"

A long sigh from the big man.

"Getting divorced would cost you twenty-five million dollars and ninety percent of your time with your kids."

"Ninety percent?"

"If Luvy takes the position you've outlined—and David Bliss represents her—that's correct. You can expect to see them every other weekend, and then a special arrangement for holidays, of course. A few extra hours. I can almost guarantee Father's Day."

"*Father's Day?* I was planning on flying Jake up to half the NASCAR races this year. Boy . . . that just ain't right."

"Morally, I couldn't agree with you more. But legally . . . I'm afraid it is right. In the great sovereign state of Mississippi anyway. No such thing as no-fault divorce here."

"Hell, I'll take the *blame*. I just want to end this thing and be friends."

Rusk shook his head sadly. "A pipe dream, Carson. Let me ask you this. Have you and your new love been careful?"

Barnett actually squirmed in his seat. "Pretty careful . . . you know."

"Ever bought her a present?"

"Well, sure."

"Ever use your credit card for that?"

"Hell, they make it damn near impossible to buy anything with cash these days. You know?"

"Yes. What about phones? Have you called her on your cell phone?"

Barnett nodded, a desolate look on his face.

"You can count on Bliss bringing suit against your girlfriend for alienation of affection."

"What?"

"Oh, yes. They'll drag her through the papers and try to get a financial judgment against her as well."

"She don't *have* nothing!"

"As your wife, she will. They can garnish all her future earnings."

"Well, I don't give a damn about the money. But to put her through that for spite—"

"How long were you planning on waiting to marry this girl?"

"I know it can't be right off. But we're getting pretty itchy, you know."

Rusk could imagine the girl in question being *very* itchy to tie the knot before her "soul mate" got distracted by another sweet young thing in another restaurant somewhere.

"You should also be prepared for a lot of anger on the part of your kids."

He had Barnett's full attention now.

"They'll be made painfully aware that you're abandoning their mother for a younger woman, and they'll know who that woman is."

Barnett was sullenly shaking his head.

"Do you think Luvy will make an effort to integrate your new love into the life of the family?"

"She'll scream 'harlot' or 'Jezebel' every time she sees her. And you're right about something else. Luvy'll do everything she can to poison the kids against me. She's already told me she wished I'd drop dead from a heart attack. Says she's praying for it every night."

"You're not serious."

"I swear on the Bible. She says it's better for the kids to think I'm dead than gone off to leave them."

"But you're not leaving *them*, Carson."

"Try telling that bitch that!" Barnett screamed, coming up out of his chair. "Goddamn it, I'm sorry, Andy. Sometimes I get so damned frustrated, I could just . . ."

"What?"

"I don't know."

Rusk let the silence stretch out. Now that Barnett's anger had reached critical mass, it wasn't going to cool anytime soon.

Rusk stood up and rolled his chair around his desk, then arranged Barnett's chair so that it faced his—very close, too. The big oilman stared at him with obvious curiosity, even suspicion, as though wondering if Rusk might be queer.

"Please sit down, Carson. I want to talk to you, man-to-man."

This was a language Barnett understood. He turned his chair around and straddled it, his big forearms inches from Rusk's face.

"What I'm going to say may shock you, Carson."

"No, you go right ahead."

"I'm guessing that a man like you has come across some unusual situations in your business."

"How do you mean?"

"Well . . . *difficulties*."

"That's for sure."

Rusk nodded soberly. "Some difficulties, I've found, are solvable by conventional methods. While others . . . others take some creative thinking. Extraordinary measures, you might say."

Barnett was watching him carefully now. "Go on."

"I've handled a lot of divorces. Hundreds, in fact. And a few of those cases had some similarities to yours."

"Really?"

Rusk nodded. "And some of those cases, well, they just broke my heart. More than once I've watched a liberal-biased judge take away half a man's lifetime earnings—or more—and then stop him from seeing his own children to boot—the children he brought into the world! When you see that . . . well, it feels almost un-American, Carson."

"You're right!"

"I know I'm right. And after I'd seen enough of those cases, after fighting down in the trenches for a client and watching it all come to nothing . . . well, a thought would come to me."

"What was it?"

"I thought, 'God forgive me, but how much of a mercy would it be for this man—and for these kids—if one of the parties to this goddamn court battle was to just *disappear*?'"

Barnett's mouth was open like that of a teenage boy watching a stolen porn film, and his eyes were gleaming. Rusk could almost see the idea sinking into the slow gray cells behind those eyes. He dared not look away from Carson Barnett; he held his eyes with almost evangelical fervor.

Barnett swallowed and looked down at the carpet between them. "You mean—"

"I mean what I said. No more, no less. If a vicious and unforgiving person was doing their utmost to stop a person they supposedly loved—a person with whom they had had children—from even seeing those children, and also trying to take away everything that person had worked for all his life . . . well, then, it just seemed like almost divine justice if some force—fate, maybe—were to intervene to stop that from happening."

"Jesus," Barnett said quietly. "You said a mouthful there."

"I don't say this to many people, Carson. But you're in a desperate situation."

The big man looked up with dark animal intelligence. "Has something like what you talked about ever happened? I mean, has the other person just . . . disappeared?"

Rusk nodded slowly.

Barnett opened his mouth to speak again, but Rusk stopped him with an upraised hand. "If that idea intrigues you, you should never come back to this office again."

"*What?*"

"You should go to the Jackson Racquet Club the day after tomorrow at two p.m. and ask to take a steam bath."

"I ain't a member," Barnett said awkwardly.

Rusk smiled. "A ten-dollar guest fee will get you in."

"But—"

He put his left forefinger to his lips, then stood and offered Barnett his right hand. "Carson, if you want to get a divorce, I'll be happy to represent you. Given Luvy's attitude, it could take a year or more to resolve everything, but I promise I'll do my best for you. And as you said, you could give her twenty-five million dollars, and you'd still have a lot of money."

Barnett was opening and closing his mouth like a man in mild shock.

"A guy like you, a guy who's made and lost several fortunes, money probably doesn't mean the same as it does to a guy like me."

"I ain't as young as I used to be," Barnett said softly.

"That's true." Rusk smiled. "Time works on us all." He rolled his chair back behind his desk.

Barnett was watching him like a man who had thought he was sharing space with a dog, then discovered that his roommate was a wolf.

"You take it easy now," Rusk said. "Don't let her get you down."

"The Jackson Racquet Club?" Barnett murmured.

"What's that?" Rusk said. "I didn't hear you."

Barnett's eyes flickered with comprehension. "Nothing. I was just mumbling."

"That's what I thought."

The oilman looked at Rusk a moment longer, then turned to go. When he reached the door, Rusk called after him, "Carson?"

When Barnett turned back, he looked exhausted.

"I don't think you ought to share this with your future bride." And then, in the truest moment of their meeting, Rusk added, "You never know how things will go down the road."

Barnett's eyes widened, then he hurried out of the office.

CHAPTER

21

Chris pedaled past the Little Theater, then turned his Trek onto Maple Street and pumped hard up the long slope toward the Natchez Cemetery. Soon he would break out onto the bluff, with miles of open space to his left and the pristine cemetery on his right.

Chris had prescribed a lot of antidepressants in his career, but he had never experienced depression. He'd read deeply on the subject and asked the most penetrating questions he could to patients, but until today he'd had no true inkling of the condition those patients had described to him. Plath's metaphor of a bell jar seemed strikingly apt: he felt as though all the air had been sucked out of his life, that he was moving in a vacuum, and that his actions, whatever he might choose to do, would have no meaning or positive consequence in the world.

Tom Cage, as perceptive as ever, had noticed Chris's dazed mental state and told him to take the afternoon off. Since Thora had left for the Delta before daybreak (despite having promised to take Ben to school), his only remaining obligation—barring evening rounds—

was to deliver Ben to the birthday party at the bowling alley at 4 p.m. And even that could be handled by Mrs. Johnson with a single phone call.

After leaving the office, Chris had driven home, suited up, and without really intending it had begun a ride from Elgin to the Mississippi River. He'd covered fifteen miles in thirty-six minutes—a record time for him—yet he felt neither tired nor elated. He felt like a machine endowed with the capacity for thought. Yet he did not want to think. With a rogue wind blowing out of the west, he wanted only to crest the hill and hit the breeze shooting up the face of the two-hundred-foot bluff that lined the Mississippi River.

Ten seconds after he hit Cemetery Road, the vast river valley opened up on his left. He knew then that he would not sidetrack and ride the cemetery, as was his habit, but rather continue past the shotgun shacks that lined the road beyond the cemetery and ride on to the Devil's Punchbowl, the deep defile where notorious outlaws had dumped the bodies of their victims in past centuries. He was staring so intently over the endless miles of Louisiana cotton fields on his left that he almost slammed into a car that had turned broadside across the road.

Chris braked so hard that he nearly went over the handlebars. He was about to start screaming at the driver when she jumped out and started screaming at him. He stood with his mouth hanging open.

The driver was Alex Morse.

She looked as though she hadn't slept for days. Her voice was shockingly hoarse, her eyes ringed with black, and for the first time since he'd met her, she appeared to be out of control.

"Why haven't you been answering my calls?" she shouted.

"I don't know."

"You don't *know*?"

"Because I already know what you're going to say."

"You *don't* know what I'm going to say, goddamn it! Something terrible has happened! Something I couldn't have predicted in a million years."

Chris pedaled up to her open door. "What?"

"One of the husbands that murdered his wife tried to commit suicide last night."

This took Chris aback. "Tried how?"

"Insulin overdose."

"He's still alive?"

Morse nodded.

"In a coma, right?"

"How did you know?"

"I saw that a lot during my residency. People try insulin because it offers hope of a painless death. More times than not they wind up in a permanent vegetative state. Was he diabetic?"

"Yes. Two injections per day."

Chris looked toward the river. "Could have been an accidental overdose."

"I don't think so. But then I don't think it was suicide either."

He said nothing.

Morse took a couple of steps toward him, her eyes boring into his. "What's wrong with you?"

"Nothing," Chris replied.

"Why aren't you at work?"

"Didn't feel like working. Why don't you think it was suicide?"

She studied him as though unsure whether to drop the issue of his mental state. "The guy's name is William Braid. He's from Vicksburg. His wife suffered terribly before she died. If I'm right, and Braid paid for her murder, then we have two possibilities. One, Braid was so consumed by guilt that he couldn't stand to live with himself one more day. Some local gossip supports that scenario. But a couple of his close friends say Braid's ego was so big that he could never kill himself."

"Go on."

"It could also be that whoever Braid hired to murder his wife—Andrew Rusk, for example—decided that an unstable, guilt-ridden client was an intolerable liability. Especially now, with me poking around." Morse looked up and down Cemetery Road. "How hard would it be to put Braid into a permanent insulin coma?"

"Child's play compared to giving someone cancer. Think of the Klaus von Bülow case. Same thing."

Morse's eyes flashed. "You're right. Only in this case, there's no family to get pissed off. So by putting Braid into a coma rather than killing him, the attacker greatly reduced the amount of police scrutiny on the case."

An ancient pickup rumbled by, spewing blue-black exhaust from its tailpipe.

"You look terrible," Chris said. "Why haven't you slept?"

"I drove to Jackson last night. To see my mother. They had to put her into UMC again last night. Her liver's going. Kidneys, too."

"I'm sorry."

"She's close to the end this time. Tons of edema . . . she's heavily sedated now."

Chris nodded. He'd seen it many times.

"It's weird," Morse said. "Put me on a plane, and I can sleep from wheels-up to the arrival gate. But hospitals . . . I can't do it."

She seemed to expect him to make conversation, but Chris didn't know what to say.

"I did sleep in my car for a couple of hours," she added.

"Sounds risky."

"Not really. I was in the parking lot of your office. I was still asleep when you left."

He felt a prick of guilt.

"I figured you might come out here," she went on. "I've followed Thora when she ran out here."

"Look, Agent Morse—"

"Would you call me Alex, for God's sake?" Exasperation colored her face, darkening the scars around her right eye.

"Okay. Alex. I've heard everything you've told me, okay? I've seen what you've shown me. I know what you want me to do. I've even thought a bit about the feasibility of inducing cancer in human beings. But I didn't feel like listening to any more about it today. That's why I didn't answer your calls."

Her expression had changed from exasperation to something like empathy. "What do you feel like doing?"

"Riding."

She turned up her palms. "Fine. Why not?" She nodded at an approaching car. "But we should get off this road. Where were you going from here?"

He didn't want to mention the Devil's Punchbowl. "I was going to do some sprints in the cemetery, then sit on Jewish Hill for a while."

"What's Jewish Hill?"

Chris pointed to a thirty-foot hill topped with marble monuments and a tall flagpole. The American flag was shamefully weathered, even tattered at the ends of the stripes. "Best place to watch the river go by."

"I can't ride with you today," Alex said, nodding at the empty bike rack attached to her rear bumper. "Could we just take a walk in there? I won't even talk if you don't want me to."

Chris looked away. Could she walk beside him without bringing up her obsession? He doubted it. And talking to Alex Morse would certainly drive him deeper into depression. Yet, oddly enough, she was the only person who might remotely understand what was eating at him. "We're liable to run into people who know me in there, believe it or not. A lot of people run in this cemetery."

Alex shrugged. "If we do, tell them I'm a doctor from out of town. You and Tom Cage are thinking of bringing in a new associate."

Chris smiled for the first time in many hours, maybe days. Then he mounted his bike and pedaled slowly toward the nearest cemetery gate, a wrought-iron monster attached to heavy brick pillars. The whole cemetery was filled with beautiful ironwork from another age. Alex drove through the open gate and parked her Corolla on the grass. Chris chained his bike to her rack, then led her down one of the narrow lanes that divided the tall and silent stones.

They walked some distance without speaking, penetrating ever deeper into the cemetery's interior. Like much of old Natchez, the cemetery had a classical Greek feel to it, thanks largely to the Greek Revival architecture favored by Anglophile cotton planters before the Civil War. Confederate dead were buried here, and also many Americans of national reputation, but the graves of the common people had always interested Chris most.

"Look," he said, pointing toward a dark stone covered with moss.

"Who's buried there?"

"A little girl who was afraid of the dark. She was so afraid that death would be dark that her mother buried her with a glass lid on her coffin. Little steps lead down to the tomb. The mother would go down there every day and read to the dead child from her favorite book."

"My God. When was this?"

"About a century ago."

"Can I see her?"

"Not anymore. They finally had to block it up, because of vandals. Assholes come out here all the time and destroy things. I wish I had the time to sit out here for a few nights in a row. I'd kick the shit out of anybody who tried to desecrate this place."

Alex smiled. "I believe you."

She took the lead and started up a lane that sloped toward the high ground over the river. "You said you've given some thought to my cancer theory."

"I thought you weren't going to talk about that."

"You opened the conversation."

Chris heard himself chuckle. "I guess I did." He walked on for several yards, then said, "I've been doing a little reading in my oncology texts between patients."

"What have you learned?"

"I was right about the complexity of the blood cancers. We don't know what causes ninety percent of them. We *do* know that most of them have different causes. They can tell that from the changes in various blood cells, and by other factors like tumor-suppressor genes, cellular growth factors, et cetera. This is bleeding-edge medicine we're talking about."

"Was I right about radiation?"

"As far as you went, yes. You could definitely cause a whole spectrum of cancers with radiation. But"—Chris held up a forefinger—"*not* undetectably. You fire gamma rays into somebody without a qualified radiation oncologist directing the beam, you're going to have severe burns, skin rotting off, vomiting around the clock. Even with qualified personnel, you get serious side effects from radiation therapy. And I'm talking about minimum doses given to *cure* people."

"But it's *possible* with enough expertise," Alex insisted. "Did you come up with any other options?"

"Chemicals," said Chris, making steadily for Jewish Hill. "As I suspected, the toxins known to cause cancer are some of the most persistent on the planet. You put one nanogram of dioxin into somebody, it'll be there on the day they die. Detailed toxicology studies on autopsy would turn up things like that very quickly. As for volatile compounds like benzene, which you mentioned the second time we met, you'd have the same problem you have with radiation. Using enough to reliably kill people would almost certainly cause acute illness. So basically, as a class, chemicals are a less reliable oncogenic murder weapon than radiation, but more likely to get you caught. I suppose—"

"I'm sorry. *Oncogenic*?"

"Cancer-causing," Chris clarified.

"Sorry. Go on."

"I suppose someone could come up with an untraceable oncogenic poison—the CIA or the army, I mean—but in that case you'd have almost no practical hope of discovering it."

Alex looked thoughtful. "But it's something to consider. I haven't been profiling intel or military officers as suspects, but maybe that's a realistic option."

"Not around here. Fort Detrick, Maryland, is where they keep the germs and toxins. You really need to talk to an expert, Alex. And I don't mean a garden-variety hematologist. You need somebody from NIH or Sloan-Kettering or Dana-Farber." Chris stopped and watched a half dozen butterflies flitting around a bush bursting with purple flowers. One had marks on its wings that looked almost psychedelic, rounded spheres of electric blue. "M. D. Anderson is probably the closest place."

"That's Houston?"

"Right. Seven hours by car."

Alex held out her hand, and one butterfly danced around her extended finger. "And what do I ask these experts? What would *you* ask them?"

Chris started walking again. "If we dispense with radiation and chemicals in our little hypothetical, that leaves only one possibility I know of. And it's a biggie."

"What is it?"

"Oncogenic viruses."

She turned toward him. "A professor I spoke to last week mentioned viruses, but a lot of what he said was over my head."

"Do you know anything about retroviruses?"

"Only that AIDS is caused by one."

"Reverse transcriptase?"

Alex looked embarrassed.

"Okay. Some viruses in the herpes family are known to cause cancer. And there's at least one retrovirus that's known to be oncogenic. If there's one, there are probably more. There are theoretical models about this stuff, but it's not my area. I was thinking of calling my old hematology professor from medical school. Peter Connolly. He's up at Sloan-Kettering now. He's done groundbreaking work on gene therapy, which actually uses viruses to carry magic bullets to tumor sites. It's one of the newest forms of cancer therapy."

"From Jackson, Mississippi, to New York?"

Chris laughed again. "It happens. Didn't you know that the first heart transplant in the world was done in Jackson?"

"I thought that was in Houston, too."

"The Jackson transplant was done on a monkey. But the technology was the same. The difficulty was the same. Kind of like the first space shot. Michael DeBakey and Alan Shepard—monkeys helped blaze the trail for both of them."

They had reached Jewish Hill at last, but as they started toward its forward precipice, and the immense vista it offered, Chris glanced at his watch.

"Alex, I hate to say this, but I've got to run. Ben's at a birthday party, and with Thora gone, I've got to pick him up."

She smiled. "It's okay. We can jog back to the car."

They started trotting downhill, but Alex clearly didn't intend to squander her remaining time with him. "I've wondered about someone simply injecting tumor cells from a sick person into a healthy one. I saw that done with mice on the Discovery Channel."

A little knowledge was a dangerous thing, Chris

reflected. "They can do that because the mice used for cancer research are either nude mice, which means they have no immune systems, or because they're genetic copies of each other. Clones, basically. That's like injecting cells from a tumor in my body into my identical twin. Sure, those cells would grow, or they'd have a chance to, anyway. But if I injected cells from my tumor into you, your immune system would quickly wipe them out. Very violently, too, on the cellular level."

"Are you positive? Even with really aggressive tumors?"

"I'm pretty certain. Even with what we call undifferentiated tumors, those cancer cells began as part of a specific person, from their unique DNA. Any other person's immune system is going to recognize that foreign tissue as an alien invader."

"What if you somehow beat down your victim's immune system beforehand?"

"You mean like with cyclosporine? Anti-organ-rejection drugs?"

"Or corticosteroids," Alex suggested.

She had been doing her homework. "If you compromised someone's immune system sufficiently to accept cancer cells from another person, they'd be vulnerable to all sorts of opportunistic infections. They'd be noticeably sick. Very ill. Do the medical records of your victims show strange illnesses before their cancer diagnosis?"

"I only have access to the records of two victims. But, no, those records don't show anything like that."

The Corolla was forty yards away. Chris cut across the grass, picking his way between the tombstones. "If you had the records of every victim, you might be able to learn a lot. You could really move this thing forward."

Alex stopped beside a black granite stone and looked

at him with complete candor. "I feel so inadequate in this investigation. I mean, my genetics stops at the high school level. Mendel and his peas. But you speak the language, you know the experts we need to talk to—"

"Alex—"

"If I can get hold of the other records, will you consider helping me analyze them?"

"Alex, listen to me."

"*Please*, Chris. Do you really think you're going to be able to avoid thinking about all this?"

He grabbed her hands and squeezed hard. "Listen to me!"

She nodded almost violently, as though aware she had crossed some line.

"I'm not sure what to do yet," he said. "Everything that's happened is swirling around inside me, and I'm trying to come to terms with it. I'm working on it, okay? In my own way. I am going to call my friend at Sloan-Kettering tomorrow."

Alex closed her eyes and exhaled with relief. "Thank you."

"But right now I need to pick up Ben, and I don't want to be late."

"Let me give you a ride to your truck. Where is it?"

He dropped her hands. "At home."

"Home! It'll take you an hour just to get there."

"A half hour."

"You have to let me take you."

He walked the rest of the way to the car, and she followed. "I need to be alone, Alex. I've had all I can take for now." He unlocked his bike and took it off her rack. "I'm going to call in a prescription for you, to help you sleep."

"Those things don't work for me. Not even Ambien."

"I'm going to give you Ativan. It can't not work, unless you're already addicted to it. If you don't sleep, you'll still relax. Is Walgreens pharmacy okay? That's near your motel."

"Sure."

He climbed onto the Trek and held out his hand. When Alex took it between both of hers, he felt her hands shivering.

"Promise me you'll be careful," she implored. "Stay away from the traffic."

"I'll be fine. I do this all the time. Now, let me go. We'll talk later."

"Tonight?"

"Maybe. By tomorrow for sure."

"Promise?"

"Jesus."

Alex bit her bottom lip and looked at the ground. When she raised her head, the sclera of her eyes were shot with blood. "I'm out on the edge here, Chris. You are, too. Only you don't know it."

He looked back long enough for her to see that he meant what he was going to say. "I do know."

She obviously wanted to say more, but before she could, he kicked his right foot forward and sprinted for the cemetery gate.

CHAPTER

22

Eldon Tarver exited from I-55 South and drove his white van deep into the low-rent commercial sprawl of south Jackson. Soon he was lost in an aluminum jungle of small engine-repair shops, pipe yards, automotive-repair shacks, and the few sundry retail shops that had survived the coming of Wal-Mart and the other bulk retail outlets. His destination was an old bakery building, one of the only brick edifices in the entire area. Built in the 1950s, it had once filled the idyllic neighborhood with the rich aroma of baking bread every morning. But the bakery, like the neighborhood, had died a slow death in the late 1970s, and a succession of owners had failed to make a go of whatever businesses they installed there.

Dr. Tarver pulled up to the gate of the high Cyclone fence that guarded the parking lot, got out, and unlocked a heavy chain. He had thought someone might remark on the razor wire mounted atop the fence, but no one had. Everyone knew that this area suffered some of the highest crime rates in the

United States. Dr. Tarver closed the gate behind the van but did not lock it, as he was expecting a delivery.

In this neighborhood, he was known not as Eldon Tarver, MD, but as Noel D. Traver, DVM. The bakery was ostensibly a dog-breeding facility, selling beagles, mice, and fruit flies to research institutions around the country. Because "Dr. Traver" accepted no federal funds, he was not subject to many of the oversight regulations that caused other breeding facilities such inconvenience. This was a necessity since the dog-breeding operations were merely a cover for what really took place inside the old bakery.

Dr. Tarver had not chosen the old bakery for its location. He had chosen it because beneath the factory floor lay one of the most extensive bomb shelters he had ever seen. The owner of the bakery, a right-wing zealot named Farmer, had feared the Soviet Union as much as he hated it. Consequently, he had constructed an elaborate shelter capable of protecting not only his family from a nuclear attack, but also selected members of his workforce. While Eldon believed that the bomb shelter might well save his life in the next ten or fifteen years, his primary reason for purchasing it was as a clandestine primate research facility.

He unlocked the front door and walked quickly through the large holding area in the front of the building. Two hundred beagles began barking wildly in their cages. Dr. Tarver had grown inured to the racket, and indeed was thankful for it, as it masked the more curious noises that sometimes emerged from the bowels of the old bakery. He had passed into the breeding area and was searching for his adoptive brother when the blare of a horn penetrated the walls of the building.

Cursing, he turned on his heel and hurried back outside. A refrigerated panel truck with ice cream sundaes painted on its side was rumbling up to the front door. Dr. Tarver waved his arm, indicating that the truck should drive around to the delivery entrance. The truck swerved accordingly, and Eldon jogged along in the foul wake of its exhaust. He was eager to see what the Mexicans had brought him this time.

Luis Almedovar jumped down from the cab and nodded excitedly to the doctor. A heavyset man with a black mustache, Luis wore an almost perpetual smile, but today Dr. Tarver saw anxiety in the taut flesh around his black eyes.

"Did you just get here?" Dr. Tarver asked.

"No, no. We've been here for hours. Javier wanted a hamburger."

"How many do you have for me?"

"Two, *señor*. This is what you asked for, no?"

"Yes. Open the truck."

Again the shadow of anxiety crossed Luis's face. He unlocked the door at the rear of the truck, and Dr. Tarver stepped up onto the bumper. The stench hit him in a solid wave that would have incapacitated anyone but a pathologist.

"What the fuck happened?" he asked.

Luis was wringing his hands in obvious terror. "The refrigerator, *señor*. He broke."

"Jesus." Dr. Tarver pressed his shirt over his nose and mouth. "How long ago?"

"At Matamoros, *señor*."

Dr. Tarver shook his head in disgust and marched into the truck. It was filled with animals of various species, with at least a dozen NHPs, or nonhuman primates, locked in cages against the front bulkhead. The smell of excrement was almost suffocating in the heat, which had probably built to above 160 degrees under the Mississippi sun. Flies had gotten into the truck, and their buzzing droned at an intensity that would drive a human mad were one confined in the truck with it.

Walking forward, Eldon saw that two Indian-origin rhesus monkeys had died in their cages. That would cost the Mexican traders dearly, but the loss to his research was what concerned him. Indian-origin macaques were the best animals for HIV research, and he had made good use of them in his own studies. But Eldon's prize cargo lay against the front bulkhead. In a single large cage sat two lethargic chimpanzees, their eyes gazing up at him with exhausted reproach. The cheeks of one chimp were covered with mucosal drainage, and the coat of the other had several bald patches that might indicate any number of diseases. It was obvious that the chimps had not eaten for days, and possibly weeks.

"*Goddamn idiots,*" he muttered. "Fucking Mexican morons!" He turned in the darkness and roared at the squat shape silhouetted in the door. "Get these cages out of here!"

Luis nodded again and again, then forced his way past Dr. Tarver in the narrow aisle between the cages.

"You stupid bastard," Eldon said to Luis's back. "Do you know what kind of delay this causes? I have to get them back to normal weight before I can run any tests. And I can't begin to measure the effects of the stress you put them through. Stress directly impacts the primate's immune system."

"*Señor—*"

"If you were delivering a sixty-thousand-dollar car

in your fucking truck, you'd take care of that, wouldn't you?"

"*Sí, señor!*" Luis grunted as he struggled to lift the cage. "But these monkeys—"

"Chimpanzees. Where's your retarded partner?"

"*Señor,* these are vicious animals."

"They're wild animals, Luis."

"*Sí,* but they're smart. Like *people* smart."

Probably smarter than you are, Eldon thought.

"They fake you out, make you think they're sleeping, or that they've given in, and then, *Dios mio!*—they rip your head off and try to make a break for it."

"Wouldn't you do the same if you were being starved?"

"*Sí,* but . . . I am human. Javier nearly lost his eye after one of these chimps went at him. That eye was hanging out of Javier's head. I do not lie, *señor.*"

Tarver smiled at this image.

"What do you do with these monkeys, anyway?"

"I make them sick," said the doctor.

"*Señor?*"

"Then I make them well again. The work I do here could save your life one day, Luis. It's worth losing an eye over."

Luis nodded, but it was clear that he questioned this assertion.

Unable to remove the cage on his own, Luis finally coaxed Javier Sanchez from the cab of the truck. It took a $100 bill from Dr. Tarver's pocket to get Javier to enter the trailer, but together the two Mexicans finally manhandled the cage out of the truck and into the bakery. Dr. Tarver resented having to bribe his drivers, but after paying $30,000 apiece for the black-market chimps, what did a hundred bucks matter?

He escorted the Mexicans outside and sent them on their way. No deliveryman had ever penetrated deeper into the bakery than the shipping area just inside the door. When Eldon walked back in, his adoptive brother Judah had loaded the cage onto a piano dolly and was moving it toward the lift platform that led to the bomb shelter. One of four brothers in the family that had adopted Eldon as a boy, Judah could easily have carried the cage downstairs. At fifty-five, he was still as wide and hard as a tree trunk, with a shock of black hair and pale eyes beneath his low forehead. He had been a willful child until his father decided to break him. Since then, Judah had not spoken much, but he was devoted to his adoptive brother, who had always taken care of him in the "outside world," which was so unlike the one they had known as children in Tennessee. As the lift groaned downward, Eldon instructed Judah to delouse and bathe the chimps, then sedate them for a complete physical examination. Judah nodded silently.

When the lift hit bottom, Eldon turned the wheel that opened the air-lock door and walked into the primate lab. No one driving on the surface streets above could have guessed that such a facility existed beneath them. An obsessive-compulsive with a cleanliness fetish could happily eat dinner off of any surface in the lab; Judah cleaned it daily with ritualistic attention to detail. Sterility was essential when one considered the opportunities for cross-contamination in a lab like this. Dr. Robert Gallo had learned as much in his AIDS lab; and only two years ago, half the nation's flu vaccine had to be destroyed because of such a mistake.

The west wall of the lab held the primate cages, luxurious custom-built affairs designed by Dr. Tarver and welded together by Judah. At the moment, they held four chimpanzees, two dozen macaques, four marmosets, two baboons, and a cottontop tamarin. All the primates, even those suffering from terminal diseases, rested in obvious comfort. Dr. Tarver provided round-the-clock climate control and music to keep the social animals happy. Even now, Mozart's Seventh Symphony was rising to a crescendo in the background.

The mouse cages—prefab plastic things—were stacked against the north wall. Near the east wall hung breeding bubbles for the fruit flies: *Drosophila melanogaster.* Beneath these stood three stacks of aquariums that seemed to contain nothing but foliage. But close inspection would reveal the scaled bodies of some of Dr. Tarver's prize serpents.

Most of the floor space was occupied by massive refrigerators used for storing cell cultures, and testing machines built by the Beckman Coulter company. Two were newer models of analyzers in the oncology and genetics departments at UMC. Dr. Tarver had initially tried to carry on his experiments at the medical school, under cover of his legitimate work, but budget constraints had resulted in a level of oversight that made this impossible. On occasion he ferried samples from this lab to the medical school to view them under the biochemistry department's electron microscope, but for the most part he'd had to construct a virtual mirror of the UMC labs right here. He could do PCR amplification on the spot, and with remote connections to the computers in the commercial pathology lab he operated in north Jackson, he could use Sequence software to do genetic analysis. To date, he had spent more than $6 million on the facility. Some of the money had come from his wife, an early believer in his talent, but after her death he'd been forced to find more creative sources of financing.

Like Andrew Rusk.

There were other sources happy to provide him with funds, of course, but all were foreign—usually foreign governments—and Dr. Tarver would have no truck with them. Not that he wasn't tempted. The United States had adopted an almost suicidal policy regarding medical research—nearly as bad as the Brits, though not quite. In Britain you couldn't experiment on chimps *at all,* which pretty much guaranteed that Britain would not be a player in the pharmaceutical field in future. But it was bad enough in America. Chimpanzees were on the endangered species list, but they had been "split-listed" by the government, which allowed them to be used for medical research. Still, fewer than sixteen hundred chimps were being used for research at any moment in the United States. Most had been bred domestically, at highly regulated breeding centers. One of those centers was only 250 miles away, at New Iberia, Louisiana. But Dr. Tarver couldn't use those animals, not for what he was doing. Wherever those primates went, government inspectors would follow.

Your Chinese, on the other hand, didn't give one goddamn how many chimps were left in the wild. They would send an army of biologists to strip every tree in Africa if they decided it was necessary. The animal rights fanatics could go straight to hell, for all they cared. Dr. Tarver shared this view. In his experience, the moral convictions of animal rights activists lasted about as long as it took them to get a fatal disease that could be cured by receiving a valve from a pig's heart.

Suddenly that pig didn't seem so goddamned sacred after all. Your animal rights fanatics weren't like Jehovah's Witnesses, who would lie there and die within ten feet of a bag of blood that could save them. They were liberal arts pussies raised by Summer of Love hippies; they'd never gone without a life-essential since the day they were born. Jehovah's Witnesses had been some of the toughest resisters to Nazi tyranny, Eldon knew, especially in the death camps. He figured the average animal rights activist would have lasted about three days at Auschwitz.

Animal experimentation had a long and venerable history. Aristotle and Erasistratus had experimented on live animals, and Galen had dissected countless pigs and goats in Rome. Edward Jenner had used cows to develop the smallpox vaccine, and Pasteur had cured anthrax by purposefully infecting sheep. How the hell anyone expected scientists to cure cancer or AIDS without using animals to set up testable models was beyond him. But Dr. Tarver didn't stop there. Because the truth was, animal models only took you so far. When you got into neurological diseases or viral studies, it wasn't enough to experiment on a *similar* metabolism. You had to use the real thing. And the real thing meant *Homo sapiens*.

Any serious medical researcher could tell you that. Only most of them wouldn't. Because research dollars were often controlled by foggy-minded liberals who hadn't a clue to what science really was, and no one wanted to risk his research budget for something so politically dangerous as the truth. The conservatives could be just as bad. Some of them didn't even believe in *evolution*! It staggered the mind.

Dr. Tarver walked across the lab and watched Judah bathe a sedated chimp. It gratified him to see his adoptive brother carefully scrubbing the chimp's snotty cheeks. After patting Judah on the shoulder, he walked over to the metal table he used as a desk in here. On the right side of the big table lay a stack of thick file folders. Each folder held a unique compilation of documents and photographs that added up to a person's life. Each had been delivered to Eldon by Andrew Rusk, who had ordered them compiled by various clients over the past two years. The files held daily schedules; medical histories; keys labeled for what they opened, which included cars, houses, offices, and even vacation homes; lists of important numbers, such as Social Security numbers, passport numbers, phone numbers, PINs, and credit card numbers; and of course there were photographs. Eldon didn't spend much time looking at the photos until right before an operation. He spent most of his time poring over the medical records, searching for anything that might negatively affect his research, or something that might make someone a candidate for a particular approach. Dr. Tarver was as meticulous in this work as he was in all things.

Everyone was in such a hurry. Everyone wanted it done yesterday. Everyone believed that his case justified special consideration. But that was the twenty-first-century man for you. No notion of patience or deferred gratification. When Eldon had faced a similar situation, he'd handled it himself. He was uniquely qualified to do so, of course. But he had never let unfamiliarity stop him before. When a mechanic tried to gouge him on the price of repairing an engine, Dr. Tarver had ordered a maintenance manual from the Ford company, studied it for four days, then disassembled the engine, repaired it, and reassembled it himself in perfect working order. This kind of thing was beyond most Americans now. And because of that, the day was coming when conventional war would not be an option against any major power. Only a special weapon would suffice.

Dr. Tarver intended to be ready.

CHAPTER
23

Chris was working late in his studio when he sensed that he was not alone. He'd been running footage on the Apple, using the familiar routine of reviewing and editing video to occupy his conscious mind, while on a deeper level his brain worked out what his next step should be. His first thought upon sensing another human presence was that Ben had awakened. Chris saved the file he was working on, then walked down the hall toward the back room of the converted barn. Any other night, he would have put Ben to bed and then come out to the studio to work alone. But fifty yards of darkness separated the studio from the house, so tonight he'd let the boy fall asleep on the sofa where he and Thora had made love two nights ago. Once Ben was dead to the world, Chris had moved him to an old twin bed in the back room.

"Ben?" he called softly, opening the door.

Ben lay stomach-down on the bed, fast asleep. Chris stared for a second, then rushed back to the front room and switched off the light. After listening carefully for twenty seconds, he edged up to the win-

dow and drew back the curtain. The darkness just outside the studio slowly revealed itself to be empty.
Beyond that lay the black gulf between the studio and
the house. Feeling a little foolish, he switched on the
light and went back to his workstation.

He was reaching for the flywheel when a sharp
knock sounded at the studio door. He had no firearms
out here, but an aluminum baseball bat was propped
beside the door, left there after an informal batting
practice. He jumped up, grabbed the bat, and went to
the door.

"Who's there?"

"It's Alex," said a recognizably female voice. "Alex
Morse."

He yanked open the door. Alex stood there in the
same clothes she'd worn in the cemetery that afternoon, and she looked still more drawn and confused, if
that was possible. In her hand was a black automatic.

"What the hell are you doing?" he demanded. "If
I'd had a gun, I might have shot you!"

"I'm sorry for just showing up like this. I tried to
call. I know I said I'd wait, but . . . Can we go inside?"

"The published number only rings in the main
house."

Alex nodded an exaggerated apology. Her eyes were
still ringed with black shadows. "Can we go in?"

"Yeah."

She pushed him backward and closed the door
behind them.

"Have you slept at all since I saw you last?" Chris
asked.

"No. I picked up the prescription, but I was afraid
to take it. I had to drive back to Jackson to see my

mother. She's going down fast, but she was awake for a little while, and she was asking for me."

He motioned for Alex to sit on the sofa opposite his workstation. After she did, he rolled his chair across the hardwood floor and sat in front of her.

"Why are you carrying your gun?"

She set the pistol on the sofa beside her. "I'll tell you in a minute. Has Thora called you tonight?"

"Oh, yeah. She's having a great time. She and Laura had full-body mud baths this afternoon."

"How long ago did she call?"

"I don't know. A good while ago. Ben was awake."

"Did she ask if you were in the house or the studio?"

Chris leaned back in his chair. "She wouldn't have to. My private phone only rings out here. What are you doing here, Alex?"

"I came back from Jackson because I knew that once Thora left town, someone might make a move against you. I've been watching your house for the last three hours."

"Why? And from where?"

"I parked across the road, in the carport of that house that's for sale."

"Did you see anything?"

"When I pulled into Elgin, I passed a vehicle coming out. The driver had his brights on, but it looked like a van. A white van. Does anybody who lives back in here own a white van?"

He thought about it. "I don't think so. But there are about sixty houses out in these woods, even though it looks like wilderness. Also, we get a fair number of strangers out here. Kids parking, or nosy people just trying to check out the houses."

This didn't mollify Alex. "About fifteen minutes ago, another vehicle drove slowly down the road. It came around the last curve, but instead of going on toward your house, it nosed into the drive of the house where I was parked. It came far enough up the hill for its lights to illuminate my car, then stopped and backed out."

That sounded like teenagers looking for a place to make out. "Did they see you?"

"I don't think so. I took cover pretty quickly."

"Could you ID the vehicle?"

She shook her head. "When he backed out, he didn't turn around. He backed all the way around the curve."

Chris saw genuine fear in her bloodshot eyes. "I know that seems suspicious to you, okay? But I've seen exactly that kind of thing happen out here at night. Poachers drive out here to spotlight deer. They'll shoot right into your yard, and the residents out here will shoot back. The poachers know there's only the one road in and out, so they're paranoid as hell."

Alex was watching him carefully.

"You're too tired to think straight," he said gently. "You told me yourself that we have a margin of safety before anybody tries anything. Remember? The first day we met."

"That was before William Braid and his insulin coma."

"Alex, if you want me to, I can call the neighborhood watch captain. He's got a big John Deere that he can pull across the road and block all access in or out."

"Really?"

"Absolutely." Chris looked at his watch. "And if it weren't so late, he'd love to do it for us."

She looked as if she wanted Chris to make the call, but she said, "I admit, I didn't see the vehicle that second time. I don't know if it was a van."

"You said you weren't even sure about the first vehicle you passed."

"I know that was a van. I just wasn't sure about the color."

He reached out and squeezed her knee. "You know what I think?"

"What?"

"I think that even if some guy drove here to kill me, once he saw you parked across the street, he'd realize the game was up."

Alex didn't look convinced.

"I mean, he has to make it look like an accident, right? That's the deal, according to your theory. Not even an accident, but a *disease*. There's no way he can pull that off now."

She was shaking her head. "Three of the victims didn't die of cancer, remember? One heart attack, one stroke, one pulmonary embolism."

"You don't *know* those were murders. And they don't fit in with the other deaths, do they?"

"I think those deaths show that if the fee is high enough, the murderer will take the risk of killing someone quickly."

Her stubbornness was starting to wear on him. "Even if you're right, you contacting me—not to mention hanging around and ambushing me for the past three days—has wiped out any chance of someone murdering me for money and making it look like an accident. That's just not an option anymore. You told me yourself that someone trying to kill me would be watching me, tapping my phones, that kind of thing. If they have any sense at all, they're lying low and hoping you'll get tired of chasing them."

"I won't."

He smiled. "I know that. But tonight, you can take a break. A short rest. I'm going to fix up a bed for you in the main house, and—"

"No. I don't want to upset Ben."

"Ben will never see you. No argument, Alex. You're going to take an Ativan and crash for the next twelve hours. All this is going to look different after you wake up, I promise."

He could tell she was considering it.

"If I do that," she said, "I want you and Ben in the main house, too. So I can—"

"What?" He laughed. "Watch us? Forget it. You're going to sleep."

Alex opened her mouth to keep arguing, but her cell phone preempted her. She checked the LCD, and her face darkened.

"Who is it?" Chris asked.

"My father's old partner. He's a private detective." She opened the phone. "Uncle Will?"

Alex listened, her face growing taut. She put her elbow on her knee and cradled her forehead in her hand. After a short while, she asked some questions about her mother's prognosis, then hung up.

"What is it?" Chris asked. "It sounded like renal failure."

She nodded. "The doctors think this is the end. She has two or three hours, barring a miracle. They told me that once before, but this time Will agrees."

"You can't drive to Jackson now. Not in this state."

Alex stood and put the phone in her pocket, then lifted her gun off the sofa. "I don't have a choice. It's my mother."

He stood and took hold of her free hand. "Do you think she would want you to risk your life to be there when she's not even conscious?"

Alex looked up at him with determined eyes. "She'd do it to be there for me."

He saw that there was no arguing the point. "If I didn't have Ben to worry about, I'd drive you myself."

"You don't need to do that. But . . ."

"What?"

Embarrassment made Alex look away for a moment. "Do you have anything that could help me stay awake? I hate to ask, but I'm dead on my feet."

"I'd be glad to prescribe something, but all the pharmacies are closed."

"You're kidding."

"Nope. The last one shuts down at nine p.m."

Alex hung her head, obviously dreading the coming ordeal.

"Wait, I think I may have something. Before I became his doctor, Ben had been diagnosed with ADD. He was taking Ritalin, and too much of it. I think we still have some in the house."

"I thought Ritalin calms you down."

"It has the opposite effect on adults. I figured you'd know that from handling drug cases."

"I mostly worked the money side in Miami. Forensic accounting. Although I did go on a few raids."

Chris walked to the door. "You stay here with Ben, and I'll get the pills."

She shook her head. "We all need to go together."

"Alex, you're about to leave town. What does a walk to the house matter?"

"You have a gun in the house, don't you?"

He nodded.

She handed him her automatic. "You know how to use this?"

He hefted the pistol in his hand. It was a Glock, .40 caliber, but smaller than the ones he'd held in the sporting goods shop. "Yes."

"Take it with you. Bring your gun back with the pills. I'll watch Ben till you get back."

"I will. If he wakes up—"

"I can handle it. Go."

Chris closed his eyes long enough to dilate his pupils, then walked out into the darkness. He felt no fear, but even on normal nights he kept his eyes open during this walk. There were always deer in the yard, not to mention the occasional coyote, and he'd killed a six-foot rattlesnake on the patio only last spring. He covered the distance to the house in thirty seconds, then slipped through the back door and went to the master bedroom.

He had several rifles in his gun cabinet in the study, but his only handgun was a .38 kept locked in a small safe in his closet. He retrieved it, then pulled down an old box from the top shelf of the closet, where he kept old medicines and samples he'd brought home from the office. Sure enough, a bottle of Ritalin lay at the bottom, a drug that Ben should probably never have been taking. Chris slipped the bottle into his pocket, shoved Alex's gun into his waistband, then left the house and jogged back to the studio with his .38 in his right hand.

"Take one of these," he told Alex. "Take another later if you start to fade. I'll get you some water."

"No need." She dry-swallowed one of the pills, then put the bottle in her pocket.

"You're pretty good at that."

A wry smile. "Birth-control pills."

"Ah."

"Not that I've needed them lately." She looked up, suddenly self-conscious. "Too much information?"

"Not at all. You just focus on staying awake."

She nodded thankfully, then took her gun back and went to the door. "I'll talk to you tomorrow, okay?"

"Tonight," he said. "Call me when you get to Jackson. Call before that if you can't stay awake."

"I will. But I'll be all right."

She lingered for a moment, as though she wanted to say more, but then she turned and walked away. In seconds she was swallowed by the blackness. Chris stood looking at the lights of the main house, wondering if he would ever truly leave it to move to Avalon with Thora. Even before Alex arrived in Natchez, the idea had not seemed quite right, but now it seemed truly tainted. He was thinking of the night he'd carried Thora over the threshold of this house when he heard an engine start in the distance. It revved a couple of times, then slowly faded away. He breathed in the night smell of spring leaves and sweet olive, then turned and went back into the studio.

CHAPTER
24

Alex turned left out of the driveway across from Chris's house and headed toward Highway 61. It was nearly a mile to the turn, with much of the narrow lane threading between high, wooded banks. Thankfully, she didn't see a single headlight on the road, nor any vehicles parked in the darkness on the few driveways she passed.

Turning north on 61, she soon passed St. Stephen's Prep, then half a mile farther the Days Inn. She felt an impulse to stop and get her computer, but since she already had fresh clothes in the bag from her earlier trip, she decided to go on without stopping. If her mother died tonight, she could use Uncle Will's computers for any necessary e-mail. If by some miracle Margaret survived the night, then Alex would probably be back in Natchez by noon tomorrow.

As she passed the fork where Highway 84 veered away toward the Mississippi River, she realized that a pair of headlights was pacing her from behind. Her first thought was "cop," because the car seemed to have come up suddenly, then remained at a uniform distance behind. He was probably radioing her tag in now. But after watching the lights for a while in her rearview mirror, Alex decided they were too high off the ground for a police cruiser. More probably a pickup truck or a van.

A Baptist church with a tall steeple drifted by on her right. Then the road narrowed to a single lane—construction where a new stretch of the Natchez Trace highway intersected Highway 61. Alex could see the Super Wal-Mart ahead on her left. She accelerated steadily, then whipped the Corolla across the oncoming lane of traffic and into the Wal-Mart lot.

The vehicle behind kept on at a constant rate of speed. As it passed the turn, she saw that it was indeed a van—a white van covered with patches of mud and primer. The driver's window appeared almost black. She didn't have the angle to see the license plate, but something told her that mud would be covering it.

She parked thirty yards from the store, the nose of the Corolla pointed toward the highway. *What do I do now?* she wondered. She could call the local police, complain of harassment, and have them stop the van—if they could find it—but she didn't want to do anything that would force her to reveal her FBI credentials if she could avoid it. But neither did she want to blindly begin a hundred-mile journey to Jackson over a mostly deserted highway. She needed to know if the van represented a real threat or an overactive imagination.

The idea that Grace's killer might be in that van was almost too much to hope for, but she cradled her Glock in her lap nevertheless. Occasional cars passed on the highway, and two turned into the parking lot, but she saw no further sign of the van.

"That's long enough," she said aloud.

She put the car in gear and drove out to the highway, but there she turned right instead of left, which would carry her away from Jackson. She hadn't gone more than fifty yards when an approaching vehicle made a U-turn between orange-and-white traffic barriers immediately after passing her. She hadn't seen the make, but she made a quick right turn anyway, which put her on Liberty Road. If memory served correctly, this road would take her past a few of the town's premier mansions, then into the heart of downtown.

A set of headlights appeared behind her. They sat high enough to be a van. She took the first right turn she came to, this time into what appeared to be a residential subdivision: tract homes that looked as though they'd been built in the 1950s. She gunned the motor for five seconds, then waited to see if the headlights followed her into the neighborhood. They slowed, stopped, then rolled into the road behind her.

Alex wrenched her wheel left, sped up a low incline, then took another left into a lane that wound beneath a pitch-black canopy of trees. A mansion like something out of a Technicolor period piece materialized out of the darkness on her left. She could almost see gray-clad officers and ladies in hoop skirts strolling across the wide veranda. She idled past the broad front steps, then accelerated and found herself at another intersection. She sensed this was the same road she had been on before, looping around the estate at the center of this strange subdivision. As she pondered which way to go, the high headlights floated toward her from behind.

Sensing that a left turn would carry her back to Liberty Road, she jerked the wheel right and sped around a curve that swept through 180 degrees. At the end of the curve, she turned left, then right, and reduced speed again. The headlights had fallen farther behind, but they were still there. There could be no doubt now.

She drove thirty more yards, then on impulse turned into a long driveway beside a one-story ranch house. The driveway actually ran past the house, which was set far back from the road. She shut off her engine and got out, moving quickly underneath a carport that held two American-made sedans. She'd worried that the occupants of the house might wake up, but no lights came on.

She cycled the slide on her Glock and waited.

The headlights glided up the road, then passed the driveway without slowing down. Alex leaned back against the clapboard wall, her pounding heart resonating through the wood. Was she going crazy? Her left hand went to the cell phone in her pocket. Who could she call? Chris? He couldn't leave Ben. Even if he did, he wasn't trained for this kind of situation. Will Kilmer was too far away to help. Christ, even if she called 911, she couldn't direct help to her exact position. She only knew where she was in general terms. In the last ten minutes, she had broken half the rules in the FBI book.

"They *ought* to fire me," she whispered.

Her heartbeat slowed steadily and, when no headlights appeared, stabilized at something like high normal. To pass the time, she counted the beats per minute: *seventy-five*. As she stood there waiting, it occurred to her that the driver of the van might only have been insuring that she was out of the way before attacking Chris.

"Fuck," she muttered, digging out her cell phone. She dialed Chris's cell phone, and this time, thankfully, he answered.

"Hey, you doing okay?" he asked.

"No. Listen to me. The white van followed me after I left your place. I'm parked in a neighborhood off Liberty Road, and he took off about five minutes ago. He couldn't be at your place yet, but it's possible that he could be headed there. Are you still in the studio?"

"Yeah."

"Your gun close by?"

"In my hand. Should I call the police?"

"It wouldn't hurt. You could just say you saw a prowler."

"I've done that before. It took fifteen minutes for anybody to show up. This is the country, not the city."

"Make the call now."

"Okay."

"I'll call you back in a few minutes."

"What are you going to do?"

"Find the van. Anybody approaches that studio, you shoot to kill."

"Alex—"

"I'm hanging up now."

She was reaching into her pocket for her keys when her threat radar redlined. There was no warning, no sound, nothing tangible to make her freeze—yet she had. Something had changed while she was on the phone. Her conscious mind had not registered it, but deep in her reptilian brain, some ancient sensor had been triggered. Adrenaline was flushing through her as though she had an infinite supply. It took all her self-control not to burst into panicked flight. A normal person would not have been able to resist the urge, but Alex's training had set deep; she knew that to run was to die.

Her heartrate had doubled. Thirty yards away, the asphalt street was dimly lit by the spill from a distant streetlight. The nearby houses had single bulbs on their porches, nothing more, and there was no moonlight to speak of. Her world was black and gray. She crouched and moved swiftly to the inside corner of the carport, sweeping the area with her Glock as she moved. It took an act of will not to push the doorbell button beside the screen door.

Her ears were attuned to the slightest sound, but she heard only the steady thrumming of air conditioners in the humid darkness. Then it came: a percussive skating sound, like a stone skipping across cement. Her pistol flew to the right, where the carport opened to the driveway. She stared into the blackness like a trapped miner searching for light. She stared so hard that she was almost entranced when a leather-gloved hand seized her throat.

Before she could react, another hand slammed her Glock against the carport wall. She fought with every fiber of muscle in her body, but her struggles had no effect. She couldn't even see her attacker; his enormous bulk blocked out the light. She tried to lunge upward with her right knee, but this only revealed the helplessness of her position. Her assailant had pinned her lower body against the wall. She tried to scream, but no air could escape her windpipe.

Think! What can you do? What weapon do you have? One free hand—

She struck again and again where she thought a face

should be, savage blows, yet they had no effect. Her fist collided with flesh and bone, yet her attacker didn't even move to avoid her blows.

He was choking her to death. In seconds she would lose consciousness. Fear welled up with debilitating force: she was stunned to realize that it had no limit. It shot up into terror and rocketed free, like a missile breaking away from the earth's gravity. She tried to gouge the invisible eye sockets with her fingernails, but the man simply drew back his head, putting them out of reach. Had she heard an appreciative chuckle? Tears of rage blurred her eyes. The already faint image of the distant street began to go black. . . .

A ringing crash of metal on metal heralded a barrage of canine fury. A huge dog had launched itself against the Cyclone fence at the end of the driveway. The animal was fifteen feet away, but his thunderous barking made an attack sound imminent. The grip at Alex's throat lessened for a moment, and the massive thigh pinning her to the wall torqued away. With all the strength left in her body, she twisted into the attacking shadow and hammered her knee into the apex of faint light at its center.

Testicles crushed beneath her knee, and an explosive grunt burst from the shadow. The grip at her throat loosened, and she screamed with the piercing shriek of a panicked five-year-old. Even the dog fell silent. But before she could exploit the instant of uncertainty, the glove closed around her throat with redoubled force, and the hand pinning her arm slid down toward her Glock.

If he gets my gun, I'm dead . . .

The hand tried to wrench the pistol from her grasp. In desperation she thrust her left hand deep into her pocket, dug past her cell phone, and jerked out her car keys. Raising her hand high, she stabbed again and again, like Norman Bates in *Psycho*. She felt the Glock tear loose from her hand, but her next blow struck something vital—something soft and yielding anyway—and a gasp of pain gave her hope. Praying she'd hit an eye, she whirled away from the blast of her Glock.

In the same instant, the carport light switched on.

What she saw disoriented her: not the face of a man, but a huge maroon shape sitting on a massive pair of shoulders. A door flew open behind her. A man shouted a warning, but the Glock flashed up to her face with eerie slowness and blotted out the light.

"Hey, miss? Hey! Are you okay?"

Alex blinked her eyes open and looked up at the face of a bald man wearing pajamas. In his right hand was a pump shotgun, in his left her Glock 23.

Her right hand flew to her face. There was blood there, lots of it. For a moment she was back at the Federal Reserve bank; she'd fallen on her back then, too, only the sound track had been the automatic weapons and grenades of the Hostage Rescue Team, not a Southern drawl uttered by a man in pajamas.

"Am I hit?" she asked. "I heard shots."

"You're not hit," said the man with the shotgun. "That fella fired one shot, but when I jammed my twelve-gauge through the door, he knew he'd better not shoot again. He slammed this pistol into your head, so I aimed my Remington center mass. He dropped the pistol and took off running."

"Did you see his face?"

"No, ma'am. He was wearing something on his

head. Looked like a T-shirt or something. He looked like something out of *Texas Chainsaw Massacre*!"

Alex breathed deeply and tried to calm down. Her dilemma was simple: identify herself as an FBI agent or get the hell out of here. Her instincts told her to haul ass, but if her attacker turned out to be Grace's killer, she would have squandered a real opportunity to catch him.

"Did you call the police?" she asked.

"Hell, yes! They're on their way. The station ain't but a mile from here as the crow flies. What was that guy trying to do to you?"

Alex rolled over slowly, then got carefully to her feet. "Sir, I'm Special Agent Alex Morse of the FBI."

Pajama Man took a step back.

"My credentials are in my car."

"Maybe I ought to take a look at them."

As she retrieved her purse, a laser show of blue light ricocheted off the faces of the nearby houses. Then a squad car squealed to a stop in front of the house.

"Over here!" called Pajama Man. "In the driveway!"

Alex had her creds out when the cops trotted up. They were amazed to find an FBI agent at the end of their call. The homeowner's wife appeared and offered Alex a paper towel to wipe the blood from her face, which she did with enough theatrical toughness to impress local cops. She presented the situation as an attempted rape and practically ordered them to issue an APB for the white van. She repeatedly assured them that there was no chance of lifting fingerprints from her Glock, since her attacker had worn gloves, and in answer to their questions informed them that she was staying at the home of Dr. Christopher Shepard, an old friend from school. The last thing she wanted was Natchez cops walking into her room at the Days Inn and discovering what even rookie patrolmen would recognize as the tools and logs of a murder investigation. They practically insisted that she go to the emergency room to have her head laceration examined, but she protested that Chris Shepard could sew it up just as well and for free. When she promised to be available to answer questions in the morning, they were placated. After thanking Pajama Man repeatedly for saving her life—and leaving her cell number with the cops—Alex got into her car and drove past a crowd of shocked neighbors wearing nightclothes and back to Highway 61.

Her whole body was shivering. *Delayed stress reaction,* she thought. She pulled to the shoulder and took out her cell phone. Chris answered after six rings. She apologized for bothering him again, and then—before she could explain what had happened—she heard a sob escape her throat. *It's the sleep deprivation,* she thought. *I haven't really slept in weeks—*

"Where are you?" Chris asked.

"On the side of the road. In town. I think I need stitches."

"What happened?"

"I'll tell you in a minute. I just . . ." She touched her face, which again was slick with blood.

"Can you get to my office?"

"Uh-huh."

"I'll meet you there in ten minutes."

"What about Ben?"

"I'll call Mrs. Johnson and tell her I have a medical emergency. She'll come."

Alex wiped the blood with her sleeve. "He's here, Chris. He's *here*."

"Who?"

"*Him*. The guy who killed Grace."

"Did he attack you?"

"He almost killed me."

"Did you see his face?"

"He wore a mask. Take Ben to Mrs. Johnson's, okay? Your house isn't safe. Can you do that?"

"Yes."

"And bring your gun with you."

"I am. If you think you're going to pass out, drive to the ER at St. Catherine's."

"I'm all right. Just hurry."

Alex lay flat on her back, squinting up into a surgical light like a blue-white sun. Chris had already cleaned her wound. Now he was stitching beneath her eye with surprising slowness.

"This laceration runs through some existing scar tissue," he said. "I don't know what your plastic surgeon will think about my work, but I guess you don't want to broadcast this injury to the world by going to the ER."

"Exactly. Why did you dilute the Betadine when you cleaned the wound?"

"That's a new thing. At full strength, it kills white blood cells that speed the healing process. The first responders, microbiologically speaking."

Alex said nothing. In less than a minute, Chris had tied off the last stitch.

"You can get up when you feel like it," he said. "No rush."

She eased onto an elbow, making sure that her inner

ear knew which way was up, then rose into a sitting position. "Thank you for doing this."

"You have no idea who this guy was?"

"No. The question is, was he after me or you?"

"I think that's pretty obvious," Chris said.

"No. There's a good chance he went to Elgin to kill you, but unexpectedly found me there."

Chris shook his head. "He's probably been on your tail all day. In your sleep-deprived state, you wouldn't have noticed a herd of elephants following you."

Alex got to her feet. "You're still in denial."

"One of us is. Where to now?" Chris asked. "You're not still planning to drive to Jackson, are you?"

"I don't know. But I'd like you to do me one favor, if you would."

"Sure."

"Come with me to the Days Inn to get my computer? It's not far away, and I really need it."

"What about the guy who attacked you?"

"I don't think he'll be there. That's only instinct, but I have faith in it."

Chris turned and set his instrument tray in a sink. "If you promise to stay the night at my house, I'll go with you."

When she hesitated, he said, "Obviously I'm not talking about anything improper."

"I know." She took out her cell phone and dialed Will Kilmer's cell. He answered after two rings. After she had explained the situation, Will practically ordered her to remain in Natchez. "I'm in the lounge now," he said wearily. "She's not even conscious, Alex. There's no change at all. Hell, Margaret's just liable to fool the doctors again. She's a tough old bird, like me."

Alex hung up and turned to Chris. "Your house it is. Let's go."

The Days Inn's parking lots were silent but well lit. Most of the vehicles parked there were pickup trucks or bigger rigs. Alex parked the Corolla four doors down from her room, then waited for Chris to pull up beside her in his pickup. He climbed out of his truck with his .38 in his hand.

"I really appreciate this," she whispered.

He laughed softly. "We used to eat Sunday dinner at this hotel sometimes when I was a kid. It used to be called the Belmont."

"Everything changes, I guess. Even small towns."

"Yeah, but slower. I like it that way."

She took out her room key and handed it to him. "The room's one twenty-five, right down there. I'd like you to unlock the door and turn the handle, but don't go in. I'll be right behind you, and I'm going in hard. If anything crazy happens, use your gun to protect yourself, not to help me. Just get away and call the police."

Chris stared at her in disbelief. "You're kidding, right?"

She gave him a deadly earnest look. "No. No Southern Neanderthal heroics."

"You don't know what you're missing."

He eased down the side of the building, then inserted the key and turned the handle. When Alex heard the mechanism open, she crashed through the door with her Glock leveled, sweeping it from side to side.

"*Clear!*" she called, moving toward the bathroom. Halfway there, she stopped cold. Grace's cat lay stretched on the carpet, its mouth open in a rictus of death. Alex saw no blood, but she knew that Meggie was dead. She started to kneel, but then she heard a sliding sound from behind the bathroom door.

"What the hell?" Chris cried from behind her.

Alex motioned toward the bathroom with her Glock, then waved Chris back. After he'd knelt behind the far bed, she yelled: "FEDERAL AGENT! THROW OUT YOUR WEAPON AND COME OUT WITH YOUR HANDS UP!"

Nothing happened.

"I'm Special Agent Alex Morse of the FBI! Come out or I'll shoot!"

After five seconds of crazed silence, she heard the sliding sound again. In her mind she saw a shower curtain sliding along the side of a bathtub.

"Maybe the water's on," Chris said.

Alex cursed to herself, then charged forward and kicked open the bathroom door, ready to blast a hole in anybody she found there.

She saw no one.

The sliding sound came again. She looked down, then leaped backward in terror. A brilliantly colored snake was writhing on the floor beneath the commode, its head biting empty air, its body twisting wildly through figure eights and whipping back upon itself as though it had been run over by a car.

"*Chris!*" she hissed.

He jerked her out of the doorway and thrust himself in front of her.

"*What is that?*" she asked.

"It's a goddamn coral snake. The deadliest snake in the U.S."

"Are you sure?"

"Positive. See the red bands touching the yellow ones? They teach you a rhyme in the Boy Scouts: 'Red over yellow, kill a fellow, red over black, venom lack.' "

Alex shuddered. "Is that what killed Meggie?"

"Has to be. The scary thing is, nobody would go to that trouble to kill your cat. That snake was put here for you."

Even in its current distress, the snake had an almost hypnotic beauty. "What's wrong with it?"

"I'd say Meggie gave as good as she got. Cats are good snake hunters."

"But it still killed her?"

"Coral snakes aren't like rattlers or moccasins. They carry neurotoxic venom, like cobras. They have short fangs, but one good bite to an animal as small as a cat, and it's lights out."

Chris grabbed a pillow off the near bed and blocked the open door with it. Then he went out to his truck and came back carrying a tall, white bucket filled with baseballs.

"What are you going to do with those?" Alex asked. "Stone it to death?"

He held up the bucket with both hands, then leaned over the pillow and smashed the bucket's bottom down onto the snake with all his strength. He ground the wounded reptile against the tile floor, then lifted the bucket and slammed it down again. The next time he lifted it, the snake came up with it, stuck to its bottom like a bug on a windshield.

"Is it dead?" Alex asked.

"Dead is a subjective state with a snake. Their nervous systems continue to function after death. People have died after being bitten by a dead rattlesnake."

"What about this one?"

Chris examined the half-exploded serpent on the bottom of the bucket. "Dead as a hammer."

He carried the bucket outside and tossed it into his truck bed. Alex heard baseballs roll everywhere. While she gathered up her computer and her case materials, Chris loaded Meggie's remains into a trash bag. "I'll take a look at her when we get back," he said, "see if I can find any bite marks."

"You're sure I won't cause a problem with Ben?"

"He's at Mrs. Johnson's house. Let's get out of here."

Alex started to get into her car, then paused. "Is the coral snake native to Mississippi? I mean, I grew up here, but I don't remember any."

"They're native to Mississippi, all right. But not *this* part of Mississippi. You'd have to drive two hours to reach coral snake territory, and you could still search for a week and never find one. They're very shy."

"So there's no way it could have simply wandered—"

"No way in hell. Somebody put that snake in your room. And that answers your question once and for all."

"What question?"

"The guy who attacked you in that carport came here for you, not me."

CHAPTER

25

Eldon Tarver nosed his white van through a thicket of bushes blocking the rutted track. This was the fourth route he had tried, and this time he felt lucky. Reaching the river wasn't difficult. Every fifty yards or so, dirt tracks led from the gravel road to the broad sandbar bordering the Mississippi south of Natchez. The problem was that at the end of those tracks, the sand was soft and the river shallow. Dr. Tarver needed a shoulder of land that would bear the van's weight right up to the river's edge, then a good ten feet of water in which to sink it. The river's powerful current would do the rest, rolling the van downstream with a force guaranteed to make it disappear by morning. But if he stuck it in the sand, it would still be standing there in the morning for any redneck or jig with a johnboat to see as they sped past in search of catfish and gar.

Dr. Tarver had known better than to run for Jackson. Agent Morse could easily have ordered roadblocks on the main routes leading out of town. For this reason, he'd driven back roads all the way from the subdivision where he'd fought her to the asphalt road that ran past the colossal husk of the old International Paper mill. A vast soybean field marked the place where pavement turned to gravel. The gravel paralleled the river; it led to a string of oil wells and a federal game reserve south of town. Eldon had learned all this from studying topographical maps—one small part of the intensive preparation he put into every operation. Experience had taught him that preparedness was the key to survival, and he never let himself down in that regard.

In the back of the van was a tangible symbol of the doctor's readiness for every eventuality: a Honda motorcycle designed for both street and off-road riding. Eldon had carried the Honda with him on every operation he'd undertaken for the past five years, and tonight every drop of sweat he had ever put into loading and unloading that bike would prove worth it.

The van's headlights refracted off a thousand leaves as branches stretched, then snapped back into position with a scream along the van's sides. He had always viewed the van as disposable. He had another exactly like it, except for the color, safely garaged at his primate lab in Jackson. Suddenly the twin beams shot out into unobstructed space, a pure blackness that changed to dark blue when he extinguished his lights.

As he stared into the night sky, tiny red lights on the massive towers that held telephone cables suspended across the river announced themselves. Lower down—much lower and to his right, about a mile distant—he saw the lights of a barge churning toward him. If he stayed where he was, it would soon pass him.

He shut off his engine, climbed out of the van, and

walked slowly forward, his eyes never leaving the sandy earth beneath his feet. He had a sense that he was above the river, but how far above he could not tell. An armadillo bolted from beneath his feet. He watched the moonlight on its armored back until the creature vanished into waist-high grass. Starting forward again, only ten steps carried him to a cliff.

Twenty feet below swirled the dark waters of the Mississippi River. He pulled off his blood-soaked shirt and tossed it into the current. The woman had stabbed him well and truly in the throat, but with a blunt weapon. Probably a key. Had she used a knife, he would already be dead. As it was, his beard was matted with blood.

He jogged back to the van, opened its rear doors, and mounted the aluminum ramp he used to unload the motorcycle. With all the caution due the darkness, he rolled the Honda to the ground and set its kickstand, then unloaded a small Igloo ice chest and duffel bag from behind the passenger seat. Apart from these three things, the van was empty. He had driven all the way from Jackson with work gloves on his hands, a Ziploc bag over his beard, and a plastic shower cap over his scalp.

He kick-started the Honda to be sure he would not be stranded, then climbed into the van, put it into low gear, and drove slowly toward the cliff's edge. Fifteen feet from the precipice, he leaped from the open door and rolled paratrooper-style on the sandy ground. He heard a splash like a breaching whale crashing into the sea. Running to the cliff's edge, he stared down at the absurd spectacle of a Chevy van floating like a royal barge down the Mississippi River. The van's nose collided with a little spit of land, which started the vehicle spinning in slow circles as it sank, drifting southward toward Baton Rouge and New Orleans.

Had not the circumstances been so dire, Eldon would have laughed. But laughter would have to wait. A thousand troubling thoughts fought for supremacy in his mind. He would allow none free rein until he reached a place of sanctuary. Part of him wanted to remain in Natchez, to finish the work he'd started. But in that matter, time was on his side. He had more important problems to deal with. Andrew Rusk, for example.

Rusk had lied to him. Eldon couldn't be sure about the extent of Rusk's deception, but he was certain of the lie. This angered him more than almost anything Rusk could have done. Eldon shut out the images of revenge welling up inside and focused on survival. He had always known a day like this would come. Now that it had, he was ready. Sanctuary was less than forty miles away. There he could rest, regroup, and plan his response. He strapped the Igloo and the duffel bag to the Honda. All he needed to reach that sanctuary was a cool head and steady nerves. As he climbed onto the bike and kicked it into gear, a rush of confidence flooded through him.

He was already there.

CHAPTER

26

Chris pulled his pickup into the doctor's section of the St. Catherine's Hospital lot and parked. Before going inside, he ran a cable lock through the pitching machine and generator he carried for Ben's baseball practices. There had been a time in Natchez when he would not have had to take such measures, but that time was gone.

He made his rounds as conscientiously as he could, but the events of last night would not leave him. After saying good-bye to his last patient on the medicine floor, he took the stairs down to the first floor, heading for the ICU. There he met Michael Kaufman, Thora's ob-gyn, coming up. Two days ago, Chris had sent some of Thora's blood to Kaufman for analysis, to check for hormone imbalances that might be affecting her fertility.

"I'm glad I ran into you," Mike said, pausing on the stairs. "I found something strange in Thora's sample."

"Really? What?"

"A high level of progesterone."

"*What?*"

Kaufman nodded. "She's still trying to get pregnant, right?"

"Of course. What kind of level are we talking about? Contraceptive level?"

"More. Like morning-after pill."

Chris felt blood rising into his cheeks. Mike Kaufman had probably just committed an ethical breach, and he seemed to be realizing it himself. More than this, they had both become aware that Chris's wife was not being honest with him about a very important matter. Kaufman gave him an embarrassed nod, then continued up the stairs.

Chris walked slowly down toward the intensive care unit, hardly aware of his surroundings. The implications of Kaufman's revelation did not bear thinking about. Was it possible that Thora's whole seduction of him in the studio—her talk about trying to get pregnant—had been a charade? A cold-blooded act designed to cover up an affair, and God knew what else? When Chris saw the big doors of the ICU before him, they seemed to offer escape from the burgeoning hell in his mind.

The cooler air, the hum and beeping of machinery, and the soft voices of nurses gave him a momentary respite from himself. Here he had no choice but to concentrate on work. He had a resistant bilateral pneumonia in the unit that had failed to respond to two powerful antibiotics: a teenager from St. Stephen's. Last night, during evening rounds, Chris had ordered a vancomycin drip. If the boy's condition had not improved, he intended to punt the case up to Jackson, to an infectious-disease specialist he knew at UMC. When he looked toward the glass-walled cubicles, the first thing he saw was Tom Cage coming out of one of the rooms.

"Tom! I didn't know you had anybody in the unit."

"I don't," Dr. Cage replied, writing on a chart. "I was seeing the patient Don Allen consulted me about. I wanted to take a more detailed history than the one I found in his record."

"You learn anything interesting?"

"I'm not sure. Something is telling me that this guy might have generalized scleroderma, even though the lab tests don't show it. You often see almost no external signs in men, and this guy's blood pressure is truly malignant. Nothing will hold it in check."

"If it is internal scleroderma, what can you do about the hypertension?"

When the white-haired physician's eyes rose from the chart, Chris saw a look that Dr. Cage would never show a patient: helplessness mingled with frustration, rage, and resignation. Chris nodded sadly.

"Oh, I looked in on your pneumonia," Tom said. "His white count dropped significantly during the night."

"I'll be damned!" Chris said excitedly. "I was really starting to worry. The kid's only seventeen."

Tom sighed in commiseration. "I'm seeing more and more of these atypical pneumonias, particularly in young adults."

"Are you done with your rounds?"

"Yeah, I'm headed over to the clinic."

"I'm right behind you."

Chris walked into his patient's cubicle, but he didn't need to see the chart to notice the change. There was a brightness in the boy's eyes that had not been there for at least a week, and his flesh had already lost its deathlike pallor. When Chris listened to his chest with a stethoscope, he heard marked improvement, especially in the left lung. Chris was laughing at a joke the boy had made about nurses and bedpans when he caught sight of Shane Lansing writing in a chart at the nurses' counter outside. Lansing was looking at the chart as he wrote, but Chris had a strong feeling that the surgeon had been staring at him until the instant he looked up.

Mike Kaufman's words replayed in his mind: *More . . . like morning-after pill.*

Was Lansing thinking about a patient? Or was he thinking about Thora? Chris felt some relief at finding the surgeon in Natchez this early in the morning. Greenwood was over four hours away, and it was damned unlikely that Lansing would commute eight hours every day to screw Thora at the Alluvian Hotel. He would have to have left her at 4 a.m. to be here now. Still, Chris felt an irrational urge to walk out to the nurses' station and punch the surgeon's lights out. He told his patient he'd be back to check his progress after lunch, then updated the chart and walked out to the counter.

"Morning, Chris," said Lansing. "You think any more about that golf game?"

"I can't do it this afternoon." Chris searched Lansing's eyes for signs of fatigue. "But maybe I can get away tomorrow."

"Just give me a call. Or leave a message with my service."

"You can get away in the afternoons?"

"Yeah, it's my mornings that suck."

"That's why you make the big bucks."

Lansing didn't reply.

Chris watched the handsome surgeon scan another chart, then turned on his heel and walked out of the ICU. As he trudged aimlessly down the hall, he almost walked into Jay Mercier, Natchez's sole hematologist. Like the other small-town specialists who found themselves treating everything from poison ivy to gout, Mercier served as a general-purpose oncologist, diagnosing almost every neoplasm in the county, then either treating them himself or acting as the contact person for specialized care in large metropolitan centers. He was one of the busiest doctors in town, yet Chris had always found him generous with his time, especially with consultations. Chris thought of pulling him aside and asking about the possibility of intentionally inducing cancer in human beings, but if he did, Mercier was certain to pepper him with questions about such an off-the-wall scenario.

"Morning, Chris," Mercier said with a smile. "How's that resistant pneumonia coming?"

"I think the vancomycin's going to do the trick."

"Good. That kid was looking shaky."

They had slowed enough to stop for a fuller conversation, but Chris forced himself to continue down the corridor. Once he rounded the corner, the exit was only a short walk away, but without quite knowing why, he stopped and leaned against the wall like a man taking a smoke break. Less than a minute later, he had his answer. When Shane Lansing rounded the corner, Chris stepped directly in front of him, blocking his path.

The surgeon looked surprised, but not afraid. "You reconsider that golf game?"

Chris looked hard into Lansing's eyes. "Are you fucking my wife, Shane?"

Lansing blinked, but he betrayed no deep emotion. "Hell, no. What are you talking about?"

Chris stared without speaking for a few moments. "I think you're lying."

Lansing's eyes narrowed. He started to speak, then he closed his mouth and tried to sidestep Chris.

Chris caught him by the arm and slammed him against the wall. "Don't walk away from me, you son of a bitch."

Lansing looked stunned, probably more by the directness of the confrontation than the physical attack. "You've lost your fucking mind, Shepard!"

"I'll bet you've been through a lot of these scenes, haven't you? A ladies' man like you? Well, guess what? This time you're not going to skate. If this were junior high school, I'd just whip your ass and let it go. But there's a kid at stake in this. And I know enough about you to know you don't really give a shit about Thora. Oh, you like fucking her, I'm sure. You like knowing she wants you. But the whole package doesn't interest you, does it?"

Lansing's eyes continued to betray nothing. But then, in the crackling silence, Chris saw a chink in his armor. It was smugness. Lansing could not conceal the superiority he felt—a secret superiority undoubtedly based on his intimate knowledge of Chris's wife—her body, her emotions, her intentions. And then a far more frightening scenario entered Chris's mind.

"Or *does* it?" he said. "It's the *money*. You always did love money. And Thora's got enough to make your mouth water, doesn't she?"

Lansing had abandoned all pretense at innocence— or so it seemed to Chris. He was saying something, but Chris didn't hear. His reptilian brain was reacting to the fist he felt rising from the surgeon's waist. Chris was no boxer, but he had wrestled for three years during high school. He threw himself backward with the momentum of Lansing's punch, then grabbed the extended wrist and hurled the surgeon bodily over him, smacking him to the floor.

Lansing's breath exploded from his lungs. Chris flipped him onto his stomach, shoved a knee into his back, and wrenched one arm behind his back. As Lansing yelped in pain, two nurses rounded the corner and stopped, gaping.

"Move on!" Chris shouted. "Leave!"

They scurried down the hall, but never took their eyes off the scene.

Chris put his mouth against Lansing's ear. "A friend of mine almost got killed last night. You may know that, or you may not. But remember this: you're not the only one involved here. There's Ben, your kids, your wife, Thora, and there's me. Most of those people can't defend themselves. But *I can*." He twisted Lansing's right arm until the surgeon screamed. "You do something to hurt Ben, and it'll be a year before you operate on anybody again. Do you hear me, Shane?"

Lansing grunted.

"I thought so. Now, if you're innocent, you just call the police and press charges against me. I'll be waiting at my office."

Chris heard a buzz of voices approaching from around the corner. He got to his feet and walked through the glass exit doors, then trotted to his pickup. As he drove out of the parking lot, he saw the hospital administrator standing outside the door, staring after him.

When Chris reached the clinic, he told Holly not to disturb him, then walked into his private office, buzzed the front desk, and asked Jane to get Dr. Peter

Connolly of the Sloan-Kettering Cancer Center in New York on the telephone.

Pete Connolly had risen high in the world of oncology, but six years ago he had been a professor of hematology at the University Medical Center in Jackson, Mississippi. Then Sloan-Kettering had tapped him to head a new clinical research unit focusing on simultaneous organ and bone marrow transplantation. During his stint in Jackson, Connolly had started UMC on the road to gaining the designation of National Cancer Institute—of which only eight existed in the United States.

Jane buzzed Chris's phone, and he picked up the receiver. "Yes?"

"I'm on the phone with his nurse. Dr. Connolly is teaching some residents how to harvest bone marrow right now, but he'll try to get back with you before lunch."

"Thanks," Chris said, trying not to feel disappointed. You couldn't expect to call what was arguably the best cancer center in the nation and get one of their top researchers on the phone without a wait. "Tell her I appreciate the quick response."

"She can give you his voice mail if you want to leave a message."

"Okay, yeah."

"Hang on."

After a couple of clicks, he heard a digital voice say, "Please leave a message."

"Peter, this is Chris Shepard calling from Mississippi. I've got a pretty strange question, so I'm just going to lay it out and give you time to think about it. I want to know if it would be possible to purposefully induce can-

cer in a human being in such a way that a pathologist
wouldn't detect that it had been done. I'm talking about
blood cancers, and an eighteen-month time frame from
diagnosis to death. I know this sounds crazy, but we
dealt with some pretty crazy stuff back at UMC. I know
you're busy, but I'd really appreciate it if you could get
back to me when you get a chance."

Chris hung up and buzzed Jane. "When Connolly
calls back, don't make him wait. Get me out of a room,
no matter what I'm doing."

"I will."

"Unless I'm doing a pelvic."

"I know."

"Thanks." Chris took a deep breath, walled off the
paranoid fears writhing in his brain, and walked out to
face the day's patients.

Alex jerked erect in bed with her Glock in her hand and
her eyes wide-open. Blue light streamed through a
crack in the drapes on her right. It took her several seconds to remember where she was: a guest room in
Chris Shepard's house. There was a desk against one
wall, stacked with household bills and papers. It
looked like the kind of desk housewives used to handle
day-to-day business.

As Alex stared at the desk, her cell phone began to ring
inside her purse. It had been ringing before, she realized.
That was what had awakened her. What frightened her
was that her private cell phone—the one she used to run
her murder investigation—was lying silent on the bedside
table. The phone in her purse was her official phone.

Oh, God . . .

Memories of last night's attack flashed through her

mind. She had given her real name to the Natchez
police: she'd had no choice. As she stared at the words
UNKNOWN CALLER in the message window, she felt an
impulse to answer the phone. But at the last moment she
followed her standard procedure for the past month,
which was to use her voice mail as a screening device.
Her official phone could only mean bad news. The caller
might be any number of field agents, or it might be her
SAC in Charlotte, who was supposed to be on vacation
in the Bahamas. After waiting a full minute, she dialed
voice mail to find out who was looking for her.

"Agent Morse," began a familiar voice with a prig-
gish Boston Brahmin accent, "this is Associate Deputy
Director Mark Dodson in Washington."

Alex's chest tightened until breathing was difficult.

"I'm calling to inform you that we have dispatched a
Bureau plane to bring you back to Washington for an interview with the Office of Professional Responsibility . . ."

Her blood pressure went into free fall.

". . . jet is bound for Jackson, Mississippi. If you are
anywhere other than Jackson, you should call me back
immediately so that I can reroute the plane to wherever
you are. Do not delay, Agent Morse. You will only
make matters worse for yourself."

She heard a click, and Dodson was gone. When the
voice-mail program offered her a chance to delete the
message, she did so. She would not put herself through
the hell of listening again to a mortal enemy in his
moment of triumph. *The Office of Professional
Responsibility* . . .

"Damn it!" she cried, climbing off the bed and
pulling on yesterday's pants. If they were sending a jet
for her, they must know everything. The extra sick

leave she had taken, the fake reports she had filed, the classmate covering for her in Charlotte . . . they probably even knew about last night's attack in the carport by now. That was probably what had started the collapse of her whole house of cards. And all for nothing! Every white van checked by the police last night had been legally registered to a legitimate citizen.

"Stupid, stupid, *stupid*," she cursed.

Fighting back tears, Alex dialed the main switchboard of the Puzzle Palace in Washington, better known as the J. Edgar Hoover Building. *Of course,* she thought wryly, *there's always the chance that they've sent the plane to carry me to Afghanistan, to negotiate the surrender of Osama bin Laden, or something equally as important. Possible—but unlikely.* She asked the all-too-chipper switchboard operator to connect her to Associate Deputy Director Dodson's office. When she gave her name, she was immediately put through.

"Special Agent Morse?" said Dodson.

"Yes, sir."

"Where are you at this moment?"

"Natchez, Mississippi."

There was a longish pause. "I see they have an airport there that can take a Lear."

"I believe they do, sir."

"You will be at that airport in thirty minutes, packed and ready to go."

"Yes, sir. May I ask why, sir?"

"You may not."

"Yes, sir."

"That's all."

"Sir," Alex said, but Dodson had already hung up. She looked around the empty guest room. Last night, with Chris Shepard in it, the bedroom had seemed a warm and human place. Now it was just another hollow shell. She walked into the bathroom to clean up as best she could.

When she closed the door and sat on the toilet, she found herself facing an eleven-by-sixteen-inch color portrait of Thora Shepard. Thora stared back at her with the cool indifference of a magazine model—stared right through her, really—with perfect blond hair framing the high cheekbones, sculpted nose, and sea-gray eyes that had ensnared Chris Shepard as surely as they had Red Simmons before him. Though Alex had never spoken a word to Thora, she had always felt that they were adversaries, like two agents on opposite sides of the Berlin Wall, playing a distant game of cat and mouse. But now she realized that this was a ludicrous fantasy. The cool visage before her belonged to a woman who had already won whatever game she was playing, while Alex was about to be flown back to Washington for what amounted to professional execution.

Neville Byrd delicately adjusted the joystick in his lap, shifting the laser on the roof five millimeters to the right. Then he donned his goggles to check the line of the beam. *Hello.* This time he'd done it. The green beam terminated precisely at the center of the northeast corner window on the sixteenth floor of the AmSouth Bank Tower. From this moment forward—thanks to the laser and the fourth-generation optical scope sighted along the same track—every word spoken and every keystroke typed on the keyboard inside the office of Andrew Rusk would be recorded on the instruments racked in the flight case behind Neville Byrd.

Neville took a slug of Vault and leaned against the window of his hotel room, which was separated from the AmSouth tower by only a single city street. He was here at the behest of Noel D. Traver, a well-spoken man of about sixty with a horrible purple birthmark on his face. Dr. Traver had given Neville very simple instructions, then offered double his usual rates to accomplish them. This had made Neville Byrd a happy man. High-tech security work wasn't exactly a growth business in Mississippi.

For the last few years, Byrd had worked for divorce lawyers and private detectives, hacking into e-mail accounts and eavesdropping on the cell phones of people committing adultery. A long fall from the days when he worked for Netscape. Just ten years ago he had been part of the forefront of the battle against mighty Microsoft. Now CEO Jim Barksdale was a philanthropist, and Netscape was only a shadow of its former self—much like its former software engineer.

But this job was different.

Andy Rusk was one of the top five divorce lawyers in the city, and he had actually hired Neville on several occasions. In Neville's not-so-humble opinion, Rusk was just another aging Ole Miss frat boy with too much money and more ego than was good for him. Right now he was blabbing on the phone to some guy about a cross-country motorcycle trip he was organizing—on Harleys, of course; *hawgs,* man!—but rented ones. Rented Harleys. That pretty much said it all.

Neville took another slug of Vault and giggled. Unlike Andy Rusk, Dr. Traver seemed like a decent guy, and he was certainly a hell of a lot smarter than Rusk and his ilk. (Neville knew Traver was a veterinarian because he had looked him up on the Internet: *A Breed Apart, Noel D. Traver, DVM Proprietor.*) Dr. Traver knew about a lot more than animals, too. He had known exactly what kind of gear it would take to carry out the surveillance on Rusk's office, and he wouldn't have hired anyone who didn't own it.

Dr. Traver had not hired Neville blind, either. He'd asked him to drive down to the Byram exit on I-55 South for a face-to-face. Neville hadn't minded. He'd met people in lots worse places in the five years since he'd hung out his Digital Security shingle. Over a Frescata Club sandwich from Wendy's, Neville had assured Dr. Traver that he would be able to hack into Rusk's office network, no problem. Dr. Traver had been skeptical, and so far, his skepticism had proved justified. Whoever had beefed up Rusk's security had done all right. But the laser rig would nail him in the end. Not only would it pick up all of Rusk's conversations by measuring the vibration of the window glass, but it would also track which keys were depressed on Rusk's computer keyboard—and in which order—by measuring changes in the electromagnetic field of the office. The optical scope alone could make out about two-thirds of Rusk's keyboard and monitor, which meant that much of what was typed would also be recorded onto digital video.

The tough part of this job had been the installation. The Marriott Hotel was the only building with line-of-sight access to Rusk's sixteenth-floor window, and even the Marriott lacked windows facing the AmSouth tower. To solve this problem, Neville had built a custom rig at home—sort of a plastic doghouse for the laser and optical scope—then installed it on the roof of the

Marriott. Then he'd checked into a room on the top floor and set up his wireless monitoring station.

So far its highest-value data transfer had been stunning views of Rusk's secretary's tits. The lawyer must have listed Russ Meyer tits as the prime qualification for the job, because his secretary had them in spades. She had killer calves, too. Neville wondered if maybe Dr. Traver was married to Rusk's secretary. But she was no more than thirty—and *hot*—while Dr. Traver was close to sixty and had that ugly mess of a birthmark on his face. Neville sipped his Vault and watched Rusk pick his nose as he jabbered on the phone.

"Maybe Traver's loaded," he said. "That must be it."

Neville waited for the secretary to reappear, confident that he would know everything there was to know about Andy Rusk, his secretary, and the old vet before the week was out. That was the main kick in this work, the feeling of omnipotence. A lot of game designers talked about the same thing, but that was only hackers' fantasy. This job wasn't animated chicks with comic-book bustlines; this was real life, real people. And if you were good, you got to peek into their private lives, their bedrooms, wherever you wanted. If you were *really* good, sometimes you got to peer inside their heads. *That* was the kick, man.

CHAPTER
27

Alex stood on the edge of the little concrete apron at the Natchez Airport and watched a Lear 35 make a perfect landing across her field of vision. She was only a couple of miles from the Natchez Trace, where she and Chris had stood on the bridge overlooking the creek. That seemed a week ago already.

As the jet began its taxi toward the spot where she was standing, she took out her official cell phone and tried Chris again. Her private phone had died during the night, while she slept an Ativan-induced slumber in Chris's guest room. To her surprise, Chris answered her call.

"Alex?"

"Yes. I . . ."

"Are you still at my house?"

"No, I'm at the airport. I'm about to board a jet for Washington."

"*What?*"

"They're onto me, Chris. My investigation, every-thing. They called this morning."

He was silent for a bit. "I'm sorry. I may be in some trouble myself."

"Why?"

"I saw Shane Lansing in the ICU this morning, and I confronted him."

Alex closed her eyes in disappointment. Dr. Shepard was turning out to be a poor choice for setting a trap. He didn't have the devious personality required. "What did you say to him?"

"I asked if he was fucking my wife."

"Oh, God."

"He tried to take a swing at me, so I took him down."

"Took him down? Is he hurt?"

"Maybe. But no cops have showed up to arrest me yet."

"I doubt they will."

"I hope I didn't screw you up too bad. Your investigation, I mean."

"Don't worry about it. Just try not to do anything else, okay?" The Lear was steadily approaching. "I don't have long. I just wanted you to know that you might not see me for a while."

"How bad could this be? Washington, I mean?"

Her laugh had a touch of hysteria. "Bad. Remember my screwup at the bank? When I got shot?"

"Yes."

"I went back into the bank because I thought I was right, but a deputy director ordered the HRT in on top of me."

"Right, I remember."

"That's who called me today. His name is Dodson. And the thing is . . . I turned out to be right that day. The bank robber wasn't a terrorist, he was a disaffected employee. I made a terrible procedural mistake that day, but when the truth came out, my instinct was proved correct. I was right, and Dodson was wrong. And he's never forgiven me for that. He's been after me ever since, and today is payback."

The approaching jet swallowed almost all sound in the whine of its turbines.

"What?" Alex yelled.

"I said, I put in a call to my friend at Sloan-Kettering!" Chris repeated. "I'll let you know what he says. Look, somebody up there has to know they need you. Focus on that."

"I've got to go. Bye."

Chris's reply, if he made one, was lost in the roar.

Alex hit END, set the phone to SILENT, and slid it into her pocket as the Lear stopped and its side door opened. A stereotypical FBI agent walked down the little stair. Blue suit, dark sunglasses. Even with his jacket cut a little full, she could make out the butt of his weapon beneath the cloth under his left arm.

"Special Agent Alex Morse?" he called.

"I'm Alex Morse."

As the clean-cut, blond agent drew closer, Alex suspected that he was part of one of the most exclusive agent cliques in the Bureau: the Mormon Mafia.

"Special Agent Gray Williams," he said. Williams did not offer his hand. "Are you carrying a weapon, Agent Morse?"

"Yes." Alex was afraid he would order her to surrender her sidearm.

"Do you have any other bags?"

"Nope." She bent to lift her soft-sided suitcase.

"Let's get aboard then."

Williams's tone indicated extreme reluctance to talk to her—a sure sign that she was known to be an official leper. She tossed her suitcase through the hatch, then climbed in after it, bent low, and took a forward-facing seat. She expected Williams to take the seat facing her, but he sat two seats behind her. Alex could hear him talking softly on his cell phone, confirming that she was aboard and soon to be bound for Washington. After gripping the armrests for takeoff, she took out her private phone, plugged it into an outlet beside her seat, and checked her voice mail. A ragged male voice came through the ether.

"Alex, this is Uncle Will." She clicked the volume down to minimum level using the side button. "Your mom's the same as she was last night, alive and not quite kicking. You did the right thing getting some rest. I'm calling because I got a report from my guy at the Alluvian Hotel. He couldn't find out which floor Thora Shepard was staying on, but his wife talked to her in the wet area a couple of times. Thora's girlfriend was with her, and everything seemed legit. But around five thirty this morning, my guy's wife happened to look out her window, which overlooks the main courtyard that leads to the back parking lot. She saw a guy carrying a small suitcase out to the lot. He was in a big hurry. It was fast and in poor light, but she thinks it could have been Dr. Lansing. She couldn't be positive. Said she's sixty percent sure. I'm going to check out the possibility that Lansing could be commuting back and forth to get his poontang from Mrs. Shepard. You call me as soon as—"

The line had not gone dead; voice mail had cut Will off before he finished his message. There were no more messages. Alex wondered if a few hours in bed with Thora was worth commuting four hours both ways. Most men she knew would undoubtedly say yes. She saw no point in calling Chris to pass on an inconclusive report, but she was likely to have real evidence soon. If Chris had attacked Dr. Lansing based on suspicion, what would he do if Will provided the kind of graphic evidence that he frequently obtained in his business? Alex had not expected a violent reaction from Chris. Yet he was a Southerner, and in matters of this kind, direct action was the rule among them rather than the exception.

She sat back in her seat. Summoned by the roar of the engines and the shuddering airframe, a hundred memories assailed her. How many times had she been rushed to a jet like this one and ferried to some strange city where a man with a gun held innocent people under his power? Being the person that the Bureau counted on in those situations had engendered its own sense of power within Alex. And she had justified their faith time and time again, the faith of her tribe. But now she had broken that faith, at least in their eyes—*their* being an all-inclusive euphemism for the quasi-military, superpatriotic culture known to outsiders as the FBI. It had destroyed a part of her to break that faith, to forge daily reports, to ask fellow agents to cover for unauthorized absences. What would it do to her to be expelled from the Bureau altogether? She felt hollow and afraid, like someone about to be driven out of her village and forced alone into the bush. But there was a higher duty than that owed one's tribe—the obligation to one's family. To *blood*. And no matter what it cost, she would not break faith with them. After her mother died, Alex would be the only Morse left, save Jamie Fennell. Like Alex, Jamie had no one else. Why couldn't the Bureau understand that?

Fed up with being passive, Alex took out her cell phone and clicked into text-messaging mode. If she had to sweat out the next twenty-four hours, she wasn't going to do it alone.

Andrew Rusk was surfing an Internet porn site and thinking about calling Janice into his office for some personal attention when his cell phone emitted the brief chirp that signaled an incoming text message. He looked away from the ménage à trois on his screen— two girls on a guy, his fantasy since high school—and pressed READ on his cell phone. His heart began to race as he saw the words outlined in blue:

> *You're going to pay for what you did. I don't care how long it takes. You're going to ride the needle, Andy. For Grace Fennell, for Mrs. Braid, for all the others. I don't care what happens to me. Nothing will stop me. Nothing.*

Rusk stared at the message with a sense of unreality. The letters seemed to shimmer before his eyes, like blurry waves of heat over desert sand. He checked the source of the message, but no number showed up. It didn't matter. He knew who had sent it.

His first instinct was to get up and tape two squares of Reynolds Wrap to his northeast window, but his good sense stopped him. For one thing, Dr. Tarver might not see the foil until the end of the day. For another, Tarver was already upset enough about Alex Morse. This new development would only add fuel to the fire. And the hotter that fire got, the less Rusk's life was worth.

"What the hell is she doing?" he thought aloud. "Why would she send this?"

She's trying to provoke me. It's like throwing a rock into a thicket to try to make your prey move into your sights. That means somebody's watching to see which way I jump. Waiting for me to lead them somewhere.

"Just stay cool," he murmured. "Stay cool."

Rusk toyed with the idea of sending Dr. Tarver one of their Viagra spam messages. Tarver would likely receive this within the hour, and it would prompt him to head for the country club where Rusk normally dropped off the operational packets. Annandale was exclusive enough that he could even risk a conversation with Tarver there. But he could not know how the doctor would react. He needed to think before he did anything. If Alex Morse was working with the full backing of the FBI, the usual drop point would afford no protection whatsoever.

"Stay cool," he said again. Then, in a much lower voice, he said, " 'Do you have the patience to do nothing?' " Rusk was no scholar, but he had read the *Tao Te Ching* during college—mostly to please an English major he was screwing—and that line had stuck with him. The best time to do nothing, of course, was when your adversary was about to make a big mistake—or had already made one. But Alex Morse hadn't made any recent mistakes that he knew about. "That I know about," he said thoughtfully.

He picked up the phone and dialed the number of a detective agency he sometimes used. They were expensive, but they boasted several former government agents among their operatives. Some had been IRS agents, others had worked for the DEA or BATF, while a highly paid few were former special agents of the FBI.

"It's time to find out what Agent Alex has really been up to," he said.

Chris was in an examining room checking a prostate gland when Jane called him out to take Dr. Connolly's call. He ripped off the glove, hurried to his office, and picked up the phone.

"Pete? It's Chris Shepard."

"Hey, boy! What's it been, seven years?"

"More."

"The last I heard, you were playing Albert Schweitzer in the Mississippi Delta."

"Just a phase."

"I know better."

"How's your wife, Pete?"

"Anna's good. And my daughter's starting at UVA med next fall."

"God, is she that old?"

"No, *I'm* that old. Now, what's all this about giving people cancer on purpose? That was a pretty strange message you left me. Have you switched from making documentaries to horror movies? Or did somebody get murdered down there?"

"To tell you the truth, Pete . . . I can't talk about it."

There was a long pause. Then Connolly said, "Okay, well, I did some thinking about it during what passed for my lunch. You ready?"

"Shoot."

"As for chemical agents, multiple myeloma can be caused by a spectrum of carcinogens. Herbicides are particularly damaging. But you're talking about a twenty-year incubation period before the cancer hits. Toxins could work much faster, but virtually all are detectable using gas chromatography and a mass spectrometer. The CSI guys would bust you in a hurry."

"On TV they would. I'm finding out that the real world is different."

"What the heck are you into, Chris? No one's going to be mixing this stuff up in his kitchen sink. Not even in an average university lab."

"I hope you're right," Chris replied, ignoring the question.

"Radiation is another obvious choice," Connolly went on. "There's no doubt you could induce leukemia with it."

"But could you do it undetectably?"

"Not easily. But it might be possible."

Chris felt a strange thrumming in his chest.

"X-rays would probably cause all sorts of side effects, both local and systemic, so forget that. Radiotherapy pellets would probably cause burns, skin tumors, maybe nausea early on. Although there are some alpha emitters whose effects aren't dose-related at all. Even the smallest exposure is oncogenic."

"Really?" Chris grabbed a pen and scrawled this on a notepad.

"It would take a real specialist to know that kind of thing, of course. The most interesting radiation option isn't pellets, though."

"What is it?"

"Against some tumors, we use irradiated liquids that have very short half-lives. I'm talking twenty-four to forty-eight hours."

Chris felt a chill of foreboding.

"Take thyroid cancer. We put radioactive iodine into the bloodstream. The iodine collects in the thyroid, kills the cancer cells, then is harmlessly excreted from the body. A sociopathic radiation oncologist could probably figure a way to induce cancer like that without leaving any measurable trace."

Chris wrote rapidly; his time with Connolly would be limited. "Go on."

"I know about an actual case where somebody used irradiated thallium to attempt an assassination in Africa. The radiation broke the thallium into microparticles that dispersed throughout the body. The victim nearly died, but at the last minute they shipped him here. Our best doctors treated him for over a week. He ultimately survived, but anywhere else in the world he would have died. And I seriously doubt whether anyone else could have traced the cause of death."

"I had no idea. I've been going through my oncology books, and I haven't found anything like that."

"Not everything is in the books, Doc. You know that. But listen, if I really wanted to give someone cancer with zero risk of being caught, I'd explore one of two avenues. The first is viruses."

"I've considered that myself, but I don't even know enough to be dangerous."

"You'd have to be willing to wait a while for your victim to die."

Chris nodded to himself. "Up to a point, time isn't a factor in these cases."

"Well, then. You know that HTLV has been implicated in at least one form of leukemia. The Kaposi's sarcoma associated with HIV is the result of infection with herpes eight. Epstein-Barr can cause Burkitt's lymphoma, and of course, human papilloma virus is known to cause cervical cancer. Herpes eight may also be a factor in multiple myeloma. I think that over the next ten years, we're going to discover that viruses are responsible for all sorts of cancers that we don't yet suspect have a viral etiology or mediator. Other diseases as well."

As Chris jotted down Connolly's words in the shorthand he'd invented during medical school, he talked to keep the hematologist on the line. "I knew that one of the herpes viruses had been implicated in multiple sclerosis."

"Herpes six," said Connolly. "And there are indications of a viral component in juvenile diabetes. But let's get back to cancer. There's no doubt that viruses can cause cancer. But you have to remember, getting cancer isn't a one-step process. Millions of women carry HPV, but only a few develop cervical cancer. Millions of people smoke without getting lung cancer. It wouldn't be enough to isolate and infect someone with an oncogenic retrovirus. You'd have to solve several other riddles, too. How to switch off tumor suppressor genes, how to increase cellular growth factors. It would take a massive research effort."

Chris's thoughts were already shooting ahead. "So we're talking about something beyond the reach of present-day technology."

"Not at all. I've already done it myself, right here in my lab."

Connolly's words hit him like a body blow. *"What?"*

"It's amazing, really, but we did. In trying to understand the cause of chronic myelogenous leukemia, my team and I basically carried out gene therapy in reverse.

We attached a leukemia-inducing gene to a retrovirus, then infected a mouse with the virus. The oncogene was incorporated into the mouse's genome, and within weeks the mouse had developed the rodent version of CML."

Chris was literally speechless. After several moments, he asked, "Was this mouse immune-compromised?"

"No. Perfectly healthy."

"Christ, Peter!"

"What?"

"You basically murdered this mouse by giving it cancer."

"Absolutely. And thousands of human lives will one day be saved because of that murder."

"You're missing my point. What I asked you about on the phone . . . it's *possible*."

"Well, in theory, I suppose."

"What about in the real world?"

Connolly took a few moments to consider the question. "I suppose if you had some higher primates to test your work on—or, God forbid, human beings—then, yes, it's possible."

Chris gripped the phone in stunned silence.

"I might be worried," said Connolly, "if it wouldn't cost someone millions of dollars to reach the point where they could murder someone using that method. Not to mention that they'd have to sit pretty goddamn high on the intelligence curve."

"But if they did use that method, they could be sure of getting away with murder?"

Connolly's voice took on a clinical coldness. "Chris, if I used this technology against a human being, I could kill whoever I wanted, and the greatest pathologist in the world wouldn't even realize that a crime had been committed. Even if I told him, he couldn't prove it with the science at his disposal."

A deep shiver went through Chris.

"Hey," said Connolly. "You don't think . . ."

"I don't know, Pete. You mentioned two possible scenarios in this line, didn't you?"

"Right. The second scenario is far scarier to me, because it requires much less expertise. All you'd need is a hematologist or oncologist with the ethics of Dr. Mengele."

"Go on."

"All you do is modify the process of a certain type of bone marrow transplant. Remove marrow cells from your patient; irradiate or otherwise poison them in the lab, causing your malignancy of choice; then reinject them into the patient."

"What would be the result?"

"A cancer factory powered by the victim's own bone marrow. Exactly the kind of thing you described to me, in fact. A spectrum of blood cancers."

"And no one could ever prove what had been done?"

"Barring a confession, no way in hell."

"Jesus." Chris analyzed this scenario as rapidly as he could. "Would you have to use marrow cells for that? Or could you use cells that are easier to get?"

"Hmm," Connolly mused. "I suppose you could use just about any kind of living cell, so long as it contained the patient's DNA. A hair root or a scraping from the mucosa, say. But marrow cells would be best."

Chris had received too much information to process it efficiently. "Pete, can you tell me anything about the hematology and oncology departments at UMC now? Do you know anything about your replacement?"

"Not much. It's been six years, you know? I left there in a hurry, so they made Alan Benson acting chairman until they recruited a new chief."

"I remember."

"They've got a brand-new critical-care hospital down there. The new hematology chief is named Pearson. He came down from Stanford, where he did some groundbreaking work. They've got a terrific bone marrow transplant program, but they're still a ways from getting their NCI designation, which was always a dream of mine."

"Do you know of anyone at UMC who's working on the kind of stuff we've been talking about?"

"Which stuff? Retroviruses? Bone marrow transplant? Radiation?"

"All of it."

"I don't know of any ongoing retrovirus trials there, but I'm not the best guy to talk to. I'd give Ajit Chandrekasar a call. First-rate virologist, and I was damned lucky to have him. There's another guy there, multiple specialties . . . I used him for difficult histology and culture stuff. His name was . . . Tarver. Eldon Tarver. I don't know if he's still around."

"I've got it."

Chris heard a female voice in the background. "They're calling for me, buddy. Did I help you at all?"

"You scared the shit out of me."

"Can't you tell me why you need this stuff?"

"Not yet. But if someone I know turns out to be right, I'll have some reportable cases you can write up for the journals."

Connolly laughed. "I'm always happy to do that. Keeps the research money flowing."

Chris hung up and looked down at his notes. He'd been a fool to resist Alex's theories. She might lack medical training, but she had evolved her hypothesis by observing empirical evidence and had thus come to an improbable but quite possible conclusion. He had discounted her ideas on the basis of professional prejudice, nothing more. He felt like the pompous French physicians who had ridiculed Pasteur when the country doctor claimed anthrax was caused by a bacterium. But Chris wasn't like those doctors. Shown the error of his ways, he would become a zealous convert. After all, his life was at stake.

CHAPTER
28

Alex sat in a low chair opposite the desk of one of the two associate deputy directors of the FBI. One of those deputy directors she considered a friend; the other had long ago revealed himself to be an enemy.

That man was the one she was facing now.

Outside of the Bureau's Washington headquarters, Mark Dodson was said to have been eugenically bred as a bureaucrat. He had spent little time in the field, because he'd set his sights on FBIHQ from the beginning. By judicious use of his family's political connections, Dodson had insinuated himself into the Bureau's halls of power with almost unprecedented speed. He'd honed his skills in the ethically bankrupt, cover-your-ass environment of Washington, until his character consisted only of what remained after countless compromises made not for the good of the service, but for advancement in the Bureau's rigidly delineated hierarchy. His title said it all: Associate Deputy Director, Administration.

Dodson had taken a set against Alex early during her Washington service. She had no idea why this should be so, but in the Byzantine corridors of the J. Edgar Hoover Building, one could never be quite sure why anything was so. After the fiasco at the Federal Reserve bank, Dodson had pushed relentlessly to have her fired. Had it not been for the intervention of Senator Clark Calvert—Alex's staunchest supporter— Dodson might have rammed his agenda through. Today, however, there would be no last-minute charge by the Seventh Cavalry, and Alex had only herself to blame. Dodson stared across his desk with open satisfaction.

"You had a good flight, I trust?"

"Can we not play games?" Alex asked wearily. "Can we just not do that? I'm really too tired."

The good humor instantly left Dodson's face. He leaned across the desk and spoke in a harsh voice. "Very well, Agent Morse. Tomorrow morning at nine a.m. you will meet with three representatives of the Office of Professional Responsibility. Before the interview, you will be ordered to take a drug test. Failure to submit to that test will constitute grounds for dismissal from the Bureau. Failure to answer every question truthfully and fully will also constitute grounds for dismissal. Do you understand?"

Alex nodded once.

"You're not going to skate this time," Dodson went on, prodding her for a reaction.

She gave him nothing.

"I mean, what the hell were you thinking down there?" Dodson asked. "As far as I can tell, you've been carrying on a one-man murder investigation in Mississippi. You've broken so many rules and laws that I don't even know where to begin. You've also influenced serving agents to break rules and laws, and it pains me to say that they have probably done so out of misguided loyalty to you. Do you have any comment, Agent Morse?"

Alex shook her head.

"Is there some purpose to your silence?" Dodson asked with narrowed eyes. "Are you attempting to communicate the fact that you despise me?"

Her eyes flashed. She hoped he could read her mind.

Dodson jabbed a forefinger at her. "You won't look so goddamned high-and-mighty at tomorrow's meeting. You'll be living proof that even blue flamers can crash and burn."

Alex studied her fingernails. Two had broken in last night's struggle. "Are you finished gloating?"

Dodson leaned back in his seat. "Lady, I'm just getting started." He was about to go on when the phone on his desk buzzed. He reached out and pressed a button. "Yes, David?"

"Director Roberts's office just called, sir. The director would like to speak to Agent Morse personally."

Dodson's face tightened. He leaned forward and pressed the button again, then picked up the telephone and said something too low for Alex to hear. She heard him say, "Now? Right now?" Then, as she watched in amazement, Dodson hung up the phone and spoke without meeting her eyes.

"You're to go to the director's office immediately."

She stood and waited for the deputy director to look up at her, but he never did. She left Dodson's office and walked down the hallowed corridor to the office of newly appointed FBI director John B. Roberts.

•   •   •

The director's office was considerably larger than Dodson's. His window overlooked Pennsylvania Avenue, just as J. Edgar Hoover's had done. But Hoover had watched the inaugural parades of seven presidents pass beneath his window, whereas no FBI director since had enjoyed anything like that kind of tenure. Some hadn't even lasted long enough to learn the names of their SACs. Alex wondered how long Roberts would survive.

A dark-haired man of fifty-five, Roberts had been appointed to lead the Bureau after the initial wave of post-9/11 reforms had stalled. His predecessor had spent almost two hundred million dollars on a new nationwide computer system that never worked, while terrorists roamed the country with sacks of cash to keep them off the digital grid. The street buzz on Roberts was good; as a U.S. attorney, he had taken on some of the largest corporations in the country, proving again and again that they had colluded to defraud American consumers and investors.

To Alex's surprise, Roberts wasn't the only senior officer in the room. Seated in a club chair to his left was a ruggedly handsome man of forty-eight, Associate Deputy Director Jack Moran. Moran handled investigations, not administration, and he had been a good friend to Alex during her Washington years, often running interference to keep Dodson off her back. Though there was little that Moran or anyone else could do to save her today, it warmed her heart to see him here.

"Hello, Alex," Moran said. "You look tired."

"I am."

"I don't believe you've met the new director. John Roberts, Alex Morse."

Alex stepped forward, held out her hand, and said, "Special Agent Alex Morse, sir."

Roberts took her hand and gave it a firm shake. "Special Agent Morse, I regret extremely the circumstances in which we now find ourselves. I'm a close friend of Senator Clark Calvert, and I'm well aware of the great service that you performed for his family."

The director was referring to Alex's career-making case, a kidnapping-for-ransom of a U.S. senator's daughter. The Bureau's play had ended in a dangerous standoff in rural Virginia, but after nine hours of nerve-racking negotiation, Alex had talked the barricaded kidnappers into releasing their four-year-old hostage. To preserve the illusion of the invulnerability of government officials, no word of this incident had reached the media, but Alex's career had been kicked into overdrive. Even now, her work that day was paying dividends.

"I've asked you here today," Director Roberts said, "to find out whether there might be mitigating or extenuating circumstances that I'm unaware of—circumstances that might justify your recent behavior."

Alex knew that her amazement showed on her face.

"Please have a seat," said the director. "Take your time and think about my question."

She tried to gather herself, to marshal what arguments there might be in her favor, but in the event she couldn't find any. "I have no excuse, sir," she said finally. "All I can say in my defense is that I'm convinced my sister was murdered, along with at least eight other people." Alex saw Jack Moran's face falling, but she pushed on. "I don't yet have objective evidence to prove these assertions. All my actions over the past few weeks have been directed toward uncovering such proof. Last night I was almost killed by a man attempting to stop my investigation. The Natchez, Mississippi, police department can verify that."

Director Roberts stared at her for some time without speaking. Then he said, "It's my understanding that neither the Mississippi State Police nor the local police departments in the various towns involved believe that any such murders ever took place. That view is supported by our field office in Jackson."

Alex tried to keep all emotion out of her voice. "I know that, sir. But these are not conventional crimes. They are, in effect, very sophisticated poisonings—almost in the sense of biological weapons. The deaths occur so long after the administration of the poison or biological agent that forensic evidence is difficult or even impossible to obtain."

"Weren't some of these deaths the result of cancer?"

"Yes, sir, they were. Six of nine that I know about. But I believe there have been more. Possibly a lot more."

"Alex," Jack interjected in a gentle voice. "You lost your father last December. Your sister died from an unexpected stroke only a month ago. Your mother is dying of ovarian cancer as we speak. Is it just possible—and I say *possible,* mind you—that under this phenomenal amount of stress, your mind has latched onto an explanation that's outside the realm of what's probable?"

She didn't answer immediately. "I've thought about that a lot. It's a reasonable question. But I don't believe that's the case. I also believe that I've identified the next victim of this killing team."

Jack's chin sagged onto his chest.

Director Roberts rubbed his left cheek and spoke in a harder voice. "Agent Morse, I want you to listen to me very closely. I would like you to take a voluntary leave of absence from the Bureau. We'll list your absence as extended compassionate medical leave. During that absence, I'd like you to voluntarily undergo an extensive psychiatric evaluation." Roberts glanced at Jack Moran. "If you will agree to this, I'll cancel the OPR interview tomorrow morning, pending the results of your evaluation. I'm making you this offer because of your exemplary record as a crisis negotiator for the Bureau. But as a condition of this offer, you must here and now agree to"— Roberts looked down at a piece of paper on his desk— "'cease and desist from all efforts relating to the death of your sister; the attorney Andrew Rusk; your former brother-in-law, William Fennell; and your nephew, James William Fennell Jr.'" Roberts looked up at her again. "You must also agree to terminate all contact with former agents of your acquaintance. Such contact can only damage their careers as well as yours. If you agree to these conditions, termination can be avoided. You might conceivably be reinstated as an agent in good standing in this agency."

The director sat back in his chair, obviously waiting for an answer. Above his head, the eyes of the president stared down at Alex as though he were waiting, too. Alex studied Moran's shoes as she mulled over the director's words. They were cordovan wing tips, new and shiny, a far cry from the Rockports he used to wear in the field. She could not deny that the offer was remarkably generous. In it, she felt the hands of both Jack Moran and Senator Calvert. She didn't want to disappoint the new director, who was obviously a considerate man. Even less did she want to disappoint Moran, who had done so much for her as a mentor.

After a couple of minutes, she looked at the director and spoke in a quiet voice.

"Do you have a sister, sir?"

"Alex," Moran cut in. "Don't make it—"

"It's all right, Jack," said the director.

"I don't mean to be presumptuous, sir. I just want you to understand my position, if you can. You see, as my sister lay on her deathbed, she told me that she'd been murdered by her husband. My sister wasn't the imaginative type, but I was still skeptical. However, in a matter of days I discovered that her husband *did* have a motive to get rid of her—a very attractive female motive. Sir, I promised my sister that I would do everything in my power to save her son from his father. And the only way I can see to do that is to solve her murder. As far as I can tell, nobody else is going to do that." Alex turned up her palms. "So that leaves me here. I promised her, sir. It was her last request. Do you understand?"

The director stared intently at her. "I do have a sister, Agent Morse. And truthfully, I can't answer for what I would do if I were in your shoes." Roberts picked up a paperweight from the desk—a glass cube enclosing a clock—and turned it in his hands. "But this is the FBI, and we can't tolerate the kind of off-the-reservation things you've been doing."

"I understand, sir. I don't want to be off the reservation. I'm no rogue agent. I wish you would throw the weight of the Bureau behind me. I've got good instincts—Jack can attest to that."

Moran nodded with obvious affection.

"I know I'm right about this. The same way I was right about the Federal Reserve bank, which still bothers some people, I'm afraid."

Moran winced at this veiled reference to Dodson.

Alex touched her scarred cheek as she went on. "I paid a heavy price to go with my instincts on that day. A lot heavier price than my face. And whether you help me or not, I'm going to fulfill the promise I made to my sister. No matter what you do to me, I'm going to get to the bottom of her death. I hope that I'm still an FBI agent on that day, but whether I am or not, that day is going to come."

Director Roberts sighed wearily, then looked over at Moran. "I think we're done here, Jack."

Moran got up and escorted Alex into the hall. As soon as the door closed, he put an arm around her shoulders and hugged her tight. She struggled to hold back her tears, but when she felt Jack stroking her hair, a sob broke from her throat.

"What was it?" she asked. "What finally did it?"

"The Charlotte apartment. When you broke that lease, Dodson knew you were never going back. He started asking questions in Charlotte, and that was that."

She nodded into Jack's chest, then leaned back and looked into his eyes. "Do you think I'm crazy?"

"I think you're exhausted. I've been tired that way myself. I had to be hospitalized in Minneapolis once, I was working so hard. By a strange coincidence, that was just after my wife died. You hear what I'm saying? There's a connection between personal loss and . . . losing your grip on things. You've lost a lot in the past few months, Alex. More than anybody should have to lose."

She nodded in agreement, then tried to wipe away her tears. "I concede all that. But—"

Jack put a finger up to her lips. "Just promise me one thing."

"What?"

"You won't hurt yourself any more than you have to tomorrow morning."

She laughed strangely. "What does it matter now?"

Moran squeezed her upper arm. "You've still got friends in this building. That's all I'm saying. Don't give that prick Dodson the rope to hang you with."

Alex nodded, but her mind was already far away. As she pulled away and walked down the hall alone, she saw an image of Chris Shepard practicing baseball with his adopted son. Superimposed over that picture like a descending shadow was a scene of Thora Shepard copulating with Dr. Shane Lansing. Thora's eyes, blazing with desperate lust, were the brightest things in Alex's head. Standing in the shadows behind Thora was Andrew Rusk, his face a grinning mask of greed, and behind him, almost beyond the realm of sight, hovered an even darker figure—far more threatening yet utterly faceless.

"I know you're there," Alex murmured. "And I'm going to find you, motherfucker."

CHAPTER

29

While Alex was walking out of the Hoover Building, Eldon Tarver was squatting beside a sandy stream, waiting for his bowels to move. He had spent the last eighteen hours in the woods of Chickamauga, while forty miles away the Natchez police, the Adams County Sheriff's Department, and the Mississippi Highway Patrol combed the area for a white van that was tumbling along the bottom of the Mississippi River toward Baton Rouge.

The doctor's motorcycle was parked beneath a sycamore forty feet away, and his duffel bag lay beside it. Eldon had come down to the stream to escape the sun, and to do his business in peace. As he rocked and strained on his haunches, he kept his eyes peeled for movement near the stream. Snakes liked this kind of ground, down in the cool hollows near water. They needed to drink just as people did. That was one of the secrets of handling them: knowing that they weren't so different from people. Cold-blooded, yes, but Eldon had learned young that many humans shared this trait. Snakes lived to eat, sleep, and mate, just as humans did. To eat, they had to kill. And to kill, they had to hunt.

Most humans hunted, too, those who weren't so alienated from their natures that they retained nothing of their ancient selves. People hunted in different ways and places now: in offices, financial markets, laboratories, and dark city streets. A few still carried the spirit of the true hunter within their breasts. Alex Morse was one of these, and that only made sense. She had been born from a hunter's loins, and she was simply fulfilling her destiny, as her genes bade her to do.

Right now she was hunting *him*.

Morse had a tough job ahead. Eldon knew ways of hiding that even animals did not. There had been times, he believed, when he had made himself literally invisible to people passing within a foot of him. Today was a good example. He wasn't tearing across the country in a panic, as so many people who had killed would now be doing. He was living quietly, close to the earth, and still near the sites of his attacks.

He often felt a deep lethargy after a kill, the way snakes did after devouring large prey. It took time to digest the big things. Later, of course, he would begin to stir, to focus on research again. But now he felt a deep slowness in his veins, a reluctance to engage with life that almost frightened him. The feeling wasn't new. Sometimes he felt like a retrovirus himself, neither alive nor dead, but rather half a helix—half a chain—eternally searching for a tie that would bind. He suspected that most human beings were like that: dormant, drifting, like living corpses until they infiltrated the barriers of another person. By insinuating themselves into that other life, they began to function, to act, to feel, and ultimately to reproduce. But after a time (varying in every case, but always inevitable) they began to kill the host body. Look at the desperate men and women who went to Andrew Rusk for help. Most had already attached themselves to a new host and were now consumed by a frantic impulse to flee the dying husk of the old one, the husk that they themselves had sucked dry. And they would not scruple to kill if necessary.

Eldon listened to the whisper of the creek and let his mind drift downstream. Sometimes he had trouble evacuating his bowels. Before his adoptive father came to believe that Eldon had been ordained by God to handle serpents, he had flown into rages and beaten the boy without mercy. All the anger that would have crashed onto the thick heads of his biological children was diverted onto Eldon by his wife, a living monument to passive aggression. But Eldon had understood none of that then; he understood only pain. Even now, he had more than a dozen burn scars on his body, souvenirs of his father's Kafkaesque efforts to "prove" that he was not one of the elect, that he had been touched by the Evil One. (Being burned by the flame constituted damning proof of sin.) The red-hot iron had scourged Eldon in places he had not touched himself back then—the very iron they used in church to fulfill Luke 10:19: *Behold, I give unto you power to tread on serpents and scorpions, and over all the power of the enemy: and nothing shall by any means hurt you.* And for the skeptical, there was Mark 16:18, which Eldon had heard repeated ten thousand times before he was fifteen: *They shall take up serpents; and if they drink any deadly thing, it shall not hurt them; they shall lay hands on the sick, and they shall recover—*

The sound of a cell phone was alien in these woods, and many creatures stopped to listen. Eldon let it ring three more times before he answered.

"Yes?"

"Dr. Traver?"

Eldon blinked three times, slowly. "Yes."

"It's Neville Byrd."

"Yes?"

"I think I may have him, sir. Or it, rather."

"Go on."

"The thing you were waiting for, you know? The *mechanism.*"

"Go on."

"Andy Rusk just logged on to this Dutch Web site. It seems to me he's going through an authentication protocol of some kind. You know, verifying his identity."

"And?"

"Well . . . I mean, if he does that tomorrow, I'd say we've found the trigger, you know? Like, if he didn't log in the next day, all hell would break loose. Or whatever it is you're expecting."

Eldon found it hard to adjust to the sudden intrusion of modernity. "Very good. Call me when . . . you're certain."

Neville Byrd sat breathing into the phone—he was almost panting, really, and obviously puzzled by his employer's apparent detachment. "I'll do that, Doctor. Is there anything else?"

"No."

"Okay, then."

The connection went dead.

Eldon hit END, then wiped himself with some broad leaves and walked slowly back to his motorcycle. He saw a shiver in the pine straw as he walked, a shiver that filled him with anticipation. Instead of halting, as most people would have, he threw out his right foot.

A thick black snake reared up before him, exposing the milky lining of its mouth and two long fangs. A cottonmouth moccasin. The tip of its tail vibrated like a rattlesnake's, but there was no sound. This viper had no rattle like its cousin. Still, it stood its ground more fiercely than a rattler would have done.

"*Agkistrodon piscivorus,*" Eldon murmured. "Are you a sign, my friend?"

The cottonmouth seemed perplexed by his lack of fear. As Dr. Tarver moved forward, he opened his mouth and flicked his tongue in and out, an old habit from his snake-hunting days. The cottonmouth was not brilliantly hued like the coral, but corals were rare, and the one he'd found in the park was probably dead by now. Agent Morse would almost certainly survive, even if she'd been bitten. But she would never be the same. She would have tasted the enmity that God had promised in Genesis, and she would know that her present hunt was like no other.

The cottonmouth advanced in a quick rush, showing that he meant business. Eldon laughed and sidestepped the snake, whose body was nearly as thick as his forearm. Its diamond-shaped head was big as an average man's fist. A snake like that could generate a lot of fear. In some contexts, it could be a very persuasive tool.

"I believe you are," he said. "A sign of rebirth."

As he shouldered his duffel bag and climbed aboard the Honda, his laughter echoed strangely through the trees.

CHAPTER

30

Chris was sitting at his kitchen table dictating charts when the cell phone Alex had given him began to ring. Ben was in the den playing *Madden NFL* on his Xbox, but they could see each other through the open door. Ben had already asked about the unfamiliar cell phone, and Chris had played it off as something the hospital had lent him. He debated not answering, then calling Alex back after Ben went to sleep, but that might be some time. He glanced at Ben, then got up and reached to the top of the refrigerator, where he'd stashed his .38. Slipping it into his pocket, he picked up the cell phone and a flashlight, then walked to the front door, calling, "I'm going outside for better reception, okay?"

Ben didn't even look in his direction.

"Alex?" he said, walking across the driveway. "How's it going up there?"

"Not so good."

"You sound shaky."

"Not my best day."

"I'm sorry. Take another Ativan."

"I'd like to, but they're giving me a drug test in the morning. And it's not voluntary."

"Ativan's no big deal. You've got a prescription."

"Not in writing."

"I'll fax one up there tomorrow."

"That won't help. They don't want me talking to you, Chris. They don't want me talking to anybody associated with any of the cases. Actually, 'noncases' would be more accurate."

"They still don't believe you?"

"For a second, I thought I saw something in an old friend's eye, but I was wrong."

Chris switched on the flashlight and scanned his front yard. Two pairs of yellow-green eyes glowed to life on a hilltop sixty meters away. The deer reassured him, for the skittish animals would instantly vanish if someone were prowling the area. "Well, your big worry was that they would fire you. Have they done that?"

"Not yet. They offered me a deal."

"What deal?"

"If I give up everything, stop trying to find out what happened to Grace, they probably won't fire me."

Chris didn't know what to say.

"They want me to go to a goddamn psychiatric hospital. They think I'm having some kind of break-down."

Though he didn't want to confess it, Chris had suspected the same thing for a while.

In a small voice, Alex said, "Is that what you think?"

"Absolutely not. Listen, I spoke to my old hematology professor up at Sloan-Kettering today. He scared me to death, Alex. Murdering someone by giving them cancer is more than just theoretically possible. Connolly has done it himself, to mice."

"How?"

Chris quickly recounted the scenarios Pete Connolly had outlined for him.

"My God. I wish I had talked to him a week ago."

Chris walked through a flower bed and up to the den window. Ben was still glued to the television, his mouth taut, his hands flying over the game controller.

"Listen," Alex said, "I called to let you know that I'm sending someone down to watch over you and Ben tonight."

"Who?"

"Will Kilmer, my father's old partner. You've heard me talk about him. He's an ex–homicide detective, now private. He's about seventy, and really nice. He's also sharper and tougher than he looks. I just want you to know he's going to be outside."

"I'm not going to turn him away. I'm walking around with my gun, nervous as a cat."

"That's good. Just don't shoot Will."

"Don't worry."

There was a brief silence. Then Alex said, "I also want you to know something else."

His stomach tightened in dread.

"Will has a detective staying up at the Alluvian Hotel. He's watching Thora."

Chris felt a surprising ambivalence about this. "Really?"

"I didn't tell you because it's easier to ask forgiveness than permission. But I had to do it, Chris."

"I understand. Has the guy seen anything suspicious?"

Another hesitation. "The detective's wife thinks she

may have seen Shane Lansing leave the hotel about five thirty this morning. She's not positive, though."

The knots in Chris's stomach eased a little. "I told you, I saw Lansing early this morning in Natchez. He couldn't have made it back here from Greenwood in that time."

"Unless he flew."

"There's no commercial service to Greenwood, and Lansing isn't a pilot."

"You've been giving this a lot of thought, haven't you?"

Chris colored. "Of course. I even waited outside his office in my car this afternoon, to make sure he was really there working."

"Was he?"

"Yes. But the fact that he hasn't pressed assault charges is pretty goddamn suspicious."

"We'll know the truth soon enough, I think. Be nice to Will, if you see him. He practically raised me, and he's doing this for free."

"When will he be here?"

"Probably within the next half hour."

"What am I supposed to tell Ben?"

"What time does he go to bed?"

"Probably an hour from now."

"I'll make sure Will doesn't come up to the house until after that."

"Thanks. When are you coming back?"

"I'm meeting with the OPR in the morning. They'll probably ask for my badge and gun. There may be paperwork to do up here, but I'm going to try to get back as soon as I can. You just make sure you're alive and well when I get there."

Chris turned and looked over at the hilltop. The eyes were still there, like golden spheres floating in the night. "Don't worry about that." He started to hang up, but he felt that he should say one thing more before he did. "Alex?"

"Yes?"

"Maybe you should think about taking that deal."

He heard only the hissing silence of the open connection.

"If we concentrate on the medical side of things," he said, "if we use people like Pete Connolly, I think we'll eventually have enough evidence to convince your superiors to look into this themselves."

"Not soon enough," Alex said bitterly. "Not for Jamie. I think he knows what his father did, Chris. He doesn't admit it to himself, but at some level, he knows."

"Have you made any progress getting the medical records of the other victims? From the families, maybe?"

"When could I have done that?" she replied testily.

"I understand. Look, just try to find out who their doctors were. Maybe I can get hold of them through a backdoor route."

"That's unethical, isn't it?"

"No. It's illegal."

"Well, well. Things change when it gets personal, don't they?"

A rush of anger went through him. "Look, if you don't—"

"I'm sorry, Chris. I couldn't resist. I've been alone in this for so long. You know I'll do anything to get those records."

"Okay. I need to get back to Ben. Don't do anything crazy in that meeting tomorrow."

Alex laughed, the sound strangely brittle through the cell phone. "That's what everybody tells me."

Chris hung up and looked over at the hilltop. Now there were five pairs of eyes. He clapped his hands together once, hard. As if controlled by a single mind, the eyes aligned themselves and focused on him. The cheep of crickets died, and even the frogs down at the pond fell silent. Chris whistled once, long and low, utterly perplexing the deer. They stared for a moment that dilated into something immeasurable, then bolted into the woods with a drumming of hoofbeats.

Gone.

As he walked back into the house, the floating eyes hovered in his mind like the afterimage of an exploding flashbulb. At about the same intensity, a shadowy film was running through his mind: Thora sitting astride Shane Lansing in a darkened hotel room, the air fetid with humid Delta heat, her body glistening with sweat, her eyes wild with abandon—

"Dad?" Ben called. "Where you been?"

"Watching some deer."

"How many?"

"Five."

"Yeah? Come play me a game."

Chris stepped around the refrigerator and laid the .38 on top again. "Okay, buddy. I want to be the Colts this time."

"No way!"

Chris lay on the sofa bed in his home theater, just up the hall from the master bedroom suite, and listened to the slow, regular sound of Ben's breathing. Ben had asked him to open up the bed on the pretext that it was more comfortable for watching a movie, but Chris knew that with his mother gone, the boy wanted to sleep down here rather than upstairs in his room. Chris picked up the remote and switched off the TV, then got out of the bed carefully, so as not to wake Ben.

Thora had called from Greenwood about twenty minutes after his conversation with Alex. Her tone was light and breezy as she gushed about the quality of the spa, and she laughed as she read the names of treatments to Ben, who by then was on the other extension. The experience seemed surreal to Chris, who was thinking about the morning-after pill and his scuffle with Shane Lansing while Thora giggled out names like the Mississippi Mudpie, the High-Cotton Indulgence, the Sweat Tea Soul Soak, the Muddy Waters, and the Blues Bath. He thought she might get serious once Ben was off the line, but to his amazement, she told him that they should both return in a month or so for the Couple's Renewal Treatment. No mention of Shane Lansing— nothing but sweetness and light. Chris wasn't about to get into anything while Ben was awake, so he'd matched his tone to Thora's and ended the conversation.

An hour had passed since that call, so he walked to the front door, opened it, and poked his head outside. "Mr. Kilmer?" he called. "Are you out there?"

No response.

He called out again, but no one answered. Mildly annoyed, he walked back to the kitchen to make himself a sandwich. He was taking his first bite when someone knocked at the garage door. He walked through the pantry and put his eye to the peephole. Through its bubble lens, he saw a gray-haired man wearing glasses.

"Who is it?" he called loudly.

"Will Kilmer," said a strong male voice. "Alex Morse sent me."

Chris opened the door. Kilmer was about five feet ten, and in surprisingly good shape for a man his age, except for a paunch above his sagging belt. He wore khakis, a generic polo shirt, and gray running shoes. When he smiled and offered his hand, Chris shook it, getting the iron grip he expected from an ex-cop.

"I'm sorry you had to drive all the way down here, Mr. Kilmer."

"Call me Will, Doctor." Kilmer released his hand. "It's no problem. I'm getting to where I can't sleep more than three or four hours a night these days."

"That's pretty common with the onset of age, I find. The opposite of teenagers who want to sleep twenty hours out of twenty-four."

"I was out here when you called from the front door, but that was the first time you'd showed yourself since I got here, and I wanted to see if anybody made a move."

"You don't really think somebody's out there, do you?"

"From what Alex told me, I'd say it's reasonable to expect trouble."

"If someone were out there, wouldn't they have seen you come up?"

"I walked in," Will said. "And I'm pretty quiet when I put my mind to it. Parked out by that restaurant built in the shape of a black mammy, and I've got a night scope in my pack."

There was an awkward silence. "Can I offer you something to drink?" Chris asked. "I was about to eat a sandwich."

"I don't want to put you out."

"You can guard us just as well from inside as out, can't you? Get your pack, and I'll make you a sandwich. You can tell me why Alex Morse isn't crazy."

Kilmer chuckled softly. "Hard to turn that offer down. I'll be right back."

Chris walked back to the kitchen, leaving the door open behind him. Before he finished making the second turkey-and-Swiss, Kilmer had joined him in the kitchen. The detective set a camouflage backpack on the floor and sat on one of the barstools at the counter. Chris slid a plate over, then opened a Corona and passed it to the detective. Kilmer's eyes lit up when he saw the beer.

"Thanks, Doc. It's pretty damn hot for May."

Chris nodded and went back to his own sandwich.

"You've got a nice place out here," Kilmer said. "But I hear you're moving."

"My wife's idea. Keeping up with the Joneses, I guess."

Kilmer took another swallow of beer, then started on his sandwich.

"So you used to work with Alex's father?" Chris prompted.

"That's right. First at the PD, then at our detective agency. Never knew a better man in a tight spot."

"He was killed recently?"

"Yessir. Trying to help some people in trouble, which is about what I'd of guessed."

"Crime's pretty bad in Jackson, I hear."

"Bad? You take the Jackson I grew up in as a boy and compare it to now, it's like the end of the world. It started in the eighties with the crack. Now the inmates are running the asylum. Now that Jim's gone, I doubt

I'll stay at it more than another couple years. Close the agency, retire up to Virginia."

Chris nodded. "You've known Alex her whole life?"

Kilmer's eyes sparkled. "From the day she was born. Worst tomboy I ever saw in my life. Been handling guns since she was eight. And smart?" Kilmer shook his head. "By the time she was fourteen, she made me feel stupid. Not just me, either."

Chris laughed. "What about that murder theory of hers?"

Kilmer pressed his lips together and sighed. "I'm not sure what to think. The technical side is over my head. But I'll tell you this: I worked homicide for more years than anybody ought to, and I think a lot more people have been murdered in divorce situations than anybody knows or even suspects—especially before the forensics were what they are now. I had lots of cases where I just *knew* the husband had offed his wife and made it look like an accident. Same way I knew it was sex abuse when I'd find a mama and her daughters over a dead husband. But divorce is a lot more common than child abuse." Kilmer looked suddenly abashed. "Look, just because I think Alex may be onto something don't mean I think your wife is doing you wrong. I'm just here as a favor to Alex."

"I understand. I've only known Alex a few days, but I can see why you like her so much." Chris took a swallow of beer. "But I have wondered if she hasn't gone through so much in the past few months that she's not quite in control of her faculties."

Kilmer raised his eyebrows, as though considering this possibility. "She's been through a lot, all right. And you may not know the worst of it. I believe Alex loved that fella who got killed the day she was shot. But he was married, and she wasn't the type to break up a family. So that day was pretty rough. She lost half her face and the man she loved in about five seconds. She feels guilty that she loved him, and guilty that she got him killed. A lot of people *would* crack under strain like that. But excepting her daddy, Alex is the last person out of anybody I ever met who would lose her grip on reality." Kilmer met Chris's eyes. "If she believes you're in danger, watch out. She ain't down here to waste her time or yours."

Kilmer's furrowed face had been hardened by years of smoking cigarettes, and his belly had probably grown during years of eating bad food on stakeouts. How many years had he taken off his life by choosing the life he had? Would Alex look that rough when she was seventy? It seemed unlikely, but her facial wounds had already taken her partway down that road.

"Well," Chris said, getting up and taking his plate to the sink, "I'm going to hit the rack pretty soon. You're welcome to sleep in the house tonight. There's a guest room right off that hall over there."

"Where's your boy?" Kilmer asked.

"He fell asleep in the TV room." Chris pointed. "That glow right down there. I'll be just past it."

"If he wakes up and sees me, what should I tell him?"

"He won't. But if he should, just come get me."

As Chris reached up to the top of the refrigerator, a sudden thought struck him. He brought down the .38 and said, "Do you have any identification on you, Mr. Kilmer?"

Kilmer stared back for a long moment, then nodded, walked to his backpack, and reached inside. Chris felt himself tense, as though preparing for violence, but Kilmer only brought out a wallet. He showed Chris a Mississippi driver's license. The good-natured face on it matched the man in front of him.

"Look here," Kilmer said, flipping open a plastic picture holder. "This is Alex in her younger days, with me and Jim."

Chris looked down at three figures huddled in what appeared to be a duck blind in the dead of winter. Sandwiched between two handsome men in their prime was a girl whose arms were wrapped around the neck of a black Labrador retriever. Her grin revealed two missing teeth, and her eyes shone as though they couldn't possibly hold more happiness than they did in that moment. Despite her youth, Chris could see hints of the woman that Alex would become in the future.

Kilmer flipped up the picture, revealing a snapshot of Alex at what looked like her high school graduation. She was pressed between the same two men, older now and this time wearing dark suits. There were two women in the picture also, classic Mississippi wives with too much makeup and wide, genuine smiles.

"Ain't she something?" Kilmer said.

"Do you have kids, Will?"

The older man swallowed. "We had a girl, a year behind Alex in school. We lost her on homecoming night the year Alex graduated. Drunk driver. After that . . . I guess Alex kind of took her place in my heart." Kilmer closed the wallet, went back to the counter, and drank off the rest of his beer.

"I'm sorry," Chris said.

"Part of life," Kilmer said stoically. "You take the

good with the bad. Go on to bed, Doc. And don't worry about nothing. I got you covered."

Chris shook the detective's hand, then walked down the hall toward his bedroom.

"Appreciate the sandwich," Kilmer called.

Chris waved, then backed up and stepped into the home theater room. Ben's breathing hadn't changed, but he had managed to tie the bedclothes into a knot around him. Chris tried to imagine getting a call like the one Will Kilmer must have gotten on that long-ago homecoming night, but he couldn't do it. As he stared down at Ben's gentle face, he thought of the trauma the boy would suffer if it turned out that his mother was not the woman that either of them believed her to be. Praying for a miracle he no longer believed in, Chris quietly shut the door and walked down to his own bedroom.

CHAPTER

31

Eldon Tarver stood in the deep moon shadow beneath the low-hanging limbs of a water oak and watched the lights go out in the house on the hill. His motorcycle lay in the underbrush back near the highway. A backpack lay on the ground at his feet. He had spent the day at the Chickamauga Hunting Camp in Jefferson County waiting for night to fall. He had done many things during the day, but one he had not done was answer the calls of Andrew Rusk.

When he arrived last night and found a woman here, his first thought was that he had made a mistake about the house. The wife was supposed to be out of town. But when he checked the coordinates on his pocket GPS unit, they had matched his notes exactly. He had moved closer, close enough to see the woman clearly and compare her to the photos in his backpack. She did not match. However, she did match an image deep in Eldon's mind—one he had seen only briefly in the Fennell file supplied by Rusk. The woman in the house was Special Agent Alexandra Morse, the sister of Grace Fennell. Her presence there—talking to his next target—had such profound implications that he had almost panicked. But life had taught him to expect the unexpected.

He'd thought Morse would be easy prey, despite whatever training the Bureau might have given her. She was a hostage negotiator, after all, not a tactical specialist. But she had fought like a demon when he moved in for the kill. He hadn't been sure he meant to kill her until he was less than ten feet away. Killing an FBI agent was a serious matter. Institutional memory was long, and the Bureau did not forget such crimes. But the way she had played it—slipping into the driveway in an amateurish attempt to trick him—told Eldon one thing: Morse was alone. She had no backup. There or anywhere else. Yet she had taught him a painful lesson and almost exposed him.

Tonight, it seemed better that she had survived. Had Alex Morse died in that carport, a hundred FBI agents would have descended on this little corner of Mississippi. Now he had time to do what was necessary for a clean escape.

Eldon shouldered his backpack and walked slowly up the hill. As he neared the house, he veered right and moved around dense azaleas to the cluster of air conditioners that served the house. He had studied the blueprints provided by Rusk until he knew this house inside and out. He knew which air-conditioning units cooled which zones, for example, and he would soon make use of that knowledge. He continued circling the house, moving past an outdoor hot tub, then the swimming pool, then into the breezeway that led to the storeroom. There was some risk that he could be seen from the darkened windows inside, but instinct told him he was all right. Moving quickly into the storeroom, he pulled down a collapsible stairway and climbed into the attic. From here, he could reach the attic of the main house.

After squeezing his bulky shoulders through one crawl space, he entered a forest of rafters and ceiling joists. By walking carefully on the joists, he traversed the forty feet that took him to the duct he needed. Digging into the backpack, he removed a respirator gas mask and fitted it closely over his nose and mouth. Then he fitted a pair of foam-lined goggles over his eyes. After donning a pair of surgical gloves, Eldon reached into his pack and removed a heavy, oblong canister. It looked like the CO_2 cylinders that kids used to charge paintball guns. He laid a heavy rubber mat over the duct to dampen vibration. Then, with a small, battery-powered hand drill, he bored a hole in the duct. After laying a thin piece of rubber over the hole, he lifted the cylinder and punched its sharp nozzle through both rubber and hole, creating a seal. Once he was certain of his setup, he drew a deep breath, then opened the valve on the cylinder.

The soft hissing that followed gave him intense satisfaction. Within two minutes, both men and the boy below would be unconscious. They would remain that way until morning, long after Eldon had left the house. The gas in the cylinder could not be purchased anywhere in the United States unless the buyer was the U.S. government. It had been provided to Dr. Tarver by Edward Biddle, an acquaintance from many years ago. Biddle had once been an army officer associated with a project Dr. Tarver had worked on. Now Biddle was an officer of a large corporation that handled critical defense contracts for the United States. The gas was an agent similar to that the Russians had used in their attempt to free the seven hundred hostages trapped by terrorists in a Moscow theater. Quite a few people had died from the gas in that instance, but most were elderly, and the dosage had not been precisely calculated. Unlike the Russians, Dr. Tarver knew exactly what he was doing.

He sat absolutely still for two minutes, then moved deeper into the attic to the folding-ladder steps over the closet of the master bedroom. So confident was he of the gas that he had not brought a firearm tonight. An unregistered weapon was the quickest path to arrest during a random traffic stop. Bracing both hands on a ceiling joist, he pushed down the spring-mounted steps with his legs. After unfolding the ladder, he carried his backpack into the closet and unpacked an aluminum thermos. Inside the thermos were two preloaded syringes. One contained a mixture of corticosteroids to suppress the human immune system. The other contained a solution that had taken Dr. Tarver over a year to develop. Twenty years, really, if you counted the research that had gone into it. But this specific solution had been a year in the making. It was different from those used on the other targets. And for that reason, Eldon was excited. He felt a hyperalertness that even the knowledge that this would be his last operation could not diminish. For there could be no doubt of that. Either Rusk had been lying to him, or Rusk was a fool. Either way, the connection had to be severed. But there were things Eldon had to do first. Some would be unpleasant, but not this. This was something he had waited for, for a very long time.

He walked into the master bedroom without even

trying to be quiet. Dr. Shepard lay on his side in the bed, his mouth open wider than appeared normal, but this was common after the gas. Dr. Tarver took a mental snapshot of the bed to make sure he would leave everything exactly as he found it. Then he set the syringes on a dresser, pulled the covers off Shepard, and rolled the internist onto his stomach.

Dr. Tarver took a small LED flashlight from his pocket, switched it on, then got the steroid injection from the dresser. Kneeling between Shepard's thighs, he pulled down his boxer shorts and pushed one cheek aside, exposing the anus. Holding the light between his teeth, he opened the doctor's anus enough to insert the needle, then injected the steroids an inch inside the rectum. Dr. Shepard hardly stirred. Eldon repeated the procedure with the other solution, but at the last instant Shepard's lower body flinched in an involuntary muscle spasm. Eldon found his needle embedded at the entrance to the rectum. A bad mistake, but now that the hole had been made, there wasn't much point in removing it to find a site deeper in.

He hesitated before depressing the plunger. Several times today he'd thought of extending his experiment. He'd known the boy would be in the house, and since his research was likely to be cut short, the boy offered a unique opportunity. Eldon had not prepared enough solution to inject both Shepard and his son with the precalculated dose, but instinct told him there was probably enough. On the other hand, a juvenile immune system might be resilient enough to overcome the virus. Given the unknowns, Eldon depressed the plunger to the bottom of the syringe's barrel and gave Shepard the full dose.

The boy would live.

Eldon turned Shepard back on his side, pulled the covers over him, then loaded everything back into the pack and walked quickly down the hall. He found the boy on a sofa bed in the home theater. To his surprise, he discovered an older man sleeping in an easy chair in the den, three empty beer bottles beside him. Eldon did not know the man. He took a cell phone from his pack, aimed its tiny lens at the stranger's face, and shot a picture of him. Then he forced his hand into the stranger's back pocket and took out his wallet.

Eldon looked around the room. Leaning against the sofa by William Kilmer's feet was a camouflage backpack. When he opened the backpack, a strange numbness began spreading outward from his heart. Inside was a handgun, a starlight scope, a canister of pepper spray, a camera, and a pair of handcuffs. It took several moments for Eldon to gather himself, but he put everything back exactly as it had been before he arrived.

He left the house by the ladder in the closet, retracing his steps back to the duct, where he sealed his tiny hole with duct tape. Ten minutes after he injected Shepard, he was walking swiftly through the trees toward the highway. The sense of exhilaration he'd felt inside had vanished, now replaced by anxiety, anger, even fear.

Tonight, everything had changed.

Alex sat with her elbows propped on the desk of her hotel room in Washington, drunk on Ativan and room service wine. She'd been staring at her computer for hours, afraid that the announcement bell wouldn't ding when Jamie logged on to MSN. The bell had not dinged yet, but not because of a malfunction. For whatever reason, Jamie simply had not logged on. The reason might be as simple as a power outage in Jackson, but Alex couldn't make herself believe it. Given what Jamie had told her during their last video chat, she feared that he might have tried something desperate. . . .

Like running away.

A half hour ago, she had broken down and called the landline at Bill Fennell's house. She had a right to talk to her nephew (and she'd meant to tell Bill so, in no uncertain terms), but she never got the chance. All she got was an answering machine.

She looked over at the hotel bed and considered climbing into it. She had an early interview tomorrow with the OPR people, and she needed to look her best. Solid. Reliable. Deserving of institutional trust. *Ha!* She wasn't going to take a chance on missing Jamie.

No way, nohow.

CHAPTER

32

"Have you got enough silk?" asked the nurse.

"I think so," said Chris, tying off the last of twenty-three stitches.

The lacerated arm under his light belonged to a fifty-year-old handyman named Curtis Johnese, a huge man in stained overalls, with a pumpkin-shaped head and a dip of Skoal tucked behind his lip. An hour ago, Mr. Johnese had contrived to open an eight-inch gash on his forearm using a table saw. In the custom from time immemorial, he had come to Tom Cage's office to be sewn up rather than visit the emergency room, which would have cost four times as much and taken four times as long. Johnese would have preferred Dr. Cage, but Tom had stepped into Chris's office and asked if he would suture the wound. Among Tom's many chronic illnesses was psoriatic arthritis, and with a recent bout with cataracts under his belt, he didn't feel he was ready for detailed work.

Chris set down his forceps, lifted the paper drape, and examined his work. As he stared, a sharp throbbing stabbed the base of his skull. He'd felt this intermittently since waking this morning, and it was strong enough that he'd taken three Advil. Surprisingly, the pain had grown worse, not better. At first he'd thought it was a tension headache—Thora was set to return tomorrow, and there was bound to be trouble when he confronted her—but this pain had a relentless quality to it, as though it signaled the onset of a fever.

"Looks great, Mr. Johnese," he said, rubbing his neck. "Just let Holly give you a tetanus booster, and you can be on your way. Come back in a week, and I'll take them out for you."

Johnese smiled and said, "I shore appreciate it, Doc. Dr. Cage is all right, ain't he?"

"He's fine. We're just backed up this morning."

The handyman looked down at his tanned forearm as Holly applied a bandage. "That's pretty good work for a young fella. You keep at it and listen to Dr. Cage, and you can't go far wrong."

"I'm with you there," Chris said, patting him on the back.

Chris left the surgery, walked into his office, and shut the door behind him. Sitting in his chair, he massaged his temples with his thumbs, then tried to work the muscles at the base of his neck. This brought no relief. He reached into his desk and popped another Advil, upping the dose to eight hundred milligrams.

"That ought to do it," he muttered.

He'd intended to call the University Medical Center to try to speak to a couple of the doctors Pete Connolly had mentioned, but he was in no mood to do that now. He leaned back in his chair, recalling Ben's fright this morning when he'd discovered Will Kilmer sound asleep in the easy chair in the den. Ben had raced back

to Chris's bedroom and shaken him awake. But once
Chris had explained that Kilmer was a distant cousin
who was passing through town on his way to Florida
(and once Ben saw that his dad wasn't worried), the boy
put it out of his mind and started getting ready for
school. Kilmer had apologized profusely and quickly
left the house.

On the way to school, Ben told Chris he'd seen three
empty beer bottles beside "Cousin Will's" chair. Chris
hadn't seen the bottles, but he figured that was why
Kilmer had fallen asleep before reaching the guest
room. *Not much of a watchdog,* he thought wryly. The
only question remaining was what he'd say to Thora if
Ben mentioned their visitor.

"Dr. Shepard?" Holly's voice intruded into his reverie
like a shout.

As he jumped in his chair, Chris wondered if he might
be getting a migraine. He'd never had one before, but
the hypersensitivity to sound and light seemed to signal
the onset of something in that line. "What is it, Holly?"

"You've got patients waiting in all four rooms."

Chris rubbed his eyes and sighed heavily. "I'm on
my way."

"Are you okay?" she asked, breaking through the
professional barrier, which she didn't observe much
anyway.

"Yeah. I've just got a headache."

The nurse nodded. "I'll try to pace things a little better today."

Chris heaved himself out of his chair, put on his
stethoscope, and walked into the hall. Between his
door and that of Exam Room 1, he felt a surge of sympathy for Alex Morse. Right about now, she was prob-

ably watching her career get flushed down the toilet. He wished there were something he could do to help her. If only she could be patient, there might be. But Alex had been under so much strain for so long that patience seemed not to be an option for her.

Just as he'd done on the day he met Alex, Chris lifted a chart from the file caddy on the door and walked into the examining room. What awaited him was not a mystery woman with a scarred face but a 280-pound man with a pilonidal abscess. Chris forced a smile, steeled himself against the coming stink, and went to work.

Alex sat in a straight-backed wooden chair before a stone-faced tribunal of OPR officials. There were two men and a woman, the men bookending the woman behind a long table. They had introduced themselves at the opening of the proceedings, but Alex had paid no attention to their names. Nothing she said today would change the outcome of this hearing, and taking part in their little charade would only demean her further.

Almost no FBI agent got through his or her career without a few OPR reviews. Usually they resulted from minor infractions of the rules, and sometimes from tattletale gossip anonymously provided to the OPR by jealous fellow agents (common enough behavior to have a slang term describing it: *jamming*). But today's hearing was different. One of the worst offenses in the eyes of the OPR was "lack of candor," which meant deception of any kind and degree by an agent, including trivial lies of omission. Judged by this standard, Alex's offenses were grave. She had not yet been ordered to take a polygraph, but she had been placed under oath.

One of the male officials had recounted all the

charges that Associate Deputy Director Dodson had leveled against her, then added a few technicalities for good measure. It was all the equivalent of an auditory blur until the woman held up a copy of the threatening text message Alex had sent to Andrew Rusk yesterday during her initial fury at being called to Washington. She had no idea how Mark Dodson could have come into possession of that message, but she was an old enough hand not to ask. The bureaucrats behind the table would tell her nothing. But now they were coming to a part of the proceeding that she could not ignore.

"Special Agent Morse," said the woman, "do you have anything to say on your behalf before we close this hearing?"

"No, ma'am."

The woman frowned like a reproachful church matron, then conferred quietly with her colleagues. A stenographer sat patiently at a desk to Alex's right. Alex filled the time by studying the stenographer's shoes. They were low heels from Nine West, or maybe Kenneth Coles, if she'd saved her money—still a far cry from the Manolo Blahniks covering the feet of the OPR bitch behind the table. It took Italian leather to shoe ambition like that in the Washington OPR.

"Special Agent Morse," said the woman, "as a result of this preliminary hearing, we are suspending you from all further duties until final and formal disposition of your case. You will turn in your credentials and your weapon, and all further contact with the Bureau should be handled through your attorney."

Alex said nothing.

The woman glanced at the stenographer. "I'm going off-the-record."

The stenographer's fingers rose from her machine.

"In view of your exemplary record," said the Blahnik-shod woman, "—excluding the incident at the Federal Reserve bank, of course—I regret extremely that we've been forced to take this action. It's my understanding that an effort was made to come to a compromise whereby your termination would not be necessary."

Alex suffered silently through the pregnant pause that followed this remark. The triumvirate of bureaucrats stared for what seemed an eternity. How, they must have been wondering, could someone voluntarily walk away from the agency to which they were giving their lives?

"I'm sorry you chose not to take advantage of that offer," said the woman.

Alex lifted her purse off the floor, removed her FBI identity card and her Glock, then walked forward and laid both on the table.

"You don't turn those in to us," said the woman. "You turn them in on the first floor."

Alex turned away and walked to the door.

"Agent Morse," the woman called after her. "You're not to leave Washington until this matter has been fully resolved. Agent Morse?"

Alex walked out, leaving the door open behind her. For good or ill, she was free now.

Chris was examining a man in congestive heart failure when Jane knocked at the door and told him he needed to come to the phone.

"It's the secretary at St. Stephen's, Doctor. The middle school."

Alarm hit Chris with surprising force. "Is it Ben? Has something happened?"

"Nothing terrible. Just a headache, but it's bad enough that he wants to come home."

"A headache?" Chris echoed. "I've got a headache, too." He walked into the reception area and took the receiver Jane handed him.

"Dr. Shepard? This is Annie out at St. Stephen's. Ben's had a headache all morning, and I think it's bad enough that he ought to go home. I knew your wife was out of town, so I called your office."

Everybody knows everything in this town. "Is he having visual disturbances or anything like that?"

"I don't think so. All I know is, he came to see me during recess, and Ben wouldn't do that unless he was really hurting."

"I'm on my way. Please keep him in the office until I get there. Is he there now?"

"Here he is."

"Dad?" said a shaky voice.

"Hey, buddy. Your head hurts?"

"Uh-huh. Real bad."

"I'm coming to get you right now."

"Where will you take me? Mom's not home."

"You can stay at the office with me. Miss Holly will take care of you. Okay?"

"Okay." The relief in Ben's voice was plain.

Chris hung up and started toward his office. Then he stopped, reversed direction, and walked down the hall to Tom Cage's office. The white-bearded doctor was saying good-bye to a drug rep.

"Excuse me, guys," Chris cut in. "Tom, I've got to run pick up Ben from school. He's got a bad headache. Can you hold the fort while I'm gone? My rooms are full."

"No problem. Take off."

Chris tried to recall who was in each room. "I've got Mr. Deakins in three with congestive heart failure. I've got Ruth Ellen Green in four with a diabetic neuropathy—"

"They'll tell me what's wrong," Tom said with a smile. "Go take care of Ben."

As Chris shook Tom's hand, the drug rep said, "Are you the guy who punched out Shane Lansing?"

Chris reddened. He and Tom had not yet spoken about this, though Tom must have heard about it by now. "We had a little disagreement. Nothing major."

The drug rep stuck out his hand. "Well, I want to shake your hand. I hate that arrogant son of a bitch."

This was risky talk for a detail man, especially in front of two doctors, but the rep probably knew that Tom wasn't the type to talk out of school.

"I'd guess Lansing had it coming," said Tom, giving Chris a private wink. "Let the man go, Tony."

The rep grinned and withdrew his hand.

As Chris strode down the hall, he heard the rep imploring Tom to prescribe whatever drug he was hawking that day.

"You know me, Tony." Dr. Cage laughed. "I'm happy to accept all the free drugs you'll give me, but I'm going to prescribe the cheapest drug that works for the patient."

Chris smiled as he darted into his office to retrieve his keys. Alex's cell phone was blinking on the desk. She'd left three voice messages in the last fifteen minutes. As he walked out to his truck, he speed-dialed her.

"Chris?" she answered.

"Yeah, what's up?"

"I'm history."

"They fired you?" he asked in disbelief.

"Pending final disposition of my case. But I'm basically a private citizen now, just like you."

Shit. "What are you going to do?"

"I'm supposed to stay here in the District."

"Didn't you tell me you have a condo up there?"

"Yes. But I don't want to go there. I can't."

"What do you want to do?"

"Come back to Mississippi and keep working the case."

"What's stopping you?"

"They're monitoring my credit cards. Probably my cell phone, too. But they don't know I have this phone."

Chris got into his truck, backed out, and pulled onto Jefferson Davis Boulevard, thinking quickly. "How soon can you fly out?"

"I could go straight to the airport."

"Then I'll book you a flight. I mean, I'll get my secretary to do it."

"Chris, you—"

"No argument, okay? Do you want to fly into Baton Rouge or Jackson?"

"Jackson. There's a nonstop flight."

"I can't pick you up," he said, thinking of the two-hour drive each way. "But I'll rent you a car."

"Thank you, Chris. I don't know what I would have done. Did Will show up last night?"

"Yeah. We got along great." He thought of adding, *He drank three beers and fell asleep in my den,* but Alex was having a bad enough day. "Will sure thinks the world of you. Call me when you land, okay?"

"I will."

He hung up and stepped on the gas, heading south toward St. Stephen's. He couldn't remember the last time Ben had had a headache. He couldn't remember the last time he'd had one either.

That kind of coincidence was almost never random.

CHAPTER

33

Wearing only a towel around his trim waist, Andrew Rusk opened the glass door of the Racquet Club steam room and walked into an almost impenetrable cloud of water vapor. Behind him a club employee slapped a DO NOT ENTER CLOSED FOR REPAIRS sign on the door. Rusk waved his hand through the cloud, trying to disperse enough steam to catch sight of his quarry, Carson G. Barnett.

"Rusk?" said a deep voice, low and utterly devoid of good humor.

"Yes," he said. "Carson?"

"I'm in the corner. Over by these goddamn rocks. Damn near burned my pecker off a second ago."

Rusk could tell by the latent anger in the oilman's voice that this would be a tough meeting. But anger wasn't a bad sign. Anger meant that Barnett was considering going forward; he had come to the meeting after all. Rusk had to get rid of the steam. He had to be sure Barnett wasn't wearing a wire.

He walked to the corner where Barnett's voice had spoken and knelt by the machine that controlled the steam. The air was thick with the scent of eucalyptus. At last the control knob appeared, and he dialed it back 50 percent.

When he stood up, he caught sight of Barnett's bull-dog countenance floating in the whiteness. The man's jaw was clenched tight, and he glowered at Rusk through the haze.

"I been thinking about what you said," Barnett muttered.

Rusk nodded but said nothing.

"You got a pair of balls on you, boy."

Still Rusk did not respond.

"I reckon you got 'em from your daddy. He had a pair, too."

"Still does."

"I don't reckon I'm the first one who ever heard that pitch you made me."

Rusk shook his head.

"You ain't sayin' much today. Cat got your tongue?"

"Would you mind standing by the door, Mr. Barnett?"

"What?" The tone suspicious. Then: "Oh."

The big man got up and walked into the clear air by the glass door.

"Would you mind removing your towel?"

"Shit," grunted Barnett. He pulled off the towel and stood glaring. Rusk's eyes moved quickly up and down the oilman's stumpy body.

"You wanna see where I burned it?" Barnett asked.

"Would you turn around, please?"

Barnett did.

"Thanks." Rusk recalled the unpleasantness of Eldon Tarver making him strip. "Mr. Barnett, you would be surprised at the people who have heard that pitch before, and even more surprised at those who have taken me up on it."

"Anybody I know?" Barnett climbed onto the top bench.

"Yes, sir."

"Well, if that's so, tell me what question I'm about to ask you."

Rusk waited a few moments so as not to make it seem too easy. Then he said, "How much is this going to cost me?"

"Goddamn," muttered Barnett, laughing softly. "I can't believe it."

"Human nature. The same all over."

"I guess so. What's your answer?"

"My answer is 'What do you care?' It's a hell of a lot less than half your net worth."

"But still pricey I bet."

"Oh, it'll hurt," Rusk conceded. "But a lot less than the fucking you'll take if you go the other way."

"You know, you pitch this kind of thing to the wrong man, and he's liable to beat the shit out of you."

"Hasn't happened yet. I'm a pretty good judge of character."

"A good judge of bad character," said Barnett. "It's a damn low thing what we're talking about. But nobody can say she didn't ask for it."

Rusk sat in silence. He wasn't thinking about Carson G. Barnett or his doomed wife. He was thinking about Eldon Tarver, MD. He had been unable to reach Tarver since their meeting at the hunting camp, seventy-two hours ago. Tarver had neutralized the threat from William Braid, as promised. But he must have done something to Alex Morse as well. Otherwise, why would Morse have sent the threatening text message? Rusk felt he had done right by turning over the message to the Bureau. His FBI contacts had painted a picture of Morse as a rogue agent, already in deep trouble because of the Federal Reserve bank debacle, and with powerful enemies in the Hoover Building. The Bureau as a whole represented no danger to him or Tarver; the obsessive Morse on her own was the threat. Every little straw Rusk could pile onto that particular camel's back would push her spine closer to breaking. Being out of contact with Tarver was disconcerting, but he could not afford to let Barnett get away. They could earn two to four times their normal fee for this job. All he had to do was close the deal. And to do that he had to broach the time issue. For some, it was a deal breaker. For others, not. Barnett seemed an impulsive man, but he might possess surprising reserves of patience.

"What you doing?" asked Barnett. "Look like you're in a goddamn dreamworld."

"I assume that your intent is to proceed?" Rusk asked.

"I'd like to hear a few more details first."

It was a natural question, but again it conjured images of a grand jury listening to taped testimony.

"Mr. Barnett, have you had any contact with any law enforcement agency about this matter?"

"Hell, no."

"All right. There's something you need to understand. No one is going to murder your wife. She will die of natural causes. Do you understand?"

There was a long silence. "I guess I do. How fast would it happen?"

"Not fast. You want fast, hire a nigger from west

Jackson. You'll be in Parchman prison three months from now."

"How fast, then?"

"The likely time frame is twelve to eighteen months."

"Jesus."

"If it can be sooner, it will be. But you should prepare yourself for that wait."

Barnett was nodding slowly.

"Another thing. It won't be pretty."

"How bad?"

Rusk didn't like to use the C-word if he could help it. "Terminal illness, obviously. There doesn't have to be a lot of pain, but it takes some fortitude to handle it."

"What about the legal side of things? The divorce and all?"

"There won't be a divorce. There won't be any legal side. You and I will not meet again after today. One week from now, I will park a silver Chevrolet Impala in the lot of the Annandale Country Club. In the trunk you will find a legal-sized envelope with printed instructions regarding payment. Payment is handled in different ways, but in your case, it will be made using rough diamonds."

Barnett looked as if he was about to ask a question, but Rusk held up his hand.

"That will all be in your instructions. When you pick up that envelope, you will leave me a box in that trunk. Inside the box will be a complete copy of your wife's medical history, including everything you can find out about both sets of grandparents; copies of all the keys that have any importance in your wife's life—cars, houses, safe-deposit box, home safe, jewelry boxes; blueprints of your house; the passwords of your security system and any passwords required to get access to your computers; also, a weekly schedule of your wife's activities, including any planned trips in the next three months; in short, that box should contain everything remotely related to your wife's life. Do you understand?"

Barnett was staring at him with horror on his face. The reality was sinking in at last. "You want me to hold her arms while you stick the knife in."

"This is between you and your conscience, Mr. Barnett. If you have any doubts, you should express them now, and we should not go forward. I want to be clear. If you agree to go forward now, there will be no turning back. From the time you leave this building, you will be subject to surveillance, to insure my safety and that of my associates." Rusk took a deep breath of wet, dense air. "Would you like some time to think about your answer?"

Barnett was cradling his face in his hands. His dark hair was plastered to his skull, and his big shoulders appeared to be shaking. Rusk wondered if he had pushed too hard. Sometimes he offered prospects tea and sympathy, but with his anxiety about Tarver simmering in his gut, he hadn't the patience for it.

"How long would a divorce take?" Barnett asked in a cracked voice.

"If your wife agrees to file under irreconcilable differences, sixty days. If she doesn't, it could take forever."

"She won't agree," he said, his voice desolate. "She won't."

"We've reached the point where I can't advise you, Carson. If you're unsure, we could let the box be your decision. If the box is there a week from today, I'll know we're going forward. If it's not, I'll know the opposite."

"What if you went to get the box and found the sheriff waiting by your car?" Barnett asked in a stronger voice.

"It would be a shame about your twins."

Barnett came off the bench quicker than Rusk could react. The oilman slammed him against the wall and seized his throat with a hand like an iron claw. Rusk was six inches taller than Barnett, but the fury burning behind the oilman's eyes left no doubt that he could rip the lawyer's heart out if he chose.

"That's not a threat," Rusk croaked. "I just want you to be aware that my associates aren't the kind of people you cross."

Twenty seconds passed before Barnett released his grip.

"Is that a yes or a no?" Rusk asked, massaging his voice box.

"I've got to do something," said Barnett. "I guess this is it. I'm not going to give up the one woman in this world who can bring me some peace."

There was nothing else to say. Rusk knew better than to offer his hand; you didn't shake hands over a deal as unholy as this. He gave Barnett a curt nod, then reached for the doorknob.

"How do I get into the car?" Barnett asked. "The Impala."

"I'll leave a spare key on the left front tire of your car when I leave here."

"You know which vehicle I'm in?"

"The Hummer," Rusk said.

"The red one," Barnett clarified.

Rusk held up his hand in acknowledgment on his way out.

CHAPTER
34

Alex spent the first hour of her return flight in shock, sipping vodka and reliving incidents from her truncated career. Her sense of being on the outside, of no longer being a player in the critical events of the nation, was overwhelming. But somewhere over eastern Tennessee, she found herself unable to remain disconnected any longer. After the flight attendants finished their beverage service, she leaned against the window and surreptitiously switched on her cell phone, keeping an eye out for roving glances. This was against the law, and she no longer had FBI credentials to flash for special treatment. Finally, the phone connected to a network and three voice-mail messages popped up. She covertly held her phone to her ear and dialed voice mail.

The first message was from Will Kilmer: "I figured I'd hear from you this morning, girl. Since I didn't, I'm guessing it's bad news. But you can't let that get you down. About four this morning, my man in Greenwood shot a video of Thora Shepard and that surgeon in flagrante delicto. I'm e-mailing a clip of

the video to your computer, and I'm gonna send a captured still to your cell phone. No sign of Andrew Rusk
or anybody else suspicious in Greenwood. But that
video's a doozy, girl. I feel bad for the doc. He's a nice
guy. Anyway, I hope I'm wrong about the hearing. You
get your tail back home. Your mama's still hanging on,
and we miss you."

Alex felt alternating waves of relief and sadness, but
she had no time to reflect. The second message was
from Chris Shepard's receptionist: the rental car information Alex would need in Jackson. She scrawled it on
the back of an FBI card from her purse, then leaned
against the window.

When she heard the voice on the third message, her
heart nearly stopped. The speaker was John Kaiser,
one of the top field agents in the entire FBI. Kaiser had
spent several years working serial homicides for the
Investigative Support Unit in Quantico, Virginia, but
had returned to normal duty at his own request some
years ago. Widely respected throughout the Bureau,
Kaiser had spent the past few years based in New
Orleans, where he'd solved an art-related murder case
that made international news. Alex had tried to reach
Kaiser ten days ago, when she'd first realized what she
might be dealing with, but he hadn't returned her
calls. Agents at the New Orleans field office claimed
he was on an extended vacation with his wife, a
war photographer named Jordan Glass, so Alex had
dropped it.

"Alex, this is John," said Kaiser. "I'm only just now
getting back to you because I've been working under-
cover. I haven't even been able to contact Jordan for the
past six weeks. When I heard your messages, I couldn't

believe it. I want to hear what else you have. You've got my cell number. Call me anytime."

Alex tried to control the emotions welling up within her. There was enough relief to bring tears to her eyes. But then a terrible thought struck her: Kaiser had probably left that message before hearing that she'd been suspended.

She slumped down in the seat and cradled her face in her left hand. Of all the people in the world whose help she could have wished for, Kaiser was the man. Not only that, he owed her.

Two years ago, Kaiser had been taken hostage by a pair of New Orleans homicide detectives under investigation for murder. For decades the NOPD had been crippled by a system of graft so pervasive that it tarnished the city's national reputation. In the early 1990s, several Crescent City cops were convicted of murder, and the federal government almost took over the policing of the city. Ten years later, the corruption was still deep-rooted. Kaiser had been pursuing some detectives who were facilitating the flow of hard drugs into the city, when one of his informants wore a wire to a meeting in the French Quarter. The wire was discovered, and Kaiser burst in to try to prevent his informant from being killed. Kaiser himself was taken hostage, and the detectives barricaded themselves in an apartment on Royal Street. Alex had been doing some extra training in Atlanta at the time, but her rep within the Bureau was at its peak. A Bureau jet flew her to Lakefront Airport, which was right next door to the New Orleans field office, and then she was rushed to the French Quarter in the SAC's personal car. The negotiation lasted just seven hours, but her psychological duel with the sociopathic detectives proved the most grueling of her career. Twice during the ordeal she had believed that Kaiser was about to be executed, and once had even believed him dead. She learned later that one of the detectives had held his weapon to Kaiser's head and discharged it at a slight angle, which resulted in permanent hearing loss in the FBI agent's right ear but preserved his life. Kaiser had overheard the entire negotiation, and he gave Alex sole credit for saving his life. The two detectives were still serving out the sentences that resulted from the deal that ended the incident.

As Alex thought of Kaiser, she realized that a digital image had been downloading to her phone. After it finished, she studied the tiny screen with absolute concentration. Though the resolution was poor, the picture showed a nude blond woman standing with her elbows on a balcony rail, while a naked man thrust into her from behind. The woman was unmistakably Thora Shepard. The balcony glinted dull silver, as though made of steel, and its architectural look gave Alex the feeling she was seeing a balcony of the Alluvian Hotel. If a still photo carried this kind of punch, what would watching the video do to Thora's husband?

She took several deep breaths, then called John Kaiser's cell phone.

"Kaiser," he answered.

"It's Alex Morse, John."

He didn't respond at first. Then he said, "I heard what happened this morning. I'm sorry."

"Not a good day, amigo."

"Something's fucked up when this kind of thing goes down."

"I'm afraid you're the only one who thinks so."

"I doubt that. Do you plan to stop working your case?"

She hesitated. "Are you going to report anything I say today?"

"You know better than that."

"I can't stop, John. I know I'm right, and now the doctor who's the next target believes it, too. He started out skeptical, but now he knows. This case is crazy. You wouldn't believe the crime signature. It's a team scenario—a lawyer and a medical professional—and they're killing people by giving them cancer."

"Cancer," Kaiser said softly. "Alex, are you sure?"

She closed her eyes. "Positive."

"What's the motive?"

"I think it's mixed between the perpetrators. But at bottom, it's a divorce attorney saving rich clients millions of dollars by killing their spouses."

There was a long silence. "What exactly do you want me to do?"

"You're not supposed to do anything."

Dry laughter came through the ether. "Let's say I don't know that. What would you want me to do then?"

"Are you in New Orleans now?"

"*Sí.*"

"Drive up to Jackson, Mississippi. I'm on my way there now, nonstop flight. And, no, the Bureau doesn't know."

"What would we do at this meeting?"

"I want you to meet this doctor. Listen to him, then listen to me. I need your brain, John. Your experience with homicide. It's three hours by car. Please tell me you'll come."

After a long silence, Kaiser said, "Where do you want to meet?"

Alex suggested the Cabot Lodge near the University Medical Center. Kaiser said he could make no promises, but that he would try to be there. Then he hung up.

Energized by the prospect of Kaiser's assistance, she started to dial Chris. Then she remembered the balcony photograph. Chris would demand to see the video as soon as he heard of its existence. What would he do after he saw it? Drive to Shane Lansing's office and beat him senseless? Get drunk and simply shut down from despair? She had seen men react both ways, and there was no way to predict the reaction. Of course, she could "forget" to mention the photo when she asked Chris to meet Kaiser, but she would pay a price for that later. No . . . she should let Chris deal with the pain now. That way, by the time he got to Jackson, he might be as committed as she to nailing Andrew Rusk and his accomplice. Alex glanced around the cabin again, then speed-dialed Will Kilmer.

CHAPTER

35

Chris and Ben were sitting on the leather couch in Chris's medical office when the cell phone rang. Chris had taken eight hundred milligrams of ibuprofen, and his head was still pounding. Ben's headache was just as bad. Chris was starting to worry about food poisoning, but neither of them had any gastrointestinal symptoms.

"It's that hospital phone," Ben said. "Are you going to answer it?"

Truthfully, Chris didn't feel like it. But since there was no way Alex could have landed in Jackson yet, the call had to be important.

"Dr. Shepard," he answered for Ben's benefit.

"Chris," said Alex, "I need to talk to you. Are you alone?"

"Hang on." He touched Ben on the thigh. "You lie down here. I'm going to turn off the lights and go in my bathroom to take this call. Okay?"

Ben nodded dispiritedly.

Chris switched off the lights and stepped into his private cubicle. "Okay, go ahead."

"Will sent me a digital photograph a few minutes

ago. It's a still image captured from a videotape. He's probably e-mailing the video to your address right now. It's not something that you want to see, but you need to see it."

"What is it?" he asked, fear roiling his gut.

"It was shot last night at the Alluvian Hotel."

Chris wanted to curse, but Ben would pick up the fury in his voice, even through the door. He looked at himself in the bathroom mirror. His eyes looked like those of a stranger. "Okay, thanks," he heard himself say. "I'm going to check my e-mail."

"Can you stay on the phone while you do it?"

He rubbed the base of his throbbing skull. "I'd rather not. Is there anything else?"

"Yes. I need you to come to Jackson this afternoon. Tonight at the latest."

"Why?"

"To meet an FBI agent named John Kaiser. He's going to help us."

"Who is he?"

"One of the top agents in the Bureau. Kaiser's a specialist in serial murder."

"Why would he help you? I thought they fired you."

"They're going to. But Kaiser owes me big. Just watch the video, Chris. After you see that, you're going to want to do something. The best thing you can do is come to Jackson. You owe it to yourself, and to Ben."

"I can't go anywhere, even if I wanted to. Ben is sick. I had to pick him up from school."

"What's wrong with him?"

"He's got a headache. A bad one."

There was a pause. "You told me earlier that you had a headache, didn't you?"

"Yeah. Since this morning."

"Huh."

"I need to go, Alex." Chris hung up, pocketed the phone, and left the bathroom.

"Who was that?" asked Ben.

"A doctor in New York that I'm consulting on a case."

"A lady doctor?"

Chris sometimes forgot how acute the senses of children were compared to those of adults. "That's right. How's your head?"

"It still hurts. Where does she want you to go?"

"Jackson. I sent a patient up there."

Ben looked pensive. "Can we go home now?"

"Not yet, buddy." Chris sat beside him and looked at the screen saver on his computer. It showed Ben sliding into home plate during a game last year. The boy had already grown four inches and put on ten pounds. Chris squeezed Ben's arm. "Son, I need to bring a patient in here. Let's take you out to Mrs. Jane's office. You can play games on her insurance computer, okay?"

Ben shrugged apathetically.

Chris led him to the front office, then returned to his own. On the way back, Holly tried to steer him into one of the examining rooms, but he held up his hand to ward her off.

Back at his desk, he typed in his password and opened his e-mail account. The newest message had come from wkilmer@argusoperations.com. He opened the mail, which simply read, *I'm sorry, Doctor Shepard. Sincerely, Will Kilmer.* At the bottom of the message was an icon indicating that a file was attached. Chris opted to save the file to his hard drive. A little meter popped up on his screen, indicating the pace of the download. His blood pressure mounted in synchrony with the right-moving meter; then the process was complete, and he opened Windows Media Player.

He sat with his forefinger poised over the mouse button, painfully certain that opening this file would change his life forever. He felt like one of the patients who sat anxiously on the sofa across from his desk, afraid to ask for the test results on the sheet of paper in the doctor's hand. But there was no use putting it off, not in either case. There was nothing to be gained, and a hell of a lot to lose.

"Fuck it," he muttered, and opened the file.

First he saw only a steel balcony rail in what appeared to be an enclosed courtyard, shot from about twenty feet below it. A half-open French door stood behind the rail. The cheep of crickets came from Chris's computer speakers, but there was no other sound. Maybe the hum of an air conditioner. Then a woman's laughter shattered the silence, chilling Chris to the core of his being. Even before he saw her, he knew. A muffled female voice protested something, but not too seriously. Then the door flew inward, and Thora shot from the door to the balcony rail, as though she'd been pushed.

She was stark naked.

Squealing like a sorority girl at a Chippendales show, she tried to run back inside, but a man eclipsed in shadow barred the door. He grabbed her arms and spun her back to the rail. Chris's hands clenched into fists as Shane Lansing stepped onto the balcony, his penis jutting out from his body. Before Thora could turn again, he grabbed her hips and plunged into her from behind. She gasped, squealed once more, then gripped the rail and braced herself against his thrusts. Her muscles stood out in stark relief as she endured what quickly became a brutal onslaught, her mouth hanging open, her eyes almost bulging from her head. Chris had seen her look that way during the final kick of a marathon, when she tested the very limits of her endurance. She began to grunt in time to Lansing's lunging hips, her face more animal than human. When she began to moan, her cat-like howls reverberating off the courtyard walls, Chris glanced worriedly at his office door. He reached for the volume knob on his speakers, but before he could turn it, Lansing covered Thora's mouth with his hand, yanked back her head, and began pounding her taut abdomen against the rail. As Chris waited for the inevitable climax, a wave of nausea suddenly overcame the shock that had held him rooted to his chair. He jumped up and ran into his private bathroom, where he dropped to his knees and ejected what remained of his lunch into the toilet.

"Dr. Shepard?" called a female voice. Holly, his nurse.

By the time he got back to his desk, the screen had mercifully gone black. "What is it?" he called, knowing his face was probably red with anger.

"Are you all right?"

"Yeah, come in."

He got up and stepped back into his bathroom, where he wet a towel and wiped his face. "I'm just feeling a little tired."

"I don't blame you. All that baseball at night. I'm worn slap out myself."

When Chris looked back, Holly was sitting in front of his computer, fanning herself with a magazine. If she clicked his mouse, the balcony video would start to roll. He moved behind her and squeezed her shoulders, which surprised her, but which also got her out of the chair more quickly. His only thought was getting back into that chair to extinguish the possibility of the nightmare being displayed again.

"I've been looking for those results on Mrs. Young," Holly said. "Have you seen them?"

"No."

She studied him without speaking. Then, hesitantly, she said, "Nancy finished with Mr. Martin's X-rays. He's been waiting in room three for a good while."

"I'm coming!" Chris snapped.

Holly's mouth dropped open. She turned and left without a word.

Some morbid part of him wanted to reopen the video file, but he resisted the urge. His mind was filled with images dating to the day he had first noticed Thora Rayner on a ward in St. Catherine's Hospital. The video now residing on his hard drive seemed incomprehensible in light of all they had done since that day. How could the woman who had so devotedly cared for her dying husband so casually betray a man who loved her as Chris did? How could she throw away a father who had bonded so deeply with her son? It was beyond him. The denial that had slowly been crumbling since Alex Morse's arrival finally lay in ruins at his feet. Yet anger had not replaced it. He had moved directly into grief, an unbearably heavy pall that brought with it paralyzing numbness.

His cell phone was ringing again. Alex, of course. He picked up the phone but did not answer, a juvenile response. He couldn't afford paralysis. Any moment now Holly would knock at the door again. *Patients waiting.* He also had Ben up front, playing computer games but wanting more than anything to go home with his dad. *His dad?* Chris thought. *I'm not his dad. Not really. He's not flesh of my flesh. I've legally adopted him, but what would happen in a divorce? I know what Ben would want, as crazy as that seems. Even Thora has attributed his newfound happiness and improved grades to having me in his life. But what would a judge say?*

The cell stopped ringing. As though moving underwater, Chris opened the clamshell phone and pressed the button that would connect him to Alex. She answered on the first ring.

"Are you all right?" she asked. "I know seeing that was rough."

"Yep."

"I'm so sorry, Chris."

"Are you?"

"Of course. All I care about in this is you and Ben."

"That's not true. You want to nail Andrew Rusk."

This gave her pause. "Well, yes, but not out of some cheap sense of vengeance. It's for Grace, and for you, and for all the other people whose lives have been destroyed."

Chris said nothing. He waited for a fresh sales pitch, but none came. Alex waited in silence as well. He was about to speak when she said, "Whatever you do, please don't tell Thora what you know."

"Stop worrying. We already talked about that."

"But it's different now. Isn't it? Listen to me, Chris. I'm assuming you want to be the one Ben lives with when this is all over?"

He remained silent.

"I'm not just an FBI agent, you know. I'm also a lawyer. And the best way to ensure that you get custody of Ben is to make sure Thora is punished for attempted murder."

Anger flooded through him. "I'm supposed to help Ben by putting his mother in jail?"

"In a word? Yes."

"That's great, Alex."

"There's something else. Something that's scaring me."

"What is it?"

"You and Ben both have headaches, right?"

"Yes."

"Uncle Will has one, too. A bad one."

Chris thought about this.

"He's had it since this morning," Alex continued. "He took some aspirin, but it won't go away."

A strange buzzing started in Chris's head.

"Did you hear me?"

"I heard you."

"What do you think?"

"I don't like it."

"It seemed like too much coincidence to me, too. But I don't see what could have happened. I mean, Will was guarding you all night, right?"

"He was passed out in my easy chair all night."

"*What?*"

"He drank three beers and went out like a light."

"Shit."

A sudden image of Alex's room at the Days Inn flashed into Chris's mind: the wounded coral snake writhing in the bathroom, the dead cat lying on the floor. "Alex, is there anything I need to know that you haven't told me?"

Another pause.

"Goddamn it, what are you holding back?"

"Nothing. I just—"

"Tell me!"

"I spoke to Will again, right before I called you. His detective found out how Lansing has been getting here and back. There's a small charter service out at the local airport. Crop dusters mostly, but the local farmers use it to fly to Houston and Memphis, stuff like that. Lansing called from Natchez a few days ago and arranged to get round-trip flights from the Natchez airport to Greenwood and back. He flies in there after dark and flies out about dawn. He's been commuting to—"

"Screw Thora's brains out."

"Pretty much, yeah."

"Is her girlfriend even up there? Laura Canning?"

"Yes. She's covering for Thora."

Chris slammed his hand down on his desk. Anger was finally coming to the surface. "God*damn* it!"

"Chris, wait. Hold on a sec."

"What?"

"Will's calling me back. It must be important."

She clicked him into hold mode. The wait seemed to stretch forever. "Chris?" she said, after another click.

"Yeah."

"There's more, and it's bad."

Some deep part of him tensed against the unknown. "Tell me."

"Will has been checking into Shane Lansing's business affairs. You know Lansing has his hand in a lot of stuff, right?"

"Yeah. Truck stops with gambling, restaurants, nursing homes, all kinds of shit."

"Well, it seems he's also part owner of a radiation oncology clinic in Meridian, Mississippi. The Humanity Cancer Care Center."

Chris felt as though his core temperature had dropped ten degrees. "Are you kidding?"

"No. Will just found this out."

"But that means Lansing has access to—"

"I know. Cesium pellets, liquid iodine, radiation-treatment machinery—everything."

"But . . . you told me these crimes go back like five years. Right?"

"Yes."

"Then how could Lansing be a part of it? I mean, if Thora just went to see Andrew Rusk a couple of weeks ago, how could Rusk possibly have found Lansing and hired him to kill me in that time? The time frame doesn't make sense."

"Thora's an atypical client for Rusk," said Alex. "There've only been two other female clients that I know about—"

"Wait," Chris cut in. *"Red Simmons."*

"Exactly. Thora may have used Andrew Rusk three years ago, to have Red Simmons killed. If so, she first contacted Rusk at *least* three years ago, and possibly as long as seven. She could have even met Shane Lansing through Rusk."

"But Red didn't die of cancer."

"Neither did my sister."

Chris's thoughts were tumbling over themselves, but beneath the rational level of his mind something else was happening. Fear and anger were melding into a kind of dark desperation whose only outlet could be action. "What time did you say this friend of yours would be in Jackson?"

"As soon as he can get there," said Alex, relief suffusing her voice. "If you leave within the hour, you'll probably get there the same time Kaiser does."

"Good."

"You're coming?"

"Oh, yeah."

"Thank you, Chris."

"Don't thank me. This is survival now."

Alex started to say something, but he hung up and put the phone in his desk drawer. After closing his e-mail account, he walked down to Tom's end of the clinic. Tom's chief nurse, Melba Price, was standing outside the door to Exam Room 7. Melba was quick to read nonverbal clues in patients and colleagues alike. This skill had made her Tom's right hand for more than twenty years.

"I need to see him, Melba," Chris said. "As soon as possible."

"He's just finishing up." She gave Chris a sidelong glance. "I heard about you and Dr. Lansing."

Chris grimaced.

"None of my business," Melba went on, "but a lot of people's been wanting to do what you did for a long time."

Tom Cage's good-humored baritone reverberated through the heavy wooden door. Chris heard the squeak of a chair, a booming farewell, and then Tom stepped into the hall, surprise on his face. "Hey, slugger," he said. "What's up?"

"I need to talk to you."

"Let's go in my office."

Chris shook his head. "Do you have an exam room open?"

Tom looked at Melba.

"Number five," she said.

Chris led the way. After Tom closed the door, he looked at his young partner with paternal concern. "What's going on, Chris? I didn't mean to tease you about Lansing. He's just such an unmitigated prick."

Chris looked back at his mentor, realizing perhaps for the first time how much older Tom Cage really was. Tom had started practicing medicine in 1958. He'd grown up in an era when antibiotics did not exist, yet he'd lived to practice in the era of the PET scan and gene therapy.

"I need you to do me a favor, Tom. No questions asked."

The older man nodded soberly. "Name it."

"I want you to examine me. My whole body."

"What am I looking for? Are you having symptoms?"

Tom was thinking what Chris would be thinking in the same situation. Most doctors at some time in their life suspect that they're dying of a terminal illness. They know too much, see too much, and even the slightest symptom can bring on fears of fatal disease.

"I've got a severe headache," Chris said, "but that's not really the problem. I have reason to suspect . . . something. I want you to go over every inch of my body with a light. Even a magnifying glass, if you need it."

"What am I looking for?"

"Anything abnormal. A needle mark, a bruise, a lesion, a small incision. I want you to start inside my mouth."

Tom stared at him for a long time. Chris could almost see the questions turning inside his mind. But in the end Tom only said, "You'd better strip and get on the table."

While Chris removed his clothes, Tom donned a leather headpiece with a light mounted on it. Chris climbed onto the examining table and lay on his back.

"My eyes aren't what they used to be," said Tom. "But I found a melanoma yesterday, so tiny you wouldn't believe it. Start in your mouth, you say?"

Chris opened wide.

Tom took a tongue depressor from a jar and used it to expose Chris's gums and mucosa. Then he took a small mirror from a drawer and, cursing quietly, began to check Chris's mouth.

"Goddamn it," Tom muttered. "This is like spelunking."

Chris made a guttural sound of acknowledgment.

"Looks clear to me." Tom withdrew the tongue depressor. "Remember to floss after every meal."

Chris was in no mood for levity, but Tom gave him a wry look anyway.

"Okay, what now?"

"Look under my hair," Chris said, flashing back to Gregory Peck in *The Omen.*

As Tom carefully worked his way across Chris's scalp, he said, "I don't see anything but incipient male-pattern baldness."

"Good. Now my skin. Every inch of it."

Tom started at Chris's neck and moved down his trunk. "I'm glad you're not a hairy bastard," he said, moving the light across Chris's sternum. "Okay . . . getting to the family jewels now."

"Every crack and crevice." Chris felt Tom's gloved

hands lift his testicles, then check his penis. "The hole, too."

"Jesus."

Tom checked him there, then moved back to his shoulders. He checked both underarms, then the extremities.

"Between my toes, too."

"This reminds me of my internship," Tom said. "I worked several months in the Orleans Parish Prison. The cops used to have me check between suspects' toes for needle marks."

"Same deal," Chris said, turning onto his stomach.

"Let's get the worst over first," Tom said, and Chris felt cold hands pulling his cheeks apart. He expected Tom to release them immediately, but he didn't.

"What do you see?"

"I'm not sure," Tom murmured. "Looks like maybe an injection site."

Chris's breath died in his throat. "Are you serious?"

"Afraid so. Looks like somebody stuck in a needle and you tried to jerk away. Like a scared toddler, you know? There's definite bruising."

"Outside the anus or in?"

"Right at the opening. This is weird, Chris. Are you going to tell me what's going on?"

Chris got off the table and pulled on his pants. "We need to check Ben, too."

Tom's eyes went wide. *"What?"*

"I'm dead serious. He's in the front office now. Ben has the same headache I do. I'll tell him we're checking for pinworms."

Tom stared at Chris as though worried he might be drunk.

"I'm not crazy, Tom. I wish I was. Will you stay in here with me while I check Ben?"

I'm sure as hell not leaving you alone with him, said Tom's eyes.

Chris skidded into the driveway at the Elgin house, his heart pounding with anger and fear. On the passenger seat beside him was a wooden case he'd borrowed from the radiologist at St. Catherine's Hospital. The image of Ben lying on his back on the exam table haunted him even more than the video of Thora on the hotel balcony. *What are you looking for?* Ben had asked. Chris had lied, and Tom had lied to cover for him. But there was no banishing the look of disapproval on the older physician's face. Tom Cage suspected something seriously irregular, and in the same situation Chris probably would have, too. He would have to rely on the goodwill he had built up over nine months of practicing with Tom to carry the day.

After checking Ben for marks and not finding them, Chris had put the boy back in his receptionist's care and shut himself in his office. He had no idea what might have been injected into him, but the thing that kept coming back to him was Alex's revelation that Shane Lansing had access to radioactive materials. Added to this was Pete Connolly's assertion that radiation would be the easiest method of intentionally causing cancer in a human being. Given those two facts, what did the needle mark near his rectum mean? Had a radioactive liquid been injected into him? Or could pellets small enough to pass through a needle have been shot into his bloodstream? He tried to recall what Connolly had said about irradiated thallium being used to assassinate someone, but it was difficult to concentrate with fear ballooning in his chest.

Forcing himself under control, Chris walked down the hall to the X-ray room and asked Nancy Somers, their tech, to shoot an X-ray of his midsection. Nancy looked nonplussed by this request, but she wasn't about to refuse her employer. Chris grabbed a paper gown, stripped beside the big machine, then donned the oversize napkin and climbed onto the cold table. Nancy adjusted the voltage, then shot the picture. Two minutes later, Chris was jamming the X-ray into the clip of the light-box in the viewing room.

"What are you looking for?" Tom asked from behind him.

"Overexposure."

Chris could hardly speak as he scanned the X-ray. He was terrified of seeing black spots caused by radioactive emissions overexposing the film. Yet though he squinted at every inch of the film, he saw nothing abnormal.

"Looks fine to me," Tom said. "Does this have to do with the needle mark?"

Chris nodded. Then he felt Tom's hand on his shoulder.

"What's going on, son? Talk to me."

There was no hiding it anymore. Chris turned to his partner and said, "Somebody's trying to kill me, Tom."

After a shocked silence, Tom said, "Who?"

"Thora."

The older man's eyes narrowed. "Can you substantiate that?"

"No. But I'm working with an FBI agent to prove it."

Tom nodded slowly. "Is Shane Lansing tied up in this somehow?"

"I believe so. Did you know that he owns part of a radiation oncology center in Meridian?"

As Tom shook his head, Chris saw the old doc's mind working quickly behind his wise eyes. It wouldn't take him long to connect the dots.

"Sounds to me like you need some time off," Tom said.

Chris gratefully shook Tom's hand, then collected Ben and a few other things and left the office. His headache was still going strong, but Ben's had started to subside. The boy wanted to stay with his dad, of course, but Chris insisted on dropping him at Mrs. Johnson's house. The widow had cared for Ben since before Thora married Chris, and she loved him like her own. She promised to keep Ben overnight if necessary; all Chris had to do was call. He left a bottle of Advil and a stronger analgesic with her just in case Ben's headache returned.

Now that he'd arrived at the Elgin house, he charged inside with the wooden case he'd borrowed from the hospital. Cutting into the laundry room, he opened his toolbox and took out a razor-sharp Buck knife. With the knife and a pair of pliers in one hand, and the case in the other, he ran back to the master bedroom.

First he tore the bedclothes off the king-size bed, exposing the pillow-top mattress beneath. With his eyes only six inches from the cover, he examined the entire surface of the mattress, focusing on his side of the bed. He saw no sign of tampering, but that meant nothing. Kneeling beside the bed, he opened the wooden case he'd brought from St. Catherine's. Inside was a Geiger counter borrowed from the radiology department at the hospital. The radiologist had told him that, aside from checking for "spills" after certain procedures, the counter was supposed to double for civil defense use after a nuclear attack.

Chris switched on the counter, dreading the click-click-click that would herald the presence of radioactivity, but the machine only emitted a faint hum. The Geiger counter had a carrying handle and a wand attached to it by a flexible cable. Chris moved the wand over the entire surface of the bed, but he heard no clicks.

Setting the counter aside, he stabbed the Buck knife into the mattress at the spot where his head would normally lie and ripped it open from head to foot. Using the teeth of the pliers, he tore through dense foam padding, throwing chunks of it around the bedroom, but again he found nothing.

Sweating and exasperated, he stared around the room. *Where would they put it?* he wondered. *Where would I get sufficient exposure?* He picked up the Geiger counter and ran down the hall to the den, to the easy chair where Will Kilmer had spent the night in beer-induced slumber. The Buck knife made short work of the chair seat, but when Chris passed the wand over the wreckage that remained, he heard nothing. He realized then that he had almost been hoping for the telltale click.

Why? he asked himself. *Because nothing is worse than not knowing.*

That was his problem. He had no idea what the needle mark meant. Had someone injected something merely to sedate him while they violated him in some other way? That might be the answer, given that Ben and Kilmer both had headaches, too. Yet Chris had found no needle mark on Ben. Had Ben's injection site simply been more successfully concealed? Or had they all been sedated in some other way, while only Chris was attacked through hypodermic injection? He had no way to know. Not without sophisticated medical testing.

The only poison he was likely to discover on his own was radiation. And Lansing's tie to the radiation clinic in Meridian increased the odds that radiation was the method of attack. Chris stared around the kitchen, his mind spinning. *Could it be in the shower?* Sometimes he sat for half an hour on the shower seat, relaxing under a near-scalding stream of water, but . . . No, they would have had to dig out a tile to plant a pellet there.

Then it hit him: *My truck!*

He ran out to the garage and held the wand of the Geiger counter over the driver's seat of his pickup. All he heard was a steady hum. He wanted to rip open the seat anyway, but he knew that was pointless. If there was enough radiation to give him cancer in that seat, the Geiger counter would have detected it.

He started to switch off the machine, but an almost paralyzing terror stopped him. Nancy had only shot an X-ray of his trunk. What if the radiation source had been placed elsewhere? Near a marrow reservoir in his femur, say? Or what if it was moving through his body? Standing in his garage, Chris stripped naked, then held the wand at his feet and began moving up along each leg. What would he do if the machine started clicking? Probably cut out the offending pellet with the Buck knife, unless he could somehow muster the patience to drive back to the office and have Tom cut it out using local anesthetic. Despite the normal X-ray, he felt himself tense when he came to his genitals and rectum. . . . *No click.*

Almost unwilling to believe the silence, he kept moving north until he reached his scalp. Then he switched off the machine.

He felt like puking. Some childish part of him wanted to believe that it was all bullshit, that Alex Morse was as crazy as a road lizard. But Tom had found *something.* And Chris had seen Shane Lansing screwing Thora on that balcony. And Lansing was part owner of a radiation oncology center. And then there were the headaches: three out of three people on the same day. That couldn't be coincidence. There was no escaping the truth: Grace Fennell's killer had struck again last night.

His victim was Chris Shepard.

CHAPTER
36

Neville Byrd lay on the bed in his hotel room and stared openmouthed at the screen of his notebook computer. He was masturbating. Thanks to the scope he'd mounted on the Marriott's roof, he could watch Andrew Rusk's secretary lying spread-eagled on Rusk's desk, while the lawyer pounded her for all he was worth. This was light-years better than the pay-per-view porn flickering on his TV screen. This was *real*. And he was getting it all on videotape. He made a mental note to dub himself a copy for later whack use before he gave the original to Dr. Traver.

The secretary got off the desk, turned her back to Rusk, and leaned over the wood. Rusk took hold of her hips, went into her, and continued his attack. The guy must be angry at her, Neville thought, the way he was hammering her. Relentless, man. Neville had never fucked like that, personally. He wasn't sure he could. Rusk was one of those guys who worked out all the time, went surfing, mountain climbing, the works. Maybe all that shit paid off during sex.

Because this was marathon stuff. Forty-five minutes without a break, not even a pause for water.

Then suddenly it was over. Rusk pulled out of her and walked out of the frame, leaving the secretary to mop herself up with Kleenex from the desk. Neville yanked for all he was worth and brought himself to a screaming climax before she could vanish, too.

Sure enough, the secretary soon limped out of the frame. Rusk reappeared, fully dressed again. He sat at his keyboard and checked his watch. Then he lifted his right hand and started working his mouse. A few clicks, and then he typed several strokes on his keyboard.

Neville checked his other computer, the one giving the readout from the laser rig. Then he began to laugh. Rusk had typed in pi to the ninth decimal place, a password Neville could appreciate. He recorded a few more seconds, then rewound the image and zoomed in on Rusk's monitor. He saw what looked like a black hole—or the event horizon surrounding one. Then this image was replaced by the gateway of a Web site he had seen yesterday: EX NIHILO.

"Boo-ya!" Neville shouted. He had pegged EX NIHILO yesterday, but he'd needed another day to confirm his suspicion. Now Andrew Rusk was entering a deeper level of the site, and typing another password to confirm his identity. This was the key to the mechanism that Rusk had created to protect himself. Neville was tempted to log into EX NIHILO himself and do a little scoping, but Traver had told him not to waste a moment. As he dialed the number the vet had given him, he was tempted to press for a higher fee. After all, he was holding the cards now. What did he have to lose? Traver was just a gray-bearded old veterinarian. But then again . . . he had known about the laser and the scope. Your average puppy doctor didn't know that kind of shit. Such knowledge pointed to something else. Something in the intelligence line, or even the military.

Nah, Neville thought. *I'll take my money and boogie. After all, he's already paying double rates.*

Eldon Tarver sat alone in his office at the University Medical Center, studying numbers on a stack of paper in front of him. His research assistant had given him the most recent data on the in vitro testing, and all it did was point up the inherent shortcomings of laboratory-based research. But only part of Dr. Tarver's mind was occupied with this problem. On a deeper level, he was working out his next move. He had received several false spams from Andrew Rusk, the "Viagra ads" that constituted their agreed signal for a meeting at the Annandale Golf Club. But Dr. Tarver had not gone to the club. Nor had he driven the forty-five miles to Chickamauga Hunting Camp, despite the aluminum foil glinting brightly from the sixteenth-floor window of the AmSouth tower since yesterday.

He chuckled at the idea of Andrew Rusk standing in the oppressive heat of Chickamauga, waiting for someone who would never arrive. Rusk was probably freaking out because he had pitched the new potential client he had boasted about. Rusk lived for money, for the status he believed it conferred on him, and he would do anything to get it. Even with the risk quotient rising daily, all he could think about was the next big score.

Dr. Tarver knew that score would never happen.

Their collaboration was over. Christopher Shepard's injection marked the end. Eldon would have liked to have another year or so, but there was no use crying about it. It was time to move on. He was already shutting down the primate lab. The dog-breeding facility he would sell; he'd had a buyer waiting in the wings for some time. Only one problem remained.

Rusk himself.

For five years now, Dr. Tarver and the lawyer had had an escape plan in place, one that would allow them to leave the United States and live in safety and relative luxury for the rest of their lives. The only problem with that plan—until recently—was that when it came right down to it, neither of them wanted to leave the United States. The heyday of nonextradition havens such as Costa Rica and Tenerife was long past. The diplomatic corps had been working like a busy little beehive to sew up every loophole that allowed tax evaders to flee to island paradises, and by so doing they had also closed the doors to criminals of other stripes. Andrew Rusk's Jimmy Buffett fantasy of frozen margaritas and willing señoritas had died a quick death as soon as they looked into it for real. Sure there were still places that wouldn't play ball with Uncle Sam—hellholes like Mali or Chad or Burundi. But if you wanted to commit lucrative crimes and get away in style, you had to be creative.

Using intelligence connections that dated back to the late 1960s, Dr. Tarver had worked out a one-of-a-kind deal for the two of them, a deal worthy of a greedy lawyer's fantasy. But *not* worthy of a dedicated scientist. Not anymore. Dr. Tarver's primary goal was not spending his accumulated funds in the most hedonistic way imaginable. He had ongoing research projects to maintain, and he preferred to remain in the United States to do that. After all, his in vivo subjects resided in the U.S. Moreover, five years of working with Andrew Rusk had convinced him that he never wanted to see the lawyer again. Rusk was an accident waiting to happen. Eldon could see him sitting at a bar with an umbrella drink in his hand, bragging to some expatriate real estate developer or record company exec about how he had saved the rich and famous millions by snuffing their wives. No thanks.

The irony was, Eldon had always had a choice of escape routes. There had always been countries ready and willing to pay him to work for them. Some of the offers had been quite tempting. The money was staggering, and as for government interference . . . forget it. The only problem with that scenario was that Eldon Tarver was a patriot. And the countries who wanted to pay for his services were simply the wrong ones.

Eldon remembered a time when the research climate in America had been supportive, a golden age when government and industry and the military had worked hand in hand. But now you had shrieking Ivy League brats throwing cans of red paint on scientists who might someday save their pathetic lives. It made him homicidally angry to think about it.

There were still a few people in the corridors of power who remembered how it used to be—and how it would be in the future. And the golden age *would* inevitably return, because war was eternal. Cyclical, maybe, but eternal. And *real* war, not shitty little "conflicts" like Iraq or Afghanistan. All-out war that put the holy motherland at risk, that amped up even heart-on-their-sleeve liberals until they were ready to bayonet any bastard who came over the wire. And when people got like that, the research climate got very favorable very fast.

Edward Biddle remembered the good old days, and not merely with nostalgia. Biddle worked tirelessly to prepare for the day when things went bad again. It had been *Major* Biddle when he worked with Dr. Tarver at the VCP. The major had been a liaison, of sorts, between the army, corporate America, and academia. He had eventually risen to the rank of general, long after the project was terminated, of course. After retirement Biddle had joined the TransGene Corporation, one of the many granddaughters of Bering Biomedical, the chief corporate beneficiary of the VCP, the project that had brought Tarver and Biddle together.

Five years they had worked side by side. Longer, if you counted the prep work and dismantling of the project. They had accomplished some miraculous things, too, despite the fact that the technology just wasn't there yet. They hadn't lacked for ideas. But so much of the technology they'd needed to bring the ideas to fruition had simply not yet been invented. Sequencing the human genome had been a pipe dream in 1969. Even in 1974, when the army got some real control in the project, successfully mapping the genome lay more than a quarter century in the future. Yet still . . . they had accomplished so much.

Dr. Tarver looked over at his Wall of Respect, where a picture of him and Biddle hung. Biddle was wearing his major's uniform, Tarver a white coat with VCP emblazoned on its breast. In the background stood one of the lab buildings at Fort Detrick, Maryland. The VCP had started as an academic project, but they had eventually moved everything to Detrick. It was the only place that could handle the risks.

There was a woman in the picture with them: a leggy blonde named Wyck. She had represented Bering at Detrick, unusual for a woman in those days. Degrees in microbiology and statistical analysis, no less. Eldon had lusted after her until he figured out that Biddle was banging her. Quite a shock at the time, he recalled. But understandable. Wyck was fascinated by power, and Biddle had it. A free rein, within certain limits. Wyck had possessed power of her own, and you could see that in the picture. Her eyes shone with confidence, and her face practically glowed with energy, with pleasure at being there in that place at that time, bookended by two men who wanted her in their beds.

Dr. Tarver started at the sound of his cell phone. He stared a few moments longer at the photo, one of many on the Wall, then looked down at the caller ID and answered, "Dr. Traver."

"It's Neville Byrd, Doctor."

"Yes?"

"I've got it, sir. I mean, I think I do."

"Got what?"

"The thing Rusk is doing to protect himself. Two days in a row, near the end of the day, he's logged on to this one Web site and entered a series of passwords. All at the same site."

Dr. Tarver's pulse quickened. "Did you record his keystrokes?"

"Yes, sir. Every one."

"Fax them to me."

"Are you at the fax number you gave me?"

"No. Take this down." Dr. Tarver read off the fax number of his university office. "Do you have that?"

"Yes, sir. I'll send the keystrokes through. But I can give you the site right now, if you want to check it out. It's called EX NIHILO. It's a Dutch site, and it exists solely to let people be anonymous on the Net."

"This sounds very promising."

"Yes, sir. And Dr. Traver?"

"Yes?"

"This guy Rusk is screwing his secretary's brains out."

"Is he?"

Neville's voice changed. "I thought you might want to know that."

"Thank you. Please send the data through."

"Coming up, sir."

Dr. Tarver chuckled as he hung up.

Ten seconds later he was staring at the black hole that welcomed visitors to the world of EX NIHILO. One click took him to a page that listed the company's available services. It was obvious that EX NIHILO could handle the kind of arrangement that Eldon suspected Rusk was paying them to handle. If the price was right, of course. Thirty seconds later, Neville Byrd's fax came through. Two pages of keystrokes: the keys to Andrew Rusk's life.

"My God," said Dr. Tarver, using Rusk's passwords to retrace the lawyer's digital footsteps. It was just as he had suspected. Each day Rusk would log on to the site and verify his existence by entering a sequence of passwords. If he failed to do this for ten consecutive days, EX NIHILO would forward the contents of a large digital file to the Mississippi State Police and to the FBI.

Eldon tried to open the file, but the site refused to allow it. He cursed and tried again.

No dice.

He needed a separate password to open the file. Obviously Rusk had not accessed the file since creating it, which meant that Neville's laser system had been unable to record him opening it. Without the password, Eldon could not delete the file.

It doesn't matter, he told himself. As long as he logged on to EX NIHILO once a day—as Andrew Rusk—the system would not send out its destructive file, and he would remain safe. He could kill Andrew Rusk five minutes from now, and nothing would happen to him.

Eldon laughed. It started as a chuckle, then grew in his chest to a rolling, heaving barrel of laughter. EX NIHILO changed everything. By faxing him those passwords, an out-of-work software engineer named Neville Byrd had cut the thread holding the sword above his head. With those passwords in his possession, Eldon could write Andrew Rusk right out of his plans. *Or,* he thought with an unexpected thrill, *I could rewrite them with a much different ending.*

From the beginning, Eldon had demanded his fee in uncut diamonds. Rusk had groused at first, but he soon realized the wisdom of this system of payment. Unlike cash, rough diamonds were immune to both fire and water. They could be buried for years. If they had not been engraved with ID numbers in their source country, they could not be traced. Any cash deposit over $10,000 had to be reported to the IRS, but you could carry $10,000 worth of uncut diamonds in your mouth without detection, and more elsewhere in your body without discomfort. You could hold millions of dollars' worth in a safe-deposit box, but why risk it? You could bury them in your backyard and no one could ever deny you access to them with a judicial writ. Best of all, when it came time to move them, they looked like rocks. A box of rocks!

Eldon laughed again. He'd built up quite a rock collection over the past five years. Rusk had, too, albeit a smaller one. Rusk had taken his early payments in the form of inclusion in the business deals of his wealthy clients. He'd thought this was a brilliant stroke that could keep him on the legitimate side of the IRS. And he was right, to that extent. Rusk paid taxes on the earnings, and that kept the IRS off his back. It did not, however, make what he had done to earn those profits legal. And as the business connections multiplied, so accrued his traceable connections to a list of murders. And that, Eldon was almost sure, was what had brought Special Agent Alex Morse down on their backs.

Rusk had realized the error of his ways after a couple of years. He, too, had started taking his fee in uncut diamonds. Now and then he accepted a business deal as payment, as with the Fennell deal. But he had quite a box of rocks built up by now, as well. The only question was, where did he keep them? If Eldon could learn the answer to that question, he could make the transition to his next life as a much richer man. He would be a fool not to add Rusk's stash to his own if he could.

And I can, he thought with satisfaction. *Rusk doesn't have the sand to hold out under duress. All that mountain climbing and skydiving and running marathons won't add up to five minutes of guts in the face of true pain.*

It was time for drastic measures. It was time to call in his markers—all of them. And that meant Edward Biddle. Eldon hadn't spoken to Biddle in over two years, not since the TransGene man had delivered the gas canisters to him. Biddle seemed to feel that the less he knew, the safer he was. Still, the gas delivery had made one thing clear. Biddle was living up to his promise to "take care of my people." And "his people" were, of course, the former staff members of the VCP. Not everyone, but the dedicated few who had understood the true relationship between technology and life. Every scientific discovery was a two-edged sword. A scalpel could cut out a patient's tumor or slit his carotid artery. Morphine could extinguish pain or extinguish life. A viral infection could deliver lifesaving gene therapy or cause a global holocaust. It was the responsibility of some to discover and develop those potentialities; others would make decisions about how to use them. Eldon had always understood his place in this hierarchy, and Edward Biddle had valued him for that.

He flipped through the Rolodex on his desktop—he still preferred it to a computer-based organizer—and found Biddle's card. *Edward Biddle, Vice President, TransGene Corporation.* And below that: *America Leading the World.* Dr. Tarver loved them for that, for having the balls to put it right on the card in the so-called Age of Globalization. But TransGene could say it and dare anyone to gripe about it. Microbiology was one arena in which America had kept its competitive lead. Look at the Koreans and their cloning scam: *Our cloning works better because we keep human beings in our labs to babysit the cells every night.* Who did they think they were kidding with that warm-and-fuzzy bullshit? Sure enough, the truth had finally come out, as it always did in science. You could bluff for a while, but not forever. And therein lay the cruel beauty of science; there was nothing warm and fuzzy about it. Science was truth. And truth didn't care a fig for morality. Dr. Tarver dialed the number on Edward Biddle's card. It rang twice, and then a clipped voice accustomed to command answered.

"This is Biddle."

"This is Eldon Tarver, General."

An irony-laced laugh came down the line. "Hello, Doctor. What can I do for you?"

"It's time for me to relocate."

A brief pause. "Do you have a destination in mind?"

"I'd like to remain in-country."

"I see."

"I'm almost certain to require a new identity."

"I understand." Not a moment's hesitation. A good sign. "I know you've been doing research at the University of Mississippi Medical Center. I've been following that, off and on. It's interesting stuff, as far as it goes, but I can't help but feel you're not making full use of your talents there."

It was Tarver's turn to laugh. "The regulations on research are pretty claustrophobic these days. For that reason, I've been carrying out some private studies for some time. Five years, to be exact."

"Interesting. In what area?"

"Very similar to what we were doing at the VCP."

"Is that so?" Deep interest now.

"Yes, sir. You might say I picked up where we left off. Only this time, I had the equipment I needed."

"*Very* interesting."

"Yes, sir. And, ah, these are not in vitro experiments I'm talking about. These are in vivo studies."

"Primate studies?" Biddle asked.

"*Higher* primates, sir. Exclusively."

"I'm very intrigued, Eldon. I have a feeling your work might dovetail nicely with some things our more adventurous people have been doing at TransGene."

"Like-minded colleagues would be a nice change."

"I expect so. What sort of time frame do you have in mind for your relocation?"

"Two or three days, if possible. Maybe sooner."

A brief pause. "That's certainly possible. You and I should speak face-to-face. If I flew down in the next couple of days, could we meet?"

Eldon smiled with satisfaction. Biddle had taken the bait. Now he need only set the hook, and that he would do face-to-face. "Absolutely, sir."

"Good. I'll call you later."

"Thank you, sir."

"You, too, Eldon. It's good to be working with you again."

"You, too."

Dr. Tarver hung up, then logged into his anonymous e-mail account and sent Rusk a copy of their *CHEAP VIAGRA! CHEAP!* spam. In it, below the ad pitch, he inserted the line *Satisfy the youngest CHICKs!* The word *chick* in all caps meant that Rusk should meet him tomorrow at the Chickamauga Hunting Club rather than the Annandale Golf Club. It was Dr. Tarver's version of Reynolds Wrap in a window: his crisis code.

After logging out of the account, he removed Biddle's card from his Rolodex and put it in his pocket. Then he folded the faxed pages that Neville Byrd had sent him and slid them into the same pocket. His whole future in a single pocket. Only one threat to that future existed: Andrew Rusk. Without Rusk, Alex Morse could not connect Eldon Tarver to any crime. And by tomorrow night—if Biddle lived up to Eldon's expectations—Rusk would be dead, and his cache of diamonds would be part of Eldon Tarver's unreported-asset portfolio. Eldon stood and went into the hall, then locked his office and walked down the corridor to see the chief of Oncology.

CHAPTER

37

Alex was alone as she rode the elevator to the fifth floor of the University Medical Center, her excitement at the possibility of John Kaiser's help exploded by Chris's news that he'd probably been injected with something during the night. Since Kaiser was still an hour south of Jackson, and since UMC was practically across the street from the Cabot Lodge, she'd decided to visit her mother.

When the elevator doors opened, she walked down to the adult oncology wing: not a place of gladness, despite the efforts of families and nurses to nurture a hopeful atmosphere. Alex was thankful that the pediatric cases had their own hospital; she might not have been able to endure them in her present emotional state.

She found her mother much as she had left her two days ago. Her liver was larger, her skin yellower, her kidneys deader, her belly more bloated. Her ovarian cancer had proved atypical, invading areas and organs usually spared by that disease—yet still she clung to life. To life, but not to consciousness, thank God.

Alex sat beside her, holding the limp and sweaty hand, trying to fight off waves of despair. At times like this, it seemed there was no happiness in the world. If there was, it was unknowing: the happiness of children who had not yet learned what lay behind the masks of the adults they saw each day and night. The people Alex knew seemed bent on destroying whatever happiness they might have found, as though unable to tolerate the hell of living with what they'd once thought they wanted. She wondered if human beings had ever been meant to attain the things they desired. Of course, that question presupposed some divine intent inherent in the world, whereas most of the evidence she had seen contradicted this idea. She hoped that if the day ever came that she found a man who loved her as she dreamed of being loved, she would be content to love him in return. She believed she would, if only because she had lost so much, and so young. Unlike most people she'd encountered, Alex knew in her bones that existence was terribly fragile, a flickering flame that could be extinguished at any moment without cause or justice.

She checked her watch. Chris would arrive soon, and Kaiser not long after. She squeezed her mother's hand, then wrote a brief note for the nurses to read to her later. *Dear Mom, I was here. I love you. I hope it doesn't hurt too much. I'm close by, and I'll be back soon. I love you. Alexandra.*

"Alexandra," she said, getting up and walking into the hall. Never in her life had she felt like an Alexandra, yet Margaret Morse had spent most of her life trying to force her daughter to become one. Girlie outfits, pink hair ribbons, debutante balls, sorority recommendations . . . *Christ.*

Alex stepped aside for a group of white-coated doctors walking together. Most looked five years younger than she was. *Interns.* A couple of the women were staring at her face. They were curious about the scars, and they were probably wondering how they would deal with something like that. They saw people with infirmities and afflictions every day, but most of that they shut out by force of will, aided by the separation implicit in a wide age difference. But when they saw *her,* a woman like them—even prettier than they were—disfigured by fate, it scared them.

When Alex reached the elevator, she found a man already waiting in front of it. She stood behind his big white coat, waiting for the car to come. Hospital smells permeated the air: alcohol, harsh disinfectant, God knew what else. There were highly resistant bacteria on every surface in this place, waiting to find some portal into a warm, wet body so that they could multiply into the millions, then billions, until they had wiped out the host that nourished them for their brief stay on earth—

A bell dinged softly.

Alex walked into the elevator behind the white-coated man. Another white coat was waiting inside, both members of the same exclusive club, the world within the world of the hospital, inhuman humans with faces whose smiles never quite reached their eyes, who dealt each day with death and thus denied it with twice the fervor of average citizens. The man already on board the elevator backed away from the larger newcomer and stood in the car's right rear corner. The big man took the left corner. By unwritten law, Alex took one of the remaining corners— right front, near the buttons—and stood facing the door.

The elevator smelled new, and its doors were polished

until reflective. In the blurred reflection, Alex saw that the big man had a beard, and also a flaming birthmark above it. *It must be bad*, she thought, *to show even in the dim reflection.*

The elevator stopped on the third floor, and the man directly behind her walked out. As the doors closed, Alex backed into the spot that he'd occupied. The man with the birthmark looked over and nodded, but instead of looking away afterward, he continued to study her. This broke one of the unwritten laws, but Alex figured that her scars had drawn his attention— his *professional* attention.

"Shotgun?" asked the man, touching his own cheek.

She colored deeply. He was the first one to guess right. Some doctors knew that her particular kind of scarring was caused by gunshot, but since so much of the mess had been made by flying glass, most guessed wrong. Maybe he was a trauma surgeon.

"Yes," she said.

"I don't mean to make you uncomfortable. I can relate to having people stare at your face."

Alex stared back. The big, bearded man was about sixty, with a deep voice that had probably reassured ten thousand patients over the years. "Is that a birthmark?"

He smiled. "Not technically. It's an arteriovenous anomaly. It's not bad when you're born, but when you hit puberty, it suddenly explodes into this."

Alex started to ask a question, but as though reading her mind, the stranger said, "Surgery often makes it worse. I don't want to risk that."

She nodded. He wasn't handsome, but he would certainly have been decent-looking without that awful web of indigo and scarlet on his left cheek.

The bell dinged again.

"Good afternoon," said the man, then he walked out.

Alex stood there in a trance, thinking of the day at the bank, of the flying glass she had seen only as flashes of light, and of James Broadbent lying on the floor with his chest smashed into something his wife would weep to see—

"Miss?"

The man with the birthmark was back; he was holding the door open with his elbow. "This is the lobby."

"Oh! I'm sorry. Thank you."

He nodded and waited until she had cleared the doors to let them go. "Tough night?"

"My mother is dying."

Genuine sympathy furrowed his brow. "You got on at Oncology. Is it cancer?"

Alex nodded. "Ovarian."

The man shook his head like a consoling priest. "A terrible disease. I hope she doesn't suffer too much."

"I think she already has."

He sighed heavily. "I'm sorry. Will you be all right?"

"Yes. I'm right over at the Cabot Lodge."

He smiled. "Good. They know how to take care of people over there."

"Yes. Thank you, again."

"Anytime."

The man gave her a small wave, then walked down a hall that led deep into the bowels of the hospital. The floor had colored lines painted on it. Red lines and green lines and yellow lines and even black ones. Alex wondered whether, if you knew all the color codes, you might guess your prognosis by where you were sent. Probably not. The yellow line might take you to

McDonald's, for all she knew. There was a McDonald's in the hospital somewhere.

As she hitched her purse over her shoulder and walked out into the dusk, her cell phone chirped. It was a text message from John Kaiser: *I'm at Gallman, MS. 25 mins away. See u soon.* She needed to hurry. Will Kilmer was supposed to meet her in the lobby of the Cabot Lodge with an unregistered gun. She wanted to hide it upstairs before Kaiser arrived. He wouldn't like the idea of her carrying while suspended. Even if he understood, it would make his position more difficult. Alex caught sight of her car across the huge parking lot and started running.

Eldon Tarver stood at the window of the second-floor doctors' lounge and watched Special Agent Morse jog across the parking lot. She ran with purpose, her head well forward like a sprinter's, not like the hobbyists he saw jogging all the time. As he stared, he felt a near-euphoric sense of triumph flowing through him.

"She doesn't know me," he said softly. "She was three feet away . . . she looked right into my face, she heard my voice . . . and she didn't recognize me." The fact that his beard hid the wound she'd given him undoubtedly helped.

"Are you talking to me?" asked a female resident sitting on the couch behind him.

"No."

He heard the girl shift on the couch. She was probably pissed off that he was here. The slut had probably told some attending to meet her for a quick fuck, and now he'd screwed up their plans. Eldon felt so invulnerable in this moment that he considered locking the door and bending her over the counter of the little kitch-enette, showing her what penetration really was—

Take it easy, said his inner censor. *Everything is falling your way.*

And it was. First Neville Byrd had discovered the EX NIHILO site, and now Alex Morse had walked right into his hands. She'd even given him the name of her hotel! Eldon didn't believe in fate, but it was hard not to see Jungian patterns in all this.

Of course, it was also possible that Morse was deeper than he'd been led to believe. Rusk's judgment could not be trusted, and Morse had risen to stardom in the FBI. That she'd disobeyed orders was more a rec-ommendation than a black mark to Dr. Tarver, espe-cially in a rulebound bureaucracy like the FBI.

Yes, he decided, their whole conversation could have been a performance. And even if it wasn't—even if Morse really had no idea who he was—could he take the chance that he was wrong? His policy had always been zero risk, and that policy had served him well. He had been committing felonies almost daily for five years, some of them capital crimes, yet he was not in jail.

It was time to call Biddle back.

CHAPTER

38

Alex had to park a hundred yards from the lobby of the Cabot Lodge. When she trudged through the double doors to check in, she saw Chris sitting in a chair against the wall to her right. His head was bent over his knees, and he was rubbing his temples like a man with a migraine. She walked over and crouched beside him.

"Chris?"

He looked up with red-rimmed eyes. "Hey."

"My God. How's your headache?"

"A little better. My stomach's the problem now."

"Do you have any new information?"

He groaned softly. "I talked to Pete Connolly again. He wants me to fly up to Sloan-Kettering today."

"Then you should do that."

Chris shrugged with a fatalistic air. "Actually, I can take the same drugs here that he can give me there. Tom Cage already called in a prescription for some strong antiviral drugs. AZT, ritonavir, enfuvirtide, and vidarabine. I think that's why I'm nauseated."

"Does Connolly think those will work?"

Chris laughed darkly. "How can he know that

when he doesn't know what was injected into me? Pete thinks I should start intensive IV chemotherapy as well."

"Then why haven't you done that?"

"There are serious risks. A lot of chemotherapy drugs are carcinogenic themselves. I'm not sure I'm desperate enough to try that. But Connolly thinks that blasting me as soon as possible gives me the greatest chance of survival."

Alex tried to follow the logic. "How could chemotherapy help you, if you don't have cancer yet?"

Chris stood slowly, took hold of her arm for balance, then looked into her eyes. "It's possible that I do."

Alex paled. "What?"

"Remember Pete's scariest scenario? The one where someone gets hold of your cells, turns those cells cancerous in the lab, then injects them back into you?"

Alex nodded slowly.

"Those would be active cancer cells from the moment they entered my body."

She thought of the needle mark in Chris's anus. "What do you think happened last night? Did someone steal cells in order to alter them? Or did they inject cancerous cells into you?"

Chris's eyes held only bitterness. "I pray it's the first. But I doubt I'm that lucky."

"Why?"

"Because there are easier ways to get my cells."

Alex shook her head in confusion. "Like how?"

"Think about it. Who has constant access to my body?"

"Thora?"

"Right. And she's a nurse."

"All right. But how could Thora take your blood without you knowing about it?"

Chris moved his hand in a "Come along" gesture, urging Alex toward the truth. "Not blood."

She tried to imagine what other cells Thora could take from Chris. Hair? Skin? Or— Her mouth twisted in horror and disgust.

"You get it now?" Chris asked.

"Semen?"

"Exactly. How's that for cold and calculating?"

Alex shook her head. "I can't believe she'd be capable of that."

"Why not? Once you've made the decision to commit murder, how does the method matter? You think any of the other victims died pretty?"

She stared at him, not knowing what to say or do. The situation was simply beyond her comprehension.

"The other night," Chris whispered, "the night of the day that you and I met, Thora came out to my studio and made love with me. She told me she wanted to get pregnant. It was really out of character, with the way things had been, but I went with it, hoping for the best." Chris's jaw flexed in fury. "Three days later, I found out she'd taken a morning-after pill."

Alex felt cold.

"Thora never meant to get pregnant at all. So . . . why the sex?"

Alex shook her head in disbelief. "But surely no one could induce cancer in those cells that rapidly, not even in the lab."

"I hope not. That's one reason I haven't taken the chemo yet. But who knows what's possible?"

Alex put both arms around him and hugged tight.

Chris stiffened at first, but then she felt him go limp. When his arms closed around her back, she realized he was shivering. Was it the drugs? Or was he about to break down right there in the lobby? Anybody would, given the unimaginable strain he was under.

"Let's go upstairs," she said. "Have you checked in?"

He nodded.

She left a message at the desk for Will, and sixty seconds later they were unlocking the door to room 638. Alex had reserved a suite on the "executive" floor. Attached to the bedroom was a little den with a sofa, two club chairs, and a desk against the wall. In one corner was a sink, a minifridge, and a microwave oven.

"Is that a minibar?" Chris asked.

Alex checked the fridge. "No alcohol."

He cursed softly.

"What do you want?"

"I don't care."

She checked the bedroom. "Here we go, under the TV."

"Vodka?"

"Coming up. I'll get you some ice."

She handed him a tiny bottle of Absolut, and he drank most of it in a single gulp. Alex wasn't sure how Kaiser would react to a drunken witness, but she wasn't about to reprimand a man who had just learned he might be dying.

"Is Kaiser in town yet?" Chris asked.

"He'll be up any minute."

"Why did you pick him?"

She walked to the window and looked out at the verdant campus of Millsaps College, with its clock tower rising into the sky. She'd been offered an academic scholarship there as a high school senior. "Kaiser worked with the Investigative Support Unit for a long time. He worked with the guys who invented it, when it was still called Behavioral Science. He's seen stuff that the suits in Washington can't even imagine. Reading it in a report just doesn't communicate the horror of some things, you know?"

Chris nodded. "It's like reading about diseases in a textbook. You think you know what something is until you see a patient rotting away before your eyes."

"Exactly. Kaiser gets it. He served in Vietnam before he entered the Bureau, heavy combat. He's a first-class guy. His wife is the best, too. He met her during a serial murder case. She's a war photographer."

"What's her name?"

"Jordan Glass."

"You're kidding."

"You know her?"

"No. But I do some documentary-film work, as a hobby. Jordan Glass is up there with Nachtwey and those guys. She's won a Pulitzer."

"Two, I think."

Chris drank off the rest of the vodka and went back to the minibar. Alex started at a knock on the door. She answered expecting Kaiser, but Will stood there with a shoe box in his hands.

"Thanks," she said, taking the improbably heavy box. "What is it?"

"A Sig nine. Untraceable."

"Thanks, Will. You'd better get going."

The old detective looked as if he'd been wrestling some dark demons.

"What is it?" she asked. "What's wrong?"

"I feel like I let the doc down."

You have no idea. "Last night doesn't matter now. It's going to work out. Get going, Will."

Kilmer trotted down the hall to the fire stairs.

When Alex went back inside, Chris was drinking bourbon.

"Room service delivers shoes?" he asked.

"Nine-millimeter shoes." She took the box into the bedroom and stowed it on the top shelf of the closet. "Kaiser doesn't need to know."

Chris nodded. "My .38 is down in my car."

"I'll get it for you after John leaves."

"I can definitely see myself using it on a certain person."

Who? Alex wondered. *Thora? Shane Lansing? Both of them?* "Chris . . . you're not really thinking that, are you?"

"I was raised in Mississippi. I've got some redneck in me that'll never wash out."

Alex touched his arm. "I hope you're kidding. Because that wouldn't solve anything. It would only guarantee that Ben would be raised by someone besides you."

Chris's eyes went dead.

"What do you think caused the headache?" she asked, trying to divert him from thoughts of Ben.

"I think we were all sedated before the attack. I'm not sure how. Will ate the same turkey and cheese I did, but Ben had frozen pizza. And Ben didn't drink any beer. We have a watercooler . . . it could have been that. In the end, it doesn't really matter, does it? As long as Ben and Will aren't sick."

Three strong knocks echoed through the room.

Chris followed Alex to the door.

A tall man with deep-set eyes and longer hair than Chris had expected stood there. Chris could hardly believe the guy had served in Vietnam, because he looked about forty-five. He had to be at least seven years older.

"You gonna invite me in?" asked the newcomer.

Alex smiled and hugged Kaiser, then pulled him into the suite. Chris stepped back and watched the FBI agent set a leather bag down on the sofa. Then Kaiser turned and held out a hand to Chris.

"Dr. Shepard?"

"Yes." Chris shook his hand.

"Glad to meet you."

"You, too."

"I have a lot of catching up to do."

Alex folded her arms and looked up at Kaiser. "It's worse than I thought, John. Chris is already in bad trouble. He was hit last night."

Kaiser's eyes roamed over Chris for several moments. He was taking in the smell of alcohol, the look of fatigue, even desperation. Alex knew he would have a lot of questions, and right now Chris looked as if he wanted only to climb into one of the beds and go to sleep. Kaiser looked at Alex.

"Somebody fill me in before Dr. Shepard passes out."

CHAPTER

39

John Kaiser stood at the window overlooking the college. Alex was sitting beside Chris on the bed, holding a trash can for him whenever he vomited. He'd started about twenty minutes into Alex's summary of events, and the waves were still coming.

"It's probably the drugs," he said, clutching his cramping midsection with both arms. "My body's not used to them, and I'm taking three at once."

Kaiser didn't look away from the window when he spoke to Alex. "So you feel like you got active resistance from Webb Tyler?"

Webb Tyler was the SAC of the Jackson field office. It was Tyler that Alex had first approached with her murder theory. "You could say that. Five minutes after I walked into his office, Tyler was praying I'd disappear."

Kaiser tilted his head to one side, as though looking at something on the ground six floors below. "I'm sure he was."

"I also think he started complaining to Mark Dodson about me from that first day."

"Right again."

"What do you think, John? Is there anything you can do?"

Kaiser turned from the window at last. "You need objective evidence of murder. Some kind, any kind."

"Is there any way that you can expedite autopsies of the victims?"

"Not without an ongoing murder investigation. The local authorities don't even believe that crimes have occurred. How can they invite the FBI into a case that doesn't exist?"

"I know. But I was thinking, Chris may have been injected with some revolutionary drug that's capable of giving people cancer. Why couldn't you classify that as a biological weapon? If you did, couldn't the Bureau investigate it under counterterror rules? Like searching for a weapon of mass destruction?"

Kaiser pursed his lips. "That's actually not a bad idea. But it's too soon. Again, we have no evidence that such a drug exists."

"We have the injection site on Chris's body."

"That could be anything. You'd have to isolate the compound from his blood."

"Can we try that?"

"We don't know what to look for," Chris croaked. "A radioactive metal? A retrovirus? A toxin? Is it even traceable?"

Kaiser nodded dejectedly. "And who's going to do that for us?"

"*Fuck!*" Alex shouted. "I'm sick of having my hands tied!"

"Pete Connolly will start testing me if I fly up to Sloan-Kettering," Chris told them. "Maybe he could isolate something."

"I want to see it," Kaiser said.

"What?" asked Alex.

"The injection site."

"Are you serious?"

"I've seen a lot worse in my time."

Alex looked at Chris. He felt cold sweat pouring down his face. "What the hell?" he said. "You can look if you want."

Kaiser glanced at Alex. "Give us a minute?"

She went into the bathroom without a word.

Chris got slowly to his feet, dropped his pants, then lay down on his stomach.

Kaiser checked him as professionally as a physician. "Okay, Doctor. I'm done."

"Well?" said Chris, slowly pulling his pants back up.

"Do you have any history of drug abuse, Dr. Shepard?"

"None."

The FBI agent looked deep into his eyes. "Do you believe your wife is capable of murder?"

Chris sat on the edge of the bed. Another wave of nausea was coming. "I didn't at first. But I didn't think she was capable of cheating on me, either. And there are some gaps in her past that I know nothing about. Also . . ."

"What?"

"I adopted my son. My wife's biological son. Ben has only known me for a couple of years, but if you gave him a choice about where to live after a divorce, he'd choose me over his biological mother. What does that tell you?"

"A lot, if you're right."

Kaiser called toward the bathroom, "Alex?"

She came out, a questioning look on her face. "Do you believe me now?"

He reached out and took hold of her hand. "I believe you because I believe *in* you. But I'm not sure anyone else would."

"Is there anything you can do to help?"

"At the very least, I can pull some strings and get local surveillance on Andrew Rusk."

"Will Webb Tyler allow that?"

Kaiser snorted. "Tyler's not too popular with his own agents. I can think of a few who would help out, as a favor to me. I can't do anything that will put me on the Bureau radar, but I can get you license plates, background checks, that kind of thing. I just have to do it through the New Orleans field office."

"I appreciate that, John. But those are baby steps. These guys have been killing people for years, and knowing about my involvement hasn't even slowed them down."

Kaiser's jaw muscles flexed. "This is going to sound cold, but that's a good thing. If they went to ground now, we'd probably never get them. The best thing we can do right now is poke Andrew Rusk with a sharp stick. I'll do my part. I'm going to find out everything there is to know about that asshole. Tear apart every company he's even remotely associated with. Anybody in business with him is going to hate him within two days."

Alex's face flushed with hope.

Kaiser walked over to Chris and looked down. "I want you to get that chemotherapy, Doctor. There's nothing else you can do to help this investigation. Your only job is to survive."

Chris wanted to respond, but at that moment he doubled over the trash can and began to dry-heave.

Kaiser led Alex into the other room. Chris could hear their voices, but he couldn't make out individual words. As though compelled by some will outside himself, he pulled back the bedclothes, crawled into the bed, and pulled the sheet up to his neck. By the time Alex returned, he could hardly make out what she was saying.

"Chris? Should I take you to the hospital?"

He shook his head. "No . . . just need to rest. Kaiser . . . ?"

"He's gone."

She stared down at him, her expression vacillating between concern and outright fear. *She's lost too much,* he realized. *She doesn't want me to go to sleep . . . doesn't want to be alone—*

"Is someone taking care of Ben?" she asked.

"Mrs. Johnson," he whispered. "Number . . . her number's in my cell phone."

"I'll call her. You sleep. I'll be watching over you."

She took hold of his shivering hand and squeezed. Chris squeezed back with what strength he could muster. Then, like a mountain of storm clouds sweeping over a tiny boat, the shadows took him.

Chris awoke in the dark to the chirp of his cell phone. He blinked several times, his dry eyes burning, then turned to the right. He saw a bar of artificial light where the curtains didn't quite meet. In its faint pink glow, he saw Alex lying asleep on the other bed. She was wearing a shirt but no pants. He scrabbled on the night table until he found his phone.

"Hello?" he said, his mouth sour with vomit.

"*Chris?*" A frantic female voice.

"Mrs. Johnson?"

"It's Thora! Where are you?"

"Um . . . Jackson."

"Jackson! You left Ben with Mrs. Johnson, and she had no idea where you were!"

"That's not true. She knew I might go out of town."

"She told me that some woman named Alex called her about Ben. Who the hell is Alex?"

Chris sat up slowly, then stood and walked into the adjoining den. "Look . . . I had to drive up here to see a patient at UMC. There's nothing to freak out about. Where are you?"

"In Greenwood, where I'm supposed to be." Thora's voice had lost none of its hysteria.

He clenched his jaw but said nothing.

"Chris? Are you there?"

"Uh-huh."

"What the *hell* is going on down there?"

He stood at the center of the dark room, his throat and scrotum aching from the spasms of repeated retching, his arm almost too weak to hold up the phone, and fought to keep from screaming from the depths of his soul. He remembered Alex begging him not to confront Thora, but the truth was, he didn't care about the goddamn investigation. He could never look at Thora again and pretend that everything was fine.

"Answer me!" she shouted. "Are you drunk or something?"

"You're where you're supposed to be?" he said.

"Of course I am!"

"What about Shane Lansing? Is he where he's supposed to be?"

Now there was only silence.

"Or is he where *I'm* supposed to be?"

"What are you talking about, Chris?"

"Stop it, Thora. Just stop, okay?"

"Wait . . . I don't know what you think you know, but you don't . . . I mean, you just can't . . ." Her shrill voice faded to nothing.

"I'll tell you what I know," he said with quiet conviction. "I know you took a morning-after pill after we had sex in the studio."

He heard a gasp, then the sound of a thumb being squashed over the cellular mike.

"I've also got a nice snapshot of Shane doing you doggy style on the hotel balcony. I'm sure he'd like another trophy to add to his case. You'll be what . . . the tenth conquest this year?"

He heard a muffled scream, then a male grunt.

"Is he there now?" Chris asked, reeling from sudden vertigo. "Or has he flown home to eat supper with the wife and kids again? What's it costing him to commute up there to bone your skanky ass? I guess that makes you feel like you're worth something, huh?"

No response.

"If he's there, put him on the phone."

"Chris . . ." Thora's voice was smaller now, almost desolate. "I'm alone. There's no one here but me."

"I don't believe you. I know what you did, okay? And I may be dead in a year. But *you* . . . you and Lansing, you're dead, too. Spiritually dead. You probably don't even know what I'm talking about . . . but one day you will. You're going to prison! And you tell that motherfucker he's going to stand toe-to-toe with me before it's over. Just once."

She was sobbing now.

"How could you do that to Ben, Thora? Forget me. But he's been doing so well . . . Jesus. Do you want to turn him into a clone of your fucked-up emotional blueprint?"

Thora screamed like a woman rending her flesh in mourning.

Chris hung up and stood shivering in the darkness. He was no longer alone. Alex was standing in the door that divided the bedroom from the den, her face confused, her bare legs outlined in the light from the window.

"What did you do?" she asked.

"I couldn't pretend anymore."

"But— You may have ruined everything."

"How? You've been working on this for five straight weeks and you've got nothing. You heard Kaiser: poke them with a sharp stick, he said. Well, I just poked Thora. And my guess is, she's going to poke Andrew Rusk like he's never been poked before."

Alex raised her hand like a little girl and wiped sleep out of her eyes. "How's your stomach?"

"Better. What time is it?"

"Eleven thirty. That's p.m."

Chris swallowed painfully. "I guess we're not going back to Natchez tonight."

"Not unless you need to get Ben."

"Did Mrs. Johnson say she was okay with keeping him?"

"She said he was fine."

"Shit. Thora acted like he was in a panic. She also didn't like hearing that a woman had called. Asked me who the hell Alex was."

Alex smiled. "Screw her."

"No, thanks. Never again."

Alex walked forward and took his hand, then led him back to the bed. "I'm not making a pass," she said. "I'd just rather sleep with you than by myself. Are you okay with that?"

He lay down on his back, then scooted across to make a space for her. She got into the bed and laid her head on his shoulder, her body warm along the length of his side.

"Why did you marry Thora?" she asked softly. "Was it because she's beautiful?"

He thought about it for a while. "I didn't think so at the time. But now . . . I think maybe that had more to do with it than I knew."

Alex nodded, her cheek against his shirt.

"It wasn't only that, though," he went on. "And I still don't know why she would do this. I mean, why not just ask me for a divorce? I'd give it to her."

"I think it's about Ben."

"What do you mean?"

"She knows how much Ben loves you. She can't tell her son that she wants to take away his wonderful new father because she's suddenly bored. That she lied when she married you. Death solves all those problems for her. If you die, she's a noble widow, not a selfish divorcée. And noble widow is a role Thora already knows how to play."

"That's for sure."

"Not to mention adding a couple of mil to her bank account."

He sighed but said nothing.

"People used to think I was beautiful," Alex whispered, her hand rising to her scarred cheek. "Before this."

"You still are. You just can't see it right now. You're not the same as you were, that's all. It's like women who get chemotherapy. They're still beautiful, they're just bald. I call it the Sinéad O'Connor look."

Alex laughed softly. "You've got a pretty good bedside manner, don't you?"

"Not good enough for Thora, it seems."

"Well, we know that bitch is crazy."

Chris closed his eyes. "I'm going to be bald myself soon, if I take the chemo."

"No ifs, bud." Alex wagged her forefinger in his face. "You're taking it."

"You're my doctor now?"

"Somebody needs to be."

He took her arm and turned her on her side, facing away from him, then spooned her tight.

"Oh, no," she said softly.

"What?"

"This is my favorite thing in the world."

"Good." After only a few breaths, sleep was returning.

Alex closed her hands around his arm where it enfolded her. "Don't freak out if I cry," she said. "Because I feel like I'm going to."

"Why?"

"Because life sucks right now. It's been sucking for a really long time."

Chris squeezed as tight as he could for a few moments, then eased up. "There are worse things than this. That's one thing I've learned in medicine. It can always get worse."

She turned her head so that her cheek touched his. "I hope not."

"We need to sleep, Alex."

"I know. Are you going to puke on me?"

His laughter sounded like someone else laughing in a dream. "I'll try not to."

She tensed in his arms.

"What's the matter?" he asked.

"I forgot to check in with someone online. Jamie, actually. It's kind of a tradition."

Chris struggled to raise his arm. "Go ahead."

She pulled his arm back down and snuggled in close. "No . . . it's too late now. He'll be all right for one night."

CHAPTER

40

"Oh, *shit*," said a female voice.

Chris came awake with the bed moving beneath him. Every muscle in his body ached, but his chest and neck felt as though he had endured a car crash.

"Shit, shit, shit," cursed the woman. "I slept through my alarm."

Alex, he remembered. He blinked his eyes open and felt full daylight stab his retinas. Alex was standing beside the bed, pulling on her jeans.

"What time is it?" he asked.

"Nine a.m. I set my cell alarm, but I forgot to plug in my phone. It died during the night. I guess that snuggling scrambled my brain."

Chris sat up, and a wave of nausea rolled through his stomach. "Do you need to use the bathroom?"

She looked at his face and caught his meaning. "Just let me pee."

She disappeared into the bathroom. Chris slid his legs off the bed, then got up slowly and went to the minibar. He chose a cold Dasani, which felt good going down but made him pray he could keep it there. When he was confident that he could, he went to his bag and took his morning dose of antivirals: AZT, ritonavir, enfuvirtide, and vidarabine. As he swallowed the last pill, the toilet flushed in the bathroom.

"I'm done," Alex called. "All yours."

"I think I'm okay now. I felt like I had diarrhea, but it passed."

She walked over and sat on one of the club chairs. She had washed her face, and for the first time he saw the scars without makeup covering them. In his mind, he saw an image of someone throwing acid onto a painting of a woman.

"What are you thinking?" she asked.

"About today."

Her suspicion didn't fade. "You've got two choices. Drive back to Natchez for chemotherapy, or fly to Sloan-Kettering for chemotherapy."

"Now you're my mother?"

Alex turned up her palms. "You want to play Russian roulette with your life?"

"That's what chemotherapy would be under these circumstances. We don't know what was injected into me. My best chance for survival is to find out exactly what's killing me. Only then can I get effective treatment."

Alex considered this. "How do you plan to do that?"

"How about you and Kaiser catch the son of a bitch for me?"

"I guess you feel better this morning."

Chris picked up his pants and struggled to put them on.

"Where are you going that you need your pants?" Alex asked.

"Over to UMC, to see the researchers Peter Connolly told me about. If they're not there anymore, I'll get the names of the top people in the Hematology and Oncology departments and try to see them."

"For what purpose?"

A wave of dizziness hit him. He sat on the edge of the bed, rocking slowly. "I think we've focused too much on Shane Lansing. Okay, he owns a radiation-oncology center. He owns a lot of other stuff, too. We know that something was injected into me. If that something was radioactive, it probably would have shown up on the X-ray I had yesterday. I think it's more likely that Connolly is right. Someone got hold of my blood—or semen—then altered it and reinjected it into me. If that's the case, the odds are against Lansing. Shane cares more about money than medicine, so he doesn't have that depth of knowledge. We're looking for superdoctors, Alex. People who are experts on bone marrow, genetics, oncogenic viruses. There aren't many of those in this entire state, and the ones we do have are right across the street."

Alex leaned forward in her chair, excitement in her eyes. "How's your body? Can you function?"

"I think so. I'd better take a shower, though. I'm not going to impress anybody smelling like vomit."

"Good call." She walked to the bedside phone. "I'm going to order some breakfast. Can you eat anything?"

"Toast and a bowl of grits. And hot tea."

She smiled broadly. "You're the only man I've spent the night with in the last ten years who ordered grits in the morning."

"Welcome home."

• • •

Andrew Rusk was ten miles south of Jackson when his fear hit critical mass. A few days ago, there had been only one car following him. Now there was a motorized battalion, operating in shifts. All American cars, most of the drivers white males between twenty-five and forty-five. He was in deep shit. Cursing Alex Morse with visceral hatred, he swerved off the interstate at the Byram exit and pulled into the drive-through lane of the Wendy's restaurant there. Two cars followed him.

"Goddamnit!" he shouted.

Last night, when he received the Viagra spam from Dr. Tarver, Rusk had been elated. He didn't know where Tarver had been hiding, but he was sure that the doctor had good reason to be out of contact. After all, they had hardly spent more than a few minutes in each other's company over the past five years. Last night this trip had seemed like a leisurely drive down to the hunting camp. Now it was impossible. If he led those sons of bitches in the government sedans to Chickamauga, Dr. Tarver would kill them and him without a second's hesitation.

Rusk ordered a cheeseburger and a Coke and watched one of the tail cars park in the lot a few yards away. What the hell could he do? If they were following him like this, then they were tapping his phones as well. The office, the house, his cell phones. For a moment he wondered if Carson Barnett had turned him in.

No way, he assured himself. Barnett wanted out of his marriage, and he was willing to do anything to accomplish that. It was that fucking Morse. But was it *only* Morse? That was the question.

Last night, Thora Shepard had called his house fourteen times. After two hysterical messages had been left on his answering machine, Rusk unplugged the phone. When he arrived at his office this morning, Janice had reported twelve messages left by a Mrs. Shepard, each one more frantic than the last. Thora wasn't so stupid as to have stated her reason for needing to talk to him, but something told him that Alex Morse was involved. That, or Thora was having second thoughts about killing her husband. That wouldn't surprise Rusk. The woman might be movie-star hot, but she was also nuts, as he had seen the first time around. Typical society chick, really. She looked as if she had it all together, but underneath the facade she didn't know whether she was going or coming.

He took his cheeseburger from the girl in the window and paid with a $10 bill. "Ketchup," he said. "I need some ketchup."

He took a huge gulp of his Coke and pulled into the exit lane. One of the tails pulled right up behind him. These guys weren't even trying to conceal themselves.

The funny thing about Thora Shepard, he thought, crossing over the interstate and turning onto I-55 North, was that they hadn't even had to kill her first husband. The poor guy had died of natural causes. Of course, Rusk had never told *her* that. Thora had made her payments just as instructed, and he was happy to take her money. The irony of that woman becoming a return customer was almost too much. But Rusk didn't have time to enjoy it now. Thora was flipping out, and if she lost it in front of the wrong people, it could cost him dearly. He needed to make contact with Dr. Tarver, and soon. He had no idea how to do that, but as he roared north toward Jackson, he realized that he didn't have to—Dr. Tarver would do that for him. All he had to do was play it cool. Sometime in the next twelve hours, he would walk around a corner or step into an elevator or climb into his car, and Tarver would be there. Like magic. That was how the guy worked. And all the FBI agents in the world wouldn't be able to stop him.

Rusk looked at his rearview mirror and laughed. It was time to cash in his chips and split the country. He only hoped they could fleece Carson Barnett before D-day. Barnett would be their pièce de résistance, and he would set them up for the last couple of decades of their lives. As the interstate flowed beneath him like a gray river, Rusk saw himself on a sun-drenched beach with a dark rum drink in his hand and Lisa lying nude beside him. He hated to leave the kids behind, but there was nothing to be done about it. Business was business. He slowed down until the dark sedan behind him had no choice but to pass. As its clean-cut driver glanced his way, Rusk smiled like the Cheshire cat.

Dr. Tarver regretted the look of dumb incomprehension on his adoptive brother's face. It was exactly the look he had expected, the puzzled disbelief of a child being told that his dog has been run over by a car.

"All of them?" Judah said. "Every one?"

"I'm afraid so," said Eldon. "I'm sorry."

"Even the chimps?"

They were standing in the back room, beside the primate cages, not the best place for this discussion. "The chimps most of all. Nothing can remain that would tell anyone what we've been doing here."

Judah's face was working like that of a boy doing

sums that were beyond him. "I thought what we were doing here was good."

"It is good, Judah. But people won't understand that. You know what they're like."

"I know, but, but what if *I* kept them? Just some of them?"

"I wish you could. I really do. But you know that's impossible."

"I been studying hard. I been practically running the front this past year. Why couldn't I keep running the breeding part, you know? Just the beagles?"

"You don't really know what's involved in the *business* part, Judah. There's so much more to it than taking care of the dogs. There's ordering and records, computers and taxes. Plus, you have to be licensed. If I'm not here, the whole thing just doesn't work."

A new fear entered Judah's eyes. "Where are you going?"

"I don't know that yet. But I'm going to send for you once I get there."

"Are you?"

"Don't I always?"

Judah's eyes darted toward the cages again. "Why can't we just give the animals away?"

"Because they're sick. They're carrying special germs now. They would infect other animals, and that might be a disaster. It might even cause Armageddon, like in—"

"The Revelation of St. John," Judah said in the voice of an automaton. "Chapter sixteen. The seven vials of the angels. My name is in that book." His voice dropped in pitch. "'*And the second angel poured his bowl into the sea, and it became as the blood of a dead man. Every living thing that was in the sea, and had life, died, and—*'"

"That's right," Eldon said, cutting him off before the spirit took him. "You don't want to be called to account before God for bringing that to pass, do you?"

After long reflection, Judah shook his big head.

"I tell you what," Eldon said, as if just thinking of this idea on the spot. "You take care of the beagles and leave the primates to me. I know how hard that would be for you."

Judah bit his bottom lip. "The beagles is hard, too, you know? I know every one of 'em now. Every one has a given name."

It amazed Eldon that a man as tough as Judah could be so soft when it came to animals. For Judah was a fearsome creature, once roused to anger. He was a match for any jihad-minded suicide bomber. It was men like Judah who had taken Iwo Jima from the Japanese. Men who could bayonet their way through endless ranks of the enemy, then charge uphill into withering machine-gun fire and never question the orders that put them there. That unthinking patriotism had allowed America to survive into adolescence, and a continued lack of it would insure that she never saw national maturity.

"You don't know," Judah went on. "You're never up front with 'em. It's like they're all mine. Like June Bug when we was kids."

June Bug was an old mutt with cataracts that had lived with them for fifteen years. Judah had doted on her, right to the end.

"This is like when Daddy used to drown the runts," Judah said. "In the big washtub."

Eldon put his arm around his brother's massive shoulder and led him away from the primate cages. It was amazing that anyone had ever mistaken him for

Judah's biological brother. Intellectually, they inhabited two different dimensions; Eldon's mind probably contained four times as many neurochemical connections as Judah's. Yet his adoptive brother had proved quite useful over the years, and he would in future.

They were in the front now, with their little town of beagles, two walls of black, white, and brown fur glinting with plaintive eyes. It would take Judah most of the day to euthanize them all. Not that they would resist. One of the reasons beagles were used for medical research was that they were so docile and friendly. They would only look up with mild reproof while you stuck in needles and probes; they were living proof that the meek would not inherit the earth, at least in the animal world.

"How are you going to do it?" Judah asked. "The chimps, I mean?"

"I'm going to dart them with a barbiturate. After they're fully unconscious, I'll use potassium chloride. They won't feel a thing, Brother."

Judah was biting his lip so hard that Eldon feared he would draw blood. "Does it have to be *fire*?"

"We have to purify this place. Fire is what God used, so we shall, too."

Judah closed his eyes for a while, but when he opened them, Eldon saw that he had accepted this as his lot. After all, Eldon had defied their father and lived, so he must be anointed by God.

"You must be out by five," Eldon said gravely. "Do you understand?"

"Are you leaving?"

"I'll be back to put the apes down. But I doubt you'll be finished."

"Okay. Where do I go when it's done?"

"I'll explain everything when I come back."

"Okay."

Eldon smiled, then walked back to the primate area. He had some reading to do; explosives were not his line. Still, he was confident in his abilities. What a production it would be. An explosion, then fire—fire hot enough to melt steel—and when the firefighters arrived, they would find something they had never before seen: a dozen panicked primates crazed by the flames. Eldon figured the animals would double the time it would take to get the blaze out, which was exactly what he wanted. So . . . he would dart the animals, just as he'd promised Judah. But there would be no injection of KCl. And as a last measure, he would unlock the cages, binding the doors with a couple of twists of wire, enough to persuade the primates that the doors were still locked, until a conflagration of biblical proportions ripped through the old bakery. It would be interesting to see which species smashed their cage doors open first once the panic hit, but it was not worth dying to find out.

He looked over at a locked closet to the right of the chimps' cages. In it were four cylinders filled with acetylene. Three other closets in the old bakery held identical cylinders. By the time the fire department responded to the calls of neighbors, the building would be burning at three thousand degrees Celsius. The stench of burning beagles would be permeating the area, and crazed monkeys would be flying at anyone who approached what until recently had been their home. Eldon laughed quietly, so that Judah wouldn't hear him. It would be a spectacle worthy of Hieronymus Bosch on LSD.

CHAPTER

41

Chris held the elevator door for a nurse pushing a woman in a wheelchair, then followed Alex onto the fifth floor of the University Medical Center.

"Have you met Dr. Pearson during your mother's treatment?" he asked.

Alex shook her head. "Mom's doctor is Walter Clarke."

"You're kidding. Clarke was a year ahead of me in med school. I thought he was still at Baylor."

Alex shrugged.

They walked past the patient wards and down to the academic offices. Near the end of the hall was a door with a brass nameplate that read MATTHEW PEARSON, MD, CHIEF OF HEMATOLOGY.

Chris paused and said, "Not a word about the FBI, murder, or anything like that."

"Because?"

"This is a hospital. One whiff of litigation or even liability, and we'll be out the door. This is my world, okay? Just follow my lead."

Alex rolled her eyes. "I can do that."

He knocked at the door, then walked into the

office. A red-haired woman with a retro beehive looked up from a stack of papers. "Can I help you?"

"I hope so," Chris said in his most genteel Southern accent. "I'm Dr. Chris Shepard from Natchez. I happen to be up here visiting a friend"—he nodded at Alex—"and I was hoping to talk to Dr. Pearson about a cluster of cancer cases back home."

The secretary smiled, but the smile looked forced. "Do you have an appointment, Dr. . . . ?"

"Shepard. I'm afraid not. But I was talking to Dr. Peter Connolly up at Sloan-Kettering, and he spoke very highly of Dr. Pearson. Pete seemed to think I would have a good chance of speaking with him on short notice."

At the mention of Connolly's name, the woman's face brightened instantly. "You know Dr. Connolly?"

"I studied under him when I went to school here."

"Oh, I see." She stood up and, coming around her desk, offered her hand. "I'm Joan. Dr. Pearson *is* busy right now, but let me just slip in there and see if he can't get away for a minute."

When the woman disappeared into the inner office, Alex whispered, "Aren't you something."

The door opened, and a smartly dressed man in his mid-forties walked out with his hand extended toward Chris. "Dr. Shepard?"

"Yes, sir," said Chris, taking the hand and squeezing firmly. "Glad to meet you at last."

"You, too. I see your name on a lot of charts that pass through here. You send a lot of referral business our way. We appreciate it."

"Not as much as I used to, I'm afraid, now that we have Dr. Mercier in Natchez."

"Well, that's a good thing for your city." Dr. Pearson

grinned. "Hey, you don't have a hidden camera on you, do you?"

So, even Matt Pearson had heard about Chris's documentary on residents' work hours. "No, my days as a director are over. I'm part of the establishment now."

While the glad-handing and listing of mutual acquaintances progressed, Chris sized up the chief of hematology. Despite his coming from Stanford, Pearson seemed to be cut from the same cloth Chris had gotten to know so well during his years at UMC: a smart, clean-cut WASP who'd made a 4.0 at Ole Miss or Millsaps, then left the state for a med school with a more prestigious pedigree and returned home covered with laurels. Chris was a little surprised: in a rigorous specialty such as hematology, he'd expected a foreigner.

"Joan said something about a cancer cluster?" Pearson prompted.

"Right. But I've forgotten my manners." Chris turned toward Alex. "This is Alexandra Morse. Her mother is here in your department right now. Ovarian cancer."

An appropriately somber look came over Pearson's face. "I'm familiar with the case. I'm sorry we have to meet under these circumstances, Ms. Morse."

"Thank you," Alex said in an accent so thick that Chris could have sworn she'd never left Mississippi. "All the doctors and nurses have been wonderful."

"Is your mother part of this cancer cluster?"

"No," Chris said. "Alex is just a friend. As for the cluster, I don't have statistical backing yet, but we've had several similar cases in Natchez this past year, and it's really starting to worry me."

GREG ILES

"What type of cancer?" asked Dr. Pearson.

"Different kinds, but all blood cancers. Leukemias, lymphomas, and a myeloma."

Dr. Pearson nodded with genuine interest. "I'm surprised we haven't picked this up ourselves. We've taken over the state tumor registry, you know. Have these patients passed through here?"

"Some. Dr. Mercier has treated several, and some of the others have gone to M. D. Anderson, Dana-Farber, like that."

"Right, of course."

"The thing is," said Chris, "some local doctors have wondered if there might be an environmental factor linking these cancers."

More concerned nodding from Pearson. "That's certainly possible. It's a very complex subject, of course. Controversial, too."

"I've also wondered," Chris went on, "if there might be some other etiological link between the cases."

"Such as?"

"Well, I've been doing a lot of reading in my frustration, and I've come across a few interesting possibilities. Radiation is one. We've got two nuclear plants in near proximity, and two of these patients work at one. The others don't, though. Two of the patients have had chemo for previous cancers, though. I've also been intrigued by the role of oncogenic viruses in cancer."

Dr. Pearson looked skeptical. "That seems pretty far-fetched, given what you've told me."

Chris felt for the man. On one level, Chris was playing a type that Pearson would like to avoid: the loquacious country doctor come to town with a bunch of wild scientific theories. On the other hand, Chris could be a dream come true: a country doctor with a handful of reportable cases that would splash Pearson's name through the top medical journals.

"What I was hoping," Chris concluded, "was that you could put me in touch with faculty members who specialize in those areas, particularly carcinogenic poisons and oncogenic viruses."

"I see," said Dr. Pearson.

"Pete Connolly gave me a couple of names. Yours, of course. But he also mentioned a virologist named Ajit Chandrekasar."

"Ajit is no longer here."

"I see. He also mentioned an Eldon Tarver?"

Pearson nodded. "Dr. Tarver is still with us. He's done some great work since Dr. Connolly left. He'd probably be glad to talk to you, too. With sufficient notice, of course."

Chris let his disappointment show.

"We have some terrific people on staff," Pearson said, "both in oncology and hematology. For the environmental toxins, you'd have to go a long way to beat Dr. Parminder. For radiation, I'd suggest Dr. Colbert. Oncogenic viruses are a little tougher. Most of the virologists I know are working on AIDS. Dr. Tarver might actually be your best bet."

"Do you have anybody doing gene therapy?" Chris asked.

"Yes, but I'm not sure I see the relevance."

"Don't they use viruses to deliver modified genes to the cell?"

"That's true," conceded Pearson. "But they use very simple viruses as a rule. Adenoviruses, for example. Not oncogenic viruses, or retroviruses, which are a whole other thing, as I'm sure you know."

"I understand the mechanics of RNA viruses. Reverse transcriptase and all that. I assumed that researchers doing that kind of work would probably have the answers to any questions I might ask about viruses."

"Well, I'm happy to try to set this up, but I seriously doubt whether any of these specialists would be free *today*."

Chris looked downcast. "So . . . Dr. Parminder for the environmental stuff. Colbert for radiation, and Dr. Tarver for the viral stuff?"

Dr. Pearson rubbed his chin. "Eldon is currently developing his own nucleic acid amplification assay. He probably knows as much about retroviruses as any virologist I ever met."

"But you don't think I could talk to either one of them today?"

"I doubt it. It would certainly have to be later in the day. Why don't you give me your phone number, and I'll call you after I've spoken to them."

Chris gave Pearson his cell number. "I appreciate you taking the time to see us, Doctor. I'm going to tell Pete Connolly how helpful you've been."

"Never too busy for a colleague," said Pearson, offering his hand again. "Connolly's doing fantastic work up at Sloan-Kettering. Of course, they have all the resources in the *world*. An embarrassment of riches."

Chris nodded, smiled at Joan, then escorted Alex through the door.

As soon as the door shut behind them, Alex veered to the right, toward another row of doors.

"What are you doing?" Chris whispered.

"Finding the guys he talked about. Here's Parminder

right here. That wasn't so hard." She tested the knob. "Locked."

Chris followed as she moved from door to door, but then his bowels spasmed. He doubled over, trying to keep from defecating in his pants.

"Chris?" she gasped, running back to him. "What is it?"

"I've got to get to a bathroom."

She grabbed his arm and pulled him back the way they had come. "There's a men's room by the elevators."

He struggled to duck-walk and keep his sphincter clenched at the same time. He made a note to look up the contraindications of the antiviral agents he was taking the next time he got near a computer. After a seeming eternity, the door to the men's room appeared. Alex crashed right through and helped him into one of the stalls.

"Okay, get out," he gasped.

"Are you all right?"

"Get out!"

He tried to hold it, but he was already going before she left the room.

Will Kilmer was parked at the base of the AmSouth Bank Tower when Thora Shepard climbed out of her silver Mercedes and stormed into the lobby of the office building. Her arrival stunned him. Kilmer was only parked here because the operative tailing Rusk had reported that his target had reversed direction ten miles south of town and headed back toward Jackson. Since that operative had reported other cars tailing Rusk, Will had driven here to take over the surveillance.

The couple he had watching Thora Shepard in Greenwood had broken off contact when they saw her checking out of the Alluvian Hotel. They, like Will, had assumed that Thora and her girlfriend would be driving straight back to Natchez. But now here she was, storming into Andrew Rusk's office building with no girlfriend in sight. Where had she dumped Laura Canning? Will considered getting out and going up to the sixteenth floor, but what would that accomplish? He couldn't get inside Rusk's office. On the other hand, Rusk wasn't there himself.

Will got out of his Ford Explorer and hurried across the street. He told the doorman that he was going up to the AmSouth offices on the second floor, then got into the elevator and punched 2 and 16. As soon as the doors opened on 16, he heard a woman yelling at near full volume:

"I called here all last night, and I've spoken to you at least five times this morning! I've paid your boss one hell of a lot of money, and I'm going to talk to him one way or another."

Will stepped out of the elevator and peered through a wide door that led to an ultramodern reception area. Thora Shepard was standing with her back to him, facing an attractive blonde in her thirties, who was clearly struggling to maintain some semblance of professionalism.

"Mrs. Shepard," said the receptionist, "I've told you repeatedly that Mr. Rusk is out of town. I've tried to reach him by cell phone, but I haven't been able to. As soon as I do reach him, I will relay your message and the urgency of your situation. I promise you that."

Thora stood with her hands on her hips, looking as if

she meant to stand in that spot all day if that was what it took to see Andrew Rusk. It struck Will then that for the first time he was seeing her dressed like a normal person. No designer outfit. No fancy hairdo. Just tight blue jeans and an even tighter white T-shirt. Thora was clearly giving the receptionist the hairy eyeball, but the blonde behind the desk was giving as good as she got. Without warning, Thora whirled and marched back toward the elevator.

"You going down, ma'am?" Will asked.

"You're damn right," Thora snapped.

As the elevator whooshed toward the lobby, Thora cursed steadily under her breath. In the closeness of the car, Will saw that her neck was blotchy with red spots, the way his wife looked when she was about to explode in a fit of temper. There were dark circles under both eyes. Will needed to talk to Alex in a hurry. Something had gone down last night, and they needed to know what it was.

When the elevator opened, Thora did not march out to the street. She walked aimlessly around the lobby like the survivor of a car crash. Will had seen a lot of desperate people during his years as a cop, and all his instincts told him this lady was about to snap.

He took out his cell phone and speed-dialed Alex. Her phone kicked him straight to voice mail. He jammed the phone back into his pocket and sat down on a padded bench. For five weeks, he had been helping his best friend's daughter, out of a bottomless sense of obligation. He had worked a lot of dead-end cases over the years, and about ten days ago he had decided this was one of them. But now adrenaline was flushing through his system the way it always did when a case started to break. For a brief moment, he thought of young Grace Morse, who would never see her son graduate high school. For an even briefer moment, he thought of the daughter he himself had lost all those years ago. When he got up to follow Thora out to the street, all the aches and pains of age were gone. He felt younger than he had in years. Wherever this crazy woman led him, Will would follow.

Alex was standing outside the hospital men's room when the elevator door opened and the bearded man with the birthmark that she'd met yesterday stepped out. He walked down the hall without glancing up, his eyes on a file in his hand. But then he turned, looked back at Alex, and said, "Hello, again."

"Hello," Alex called.

The bearded man smiled, then walked down the corridor and turned toward the academic offices. Alex hesitated, then followed. As she rounded the final corner, she saw his white-coated back disappear into an office. The brass plate on the door said ELDON TARVER, MD.

She hurried back to the men's room, but she saw no sign of Chris in the hall. She cracked open the bathroom door and called his name.

"What is it?" Chris groaned.

"I just saw Dr. Tarver. I was in the elevator with him yesterday and didn't even know it."

"Where is he now?"

"In his office. You almost done?"

"Yeah. Don't talk to him without me."

"Hurry, Chris."

She shut the door and went back down to Tarver's leg of the hall. His door was still closed. She was tempted to knock, but what excuse did she have to start a conversation? The only thing they shared was facial disfigurement. The guy would think she was coming on to him.

"Okay," Chris said, rounding the corner with a pale, clammy face.

"Can you make it?"

"I think so."

She turned to the door and knocked hard, but there was no answer. She waited, then knocked again. No response.

"He's gone?" she said. "That's weird."

"Why? I'm sure he just—"

"Oh, hello," said the now familiar bass voice. "What can I do for you?"

Chris held out his hand. "Dr. Tarver, I'm Chris Shepard, an internist from Natchez."

Dr. Tarver shook his hand. "Have you come to see me?"

"I suppose so. Pete Connolly recommended you as an expert on oncogenic viruses, and specifically retro-viruses."

Tarver looked surprised. "I'm not sure I would put myself forward as that. I hold several degrees, but I'm not board-certified in virology."

"Nevertheless, both Pete and Dr. Pearson seem to think you're quite knowledgeable in the area."

"I do have quite a bit of practical experience." Dr. Tarver looked at Alex. "And you are . . . ?"

"Nancy Jenner. I'm Dr. Shepard's chief nurse."

Dr. Tarver's eyes twinkled. He looked at Chris and said, "I envy you."

Chris cut his eyes at Alex, but she ignored him.

"Why don't we step into my office?" Tarver said, glancing at his watch. "I have about five minutes before I'm due somewhere."

He admitted them to an office much less spacious than the one occupied by Dr. Pearson. Bookshelves lined three of the four walls; the fourth was studded with framed photographs, many of them black-and-white. Tarver was older than she'd thought, Alex realized. There was a picture of him with President Richard Nixon; Nixon was pinning something on his chest. Another showed Tarver standing in front of a familiar-looking building with a long banner hanging over its entrance: FREE AIDS TESTING TODAY. In one picture Tarver was surrounded by emaciated black children, all reaching for him as though he were Albert Schweitzer. Alex studied the photos while Chris questioned the doctor.

"A cluster of cancers in Natchez, you say?" asked Tarver. "I wasn't aware of that. Natchez is in Adams County, correct?"

"Yes. Blood cancers, specifically," said Chris. "Several local doctors are starting to wonder if these cases might have a common etiology."

"A *viral* etiology?"

"Well, we don't know. I was thinking radiation exposure, but we can't pin down a common source. Most of the patients work at different places and live in different parts of town."

"Which militates against an environmental cause, as well," said Tarver.

"That's how I got onto the virus angle. I know that several cancers have been proved to have a viral etiology, or at least a viral mediator."

"That's more true in animals than humans. I can't

think of a single case in which a virus has produced a cluster of cancers."

Chris looked surprised. "Surely there must be some cervical cancers like that, in urban areas with a high degree of sexual promiscuity?"

Tarver nodded in surprise. "I'm sure you're right. But those studies haven't been done. The process of viral oncogenesis is a long one. Decades long, in some cases. It's not like tracking a herpes epidemic. You could be in the midst of an HPV epidemic and not even know it. In fact, in some places I think we are. Sexual promiscuity is one of the best things that ever happened to the virus as an organism. In the Darwinian sense, I mean."

Alex was moving from photo to photo on the office wall. The birthmark made it easy to pick out Dr. Tarver, even in large group shots. Though it wasn't technically a birthmark, she remembered. It was something to do with malformed arteries and veins. As she studied the pictures, a fact she'd learned back at Quantico bubbled to the forefront of her mind. Many serial murderers suffered from some physical deformity that set them apart during their childhood. It was crazy to suspect Tarver, of course—a guy she had simply gotten onto an elevator with—and yet . . . he certainly had the sophisticated knowledge that their high-tech murders would require. And there was something about him, a quiet forcefulness and logical precision that made him seem capable of decisive, maybe even extreme, action; whereas Matt Pearson seemed more conventional.

Chris was speaking medical jargon now, an esoteric version far above her level. As his voice droned on, one photograph caught Alex's eye. In it, Dr. Tarver and a man wearing an army uniform stood on either side of a beautiful blond woman. Behind them stood a fortress-like building with a sign on its front that read VCP. The breast of Tarver's lab coat bore the same legend: VCP. Tarver was much younger in the photo, with a full head of hair and no beard. The military officer reminded Alex a little of her father. And the woman . . . she had that brainy look like the models in magazine ads for saturation language courses, the ones that made businessmen think they could get laid overseas if only they would learn a little French.

At the first pause in the conversation, Alex said, "What's VCP?"

"I beg your pardon?" said Dr. Tarver.

"In this photo, you're wearing a coat that says VCP."

"Oh." Tarver smiled. "That stands for the Veterans' Cancer Project. It was something the government sponsored in conjunction with the NIH and some private corporations, to look into the high incidence of cancer in combat veterans."

"What era?"

"Late Vietnam. But we were seeing a lot of men from World War Two and Korea as well. Pacific-theater vets, mostly. That island fighting was hell, days of shelling, a lot of flamethrower use."

"No Agent Orange?"

"Sadly, no. No one was talking about that back then. Mainly because the incubation period of the cancers caused by that compound is so long. As I was saying about viral etiologies. Same problem."

Before Alex could ask another question, Chris said,

"Do you retain blood samples from patients who've died on the oncology ward?"

This question made Alex's pulse race, but she turned away and went back to looking at the photographs. Some of "her" victims had died in this very hospital. If their blood had been preserved, might it be possible to discover some common carcinogen that would prove mass murder?

"I know it's done in some research centers," Chris went on, "so that new information can be gained after new testing technology is developed."

"I know the pathology lab retains all specimens for ten years. We probably retain samples of blood and neoplastic cells in some cases. You'd have to talk to Dr. Pearson about that."

"I could give you a list of the patients we're concerned about," Alex said.

Dr. Tarver gave her an accommodating smile. "I suppose I could pass that on to Dr. Pearson for you."

Struggling to mask her excitement, she walked to his desk and took a pen from a silver cup there. "May I write on this prescription pad?"

"Of course."

Supremely conscious of Chris's eyes on her, Alex wrote the name of each person she believed to be a victim of the killers they sought, excepting those who had not died of cancer.

"This may sound a little nuts," Chris said, "but I've been wondering if it's possible that someone might be purposely inducing cancer in human beings."

Alex looked up from her list. Dr. Tarver was staring at Chris as though he had suggested that priests might secretly be killing babies during baptisms.

"Did I hear you correctly, Doctor?"

"I'm afraid so."

"That's one of the most remarkable things I've ever heard. What makes you suggest something like that?"

"Intuition, I guess. Nothing else seems to explain these cases."

Dr. Tarver gave him an understanding look. "That's frequently the case with cancer, specifically blood cancers. They remain some of the most enigmatic and intractable opponents we face."

"The other thing," Chris said in a Will Rogers drawl—his version of Columbo?—"is that all these patients were married to wealthy people who wanted to divorce them."

Tarver looked incredulous. "Are you serious?"

"Yes, sir. I am."

"Are you suggesting that someone is *murdering* people by giving them cancer?"

"More than that. I think it's a doctor."

Dr. Tarver laughed. "I'm sorry, but I don't know what to say to that. Do any law enforcement authorities agree with your hypothesis?"

"Yes," Alex said sharply. She wasn't sure why Chris had gone this route, but she wasn't about to leave him twisting in the wind. "Dr. Tarver, I'm actually a special agent of the FBI. And I can tell you that the Bureau is looking deeply into these cases."

"May I see your identification?"

Alex reached for her back pocket, then froze. She had never felt so ridiculous in her life. It was like having her credit card denied, only the embarrassment was magnified a thousandfold. "I left my ID at the hotel," she said lamely.

Dr. Tarver was looking at them with obvious discomfort. "I'd like to do all I can to help you, Dr. Shepard. But I must tell you, if Dr. Pearson knew that this visit had anything to do with legal matters, he would be very upset. I should terminate this interview until we can continue it on an official basis." He looked at his watch. "Besides, I'm late for my meeting."

He gathered up some papers from his desk, then ushered them to the door. Once they were in the hall, he locked the door, said "Good day," then hurried down to the elevators.

"I don't know why I did that," Chris said, walking slowly up the corridor.

"A shot in the dark is better than nothing," said Alex.

"Not always. Once Pearson hears about that conversation, I'll be persona non grata at this institution."

"Not if you really refer that many patients up here. Money talks, brother. And my mother's a patient. They can't kick me out."

Chris angled toward a bench opposite the elevators and collapsed on it. Dr. Tarver had already vanished. Probably into Dr. Pearson's office.

"Are you all right?" Alex asked.

"I don't know. I need to get back to the hotel, at least until my stomach settles down."

"That's fine with me. I need to charge my phone." She pressed the elevator button. "What do you think about Tarver?"

Chris shrugged. "Typical specialist. That AV anomaly on his face is bad."

She nodded. "He gives me a weird feeling."

"He wants to get into your pants."

"Not that."

Chris chuckled as though it hurt to laugh. "I know what you mean. But we're just desperate."

The bell dinged, and the elevator opened.

Chris had already boarded the car when a thought struck her. "You go ahead. I'm going back to ask Dr. Pearson something."

Chris held the door open. "What?"

"It's stupid, really. I'm just being OCD. Wait for me downstairs."

"Tell me, damn it!"

"In one of Dr. Tarver's photos, he's standing in front of a building with a sign that says FREE AIDS TESTING. It looked familiar to me. I think it was a restaurant in downtown Jackson that my dad used to take me to when I was a kid. We'd have breakfast there. It was called Pullo's. I just want to know if I'm right."

"You're serious?"

"Yeah. And I want to know why they were testing for AIDS there. It doesn't make sense."

"I'll go with you." Chris started forward.

She gently pushed him back into the elevator. He was so weak that he could hardly stay on his feet. "I'll be right down. Sit on a bench and wait for me."

He sagged against the elevator wall. "Okay."

CHAPTER

42

Eldon Tarver stood behind the trunk of a large oak tree, his eyes locked on the entrance of the new adult critical-care hospital. He had watched Shepard emerge into the cloud of smoke generated by the patients and nurses getting their nicotine fixes outside the entrance, then retreat back into the building. Where was Morse? Was she canvassing the faculty? Or was she at this moment recounting specific suspicions to Dr. Pearson? Eldon wasn't afraid, but the part of his brain that handled threat assessment was lit up like a small city.

He couldn't go back to his office. Nor could he return to his house. Even going back to the primate lab was a risk . . . but it was one he had to take. He doubted that anyone had the Noel Traver alias yet. He didn't see how they could. But then how had they gotten this far? *Rusk,* he thought angrily. *A stupid fucking lawyer, what else?* Eldon congratulated himself on yesterday's decision to pull out early. Fate had revealed that it was not early at all.

It was very late.

The conversation with Morse and Shepard was one of the most remarkable he had ever experienced. Not only had he murdered Morse's sister, but Shepard . . . Shepard was a walking dead man! Yet there he'd stood, questioning a specialist with his pathetically inadequate knowledge of medicine. Eldon wondered if Shepard knew he was doomed. If he didn't, he would soon. But unlike the other victims, who believed they'd been randomly selected by fate for premature death, Shepard would know that the cancer devouring his body had been placed there by another human being. By his wife, in fact—or at least at her request.

Of course, the cancer did not yet exist. Eldon had simply initiated a cascade of events that, left unchecked, would terminate in carcinogenesis on the cellular level. And no one was going to stop that lethal cascade for Chris Shepard. Because the only man alive who could do so was Eldon Tarver. And for Eldon, Shepard's death represented valuable research data. Alive, Shepard was useless, and in conjunction with Alex Morse, possibly even dangerous.

Eldon needed to speak to Edward Biddle.

He couldn't risk using his cell phone; the FBI might already be monitoring it. But problems like this were easy to solve. Under a stand of trees twenty yards away stood a small knot of nurses greedily smoking cigarettes. He recognized two from Oncology. With a quick glance at the hospital entrance, he crossed the open ground and addressed the smaller of the two nurses, a short-haired brunette who had always greeted him in the halls.

"Excuse me," he said. "My cell phone died, and I need to make an emergency call. It's about a patient. Would you mind if—"

The nurse was already handing him her phone.

"Thank you," Eldon said with a grateful smile. "I'll only be a minute."

He punched in the number of Edward Biddle's cell phone. The phone rang and rang, then kicked him to voice mail. Dr. Tarver hung up. Was Biddle not answering because he did not recognize the number? Was there some problem because he was airborne? That was unlikely, since he was almost certainly in a corporate aircraft. Or was there some deeper problem? Eldon dialed the number once more and got the same response.

Cursing inwardly, he gave the phone back to the nurse, then hurried across the grass to his car. He would have to risk meeting Biddle at their original rendezvous. He didn't like the idea, but when he thought back to the demeanor of Morse and Shepard in his office, he felt that the worm had not quite turned. If they had anything concrete on him—or more important, if the FBI were handling this officially—they would have played it differently. He looked back over his shoulder as he walked. Morse and Shepard had still not emerged from the hospital.

Alex put on a smile and pushed open the door of Dr. Pearson's office. The beehive lady was still at her post, but the door to the inner office was cracked open.

"Hello again," Alex said. "I forgot to ask Dr. Pearson one question."

The secretary did not hide her irritation. "I think it's better if you call with it."

Alex raised her voice, trusting to Pearson's goodwill. "It's just one question, nothing medical at all."

Dr. Pearson poked his head out of his door, like a curious cat, though not so sleek. "Hello again."

He'd at least remembered her face. "Yes, I was actually talking to Dr. Tarver a moment ago. He invited us into his office—"

Beehive lady snorted.

"—and he had some very interesting pictures on his wall. I grew up in Jackson, and one of them is really bugging me."

Pearson looked perplexed. "Well, I grew up in California, so I doubt—"

"It's a long building with glass windows, and it says FREE AIDS TESTING on a banner in front. It looks like a restaurant my dad used to take me to when I was a little girl."

Pearson's eyes lit up; he was genuinely happy to be able to help. "Yes, of course. That used to be Pullo's restaurant, until Dr. Tarver bought it."

A fillip of excitement went through Alex, almost déjà vu, but slightly different. "Dr. Tarver bought Pullo's?"

"Yes, about four years ago, I believe."

"I've been living in Washington, D.C., for quite a while now."

"I see. Well, Eldon wanted a site that would be easily accessible to the indigent residents of the city, the homeless, the poor children, the medically underserved."

"Easily accessible for what?"

"His clinic. It's a free clinic for the poor."

"Oh. I see."

"Dr. Tarver gives a great deal of time to that clinic. He tests for many of the common viruses that afflict the lower socioeconomic classes: AIDS, hepatitis C, the herpes family, human papillomavirus, all that stuff. He treats them as well. He's won a lot of grants. Of course, the records of his work are quite valuable in a statistical sense."

Alex was nodding; she felt as though she was nearing something important. "Yes, I imagine they would be. I didn't realize we had something like that in Jackson."

"We didn't for many years. But when Dr. Tarver lost his wife, he decided he wanted to make something positive out of her loss."

"Lost his wife?" Alex echoed. "What did she die of?"

"Cervical cancer. A terrible case, I believe. Seven or eight years ago—before my time here. But Dr. Tarver inherited quite a bit of money from his wife, and he wanted to put it to good use, which he certainly did. You know, Eldon was one of the first people to suggest a viral origin for cervical cancer. I saw a paper he did on it, written *years* before the idea became generally accepted. I believe he's even considered litigation over credit for that finding."

Alex had run out of words, but her mind was racing.

"Is that all you wanted?" Dr. Pearson asked.

"Um . . . you say he spends a lot of time at the clinic?"

Beehive woman gave her boss a pointed look, and Dr. Pearson suddenly seemed to remember that Alex was an outsider.

"Dr. Shepard told me to thank you again," Alex said with her best Southern-belle smile, then she backed out of the office.

Outside, she turned and ran to the elevator. When it was too slow in coming, she took the fire stairs. Her heart pounded as she ran, but not from the exercise.

When she reached the first floor, she saw Chris standing inside the hospital entrance doors.

"Hey," he said. "I wanted to go outside, but the smoke is so thick it could choke you. There are people out there smoking through tracheostomies."

She took his arm. "Chris, you're not going to believe this."

"What?"

"That building I asked about—Dr. Tarver owns it now. Pearson told me it's a free clinic for the poor."

"What kind of clinic?"

"He tests people for viruses."

Chris's eyes flickered. "Did Pearson say which viruses?"

"AIDS, hepatitis, HPV, herpes. He also treats people there. Gets grants for the medicine. He started that clinic in memory of his wife, who died of cancer seven years ago. And guess what?"

"What?"

"He inherited a pile of money from her."

Chris's mouth fell open. "Did she die of a blood cancer?"

"No. Cervical."

"Hm."

"Doesn't that seem suspicious to you?"

"I'd say yes, except that he turned around and used the money to open a free clinic in memory of his dead wife."

"Right, but that put him down in the inner city, where he could do God knows what under the guise of treating the poor for free. How much oversight do you think there is on that kind of thing?"

Chris was nodding. "Some, but it's tough to oversee

what's actually going on in that kind of patient population. OSHA would have to have their own Eldon Tarver on-site to understand what was really happening."

Alex nodded excitedly. "I want to go down there."

"And do what?"

"I don't know. Look around, for starters. I want to find out if there's any connection between Tarver and Andrew Rusk. Don't you?"

"I think it's worth exploring." Chris grimaced. "But right now I need to find a bathroom and a bed. I'm feeling pretty rough."

Consciousness of Chris's desperate plight rushed back into her mind like a dark tide. "I'm sorry," she said, slipping under his arm so that he could lean on her. "Let's go to the car. I'll get Kaiser on Dr. Tarver when we get back."

Chris nodded, then walked slowly through the doors.

"When I'm distracted," he said, "like upstairs, I can almost put the reality out of my head. But when I'm alone, like a minute ago . . ."

Alex pressed her cheek to his chest as they walked. "You're not alone. Remember that."

"Alex—" He caught his breath as they stepped over a hole in the sidewalk. "Everybody faces death alone."

She shook her head. "Not you. You have Ben, and . . . I'll be right beside you, no matter what happens."

He squeezed her shoulder.

"But nothing bad's going to happen," she said forcefully. "We're going to find these assholes, and we're going to get you cured. Right?"

His reply was a whisper. "I hope so."

• • •

Will Kilmer sat in his Explorer, watching Thora Shepard walk angrily up and down the block beneath the AmSouth tower. She clearly meant to ambush Rusk, even if she had to wait all day to do it. Will knew that the confrontation was imminent, since one of his operatives had called and told him that Rusk was sitting in traffic only a block away.

As though she were telepathic, Thora began to concentrate on the private parking garage from which Rusk would try to leave if he had been hiding upstairs. She obviously knew what kind of vehicle he drove, for when the gleaming black Cayenne wheeled around the nearest corner and rolled up to the bar that blocked the garage entrance, Thora sprinted over, interposed herself between Rusk's window and the card reader, and started banging on his window.

Will climbed out of his Explorer and hurried across the street. Thora was hammering the Porsche's window with her fists, while Rusk gaped in shock. His only option was to back up and flee, but a Cadillac had already pulled into the lane behind him. At last, Rusk lowered his window and hissed, "What the hell do you think you're doing?"

"Give me your key card," Thora demanded.

"What?"

The Cadillac honked behind them.

"Give me your card!"

"Get out of here!" Rusk snarled. "Don't you know what's at stake?"

"You have to call it off! This instant!"

"I don't know what you're talking about," the lawyer said woodenly.

The Cadillac honked again.

Thora leaned down to the window, but by now Will was only a few feet away. "He *knows*," she hissed. "Chris knows *everything*."

"You're crazy."

"If you don't call it off, I'm going to—"

Rusk thrust his key card past her and tried to slip it into the slot.

To Will's amazement, Thora sank her teeth into the lawyer's forearm with enough force to compel a scream. Rusk yanked back his arm, and Thora grabbed the card. When the driver of the Cadillac opened his door and got out, Rusk realized how dangerous the scene was.

"Get in, you crazy bitch!" he snapped. "Hurry!"

Thora ran around the Cayenne's hood and climbed into the passenger seat. Rusk took the card from her and jammed it into the slot. When the barrier rose, he screeched into the parking garage.

Will took out his cell phone and called Alex, but again he got no answer.

CHAPTER
43

Chris was vomiting in the bathroom of their room at the Cabot Lodge when Alex's cell phone began to ring. She had only plugged it in a moment ago, and now she was supporting Chris while he puked.

"You can get it," Chris croaked, dry-heaving over the commode. "I'm okay."

"You're far from okay."

"This is just side effects from the medicine. Go."

Alex let go of his shoulders and ran into the bedroom. The caller ID listed Will's phone. The detective sounded ten years younger when he answered her callback.

"Kid, I've been trying to reach you all morning. This thing's breaking wide-open."

"What's happened?"

"Thora Shepard just confronted Rusk on the street below his office. She's lost her mind. Stood right in front of his car, screaming at him to call off the hit on her husband."

"Jesus! Where are they now?"

"Up in Rusk's office, I think."

Alex thought quickly. She had already called

Kaiser about checking out Eldon Tarver, but she didn't want to wait for answers. "Can you get someone to take your place and stay on Thora? I want you to meet me somewhere else."

"I guess so. Where are we going?"

"The old Pullo's restaurant."

"That place closed years ago."

"I know. It's a free clinic now."

"And you need me there because?"

"There's a small chance it could get dicey."

"How small?"

"Ten percent. But you never know, right? Isn't that what you tried to teach me?"

Will chuckled. "Okay. I'll meet you there in fifteen minutes."

"Let's meet a few blocks away. The park behind the Governor's Mansion?"

"I'll be there."

When Alex turned toward the bathroom, she found Chris sitting on the edge of the bed.

"What happened?" he asked hoarsely.

She didn't want to lie, but she wasn't about to tell Chris that his wife was running amok on the streets of Jackson. Not in his present state. "Will almost got into an accident," she said.

Chris gave her a sidelong glance. "You said, 'Where are they now?' "

"I meant the people who almost hit him." Alex pulled back the bedclothes and motioned for Chris to get under them. "You need rest. Come on, get in."

He looked back at her with hollow eyes, but rather than protest, he let himself fall onto the sheet and shoved his feet under the covers.

Alex set the hotel phone beside him, within easy reach. "If it gets worse, call 911 and demand to be taken to UMC."

He nodded weakly.

She leaned over and kissed him on the forehead. "I'll be back soon to check on you." As she straightened up, he caught hold of her wrist with surprising force.

"Be careful, Alex," he said, his dark eyes intense. "These people don't care about anybody. Don't throw your life away."

"I know."

He jerked her wrist, hard. "Do you?"

At last his concern penetrated the buzz of excitement in her brain. "I think so."

"Good."

When Chris let go of her arm, she removed the borrowed Sig-Sauer from the shoe box in the closet, slipped it into her waistband at the small of her back, and hurried into the hall.

Andrew Rusk stopped the elevator one floor short of his office. He wasn't about to drag a hysterical Thora Shepard past Janice. Besides, he no longer felt safe discussing anything sensitive in his office.

When the doors opened, he smelled sawdust. Several walls had been knocked out on this floor, where a remodel was in progress. Hoping to find some privacy, he marched Thora down the hall, but a guy with a ponytail was patching drywall in the area he'd hoped to use. Looking around, Rusk saw that Ponytail was the only workman in the area. He dug out his wallet, handed a C-note to the workman, and said he needed twenty minutes with the lady. Ponytail grinned and headed for the elevator.

Rusk walked over exposed concrete to a tall window, then turned and spoke to Thora with all the pent-up frustration of the past hours.

"What the hell has gotten into you, lady? Have you lost what little mind you have?"

"*Fuck you!*" Thora shouted, shaking her forefinger in his face. "You told me this was safe! You told me nothing could go wrong. You remember that, you cocky bastard? But something *has* gone wrong. Chris knows everything!"

"That's impossible."

Her eyes blazed. "You think so? He *called* me, you stupid prick. He said, 'I might be dead in a year, but you're dead, too.' He also said I'd never see Ben again, because I'd be in prison. How does that make you feel, Andy? Does that wipe the smirk off your face?"

Rusk tried not to show how deeply her words had disturbed him.

"You have to call it off," Thora insisted. "That's the only option."

He started to explain why he couldn't do that, then stopped himself. He couldn't tell this woman that he had zero control over Eldon Tarver. "You're right," he said. "Of course we'll stop it."

She burst into tears. "I can't believe this. Any of it. What am I going to do? What can I possibly tell Chris?"

"Nothing." Rusk stepped closer to her. "He can't prove anything. He's getting all this from an FBI agent who's already been fired. It's going to be okay, Thora."

"You think I believe that? What the hell do you know about marriage, anyway?"

A lot more than most people, Rusk thought wearily.

"I have to tell him something!"

Rusk shook his head with deliberation. "You're not going to tell him anything. You're not going to tell anyone anything."

Thora's despair reverted to fury in a heartbeat. "Don't tell me what I'm going to do! I'll do whatever the hell I decide to do. I was crazy ever to listen to you."

"That's not what you said after Red Simmons died and made you a multimillionaire."

She looked like she wanted to cut his throat. "That's ancient history. We're talking about Chris now. Listen to me. I'm telling you to call whatever scumbag does this stuff for you and cancel my contract. Right now! You're not going to get another cent from me anyway."

Rusk grabbed her arms and let her glimpse the fear behind his eyes. "Before you start making threats, you should know a couple of things. First, you can't hurt me without hurting yourself. But that's really not the point. The person who handles these jobs is an extremely dangerous man. He has no conscience as you know it, no compassion. You should think of him as a very efficient machine. And if you upset that machine by doing something as insane as refusing to pay his fee, you will incur his wrath. Now . . ." Rusk tried to get hold of himself. "If your husband really suspects the truth, I'll do what I can to stop what's been set in motion. But *you* will do nothing. If my partner had witnessed your behavior today, you would already be dead. No one would ever find your body, Thora. The only mother Ben would ever know would be the next woman Chris marries."

She stared wildly at him, seemingly torn between the tangible fear of having her sins discovered and the theoretical fear of being murdered herself.

"When you look at me," Rusk said softly, "don't see

me—see *him*. Do that, and you just might live through this."

Thora's eyes jinked back and forth like a strung-out addict's. But after a time, she started blinking like a woman coming out of a seizure. "What am I supposed to do?" she whimpered. "Where can I *go*?"

"You can stay in my office for now. But you can't say one word about any of this within those walls. My office may be bugged. Break that rule, and I'll hand you over to my partner. Are we clear?"

Thora wiped her mascara-stained cheeks. "I don't want to stay here. I want to see my son."

"You can't. Not yet."

"Bullshit! I haven't broken any law."

Rusk gasped in amazement. "You hired someone to kill your husband! *Twice!*"

She laughed like a child discovering a lie that would get her out of trouble with her parents. "I consulted a divorce lawyer. No one can prove I did anything else."

"You've already paid me a million dollars!"

Cool arrogance descended like a curtain over her eyes. "I followed the investment advice you gave me. That put a million dollars under your control. If anyone looks at that deal, it'll look like you stole the money. Stole it and bought rough diamonds."

Rusk was speechless.

"You're like every other goddamn contractor I deal with, Andrew. It's easy to guarantee your work. What's tough is *honoring* your guarantee."

He looked past her to make sure that Ponytail hadn't returned. If anyone heard this conversation . . .

"Now," Thora said, her voice utterly composed, "I'm going to ride downstairs and go back to my old life. *You* are going to make sure that nothing happens to my husband. But if something should—or if even one policeman rings my doorbell—I will hang your ass out to dry, Andrew. Are we clear?"

Rusk's mind was spinning. This woman had no clue to the reality of the situation. There was no going back to her previous life—not for her or anyone else. Thora Shepard was one of those beauties who had slid through life without any mud sticking to her, no matter what sins she committed. She thought she could do the same thing now. But sooner or later—probably sooner, given the escalation of surveillance by the FBI—someone would lock her in a small room and turn up the heat. And she would crack like a china doll.

"You need to see something," he said. *You delusional bitch,* he added silently. He stepped around a pile of Sheetrock lying across three sawhorses. "Let me show you why you can't just go back to your old life." He nodded toward the window, then offered to escort her with his arm. She looked contemptuously at the arm, but she did walk to the window.

"Do you see those men down there?" he asked, stepping over Ponytail's toolbox.

"Where?"

"There, on the corner. And on the steps across the street. See him?"

Thora splayed her hands on the window. "The guy reading the newspaper?"

"Yep. FBI. The woman, too. The jogger."

Thora's mouth opened. "How do you know?"

Rusk looked over his shoulder, back through the metal studs of the new office. "I have contacts at the Bureau."

"But why are they here? How much do they know?"

"I don't know yet. Do you see any other likely agents?"

As Thora stood on tiptoe, he bent and lifted a claw hammer out of Ponytail's toolbox. Something shifted in the box as he rose, and Thora turned at the sound, but by then Rusk was already swinging. The head of the hammer smashed through her skull above the ear, deeply enough that he had to yank hard to free it. She tottered on her feet, then fell, blindly trying to shield her face. With all the repressed terror of being caught coursing through his arm, Rusk swung the hammer as though chopping firewood. This spoiled bitch had threatened everything he'd worked five years to build . . . but had he backed off and called for help? No. He'd stepped up to the fucking plate. Never again would Eldon Tarver see him as a gutless middleman afraid to get his hands dirty. Rusk stopped swinging and stood over the bloody corpse, breathing the way he had on that first day at base camp on Everest. Never had he felt such elemental power. He only wished his father were here to see it.

Will was waiting for Alex when she arrived at the park behind the Governor's Mansion. She got out of the Corolla, locked it, and climbed into the passenger seat of his Explorer.

"What's the deal with this clinic?" Will asked.

"It's owned by a doctor from UMC. Eldon Tarver. I got a funny feeling when I talked to him."

Will's eyes crinkled with interest. "What kind of feeling?"

"You know what kind."

"I gotcha."

"Tarver's wife died of cancer years ago, and he inherited a lot of money. He opened up this place in memory of her. He treats a lot of poor people for AIDS, herpes, stuff like that. But I think he might be doing more. He's a cancer specialist, and this would be a perfect front for him. He could give those patients any kind of virus or toxin he wanted to, then monitor them when they come back for free medicine."

"A freako, then."

"Maybe." Alex bit her bottom lip. "Or maybe he's just a Good Samaritan."

Will barked a mocking laugh. "Haven't met too many of those in my time. They may look like angels, but they're usually getting something out of what they're doing, some way or other."

"We're about to find out, I hope. Let's go."

Will put the Explorer in gear and started driving. "I wish I knew what kind of car he drives."

"Kaiser should be able to tell us soon. I already gave him Tarver's name."

"I'll do my own check, just in case. Nothing against the FBI, you understand. Spell the name."

Alex did.

"Got it," said Will, jotting in the small notebook he carried at all times. "Hey, where's Dr. Shepard?"

"The Cabot Lodge."

Kilmer's eyes asked a silent question.

She laid her hand on the detective's arm. "He's sick, Will. Bad. But it's not your fault, okay?"

"Bullshit, it ain't. Goddamn it. Sleeping at my post. They used to shoot us for that."

"You were drugged. All three of you. Now, let go

of that and get your mind on the game. I need you."

Will rubbed his wrinkled face between both hands and sighed. "You taking your piece in with you?"

She shook her head. "Not this time."

"Shit." Will reached into the glove box and brought out a short-barreled .357 magnum. "I'm gonna be close, then."

"That's where I like you, partner."

The renovated Pullo's restaurant possessed little of its former personality. The only things Alex recognized were some curiously shaped light fixtures hanging above where the old buffet used to stand. Apart from these, the building had been gutted.

Just inside the door sat a receptionist, her coffee-colored elbows resting on a scarred metal desk. To her right was a large group of chairs, several of which were occupied by emaciated men who smelled of alcohol, cigarettes, and body odor. A narrow corridor led deeper into the building, but Alex learned nothing by glancing down it. An opaque window looked onto the waiting room from the back wall, and Alex got the feeling it was used to covertly study the patients.

"Can I help you?" asked the receptionist.

"I hope so. I was just speaking to Dr. Tarver over at the medical center. He asked me something I didn't know the answer to, but now I've found out for him. I wanted to tell him in person."

The receptionist eyed Alex up and down, trying to read her. Well-dressed Caucasian women were clearly not usual visitors at the clinic.

"What's your name?" she asked.

"Alexandra Morse."

"Well, the doctor's not here. But let me go back and talk to somebody. He may be coming in soon."

"Thank you. I'd appreciate it."

The woman got up as though she were doing Alex a huge favor and walked slowly down the corridor. Alex stepped closer to the desk and read everything she could off its surface. There were bills addressed to the Tarver Free Clinic, and one to Eldon Tarver, MD. A half-hidden magazine lay open under the appointment book: *Jet*. Written on a lined pad in an almost illegible scrawl were the words *Entergy bill late—Noel D. Traver, DVM*. Beneath this was a number: 09365974. Alex was memorizing the number when the receptionist returned.

"He ain't coming in today," she said, giving Alex a territorial glare.

"Not at all?"

"That's what I said."

The receptionist sat down and opened her magazine, as though she had done her duty and now intended to forget that Alex existed. Alex started to ask her to take a message, then thought better of it. Turning to leave, Alex almost bumped into a man wearing what had to be a $2,000 business suit.

"Excuse me," she said. "I'm sorry."

The newcomer had close-cropped gray hair and steel-blue eyes. His face triggered something in her mind. But what? He reminded her of some senior Bureau agents who had entered the FBI after leaving the army CID or the navy JAG corps.

"Not a problem, miss," the man said with the slightest of smiles.

He stepped wide for her to pass, and Alex did, despite a desire to ask what the hell the guy was doing in a dump like this. Maybe he thought it was still a restaurant. In its heyday, Pullo's had drawn some very rich men for breakfast.

Outside, Alex looked back and saw the stranger in conversation with the receptionist. He seemed to be having about as much luck as she had. Scanning the street for Will, she walked past a dark sedan that had parked in front of the clinic, then strode down to Will's Explorer and got into the passenger seat. A moment later, Will climbed behind the wheel.

"Any luck?" he asked.

"Nothing good."

He nodded. "You see that guy who just went in?"

"Yeah. You know him?"

"I know his type. Soldier."

"That's the vibe I got, too."

"Good girl. And check this out." Will pulled into the street and let the Explorer idle forward. With the slightest inclination of his head, he prompted Alex to look to her left. When she did, she saw a young man wearing an army uniform sitting behind the wheel of the sedan she had just walked past. She registered sergeant's stripes on his shoulder, and then they were past him.

"He drove the sharp-dressed guy here?"

"Yep. Did you see the door?"

"The car door?"

"u.s. government. Printed in black."

"What the hell?"

Will drove down the block and turned toward the spot where Alex's Corolla was parked. "They sure as shit ain't the IRS."

"Who are they?"

Will grinned. "I've got that same feeling you were talking about before."

Alex was thinking about the electric bill. "You ever hear of a vet named Noel Traver?"

"A military vet?"

"No, a veterinarian."

"Can't say I have. But *Traver* is pretty damn close to *Tarver,* ain't it?"

Alex pictured the notepad in her mind, substituting letters— "Shit! It's an anagram."

"Eldon Tarver and Noel Traver?"

"Noel *D.* Traver, I should have said. There was a note on a desk in there about a late electric bill."

"Now we're getting somewhere." Will's eyes flashed. "A cancer doctor with an alias. That make sense to you?"

"Not unless he's married to two women," Alex thought aloud. "Something like that."

"Or tax evasion," Will suggested with a laugh. "Maybe those guys *were* with the IRS."

"I think it's time to find out."

He grinned. "You want to go back and see how long that guy stays inside the clinic?"

"Yeah. Make the block. I wish I had my computer."

"If he's still there, maybe Tarver is inside with him."

Will hit the gas and made the block, not even stopping for a red light. The instant they turned back onto Jefferson Street, Alex saw that the dark sedan was gone.

"If I had to guess," said Will, "I'd say he's headed for the interstate."

"Let me out here. I'll jog to my car."

Will slammed on the brakes, and Alex jumped onto the pavement. When the detective floored it, the door slammed shut by itself.

CHAPTER

44

"Describe her to me," said Dr. Tarver.

Edward Biddle pursed his lips and looked around the spartan office. Dr. Tarver knew Biddle was wondering if this was the place where the "groundbreaking" research had been done. "About five-eight," Biddle said. "Dark hair, pretty, scars on the right side of her face. Almost like shrapnel scars."

Dr. Tarver tried to keep his face impassive, but Biddle could not be deceived.

"Who is she, Eldon? Another of your obsessions?"

Dr. Tarver had almost forgotten what it was like to be in the company of someone who knew his private predilections. "She's an FBI agent. She's working alone, though, no support from the Bureau."

He expected to see anxiety in Biddle's eyes, but he saw only displeasure. "An FBI agent?"

"She's not a problem, Edward. That's an unrelated matter. Is your car still out there?"

Biddle waved his hand as though making the car vanish with his gesture. "Let's get down to brass tacks. What have you got?"

Five minutes ago, Dr. Tarver had been pumped and ready to make his pitch; then Alexandra Morse had walked through the front door. "I need to take care of something first. Give me just one minute."

Biddle wasn't accustomed to waiting, but he raised his hand in assent.

Eldon left the office and walked into his private restroom down the hall. The door said PHLEBOTOMIST. He wasn't about to share a toilet seat with the scuzziest 5 percent of the population of Jackson, Mississippi. Even excluding the viruses he had given them, many of the clinic's patients carried most of the nastiest bugs resident in the American population. He closed the door and leaned back against it, his heart thudding in his chest.

A few minutes ago he had been focused on the terms of his negotiation with Biddle. Now Alex Morse had put the whole deal in jeopardy. If she weren't so goddamned observant, her visit might have meant little. But she *was*. If Morse could look at a photo of this clinic for a few seconds and make the connection to Pullo's restaurant, then she would eventually realize that the army major in the VCP photo she had noticed in his office was the same man she had seen walking into the clinic this afternoon. Thirty years had passed since their VCP days, but Biddle looked essentially the same. His hair was gray now, but he still *had* his hair, the son of a bitch. And not only had Morse seen Biddle enter the clinic—she had exchanged words with him. Yes, she would remember him, all right. And once she did, she would quickly uncover the true nature of the VCP. And *that* would allow her to track Eldon Tarver from his old life to his new one.

Eldon couldn't take that chance. He could not take on his new identity until Alex Morse was dead.

He was lucky that Pearson had called to warn him that Morse might show up. *She made a big deal about the restaurant, Eldon, and she's the type to come down and make a nuisance of herself. I probably said too much, but Chris Shepard is a highly reputable internist from Natchez. I just wanted you to know, so you wouldn't be blindsided by the girl.*

"Blindsided," Dr. Tarver murmured. "FUBAB, more like."

Killing an FBI agent was risky. If you did that, you were asking to be hounded to the ends of the earth for as long as you lived. In the carport he had acted on instinct. He would have to give it careful thought. Right now he had business to take care of: the biggest deal of his life. He flushed the toilet for cover, then walked back into his office, sat behind his desk, and folded his hands Buddha-style over his stomach.

"You want to know what I've got, Edward?"

Biddle's pale blue eyes were those of a man who had handled many critical negotiations. Bullshit did not fly in the rooms he worked. "You know me, Eldon. Straight to business."

Dr. Tarver leaned back in his chair. "I've got exactly what you were looking for all those years ago."

"Which is?"

"The Holy Grail."

Biddle just stared.

"The perfect weapon."

"*Perfect* is a mighty big word, Eldon."

Dr. Tarver smiled. He doubted they ever said "mighty big" at Yale, which was where Biddle had gone to college. He must have picked it up at Detrick.

"How about a weapon that is one hundred percent

lethal, yet which no one could ever prove was a weapon at all? It makes BW agents like anthrax or even small-pox relics of the Dark Ages. Wasn't it you who spoke of the Holy Grail at Detrick, Edward? A weapon that couldn't be perceived as a weapon?"

"Yes. But every scientist who ever worked for me helped prove that it was impossible."

"Oh, it's possible. It already exists." Eldon opened his desk drawer and took out a small vial filled with brownish liquid. "Here it is."

"What is it?"

"A retrovirus."

Biddle sniffed. "Source?"

"Simian, of course, as we always suspected. And as AIDS proved viable."

"What do you call it?"

Dr. Tarver smiled. "Kryptonite."

Biddle wasn't laughing. "Are you serious?"

"It's just a working name. The actual viral pedigree must remain my proprietary secret, for now. But if you decide to—"

"Buy it?"

"Just so. If you decide to buy it, then you can look behind the curtain and you can call it whatever you wish."

Biddle rubbed his hands together with a dry, grainy sound. "Tell me what else makes this Kryptonite a per-fect weapon."

"First, it has a long incubation period. Ten to twelve months right now, with death following in an average of sixteen months."

"Death from what?"

"Cancer."

Biddle tilted his head to one side. "Our old friend."

"Yes."

"The retrovirus induces it directly? Or is there immune breakdown first?"

"Selective breakdown. Only the necessary steps. It switches off the cellular death mechanism, granting immortality. It disguises itself from killer T cells. It begins producing its own growth factor. All the best viral strategies."

Biddle was already thinking about the larger implications. "Eldon, the indiscriminate nature of that kind of weapon renders it unusable on a large scale. You know that."

Tarver leaned forward. "I've solved that problem."

"How?"

"I've already created a vaccine. I grow it in horses."

Biddle pursed his lips. "So we'd have to vaccinate all our forces prior to using the weapon."

"Yes, yes, but we already do that. You could do it under cover of any other immunization."

Biddle was frowning now, suspicious that his time was being wasted. "But what about the general population? If we vaccinated the general population, it would set off all sorts of alarms. And don't tell me we could do it under the guise of avian flu vaccine or something. You could never keep it a secret—not in this day and age."

Eldon could hardly contain himself. "I can also sabotage the virus *after* infection, during the early stages of replication. Before oncogenesis occurs."

Biddle's poker face finally slipped. "You can kill the virus *after* infection?"

"I can wipe it out."

"No one can kill a virus once it's established in the body."

Dr. Tarver settled back in his chair, his confidence unshakable. "I created this virus, Edward. And I can destroy it."

Biddle was shaking his head, but Eldon saw the excitement in his eyes.

"After about three weeks," Eldon went on, "there's no stopping the cascade. But during that window, I can short-circuit the infection."

"So what you're telling me is—"

"I have your weapon for China."

Biddle's lips parted. He had the look of a man whose mind has just been read, and read accurately.

"I know you, Edward," Tarver said with a sly smile. "I know that's why you're here. I see what's happening in the world. I know the limits of oil reserves and strategic metals. I know where those reserves are flowing, where the heavy manufacturing is going. I'm no geopolitician, but I see the tide turning. The new cold war can't be more than twenty years off. Maybe less."

Biddle chose not to comment.

"I know the capabilities of Chinese nuclear submarines," Tarver went on. "I know about their missile program. And even high school students know the size of their standing army. Almost three million strong, and growing. The real strength of that number lies in the fact that life is cheap there, Edward. Casualties mean nothing—unlike the country we happen to be sitting in."

Biddle shifted in his seat and spoke softly. "Your point being?"

"The Chinese aren't the Russians. You won't be able

to spend them into oblivion. They already keep our economy afloat. If they decide to pull the plug now, we'll only have one option. Going nuclear."

Biddle nodded almost imperceptibly.

"And we won't do that," Tarver asserted. "You know we won't, because we won't be able to. The yellow men can afford to lose half a billion people. We can't. More important, they're *willing* to lose them. And we're not."

Biddle's eyes were half-closed. He was probably put off by the amateur strategizing, but Eldon knew he had made his point, however clumsily.

"Is this Kryptonite sexually transmissible?" Biddle asked quietly.

"One variant is, and one is not."

A tight smile. "That's convenient."

"You won't believe what I've accomplished, Edward. You want deniable political assassination? Give me one tube of blood from your target. I'll induce cancer in vitro, then you can reinject the blood into him. He'll be dead of non-Hodgkin's lymphoma eighteen months later."

Biddle's smile broadened. "I always said you were my most promising egghead, Eldon."

Dr. Tarver laughed out loud.

"So you're telling me," said Biddle, "that we could set this virus loose in a slum in Shanghai, and—"

"By the time the first cases started dying, they'd have fifteen months of exponential infection. It would be in every major Chinese city. They'd see a host of different cancers, not just one. The chaos would be unimaginable."

"It would also have leaped the oceans," Biddle observed.

Eldon's smile vanished. "Yes. We'd have to accept some casualties. But only for a while. With the example of AIDS, most countries would initiate crash programs to find a vaccine. Your company could take the lead in the U.S."

"And you could head it up," said Biddle. "Is that what you're thinking?"

"I shouldn't lead it. But I should be part of it. And after a reasonable amount of time—before the death toll climbs too high over here—we'll come forward with an experimental vaccine."

"The rest of the world would demand access to it."

"Over the objections of their medical establishments. You know the ego battles involved in this kind of research. Look at Gallo and the French. Also, no one but us could be sure that our vaccine worked. The delays could last years, but our population would be protected the entire time."

"How difficult would it be for someone else to develop a vaccine?"

"Without knowing what I know? Twenty years is optimistic. We're talking about a retrovirus. Look at HIV as a model. It's been around since 1978, and—"

"Longer," Biddle corrected quietly.

Tarver raised an eyebrow. "In any case, we still don't have an AIDS vaccine. We're not even close."

"Nevertheless, with China's population, this wouldn't be a decisive weapon, but rather a destabilizing one."

"You want apocalypse? I can give you that."

"How?"

Eldon held up his hands and drew them apart. "Simply lengthen the incubation period. I could stretch it to the scale of something like multiple myeloma. Twenty-five to thirty years."

Amazement now. "Could you really?"

"Of course. I've purposefully shortened the incubation in my work."

"Why?"

"To be able to carry out my research in a measurable time frame. Lengthen the incubation to twenty years, and I'd be dead before I saw my first results."

Biddle wet his lips with his pale tongue. "With a five-year incubation period, seventy percent of the population over fifteen could be infected before anyone got sick. Even if they had an effective vaccine, it would be too late. They'd already be battling total social breakdown."

"Yes." Eldon lowered his voice. "I'll tell you something else. I think I can make these viruses *race-specific*."

Biddle blinked in disbelief. "This is Herman Kahn territory. Thinking about the unthinkable."

"Somebody has to do it. Or all our ancestors will have lived and died for nothing. The world will be inherited by—"

"Don't even say it," said Biddle. "In whatever discussions we may have in future—with whatever people—don't mention that side of it. The Darwinian side."

"Why not?"

"You don't have to. The right people will understand the implications."

Eldon leaned forward again. "I trust your instincts. So . . . now that you know what I'm offering, I'd like to hear how interested you are."

And what I'm willing to pay, said Biddle's eyes. But his mouth said, "Obviously, I'm interested. But just as obviously, there are some issues."

"Such as?"

Biddle gave him a knowing smile, a shared look between equals. "You're ahead of your time, Eldon. You always were. You know that."

Tarver nodded but said nothing.

"*But*," Biddle went on, a note of optimism in his voice, "not nearly so far ahead as you once were. The regulatory climate has been hell since the Clinton years, but things are loosening up. Everyone's ramping up their primate-breeding capacity. They've finally realized that you can only go so far in the lower species."

"And of course China's far ahead of everyone else in that, too."

Biddle conceded this with a nod. "So far ahead that we're already doing some of our primate research there."

Eldon shook his head in disgust.

Biddle shifted in his seat. "Of course, when the other shoe drops—politically speaking—all those projects will be nationalized, and you'll be Cassandra vindicated. You'll look like the Messiah, Eldon."

"How long before that shoe drops?"

"No way to know. But that's not critical to our arrangement. As for getting you a new identity, I can take care of that in a few days. If you want money, real money—"

"I want what this technology is worth."

A look of slight surprise. "That will take longer."

"How much longer?"

"Hmm . . . three years? Maybe five?"

Anger and bitterness rose from Tarver's gut.

"It could be sooner," Biddle added, "depending on a score of factors. But I don't want you to be under any illusions. And after all, money was never your primary motivation, was it?"

"I'm fifty-nine, Edward. The world looks different than it did in 1970."

Biddle nodded. "You don't have to tell me. But think about this. You'll be going to work for a company that understands your particular needs. I'll be your sole liaison, if you like. You'll have a free hand with research."

"Can you promise that? No one looking over my shoulder?"

"Guaranteed. My concern, old friend, is the risk of waiting even one minute to move to the next phase. I want you to come with me now. Today. This minute."

Tarver drew back, his palms tingling with foreboding. "Why?"

"I don't want to risk anything happening to you before my people see your research. I want your data today, Eldon. All of it."

"We haven't agreed to anything yet."

Biddle looked hard into his eyes. When the TransGene man spoke, it was with the gravity of a soldier, not a corporate officer. His voice was edged with steel and brimming with heartfelt emotion. "Listen to me, Eldon. The money will come. Recognition will come, too, from the proper quarters. But what's most important is what you'll be doing for your country. You know what's coming. The fucking dragon is getting stronger by the day. He's already eating out of our bowl, and pretty soon—" A look of self-disgust twisted Biddle's mouth. "Shit, I'm not even saying we deserve to survive, given the way most Americans have pissed away their birthright. But those of us who remember what makes us great . . . it's up to us to insure our national survival. I've bled for this country, Eldon. You have, too, in your way. But you don't resent it, do you? I think you feel the same obligation I do."

Dr. Tarver looked down at his desk. There had never been any question of refusing, of course. He had merely hoped that the more tangible symbols of appreciation would come his way more quickly. But that was all right. With Andrew Rusk's diamonds added to what remained of his own, he would be comfortable for as long as it took TransGene or the government to compensate him fairly.

"All right, Edward. I'm on board."

Biddle's face split in an expansive smile. Then he wrung his hands together and said, "Let's talk timing. I'm serious about expediting this. I want to move you out of here today."

Eldon held up his hands. "We haven't seen each other for two years. I'm not going to step in front of a bus before tomorrow."

"You don't know that. A drunk could run you over. A punk could knock you on the head. Lightning could strike you—"

"Or I could find a richer bidder?" Eldon said bluntly.

His words hit Biddle like a sucker punch to the throat. "Are you looking for one?" he asked quietly.

"No. But I need a day, Edward. One day."

Suspicion clouded Biddle's eyes. "What kind of loose ends could possibly justify waiting?"

For a moment Eldon considered asking his old colleague to take care of Alex Morse for him. The TransGene director undoubtedly had military or intelligence contacts who could take her out and make it look like an accident. But if Biddle and the TransGene board perceived Eldon Tarver as a risk to the company, a man who had left a trail that could one day lead the authorities to their darkest secrets, they might decide to eliminate him as soon as they possessed the virus and its documentation. No, he needed to enter his new life clean, an unblemished hero to Biddle and his breed. Fucking Lancelot, for once in his life.

"You have to trust me, Edward," he said. "Tomorrow I'm yours."

Biddle looked far from satisfied, but he didn't argue further.

"How are you going to get me out?"

"Here's what I'm thinking," said Biddle. "TransGene is owned by the same parent company as the firm that's building the nuclear plant between Baton Rouge and New Orleans. If we—"

"I've wondered about that," Eldon cut in. "New Orleans already has one of the largest nuclear plants in the country."

Biddle smiled. "The power produced by the new plant will be routed across Louisiana to Texas. It's a lot easier to build a nuclear plant in Louisiana than Texas. There are laws, of course, but there's no organized resistance. Hell, there's nothing but blacks, white trash, Cajuns, and chemical plants on that whole stretch of river."

"Cancer Alley," said Tarver. "But how does that relate to me?"

"Your new identity papers will take two or three days to be processed. I'm going to airlift you to the plant construction site while we wait. Shouldn't take more than a couple of days, and you'll be very comfortable. You'll have your own trailer, like a Hollywood actor."

Tarver gave him a wry smile. "Who handles the new identity?"

Biddle answered equivocally, "It's a bit like the Witness Protection Program, only it's handled by the Pentagon."

Tarver chuckled. "It's good to be dealing with professionals again. I've felt pretty damn alone out here in the wilderness."

Biddle stood and shot his cuffs. "Speaking of that, how the hell have you managed to accomplish what you have?"

Feeling fully secure once again, Dr. Tarver finally let some of his pride show through, for inside he was as proud as Lucifer. "I'll tell you, it's more a matter of *will* than anything else. I could have done what I have twice as fast at a major research center, or at Fort Detrick. But the reality is, no one would have let me."

Biddle thought about this. "You're right. I just thank heaven we still have men like you working in the trenches."

Dr. Tarver basked in the glow of Biddle's praise; he knew from experience that it was not easily won.

"I assume we have some logistics to take care of?" Biddle said. "What do you need to bring out besides data? Special equipment? Biologicals?"

"No machinery. Too much risk involved in moving it out."

"Check. Biologicals?"

"I can bring the agents I need out in a single Pelican case, and my critical files can fit in a backpack."

"Excellent. The only question that remains is timing."

"Tomorrow, as I said. But I'd like you to be on call beginning now."

Biddle stared at him for a while. "Is there anything more I need to know, Eldon?"

Tarver dodged the meaning behind the question. "I'd like you to fly the helicopter. When I call, you come, and wherever I say."

Biddle scratched his chin. "Any risk of a hot extraction?"

Eldon smiled. He'd always loved intelligence jargon. "I don't anticipate that."

"I'd prefer not to even have an *observed* extraction. We don't want to put the company in a difficult position."

"Again, I don't foresee a problem."

"All right, then." Biddle grinned. "Hell, I'd love to fly this mission. I need to keep my hours up."

Biddle offered his hand, and Eldon took it. The old soldier's handshake was stiff, like a formal salute.

"Until tomorrow," said the doctor.

Biddle walked to the door, then turned back, his face grave. "Is it worth sticking around to handle unfinished business when you have an FBI agent poking around?"

Tarver regretted revealing Morse's true identity. "I'm afraid she's involved with that business."

Biddle's face darkened, but his cold blue eyes remained steady. "As long as you're clean as regards our business."

"Absolutely."

CHAPTER

45

Alex let herself into Room 638 as quietly as she could. Inside, it was as dark as the hotel's blackout curtains could make it. She moved carefully across the floor of the suite, trying to remember the furniture placement. As she felt her way around a chair, she heard a quavering voice.

"Ah-Alex?"

"Chris?"

"Yeah."

"Are you okay?"

"Th-think so."

As she felt her way along the bed, her eyes adjusted to the darkness, and she picked out Chris's eyes in the shadows. He was lying on his back with the covers pulled up to his neck. His forehead glistened with sweat.

"My God. What's going on?"

"Typical initial ruh . . . reaction to virus. Your marrow spits out a ton of IgG to d-deal with the invader . . . tries to kill the virus with fever. Later on . . . different immunoglobulins . . . right now . . .

classic symptoms." He shook his head angrily. "Don't think I'm critical right now . . . unless . . . poisoned. That hasn't . . . b-been the pattern . . . right?"

"No. But you need to get checked out anyway."

"I'll get Tom to p-put me through the mill."

"I think you're past that, Chris. I think it's time to charter a jet and fly up to Sloan-Kettering."

"Want someone I trust. We'll send out the tests. Everybody does fuh . . . for complex stuff."

Alex wanted to call 911. But Chris wasn't panicking, and he was the physician, not her. But was he thinking clearly? He was undoubtedly depressed given what had happened to him, and maybe even delirious. For all she knew, he might even be in shock.

"Don't worry," he said, smiling weakly. "I'll t-tell you when to panic."

She forced a smile in return. "Do you mind if I use my computer?"

He shook his head.

"The light won't bother you?"

"No."

She bent and laid her hand on his burning shoulder, but he jerked away. Anger and frustration surged through her. Never had she felt such impotence. Will Kilmer had been unable to catch the government car they had seen parked at Dr. Tarver's clinic. John Kaiser had called, but to her dismay, he had not been researching Eldon Tarver at all, instead remaining focused on Andrew Rusk. Most of what Kaiser had learned duplicated information Alex had uncovered weeks ago. Kaiser had also told her that the FBI agents tailing Rusk believed Thora Shepard was still inside the lawyer's office. Kaiser thought this would give him some leverage in trying to persuade the local SAC that Alex's suspicions were grounded in fact. She'd asked Kaiser to change his focus to Dr. Tarver and informed him of the Noel D. Traver alias. After Kaiser had promised to do what he could, she signed off.

Alex went to the hotel desk, took her laptop out of hibernation, and logged into the hotel's IP network. As the Internet portal loaded, she wrote what she had memorized at Tarver's clinic onto a hotel notepad.

Noel D. Traver, DVM
Entergy bill late—09365974

The first thing Alex learned when she tried to log into the NCIC computer was that her access code was no longer valid. The third time she tried, she got a message saying that a report was being sent to the NCIC security department. The cold fingers of exclusion reached deep into her chest. Mark Dodson was being thorough in his efforts to end her career. She could no longer check the government's national database of criminal records, a crippling blow to any investigator. She would have to go to Google, like any civilian. Cursing quietly, she did so, and typed "Eldon Tarver" into the search line.

The name returned over a hundred hits. The first twenty were abstracts of medical articles or Web announcements of various research incentives at the University Medical Center. As she moved deeper into the result pages, she found a few stories about Dr. Tarver opening his free clinic downtown. Several black leaders had praised him to the skies, and three years ago, one black citizens' group had given him their annual citizenship award. Tarver was listed as one of the top fifty physicians in the state of Mississippi. In that article, Alex learned that Tarver was board-certified in pathology and had been since 1988.

"Chris?" she said softly.

"Yeah?"

"Eldon Tarver is board-certified in pathology. Does that make sense to you?"

"Uh . . . not really. I figured hematology or oncology."

"He's certified in hematology, too, but that's much more recent. His first specialty seems to have been pathology."

"Weird." The bedclothes rustled. "Can you g-get me a towel?"

She rushed to the bathroom and got one. "Where do you want it?"

"Muh . . . mouth," he said through chattering teeth. "To bite on."

"Jesus."

As Chris opened his mouth, she saw that his entire body was shivering. She stuffed in the towel, and he clamped down hard. After watching him shiver for half a minute, she went helplessly back to her computer. Before she could continue searching, her phone rang. It was Kaiser.

"What's up?" she answered.

"Noel D. Traver has no criminal record. But when I checked into his past, I found that the vet school he claimed to have graduated from has no record of his attending it. Mississippi granted him a license based on papers he gave them from the State of Tennessee."

"He didn't have to pass a test?"

"He's not actually practicing here. He owns and operates a dog-breeding facility in south Jackson. He sells dogs to medical schools for animal research."

Alex tugged at an errant strand of hair beside her chin. "This is strange, John. Especially if he's not Noel Traver at all, but Eldon Tarver."

"Hang on a sec." She heard voices but could not make out words. "Alex, I need to call you back."

She hung up and went back to her computer. It struck her then that she had not tried the simplest method of finding out whether Noel Traver was an alias or not. She typed the name into Google, then searched IMAGES. The computer hummed and clicked, and then a row of thumbnails began to load.

The first picture that popped up showed an African-American man wearing an army uniform, Captain Noel D. Traver. The second showed a high school kid with pimples. The third image showed a square-headed man with a gray beard and a full head of hair. The picture had been shot by a photographer for the Jackson *Clarion-Ledger*. The caption read BREEDER TREATS RESEARCH PUPS LIKE PETS. The picture was grainy, but Alex had no doubt: Noel D. Traver was not Eldon Tarver.

"What the hell?" she whispered.

Her cell phone rang again. She answered without looking at the screen. "John?"

"No, it's Will."

"Do you have something?"

"Maybe. Dr. Eldon Tarver owns a pathology lab here in Jackson."

"What?"

"Jackson Pathology Associates. They do the lab testing for a lot of local doctors. They're pretty successful, apparently. They do DNA analysis on-site."

"This guy is something."

"You want me to ride out there and check it out?"

"Yes. Poke around and see if anything seems out of whack."

Will chuckled. "I know the routine."

Alex's phone beeped, indicating an incoming call. Kaiser's cell. "Call me later, Will. Gotta go." She clicked over to Kaiser's phone. "Hello?"

"I'm sorry, Alex. I'm over at the Jackson field office, and things are kind of messy right now. The SAC found out about my little off-duty surveillance club, and—"

"John, listen to me. I did an image search on Noel D. Traver, and I found a picture of him."

"Yeah?"

"It's not him. I mean, it's not Eldon Tarver."

"Really?"

"I don't get it. Two names that are perfect anagrams couldn't be coincidence—not if one name is found on the desk of the owner of the other."

"I agree. We're into something weird here. Changing subject, the SAC says that even if you're right, this is a homicide case and not under our jurisdiction."

"Webb Tyler sucks."

Kaiser laughed quietly. "Webb says I should turn over any evidence I have to the Jackson police department and go back to New Orleans. And you should find a new line of work."

"Screw him. I say we check out Noel Traver's dog-breeding facility."

"Tyler won't go for that. I already asked for a search warrant. No dice."

"Jesus, what's his problem?" snapped Alex.

GREG ILES

"Mark Dodson is his problem. Tyler knows Dodson hates your guts, and he thinks Dodson is the new director's fair-haired boy. He also thinks Jack Moran is on his way out—early retirement. So, Tyler's not about to help me, since I'm a disciple of the wrong acolyte."

"I'm starting to think I'm well out of the Bureau."

"You know better than that. We'll get the warrant. We just have to keep piling up evidence."

"How, without any support? I don't guess Tyler will try for autopsies on the past victims, huh?"

Kaiser laughed out loud.

"Do you have any idea where Eldon Tarver is at this moment?"

"No. He lives alone, and he's not at home. He's not at the university or at his clinic, either. I'll let you know when we locate him."

Alex grunted in dissatisfaction. "So, exactly where is this dog-breeding facility?"

"Don't even think about it. Not without a warrant."

"I can find it on my own, you know."

"You're making it hard enough on me already. I've got to go. Call me if there's something I need to know."

Alex hung up and dialed Will Kilmer.

"Speak," Will said.

"Noel D. Traver owns a dog-breeding facility in south Jackson. I need you to find out where."

"I already know."

"I love you, old man. Give me the address."

Will read it out. "You planning on a visit?"

"I may ride by. I'm not going in. Kaiser would have my ass. I want you to do the same at the path lab, though."

"On my way. You stay in touch."

"I will."

Alex went to Chris's bed and knelt beside him. He was still shivering, but his eyes were closed now, and he was breathing regularly. She went back to the desk, packed her computer into its case, and left as quietly as she could.

CHAPTER

46

Will Kilmer touched Alex's knee and said, "That building was a bakery when I was a boy. Hell, I think it was still one till about 1985."

Alex nodded and kept trying to get her computer to stay connected to the Internet. For some reason, the surveillance spot they had chosen was a cellular dead zone, as far as data was concerned. Will had parked his Explorer in the bay of a defunct auto repair shop, because it commanded a good view of the dog-breeding facility owned by "Noel D. Traver." Traver's building was an aged redbrick rectangle about the size of a Coca-Cola bottling plant, with an even bigger parking lot surrounding it. Glittering razor wire spiraled along the top of the fence. The only vehicle in the lot was a panel truck parked ass-end toward the wall of the building, which put its license plate out of sight. The building itself looked deserted. No one had been in or out since they'd arrived two hours ago, nor had any sound come from the building. The distance was close to a hundred yards, but still. Alex figured they would have heard barking or something.

"Yours again," said Will, in response to the chirping from the seat beside her.

"Kaiser," said Alex. "He keeps calling."

"Just answer it."

"If he knew I was here, he'd flip out."

Will sighed like a man fed up with bullshit. He had already checked out Dr. Tarver's pathology lab, and on cursory inspection it had seemed legitimate. Now he was wasting the rest of his day here, probably for nothing.

The SIM card in Alex's notebook computer made a momentary connection to the Internet, then dropped it. She slammed her hand against the door in frustration. It was that or toss her computer out the window. She'd been trying to get online to do research, but now it was late enough for Jamie to be out of school, and he might be logged on to MSN.

"I'm worried about Jamie," she said. "I haven't talked to him for almost forty-eight hours."

"He's all right," Will said. "He's ten years old, and he has to go wherever his old man takes him."

"I'm worried about Chris, too." She felt terrible guilt at leaving him alone in the hotel room.

"How many times have you tried him?" Will didn't know, because he'd gotten out of the Explorer several times to take a leak or smoke a cigarette.

"Five or six. He hasn't answered in the past hour."

"Probably sleeping, huh?"

"I hope so."

"Almost all the victims have taken over a year to die," Will reminded her.

"Not Grace."

The old detective closed his eyes and shook his head.

"I think I should go back and take him to the emergency room," Alex said. "Will you help me get him down to the car?"

"Sure. You point. I'll march him."

Alex tilted her head and pointed at the tall Cyclone fence around the old bakery. "What do you think the razor wire's for? It sure isn't to keep dogs inside. The fence alone would do that."

Will shrugged. "Crime's pretty bad out this way."

Alex's cell was ringing. Kaiser again. She expelled a lungful of air in frustration, then pressed SEND. "Hello, John."

"Christ, Alex, I've been trying to get you for hours. Where are you?"

She grimaced, then recited her lie. "I'm at the hotel taking care of Chris. He's in bad shape. Have you found something?"

"Yes and no. Tyler has really dug in his heels. I think he's basically Mark Dodson's puppet right now. I'm calling in all the favors I can to run deep checks on Shane Lansing, Eldon Tarver, and our mysterious nonveterinarian. I'm also pushing hard for a search warrant on Tarver's residence."

"Thanks," Alex said, gratified to have someone pushing in the same direction at last. "Anything new on the background checks?"

"Lansing looks clean to me. Typical surgeon. Son of a lawyer, big ladies' man. He's moved around a lot, which is sometimes a flag with doctors, but he's only thirty-six, so maybe he's just the restless type. Like Rusk, he's invested in a lot of different ventures, most medical but some not. The radiology clinic in Meridian is a legitimate concern, and Lansing seems to be a passive partner. I suppose he could get access to radioactive material if he really wanted to, but right now he seems like the least likely killer of the bunch."

"And the others?"

"You know Rusk. He's rich, well connected, and on his second wife. Lives like an international playboy when he's not working. The only grounds for suspicion are those business connections you turned up, but all of those are aboveboard. Not even the IRS has a gripe with Rusk."

"And Tarver?"

"Tarver's is a little different. He was born in 1946, in Oak Ridge, Tennessee, the illegitimate son of an army officer. He was dumped at the Presbyterian Children's Home in Knoxville, Tennessee, from which he was adopted at age seven. The adoptive family was from Sevierville, Tennessee. I worked a serial murder case around there twelve years ago. That's the Smoky Mountains. It's commercialized now, but in the 1950s it was rural, with primitive fundamentalist religion. Some of the snake churches were based there."

"Snake churches?" echoed Alex, and Will cut his eyes at her.

"Congregations that use poisonous snakes in their worship services. Drink strychnine, that kind of crap. I don't know if Tarver saw any of that, but his foster father was a pig farmer and lay preacher. Eldon went to the University of Tennessee on full academic scholarship. That got him out of Vietnam. While I was running through rice paddies, Tarver was doing high-level graduate research in microbiology at UT. Data's pretty scarce for that part of his life, but in 1974, he went to work for a major pharmaceutical company. They fired him less than a year later on sexual harassment grounds. It must have been something pretty bad to be fired for that in 1975. He didn't actually go to medical school until 1976, but he definitely found his calling there. He's board-certified in multiple specialties, including pathology and hematology. He took the job at UMC in 1985, and he married a biochemistry professor there two years later. She died in 1998, of cervical cancer. You know the rest. He opened a free clinic with the money he inherited from his wife. He's had the pathology lab for over fifteen years. So far, no information about girlfriends or live-in lovers. The sexual harassment thing gives me a little pause—"

"And the birthmark," Alex cut in.

"Yeah," said Kaiser. "It looks pretty severe in photos. I wonder why he hasn't had a buddy take it off for him."

"I don't think he can. He told me it's some sort of vascular anomaly. It's dangerous to mess with."

"I think we've got a weird one, all right," Kaiser said thoughtfully. "My antennae are quivering. We may find some kinky stuff in Tarver's house, if we ever get inside it. Webb Tyler's starting to piss me off. He's a bureaucrat to the marrow of his bones. If he has any bones."

"He sure doesn't have a backbone," Alex grumbled.

Will grabbed her knee and pointed through the windshield. Sixty yards away, a red van was pulling through the gate of the parking lot. The gate must have been unlocked, because the driver simply nosed through it without getting out and drove slowly toward the side of the building.

"Chris needs me," Alex said, trying to make out the license plate of the van. It was too far away and the angle was bad.

"One more thing," said Kaiser. "Noel Traver is a real mystery man. On paper, he didn't even exist prior to ten years ago, as far as I can tell. He's got a driver's license but no car, and his residence appears to be the same address as that dog-breeding facility."

"I really need to run, John. Anything else?"

Kaiser laughed. "Yeah, one thing. I've really been calling to make sure you don't do something stupid, like break into Tarver's house or that breeding facility."

Alex laughed, hoping it didn't ring hollow. "I wish," she said. "Keep pushing for that search warrant." She hung up before he could reply.

"Did you hear that?" asked Will. "The driver just honked his horn."

The red van had pulled up to a large aluminum door set in the side wall of the old bakery. As Alex stared, the door rose until it was high enough for the van to pull inside the building.

"Son of a bitch," said Will. "I think somebody's been in there all along."

"He may be using a remote. Did you get a look at the driver?"

"No, the damn windows are tinted."

The overhead door stayed up, but the van did not pull inside.

"What should we do?" Alex asked.

Will stuck out his lower lip. "You're the boss."

"I want to know who's in that van."

Will laughed softly. "I do, too. And we can find out. But it sure won't be legal."

"I don't give a shit." Alex reached for her door handle.

Will caught hold of her wrist. "Hold on, now. Let's don't get you in worse trouble than you're already in."

She pulled her arm free. "The bastards have already fired me. What else can they do?"

Will lowered his head and looked at her with seven decades of accumulated wisdom. "Well, honey, there's fired, and then there's *fired* fired. You just got off the phone with a special agent of the FBI. If you were *fired* fired, he wouldn't be talking to you at all."

Alex forced herself to sit back in the Explorer, anger boiling in her gut. Immediately after Grace's death, she had felt she was at a great disadvantage in her quest, but not powerless. She may have acted irresponsibly, but at least she'd been doing *something*. Now she was being restrained by the possibility that the agency that should have been investigating all along might finally get off its ass and do something.

She grabbed her computer from the floor and took it out of hibernation yet again. This time her toolbar showed a three-bar data connection. She'd already searched the names Eldon Tarver and Noel D. Traver so many times in the past few hours that her eyes blurred when she looked at the Google search page.

"I'm missing something," she said.

Will grunted.

She checked MSN Messenger, but Jamie wasn't logged on.

"What did Kaiser tell you?" Will asked.

"Not much." She thought back to Kaiser's brief biography of Eldon Tarver. "He said there was a gap in the years when Tarver was in college or grad school. During Vietnam, I guess. When did the Vietnam War end?"

"They scraped the last chopper off the roof of the embassy in '75, but for all practical purposes, the big show was over by '73."

Vietnam . . .

"Late Vietnam," Alex murmured.

"What?"

"Something Dr. Tarver said to me in his office. It was about a research project he worked on . . . something about combat veterans and cancer." She closed her eyes and saw the photograph on Tarver's office wall again, the black-and-white snapshot of the blonde bookended by Tarver and the military officer. "VCP," she said, scrunching her eyelids tight. "Those letters were embroidered on Tarver's lab coat. Also painted on the building behind him."

"What are you talking about?" asked Will.

"An acronym," she said, suddenly recalling Tarver's explanation. "The Veterans' Cancer Project."

Alex typed "Veterans' Cancer Project" into the Google search field. Google returned over 8 million links, but not one in the first fifty referred to a formally named Veterans' Cancer Project. Most of the links led to sites dealing with various types of cancer in Gulf War or Vietnam veterans. But the Vietnam links dealt almost exclusively with Agent Orange, which Tarver had said his group had not looked into.

"There's not a Veterans' Cancer Program," she said, puzzled. "Or at least it wasn't a big enough deal for anyone to remember it."

Her fingers hovered over the keyboard. "But Veterans' Cancer Project isn't what I saw," she thought aloud. "I saw *VCP*."

She typed "VCP" into the search field and hit ENTER. What appeared was a plethora of results related only by their sharing the same acronym. Next she typed "VCP" plus "cancer." The first few hits concerned a research project in India. But the fifth started her pulse racing. The first words following the acronym were *Special Virus Cancer Program*—not *Veterans'*, as Tarver had claimed—which the link description defined as a scientific program that had begun in 1964, consumed 10 percent of the annual budget of the National Cancer Institute for some years, then was renamed the Virus Cancer Program in 1973. Alex bit her bottom lip, clicked the link, and began to read.

The VCP was a massive research effort involving some of the most distinguished scientists in the United States, all probing the possible viral origins of cancer, particularly leukemia. . . .

"My God," Alex breathed.
"What is it?" asked Will.
"Wait," she said, reading as fast as she could.

A small but vocal number of physicians have suggested that simian-related retroviruses like HIV and SV 40 (which has been proved to have contaminated batches of human polio vaccine) were in fact created by the scientists of the Virus Cancer Program. While this is disputed by the medical establishment, government records confirm that tens of thousands of liters of dangerous new viruses were cultured in the bodies of living animals, primarily primates and cats, and that many of these viruses were modified so as to be able to jump species barriers. In 1973, a significant part of the Virus Cancer Project was transferred to Fort Detrick, Maryland, the home of the

United States biological warfare effort. No one denies that the VCP involved an active alliance between the NIH, the U.S. Army, and Litton Bionetics. . . .

"This is it," said Alex. "Holy shit, this is it!"

"What are you yelping about?" Will asked, staring hard at her screen.

"Dr. Tarver lied to me! He told me that VCP stood for Veterans' Cancer Project. It doesn't. It stands for a government project that researched the links between viruses and cancer, especially leukemia. It took place during the Vietnam era. And Eldon Tarver worked for them!"

"Jesus."

"He's killing people," whispered Alex. "He's *still doing research*. Or else he's using what he learned back then to make money off of Andrew Rusk and his desperate clients." Her chest swelled with fierce joy. "We've *got* them, Will."

"Look!" Will said, gripping her wrist. "Son of a bitch!"

Alex looked up. The panel truck and the van had disappeared, and the big aluminum door was sliding back down to the concrete slab.

"You know what I think?" said Alex.

"What?"

"Tarver is shutting everything down. I went to his office and declared myself as an FBI agent. I went to his so-called free clinic. I even gave him a list of the murder victims, for God's sake. Nobody on that list surprised him, either. Christ, I even asked him about the VCP picture! He *knows* I'm going to figure it out eventually. He's got to run, Will." She laid her computer on the backseat and reached for the door handle again. "I'm going down there."

"Wait!" cried Will, restraining her. "If you've got him nailed with evidence, there's no point in screwing the pooch by going in without a warrant."

"I'm not going into the building."

"Be sure, Alex," he said gravely.

"Are you coming or not?"

Will sighed, then opened the glove box and took out his .357 Magnum. "I guess."

As she got out of the Explorer, Will said, "Wait. The gate's open, ain't it? We're better off driving up to the front door and telling them we're lost than sneaking in there with guns shoved down our pants."

Alex grinned and climbed back into the Explorer. "I knew I brought you for a reason."

Will cranked the Ford, pulled across the street, and drove down to the gate of the old bakery. As he slowed down to nose through the fence, Alex dialed John Kaiser's cell phone.

"Hey," said Kaiser. "What's up?"

"I've cracked it, John! The whole case. You need to check out something called the Virus Cancer Program. It was a big research project in the late sixties and early seventies. It involved cancer, viruses, and biological weapons. Tarver was part of it."

"Biological weapons?"

"Yes. There's a photo in Tarver's UMC office of him wearing a lab coat that says VCP. The building behind him has the same acronym."

"How did you find out what it stood for?"

"Google, believe it or not. It was the picture in his office that did it, though. I'd never have known what to look for otherwise. But Tarver lied to me about what the acronym stood for. He tried to make it sound noble."

"I'll get on it. The SAC is still stalling on the search warrant for Tarver's house. Maybe this will tip the scales."

"Even Webb Tyler can't ignore this. Call me when you get the warrant."

Kaiser hung up.

The Explorer was only twenty yards from the old bakery.

"Where do you want to go?" asked Will.

"Those casement windows in front."

"They're blacked out."

"Not all of them. Look to the right. A few have been replaced with clear panes."

Will swung the wheel, and the Explorer came to rest opposite one of the windows with clear glass.

"Get out and keep your hand on your pistol," said Alex.

"You think they'd try something?"

"No doubt in my mind. This is a deeply fucked-up individual we're dealing with."

She got out and walked up to the windows. Each pane was about eight inches square, but the clear ones were too high for her to look through.

"Can you give me a step up?"

Will walked over, shoved his pistol into his pants, then bent at the waist and interlocked his fingers. Alex stepped into the resulting cradle, feeling as she had as a little girl when Grace used to boost her up to the lowest branch of the popcorn tree in their backyard. The memory pierced her heart, but she caught hold of the brick sill and pulled herself up to the clear window-pane.

"What do you see?" Will grunted.

"Nothing yet."

The pane was caked with gunk. She spat on the glass and wiped a circle with her sleeve, then pressed her eye to the glass. When her eyes adjusted, she saw a wall of cages. Dozens of them. And inside each one, a sleeping dog. Small dogs, maybe beagles.

"You see anything yet?" Will asked. "My back ain't what it used to be."

"Dogs. A bunch of dogs asleep in cages."

"That's what they breed here."

"I know but . . . there's something odd about it."

"What?"

"They're asleep."

"So?" Will was wheezing now.

"Well, they can't all be asleep, can they?"

"Haven't you ever heard, 'Let sleeping dogs lie'?"

Alex almost laughed, but something stopped her. "There must be a hundred of them. A hundred and fifty maybe. They can't *all* be asleep."

"Maybe they drug them."

As Alex peered into the darkened room, the sound of a distant engine reached her, its tone rising steadily. Even before she saw the red van racing down the fenced perimeter, the spark of instinct that had guided her through so many successful hostage negotiations roared to flame.

"*Run!*" she shouted, leaping backward out of Will's hands.

"What is it?" he gasped, trying to straighten his back and grab his gun at the same time.

"*RUN!*" Alex grabbed his arm and started dragging him away from the building.

"What about my truck?" Will yelled.

"*Leave it!*"

They were thirty feet from the building when a scorching wall of air slapped them to the ground like the hand of God. Alex skidded across the cement, the skin tearing away from her elbows. She screamed for Will, but she heard only a roaring silence.

It took most of a minute to get her breath back. Then she slowly rolled over and sat up.

Will was on his knees a few yards away, trying in vain to pull a large splinter of glass out of his back. Behind him, a vast column of black smoke climbed into the sky. All the windows in the front wall were gone. Behind the smoke, Alex saw a blue-white flame that looked more like the glow of a Bunsen burner than a roaring blaze. The heat emanating from the building was almost unbearable. As she struggled to her feet, an inhuman shriek of terror echoed across the empty parking lot. Then a dark simian shape burst from the building, running on all fours, trailing smoke and fire. Alex staggered three steps toward Will, told him to leave the splinter where it was, then fell on her face.

CHAPTER

47

Andrew Rusk had taken two Valium, a Lorcet, and a beta-blocker, yet his heart was still pounding. His head was worse. As he stared into his wife's vacuous eyes, he felt as though someone had taken hold of his spinal cord where it entered the base of his brain and was trying to yank it out.

"But I don't *understand,*" Lisa said for the eighth time in as many minutes.

"Those men outside," Rusk said, pointing to the dark patio windows of the house. "They're FBI agents."

"How do you know that? Maybe they're IRS or something."

"I know because I know."

"But I mean *Cuba*?" Lisa whined.

"*Shhh,*" Rusk hissed, squeezing her upper arm. "You have to whisper."

She jerked the arm away. "This is the first time you've ever mentioned Cuba to me. Why? Don't you trust me?"

Rusk squelched a desire to scream, *Of course I don't trust you, you silly bitch!*

Pouting like a child, Lisa retreated to the sofa and tucked her legs beneath her, yoga style. She was wearing biking shorts and a tank top that revealed the usual fleshscape of spectacular cleavage.

"Cuba?" she said again. "It's not even American yet, is it?"

He gaped at her. *"American?"*

"I mean, you know, capitalist or whatever."

Lisa's primary virtue was physical beauty combined with a ravenous libido. Rusk still had difficulty with the idea that someone of middling intelligence could experience truly intense passion, but he'd finally accepted it, based on empirical evidence. Maybe it was a vanity of intellectuals to believe that dumb people couldn't enjoy sex to the degree that smart people did. But maybe they did. Maybe they enjoyed it *more.* Still, Rusk doubted it. At bottom, he figured Lisa was some kind of prodigy, an idiot savant of sexual technique. And that was fine for the bedroom and minor social intercourse. But when it came to actual *thought,* not to mention decision making, it made things difficult.

He knelt before the couch and took Lisa's hand. He had to be patient. He had to convince her. Because there were no more options. They had to get out of the country, and fast. Thora Shepard was lying under a painter's drop cloth in the back of his Cayenne. If one of the FBI agents outside bent the law and broke into the locked garage, it was all over.

Rusk had tried to shut out his memories of the afternoon, but he couldn't do it. After the first euphoric moments of triumph, he had looked down at Thora's shattered skull with horror—but he hadn't frozen. Extreme sports had taught him one indelible lesson: hesitation killed. Knowing that Ponytail would return any moment, he'd rolled Thora into the drop cloth, then carried her featherweight body through the metal studs to a distant office in the construction area. There he'd found a gift from God: a sixty-five-gallon trash can on wheels, with the brand name MIGHT AS WELL imprinted on the lid. Thora fit easily into the can, which he'd rolled straight to the parking garage. He transferred Thora to the back of his Cayenne, and then—after returning the trash can to a different side of the fifteenth floor—he'd returned to his office as though nothing had happened.

But something had happened. And since that murderous minute, he'd felt his time as a free man draining away like blood from a severed vein. He had an escape plan, but to initiate it he'd first have to break free of FBI surveillance. He did not know how to do that. He still held out hope that Dr. Tarver would save them—if Tarver had not already bolted. The doctor had requested an emergency rendezvous at Chickamauga via e-mail, but Rusk had been unable to keep it without dragging the FBI along with him. Nearly frantic, he'd gone to a friend's office in the tower and sent Tarver an e-mail summarizing every threat arrayed against them, in the hope that Tarver could somehow cut through the closing net. But if Tarver didn't contact him soon, Rusk was going to have to take drastic measures. Like calling his father. He dreaded the thought, but at this point—without Dr. Tarver's help—it would take the legendary clout and connections of A. J. Rusk to save him.

"Lisa, honey," he said softly. "We're only talking about a few months in Cuba. I've arranged for us to live on a beautiful yacht right in the marina. Guys like

Sinatra paid through the nose to hang out there with Ava Gardner and Marilyn Monroe."

"Yeah, like in the Dark Ages."

Lisa was twenty-nine years old. "Castro's history, babe. He's going to die any day now. He may already be dead, in fact."

She looked skeptical. "Didn't JFK try to assassinate him like a bunch of times, and he couldn't do it?"

Rusk wanted to kill Oliver Stone. "That doesn't matter, honey. As soon as the heat is off, we'll move to Costa Rica under different names. And Costa Rica is a goddamn paradise."

"But I *like* my name."

Rusk squeezed her hand. "Think of it this way: With the name you've got, you're worth about five million bucks. Under your new name, you're worth twenty. That's a big difference."

This got her attention. "Twenty million dollars?"

He nodded with the gravity such an amount demanded. He could see the wheels clicking behind her gorgeous green eyes. Despite the pounding at the base of his skull, he managed a smile. "That's Hollywood money, babe."

"But why can't we go to Costa Rica *now*?" she asked in a girlish voice.

He forced himself not to scream. "Because it's not safe. We have to let the FBI check Costa Rica and find nothing. Then we can go there."

"What have you done, Andy? You said it was some kind of tax thing. How pissed off can the government be about that?"

What have I done? I killed a woman who looked a lot like you, only better. And if you keep this up, I might just kill you, too. He glanced worriedly at the dark windows. "You don't understand these things, Lisa. The simple truth is, we don't have a choice."

She gave him a long stare, surprising in its coldness. "Maybe *you* don't have a choice. But *I* haven't done anything. I can stay right here until it's safe in Costa Rica. Then I can join you there."

Rusk stared, incredulous. She sounded just like Thora Shepard! "You'd stay here without me?"

"I don't want to. You're the one making this happen, Andy, not me."

She's right, he thought. Cuba had seemed such a cool idea when Tarver suggested it five years ago. It was one of the last mysterious places on earth, the last commie outpost save China. And it had that Hemingway glamour. What more macho retreat could there be? The fucking Cold War was still going on there, for God's sake. But then Castro got sick. Nobody knew what was really going on. And forty-eight hours after having his umbilical to Dr. Tarver cut, Rusk thought the prospect of living in postcommunist chaos sounded dicey. Lisa certainly wanted no part of it. Maybe she wasn't so dumb after all.

"I can't do it, Andy," she said with sudden conviction. "I promise I'll come to Costa Rica when you get there. But I don't want to leave my mom and my friends to go to Cuba."

"Baby . . . once we get there, you'll see how great it is. Now go upstairs and pack the absolute minimum you need to leave the country. One suitcase, okay? One."

Instead of obeying, Lisa set her jaw and spoke through clenched teeth. "*I said—I'm—not—going.*

You can't make me. And if you try, I'll file for divorce."

For the second time today, Rusk was stunned speechless. Lisa had to be bluffing. He'd written an ironclad prenup. If she divorced him, she'd get almost nothing. Well . . . that wasn't exactly true anymore. Over the past three years, he had found it advantageous to transfer some considerable assets into her name. It had made a lot of sense at the time. But now . . . now he saw himself as a sucker, like one of his pathetic clients. Before he realized what he was doing, he had slid his right hand up to her throat.

"One more inch and I'll scream," she said evenly. "And when those FBI guys bust in here, I'll tell them about every tax scam and swindle you ever pulled."

Rusk stood and backed away from his wife. Who the hell was this woman? And why in God's name had he married her?

It doesn't matter, he told himself. *To hell with her. As long as I get out of the country, it doesn't matter what she does. She can have a few million. There's plenty more for me. If only Tarver would show the fuck up. . . .*

He walked toward the central hallway, meaning to check his e-mail on the computer in his study, but as soon as he entered the hall, he saw a massive shape silhouetted by the light spilling from the study.

"Hello, Andrew," said Dr. Tarver. "It's pretty crowded outside. Did you give up on me?"

Rusk couldn't see the doctor's face, but he heard the cool amusement in that voice. Nothing rattled this guy. "How the *hell* did you get through those FBI agents?"

Soft laughter from the shadow. "I'm a country boy at heart, Andrew. Remember when I shot the Ghost?"

Hell, yeah, Rusk thought, recalling the legendary

buck with a flush of admiration. "You really pissed off the old-timers that day."

Dr. Tarver unslung a large backpack from his shoulder and dropped it on the ground with a heavy rustle.

"Can we get out?" Rusk asked, trying to sound calm. "I mean, have you got something figured?"

"Have you ever known me not to have things figured, Andrew?"

Rusk shook his head. This was true, though he couldn't remember them ever being in this kind of spot before.

"I appreciated this afternoon's e-mail about Alexandra Morse. I'd suspected that she was acting on her own, but I had no idea that the Bureau was going to terminate her. Most convenient."

As Rusk puzzled over this, Dr. Tarver turned toward the study. "Call Lisa in here, Andrew. We need to get started."

Rusk started to ask why the study, but then he realized it was because the room had no exterior windows. He looked over his shoulder. "Lisa? Come here."

"You come here," came the petulant reply.

"*Lisa*. We've got company."

"Company? Oh, all right. I'm coming."

With Dr. Tarver's miraculous arrival, Rusk felt the pleasant return of male superiority. Meaning to say something witty, he turned back toward the doctor and saw the pistol rise as Tarver shot him in the chest.

Alex struggled up out of a dark sea into piercing white light.

"Alex?" said a deep voice. "Alex!"

"I'm here!" She shielded her eyes with her left hand

and reached out with her right. "Don't touch it, Uncle Will!"

"I'm not Will," said the voice, and gradually the blur above her coalesced into the face of John Kaiser. His hazel eyes held a worry as paternal as any that her father or Will Kilmer had ever revealed. "You're in the emergency room at UMC," Kaiser said. "You've got a pretty serious concussion, but otherwise you seem to be all right."

"Where's Will?" she asked, gripping the FBI agent's hand for support. "Tell me he's not dead."

"He's not. He may have some internal injuries. They stitched up his back and admitted him for twenty-four hours' observation. They're going to do the same to you."

She tried to sit up, but a wave of nausea rolled through her stomach. Kaiser eased her back down onto the examining table.

"How long have I been out?"

"Several hours. It's night."

"I'm sorry I lied to you, John. I know you told me not to go there. I know—"

"Stop wasting your energy. I should have known you'd go, no matter what. In your place, I probably would have gone, too."

"What the hell happened? A bomb?"

"You tell me."

She shook her head, trying to remember. "All I know is, I was looking inside at dogs, hundreds of them, and they were all asleep. Every last one. And it just seemed *wrong,* you know? Then I heard an engine, and out of the corner of my eye I caught sight of a van racing away. It was just like the van that followed me in Natchez, only it was red. And I just *knew,* you know?"

Kaiser barely nodded, but his eyes told her he'd experienced such intuitive flashes before.

"I knew that somehow Noel Traver was Eldon Tarver, that Tarver was bugging out, and that he had let me get that close to him for a reason."

"You saw Tarver at the scene?"

"No. But I felt him. He meant to take me out, along with whatever evidence was inside that building."

Kaiser seemed discouraged by her answer.

"Did you get the warrant for his house?" Alex asked. "Is the SAC still stonewalling on an all-out investigation?"

Kaiser sighed heavily. "Not completely. We did get the warrant for Tarver's residence, and there's a team there now."

Alex raised her eyebrows.

"So far they've found nothing incriminating. Zero."

"Nothing tying him to Rusk?"

Kaiser shook his head. "But the VCP stuff you uncovered is mind-blowing. In conjunction with the explosion at the breeding facility, that convinced Tyler to ask for the search warrant. We just need to find some evidence that's fresher than thirty years old."

"What about Rusk? You should search his residence and his office."

"Tyler won't budge on that. He keeps saying there's no probable cause even to investigate Rusk, much less search his house or office. And technically speaking, he's right."

"Come on, John. Tyler's just—"

"The special agent in charge. Don't forget that. He has authority over every FBI agent in Mississippi. Don't worry, Rusk is bottled up in his house right now, and I've got six agents covering the place."

"No idea where Dr. Tarver is?"

"None."

"Thora Shepard?"

Kaiser looked embarrassed. "She was in Rusk's office this afternoon, but somehow she slipped out without our guys seeing her."

"Come on!" cried Alex, coming off the table again.

"A lot of people work in that building, Alex. Four agents just weren't enough."

"What about Chris?"

Kaiser pushed her back down. "Dr. Shepard is here in the hospital."

A stab of fear went through her.

"He's conscious, and he's doing a little better. He has a high fever, and he's seriously dehydrated. He called 911 from the hotel, and when he got here, he asked for an old med-school classmate. Dr. Clarke."

"My mother's oncologist?"

"Yes. Between Dr. Clarke and Tom Cage, they managed to check Chris into the oncology unit here. He's just a few doors down from your mother. Now they've got an oncologist from Sloan-Kettering involved."

Alex could scarcely comprehend it all. She felt as though she had come out of heavy sedation for surgery. "What about Chris's son? Ben Shepard? He's only nine, and he's staying with some older woman in Natchez. Has anyone checked on him?"

"Dr. Shepard was delirious when he arrived, but he kept asking about the boy—and you, by the way. He finally managed to make a call. Ben seems to be fine, and Dr. Cage promised to check on him."

Alex struggled to see all angles of the situation through the fog in her mind. "Thora could be a threat to Ben," she thought aloud. "She's got to be out of her mind with fear. She's also a major threat to Andrew Rusk and his accomplice. What if she never left that building, John? What if she's hiding up there?"

Kaiser considered this.

Alex grabbed his arm. "What if Rusk killed her up there?"

"Rusk hasn't killed anyone yet, has he?"

"I have no idea. But Christ, for all we know, Tarver could have been up in Rusk's office today. You know?"

"I guess it's possible. Do you think they'd move so quickly against Thora?"

"Two words: William Braid."

Kaiser grimaced. "Damn it. All right, I'll get some people to start searching that tower."

"Officially?"

"No. But if we find a corpse, the case will break wide open. We can haul Rusk in and put his feet to the fire."

"I hope you find a very scared woman. Will Kilmer overheard Thora screaming at Rusk to cancel the hit on Chris. If she would turn state's evidence, we'd have Rusk by the balls. And I guarantee Rusk would cut a deal and give us Dr. Tarver."

"You really believe Thora would talk?"

"You show her the alternative, she'll crack. She wouldn't last a day in prison."

Kaiser squeezed Alex's shoulder. "I'm going now. It's time you got some rest."

Alex snorted in contempt. "You know I can't sleep with all this going on."

"Then I'll have the doctor sedate you."

"You can't sedate someone who has a concussion."

Kaiser shook his head in exasperation, but Alex could tell he was glad to see her healthy enough to argue with him.

"If you'll get them to discharge me," she said, "I promise I won't leave the hospital. I'll spend the night in my mother's room. That way, I can keep an eye on both her and Chris."

Kaiser stared at her for a long time. "Stay here," he said finally. "Stay right here, as in *do not move*. I'll see what I can do."

CHAPTER
48

Andrew Rusk blinked awake to a hell beyond any-thing that his subconscious had ever spewed into his nightmares. Dr. Tarver had duct-taped him to the chair behind his desk. His mouth was taped shut. Lisa was sitting opposite him on the leather sofa, her slim wrists and ankles taped together, a silver rectangle of tape sealing her lips. Her eyes looked twice their nor-mal size; more white than color was showing.

Tarver stood between Lisa and the desk, holding both arms high above his head. In his hands, twisting and curling about his muscular forearms, were two thick, black snakes with heads as big as a man's fist. A maniacal light shone from Tarver's eyes; some might have called it religious fervor, but Rusk knew better. Eldon Tarver was as far from God as a man could get. The doctor spun almost gracefully around the room, as though hypnotizing the serpents into passivity, yet the flexing tubular bodies never ceased their motion.

The room stank of urine, and Rusk soon saw why: Lisa's biking shorts were stained from her navel to her knees. Every square inch of his own skin was popping with sweat, but at least he hadn't pissed himself yet. The throbbing at the base of his skull had all but ceased, or maybe it had been blotted out by the agony radiating from his sternum. A bolt of terror shot through him when he saw the two spots of blood on his shirt, but then he saw a shining tangle of silver wire near Dr. Tarver's feet. *Taser wires.* Now he remembered the gun coming up in the hallway . . . the nearly point-blank shot at his chest. It was a stun gun. That was how Tarver had gotten him into this chair.

The doctor stopped his eerie dance and sat sideways on the desk, facing Rusk. The snake nearest Andrew was thicker than his forearm, with a diamond-shaped head and bulging poison sacs beneath its eyes. *Cottonmouth moccasin,* he thought. The knowledge made his sphincter clench. Unlike most snakes, cottonmouths would not retreat when humans approached. They were highly territorial and would stand their ground, sometimes attacking and even pursuing an intruder.

"I see you thinking, Andrew," said Dr. Tarver. "I'm sure by now you've worked out exactly why I'm here."

Rusk shook his head, but he knew all right. Eldon Tarver hadn't broken through a ring of armed FBI agents to do a fucking snake dance in Rusk's study. He wanted the diamonds. *All of them.*

"No?" said Tarver. "Perhaps you're a little distracted by my friends."

He stretched out his right arm until the nearer snake's head was within striking distance of Rusk's face. Rusk's throat sealed shut, locking his breath in his chest. The pupils of the moccasin's eyes were vertical ellipses, like cats' eyes. Rusk saw the heat-sensing pits that his scoutmaster had taught him to look for a quarter century ago. As though sensing his fear, the cotton-mouth opened its huge mouth to reveal a puffy white oval topped with lethal two-inch fangs. The stench from its mouth was sickening—dead fish and other nameless creatures—but Rusk had passed beyond thought. When the doctor moved the snake closer, the ocean of piss Rusk had successfully withheld in junior high school flooded his khakis.

"The diamonds, Andrew," Dr. Tarver said in a voice of eminent reasonableness. "Where are they?"

Lisa was whimpering steadily on the sofa, but Rusk forced himself not to look. His inability to help her might unman him at the moment when he most needed his full faculties. He wished to God Tarver hadn't taped his mouth shut. He felt powerless without his voice. He was a lawyer, after all, a wizard in the art of persuasion—or so a reporter for the *Clarion-Ledger* had once written about him. Maybe that was why Tarver had taped his mouth.

Bullshit, said his father's voice. *He taped your mouth so you can't scream and alert the FBI agents outside.* Rusk hated that voice, but he knew he had to heed it. There was no room for illusion now. Dr. Tarver was back on his feet, spinning slowly, constantly changing the elevation of his arms as he did. *Motion must have something to do with keeping the snakes from biting him. Or maybe it's just professional courtesy—one cold-blooded killer to another—*

"Where *are* they, Andrew?" Dr. Tarver asked in a singsong voice. "Do you want an up-close-and-personal experience with these creatures of God? Perhaps your lovely bride likes serpents better than you do."

Tarver danced over toward Lisa. She huddled on the sofa in a fetal position, alternately shutting her eyes and opening them wide, unable to endure the horror but too afraid she would be bitten while her eyes were closed.

"These are sacred creatures, Lisa," Tarver murmured. "They represent both life and death. Death and rebirth. I'm sure through your provincial eyes, you see the serpent of the Christian garden, who so easily corrupted Eve"—he bent and caressed Lisa's thighs with a scaly tail—"but that's such a *limited* view."

The scream that burst from Lisa's diaphragm ballooned her taped-shut lips and trumpeted from her nostrils. *A few more screams like that,* Rusk thought, *and she'll be bleeding from her nose. She'll drown in her own blood.*

Laughing quietly, Dr. Tarver took two steps back and opened the mouth of a white croker sack with his foot, then dipped and thrust one of the moccasins into the bag. Stepping on the mouth of the moving sack, he pulled it tight with a drawstring. Then, caressing the head of the remaining snake, he came around the desk and addressed Rusk again.

"I'm going to partly remove the tape from your lips, Andrew. You will not scream. You will not beg. You will not plead for your life or hers. I know the stones are here. I know your escape plan, remember? I set it up. But it's time to let go of your banana-republic dream and save yourself, like the smart man you've always thought you were."

He reached out and pulled an inch of tape from the corner of Rusk's mouth. Rusk remembered his instructions, but he could not obey them. In a parched croak, he said, "You're going to kill me no matter what I do."

Dr. Tarver shook his head with an expression of regret, then walked to the corner and picked up a putter that Rusk kept there to practice his short game. Gripping the head of the golf club, Tarver began to tease the moccasin with its padded handle. He jabbed its snout again and again, causing the snake to bare its fangs and strike at the club.

A sharp odor of musk filled the room, utterly alien and yet, after Rusk had inhaled it two or three times, eerily familiar. Some primitive part of his brain had recognized the odor of a reptile under stress, and the swampy scent sucked fear from his glands in a way he had never known before.

"He's a fearsome killer, *Agkistrodon piscivorus*," said the doctor. "Nothing like the coral snake. The elapids are deadlier per milliliter of venom, but the results of envenomation are quite different. With the coral snake, you get numbness, sweating, shortness of breath, paralysis, and death. But with these babies, you get a much nastier spectrum of consequences. The venom is a hemotoxin, a complex mix of proteins that starts destroying blood cells and dissolving vascular walls the instant it enters your flesh. It even dissolves muscle tissue. The pain, I'm told, is really beyond description, and the swelling, my God, I've seen it split the skin. Within hours gangrene sets in, and the skin turns black as roadkill on an August day. A life-altering experience altogether, Andrew, if you survive it. Are you sure you don't want to change your mind?"

Rusk stared back at Tarver with utter resignation. No matter what the doctor promised, he meant to kill them tonight. To Rusk's surprise, this knowledge freed him from much of his fear. He had tempted death often in the past, but he'd always done it by choice, usually with other thrill-seeking yuppies who knew that if the shit hit the fan, paid experts would pull their asses out of the fire or off the mountain, whatever the situation required.

This was different.

This was a battle to the death, and there were no paid allies on his side. What he knew was this: he was willing to die in agony, but he wasn't willing to let Eldon Tarver steal the fruits of five years' labor. Rusk also knew that his newfound courage was not based on a rush of endorphins that would dissipate in a few minutes. Somewhere deep within him, a remnant of the Boy Scout still survived. And that scout knew that the bites of cottonmouths and rattlesnakes, while every bit as painful as Tarver had described, were rarely fatal. If the cottonmouth coiling around Tarver's arm bit Rusk on an extremity, he might well lose an arm—or even a leg—in the morning. But he wouldn't die. And therein lay his secret advantage. He was *willing* to trade an arm for $20 million. Because by morning, the FBI agents outside would start to wonder why he hadn't left for work. And if Alex Morse was pushing as hard as she usually did, they might crash in here even sooner. Rusk looked steadily at Tarver and said, "The diamonds aren't here."

What happened next blasted all his logic to hell. Tarver leaned over Lisa, rapped the snake twice on the snout with the golf club, then let it go. The moccasin struck in a blur, hitting Lisa in the upper chest. When the blur stopped, the snake's head was clenched tight around Lisa's forearm. She leaped up from the sofa and flung her bound arms around like a woman possessed by demons. Finally, the snake let go, and its heavy body thudded against a row of books.

Dr. Tarver was on the snake in a moment. He distracted it with the flashing head of the putter, then grabbed it behind the head and held it high.

Lisa had collapsed onto the sofa and was now staring at two puncture wounds in her forearm. Her breathing grew more and more frantic until foam emerged from her nostrils. When she started jerking like an epileptic, Rusk feared she might have a heart attack.

Dr. Tarver walked back to the desk, his eyes devoid of emotion. "You see the consequences of noncooperation. I'm going to give you one more chance, Andrew. Before I do, I'm going to explain something. I have no intention of killing you. If I kill you here, that creates a host of problems for me. Your EX NIHILO mechanism, for example. Not to mention a murder investigation. But if I leave you alive, there'll be no murder investigation, and you'll take care of the EX NIHILO business for me. You can't release that confession, because your hands are tied by your own guilt. The way it's always been. You see? You can survive this night. Your diamonds are the price of life. I know you've had your heart set on spending that money, but what's money weighed against thirty or forty more years of life? You have plenty of time to earn more. But I don't. I must take what life offers."

Tarver came around the desk and sat only inches away from him. The moccasin was struggling to escape. "Put your trust in logic, Andrew. I'm much safer with you alive than with you dead."

Rusk looked across the room. Lisa lay shivering on the sofa, still staring at the holes in her arm. Two tracks of blood and yellow fluid had dribbled down to her hand, and there was already pronounced swelling at the site of the bite. As Rusk stared, her facial expression changed from the stunned shock of an accident victim to fearful curiosity. She lifted her taped hands and pulled down the front of her tank top, exposing her left breast. Where the inner curve of the breast met her sternum were two more puncture marks, an inch apart and joined by a dark purple swelling. Lisa's eyes bulged like those of a woman suffering hyperthyroidism. She tried to get to her feet again, but this time she tumbled onto the floor.

"Are you ready to tell me where they are?" Tarver asked softly.

Rusk nodded. "I'll tell you. But what about Lisa?"

"After I leave, drive her to the emergency room. Tell them you were watering your lawn. She went outside to switch off the faucet, and she felt something hit her. Once she got inside, you saw the puncture marks. Use your imagination, Andrew. Just make sure she tells the same story you do."

Dr. Tarver reached out with his free hand and pulled Rusk's chin until they were looking eye to eye. "It's time."

Rusk felt physical pain as he spoke the words, or perhaps the emotional shock was so severe that it caused pain. "Under my bed," he whispered. "In a flight case, like yours."

Tarver laughed. "You keep them under your bed?"

"I buried them like you said. I dug them up this afternoon."

"Good decision, Andrew."

Tarver walked around the desk and stuffed the second cottonmouth into the croker sack with its mate. Then he resealed the tape over Rusk's mouth and walked out of the study.

A soft mewling rose from the other side of the desk. Knowing Lisa as he did, Rusk could not begin to fathom what must be going on in her mind, if indeed any rational mind remained. He was surprised how desperately he wanted to help her, but the duct tape made it impossible.

A creaking floorboard announced Dr. Tarver's return. Grinning through his beard, the doctor set the heavy flight case down on Rusk's desk with a bang. It was bright white, and twice as thick as a normal briefcase.

Tarver pulled a corner of the tape from Rusk's mouth. "What are they worth, Andrew? I know you have at least half your money tied up in business deals. I opened it in the bedroom. These looked like about ten million to me."

"Nine point six."

Tarver resealed the tape, then picked up the croker sack from the floor and stuffed it into his backpack. Pulling a small knife from his pocket, he knelt over the spot where Rusk assumed Lisa lay. Had he lied? Was he about to sever Lisa's carotids?

"I'm cutting the tape on her wrists about three-quarters through," the doctor said calmly. "She should be able to rip it the rest of the way in a few minutes, if you can keep her conscious. She looks a little shocky to me."

Rusk heard a faint slap. Then Tarver said, "Stay awake, sugar tits."

As Rusk struggled against the tape binding his arms,

the doctor got to his feet, shouldered his backpack, picked up the flight case, and strode out of the study.

Rusk felt as though he had been raped. He flexed his jaw muscles hard, and the tape came loose.

"Lisa!" he cried. "Can you hear me?"

She didn't respond.

"I know you can hear me. Rip the tape off your hands. You've got to do it before you pass out. You've got to save us, baby."

Still no response.

Rusk heard shifting body weight. Relief coursed through him. "Rip the tape off your mouth! Use your teeth! Come on, honey, do it!"

More movement on the floor. Then he heard the blessed sound of adhesive coming loose. A low, inhuman moan filled the study.

"Lisa? Are you loose? Do your feet! Honey, can you hear me?"

Now the sound of tape coming loose was continuous. Rusk flashed back to the high school autumns when he'd had to unwind what seemed miles of tape from his ankles after football games. Lisa was doing almost the same thing now. Soon she would be free. He was surprised at how little he felt the loss of the diamonds compared with the joy of surviving and the prospect of getting Lisa medical attention.

"That's it, honey. He didn't think you had it in you, but I knew you could do it."

The ripping stopped, replaced by the sound of heavy wheezing.

"Get up, sweetheart. Get up and get me loose."

The woman who stood up on the other side of the desk was almost unrecognizable. An hour before, Lisa

Rusk had been a woman of rare beauty who had glided through life without trauma of any kind. Her eyes had shone with the complacent bliss that could only exist in the young. But the woman standing across from him now looked like a refugee from a war zone, someone who had been dragged through the pit of hell and violated in ways unknown and unknowable. Her pupils were pinned against globes of white shot with blood. Her mouth hung open as from a mindless stupor, and her left breast swung free, smeared with blood and yellowish fluid.

"Lisa, can you hear me?"

Her mouth closed and opened three times, but no sound emerged.

She's in shock, Rusk thought desperately. *Holy shit.* "Cut me loose, Lisa! I've got to get you to the hospital. There's a pocketknife on the end table by the sofa. The one I got for a wedding present."

A flicker of recognition in her eyes? *Yes!*

She turned toward the sofa. Then, with the slow tread of a zombie, she walked toward the end table. She bent down. But when she came up, she was not holding the pocketknife. She was holding the golf club.

"Lisa? Get the *knife,* honey. That's a golf club you're holding."

She looked down at the putter as though unable to identify it. Then she said softly, "I know."

As she walked toward the desk, Lisa lifted the putter high above her head. Then she swung it in a long, roundhouse arc. Strapped immobile to the chair, Rusk could only tense as the flashing silver club smashed into his cranium.

CHAPTER
49

Alex let go of her mother's limp hand and quietly left the hospital room. She had sat there for the best part of an hour, talking quietly most of the time, but her mother's face had not even twitched in response. Margaret Morse's sedation was deep, and justly so. She had reached the point where an ending was better than continuing—or it would have been, were Alex in the same situation.

Alex's hospital slippers hissed along the floor as she passed the five doors that separated her mother's room from Chris's. Her head throbbed incessantly. The ER doctors had given her over-the-counter Tylenol, which hadn't even dented the pain that accompanied her concussion. To her surprise, she found Chris awake when she entered his room. As she leaned over his bed, she saw tears on his face. She took his hand.

"What's the matter?"

"I just talked to Mrs. Johnson."

Fear awakened in the pit of Alex's stomach. The same fear she felt when she thought about Jamie.

"Ben's pretty upset," Chris went on. "Thora hasn't

called him, and he's picked up from my voice that there's something wrong."

Alex laid her hand carefully on his arm. "You need to know some things."

His eyes instantly became more alert.

"Will overheard Thora telling Andrew Rusk to call off the hit on you."

Chris started to rise from the bed, but Alex pushed him back with ease. It frightened her to realize that he had become so weak so fast. She squeezed his hand. "It's time to arrest her, Chris."

Confusion filled his eyes. "She tried to call it off?"

"Only because she knew you were onto her. Frankly, I think she needs to be arrested for her own protection. She's a threat to Rusk and Tarver. They might kill her just to keep her quiet. And not only that."

"What else?"

"I'm worried that in her present state, Thora might be a threat to Ben."

Chris's eyes widened. "I don't think she'd physically hurt him."

"Given the pressure she's under? She could be suicidal. What if she decided to take Ben with her?"

He shook his head. "I don't think she'd . . . hell, I guess I'm the worst person to ask. I've been completely wrong about her so far."

"Thora's sick, Chris. But you didn't know that. You couldn't."

"I'm a doctor. I should have seen some clue."

"We're all blind when it comes to people we love. I've done the same thing myself."

"Who would take care of Ben if Thora's arrested?"

"Mrs. Johnson?" Alex suggested.

Chris shook his head. "I'd rather Tom Cage and his wife do it. Tom will know what to do if things get crazy."

She nodded. "I'll call him for you. You lie back and take it easy."

"I don't want Ben to see his mother arrested."

"I know you don't. And I don't think he will. But the alternative could be a lot worse."

Chris stared up at her with ineffable sadness. Alex had only seen sadness like that on the night James Broadbent confessed his feelings to her. After working closely with her for three years, Broadbent had become convinced that Alex was the love of his life. He was no wide-eyed boy, but a highly decorated FBI agent of forty with a loyal wife and two children. In a voice cracking with pain, Broadbent had told Alex that he could never abandon his family, but neither could he go on without telling her about his feelings. Because he couldn't endure being close to her without possessing her, he'd planned to put in for a transfer the next week. But he never did. Two days after his confession, James Broadbent was dead.

Alex leaned down and laid her cheek against Chris's pillow. "I know it looks hopeless now. But you're going to have a life again. You're going to share it with Ben, too."

Chris raised his hand and touched her face, careful to avoid the scars. "I can't see it right now. I want to . . . but I can't."

"I can. As clearly as I see you now."

He closed his eyes.

After a moment of debate, Alex climbed onto the hospital bed and lay beside him. If Chris noticed, he made no sign. She had thought they would both feel better if they lay together, but as she stroked his still-burning forehead, she was struck by the certainty that he would not live through the night.

Eldon Tarver pulled the Dodge pickup he'd been saving for his final escape up to the Union 76 truck stop on I-55 South. Ten seconds after he parked, his passenger door opened and Judah sat heavily on the front seat. Judah had a small backpack on his lap. As soon as he closed the door, he opened the pack and took out a small capuchin monkey. The capuchin had a face like a human infant's. It looked up at Eldon with anxious eyes, then buried its face in Judah's huge chest.

"Please don't be mad," Judah said.

Tarver was furious that his brother would disobey him and sneak the monkey out of the lab, but there was likely no harm done. The capuchin hadn't yet been used as a test animal, nor had it shared any cages with sick animals.

"Nobody saw the monkey?" Eldon asked, idling a few yards away from the building.

"Naw." Judah smiled. "She didn't make one peep."

"Did you wait in the restaurant?"

"Uh-uh. Spent most of my time in the shower area, by the game room. It didn't take you as long as you said."

Eldon smiled. "Sometimes things just fall right, you know?"

"Like with this one," Judah said, rubbing the capuchin's back.

Eldon laughed, then pulled out to the frontage road. He drove underneath the interstate, then turned left and accelerated up the ramp onto I-55 North. Before long they would reach the Natchez Trace exit. For several miles, the Trace ran along the Ross Barnett Reservoir, where some beautiful homes faced that stretch of the massive lake.

"Look in the backseat," Eldon said. "What do you see?"

Judah heaved his huge frame around far enough to stare into the rear seat of the pickup. Eldon switched on the overhead light.

"Looks like a box of rocks," said Judah.

Eldon belly-laughed for almost a half mile. "That's just what it is, Brother! A box of rocks!"

Judah looked puzzled, but he seemed content to caress the monkey and watch the headlights on the interstate. By the time they turned onto the Trace, Tarver's face looked carved from stone.

CHAPTER

50

Will Kilmer was sitting in his office when his telephone rang. He'd checked himself out of the hospital and come in early to try to catch up on the cases he'd been ignoring to help Alex, but the heavy backlog and the pain in his wounded back had pushed him to open the bottle of Jack Daniel's he kept in his bottom drawer.

"Argus Operations," he half-groaned, shoving a stack of files to the far corner of his desk.

"It's Danny, Will."

Danny Mills was an ex-cop Kilmer had assigned to watch Andrew Rusk's office today. "What is it, Danny?"

"Rusk hasn't shown up for work. Usually he's in at least a half hour before now."

"Okay. Stay put. I'll holler back at you."

Will hung up and considered the situation. He could send a man out to Madison County, where Rusk lived—or he could drive out there himself. He hated that idea, because commuter traffic was hell this time of the morning, with the new Nissan plant and all.

Plus, according to Alex, the FBI was watching Rusk now. Their involvement might be unofficial, but their point man was John Kaiser, an agent whose reputation Will had long known and respected. Alex had given Will a cell number for Kaiser in case of emergency. After another sip of Jack Daniel's, Will lifted his phone and punched in the number.

"Kaiser," answered a strong voice.

"Agent Kaiser, this is Will Kilmer calling. I'm not sure you—"

"I know who you are, Mr. Kilmer. Retired homicide detective, right?"

Will sat a little straighter. "Yes, sir."

"What you got?"

"I've got a man watching Andrew Rusk's office—have had for weeks now. And he tells me Rusk is a half hour late coming in this morning. He's usually regular as clockwork."

"Is that so?"

"Yessir. I don't know what might be happening out at Rusk's house, because I didn't send anybody out there last night. Didn't want to step on your toes."

"Thank you, Mr. Kilmer. I'll find out if anything's up."

"I don't need to do anything?"

"Just call with anything else you think I need to know."

"Will do."

Kilmer hung up. That was the kind of FBI agent he liked: all business, no territorial bullshit about who got credit for what. Will thought about calling Alex, but if she hadn't called him yet, she must have found some way to get to sleep last night. Maybe Chris Shepard had something to do with that. Will hoped so. The girl had been suffering for a long time, and he didn't care how she got relief, so long as she finally did. He dragged the pile of files back and opened the one on top.

John Kaiser climbed into the back of a black Chevy Suburban parked at the edge of Andrew Rusk's property. Five agents were waiting in the Suburban—three men and two women—all handpicked from the Jackson field office.

"We don't have the warrant yet," he said, "so I'm going to go up and knock on the front door. If no one answers, I want you to spread out and check the windows. See if you can find probable cause for us to go in. Understood?"

Everyone nodded.

Kaiser touched the driver's arm. "Nice and easy."

The Suburban rolled smoothly through the trees, circling around to the front of Rusk's ultramodern home. When it stopped, Kaiser got out and walked up onto the porch. He pressed the bell first, then knocked loudly.

No one came to the door.

He rang the bell again, then looked back at the Suburban. Two agents were covering him from open windows.

Another minute passed.

"Okay," he called, already filled with foreboding. "Move out."

All the doors opened simultaneously, and the agents dispersed around the house. Kaiser kept knocking. The longer he did, the worse he felt. He'd walked into many a gruesome crime scene during his service with the ISU, and despite his belief that most mythology about "intuition" was exactly that, he had a feeling that something obscene lay behind this door.

He walked down the porch steps and circled the house. Some agents were getting creative, climbing onto ladders or air conditioners to try to see through the windows. But when the cry came, it came from the far side of the house.

Kaiser started running.

"Around here!" shouted a female agent. "The kitchen!"

"What is it?"

The agent drew back from the window, her face pale. "Looks like a female, facedown on the floor. Car keys in her right hand, and a little blood beneath it. That's the only blood I see."

Kaiser pressed his face to the glass. The scene was exactly as the agent had described it. The woman on the floor wore what appeared to be spandex biking shorts, a tank top, and pink flip-flops.

"Wait five minutes, then call the state police," he said. "And the sheriff's department. I believe we're in the county, not a municipality."

"Yes, sir."

"That sure looks like probable cause to me," Kaiser said.

"She could be in need of emergency care," said a male agent beside him. "I think I may have seen movement."

"Let's don't get carried away. Bring a ram from the truck."

"Yes, sir."

Kaiser watched a burly agent smash the door open, then moved inside with his weapon drawn. Three agents followed and spread out to clear the rooms.

Kaiser knelt and checked the fallen woman's carotid pulse.

Dead.

He rose and worked toward the center of the house, all the while wondering what had killed the woman in the kitchen. A sharp cry around a corner ahead of him made him rush forward. He stopped cold.

An unrecognizable man sat strapped into a chair behind a desk, his face horribly swollen and bloody, his skull obviously fractured. A bloody golf club lay on the desk before him. *Could that be Andrew Rusk?*

"What the fuck happened here?" asked a male agent, pointing at lines of blood drops spattering the ceiling.

"You mean, *how* the fuck did this happen?" Kaiser corrected him. "Didn't we have agents watching this place all night?"

"Yes, sir. Six. I was here myself."

"You didn't hear anything?"

"No, sir."

"Did you kill him?" Kaiser asked in a deadpan voice.

"No, sir."

Kaiser moved behind the chair, reached into the corpse's back pocket, and slowly worked out his wallet. The driver's license in the wallet identified the bloody mess in the chair as Andrew Rusk.

Damn it, Kaiser thought. *This is going to be a nightmare. A clusterfuck of jurisdictions, a turf battle within the Bureau—*

He winced at the sound of his cell phone. He expected SAC Tyler, but the LCD window read ALEX MORSE. He started to ignore the call, but then he reminded himself that this was Morse's case. Had been from the start.

"Morning, Alex."

"Hey, John. Will Kilmer told me there might be something wrong out at Rusk's house?"

Kaiser sighed. "You could say that. Rusk's dead, and a woman with him. I'm guessing she's his wife."

"*Dead?* Jesus, I'm coming out there."

Kaiser heard the excitement in her voice. "That's a terrible idea. The place is going to be crawling with agents and cops. Webb Tyler's liable to come out here. You're not supposed to be anywhere near this case—or any other case, for that matter."

"Well . . . at least now we know I was right. Rusk was in this thing up to his eyeballs."

"We don't know anything of the kind. All we know is that someone you disliked intensely—some might say even persecuted—is dead. So I think the prudent thing is for you to stay away and let me brief you later."

There was a long silence.

"Do you agree?"

"John, I've been investigating Andrew Rusk for weeks, while everyone else sat on their asses and told me I was nuts. I've been inside that house. I might see things your people wouldn't see in ten years of looking!"

Kaiser felt a chill of suspicion. "You've been inside Rusk's house?"

Alex fell silent, obviously aware that her passion had carried her into dangerous waters.

"You stay where you are, Alex. That's an order."

"I hear you. Damn it."

"I'll call you as soon as I know anything."

"You'd better."

Kaiser hung up.

•   •   •

One hour later, Alex pulled her rented Corolla into the mass of law enforcement vehicles parked outside the Rusk house. She knew Kaiser would be furious, but after six weeks of blood, sweat, and tears, she could not sit idle while others picked up the baton and went forward. *Besides,* she rationalized, *Kaiser can't give me orders if I'm no longer an FBI agent. He was only a few pay grades above me, anyway. And SAC Tyler won't come out here . . . not in a million years. He likes that air-conditioned office downtown.*

Alex fell into her official stride and walked past a cordon of sheriff's deputies. A couple of FBI agents gave her the eye, but nobody challenged her. In less than a minute, she had worked her way into the study where what remained of Andrew Rusk was still taped into his chair. Crouched behind him were two men, one of whom Alex recognized as John Kaiser. A strange blue glow emanated from behind them. Then she recognized the roar of a cutting torch. After about a minute, she heard a grunt of triumph, then Kaiser stood up and turned.

"Goddamn it," he said with genuine annoyance. "Don't you ever listen?"

"This is my case," she said doggedly.

"You don't have any cases! Do you get that?"

Alex said nothing.

"Obviously you don't. I'm lucky to be in here myself. I told the sheriff that there might be biological weapons in this house, and that we needed to check it before they do the usual homicide investigation. Webb Tyler's going to have my ass, if not my job."

"What's back there?" she asked. "A safe?"

Kaiser nodded reluctantly.

"What's in it?"

"We're about to find out."

The man with the torch had finally got the door open. He backed away for Kaiser to examine the contents.

"You haven't been inside this safe before, have you?" he asked Alex.

"No." *But not for want of trying.* "What do you see?"

"Stay back there, Alex. I mean it. You're JAFO today."

Just Another Fucking Observer. "I can't observe anything from over here."

"Take a look at the notepad on the desk."

She did. It was a miniature legal pad, and scrawled on it in pencil was what looked like a man's handwriting—mostly numbers. "What is this?" she asked. "It looks like GPS coordinates."

"I think they are. And a time and date."

She read the numbers again. "Jesus, that's today."

"Yep. Two p.m. I think your lawyer friend was about to bug out of town."

"Where are these coordinates?"

"I'm not sure yet. Hank Kelly thinks they're on the Gulf Coast, if not actually in the Gulf of Mexico. He's a GPS hobbyist. Plays those games where they track down planted clues. On his off time, of course. What a world."

"There's a name here. You saw that?"

"Looked like Alejo Padilla to me," said Kaiser, still peering inside the safe.

"Me, too."

"Sounds Cuban."

"Uh-huh. And this writing after that?"

"*C-P-T*? It could mean 'captain.' "

"You think Rusk was headed south of the border?" Alex asked.

"I do."

"By boat?"

"Probably. Or maybe seaplane."

"Why would he flee the country in a boat?"

"If you need to take out contraband, it's the best way. A large amount of cash, say." Kaiser shifted on creaking knees and laid some papers out on the floor.

"Anything good?" Alex asked.

"Would you call two Costa Rican passports good?"

"Holy shit!"

"They're not valid yet, but they look legit."

"Costa Rica," she said thoughtfully. "We have an extradition treaty with them now."

"Yes, but these passports aren't in the Rusks' names."

"But they have the Rusks' photos?"

"Yep. Take a look."

She moved forward and leaned over his shoulder. Kaiser was right. She took one of the passports and compared the smiling photo of Andrew Rusk to the bloody corpse in the chair to her left. *God, he died bad.* She looked back at Kaiser, who was wading through the usual financial papers of any affluent family. Insurance policies, wills, deeds, Social Security papers . . .

"What else have you got?"

"Looks like a boat to me," Kaiser said, holding up a photograph.

Alex looked at the four-by-five snapshot. "That's not a boat, that's a yacht. You could sail around the world in that."

"Did Rusk sail?"

"Rusk did everything. All the hobbies of the rich and shameless."

"Is this boat out at the local marina?"

"I've never seen it before. He owns a powerboat, but it usually sits on a trailer out behind this house."

Kaiser looked up from the papers. "There's no powerboat out there now."

Alex looked down at the legal pad where the coordinates had been scrawled. "What if he was planning to meet someone at sea? Power out past the twenty-four-mile mark, board that yacht, and then take off for Costa Rica?"

Kaiser was staring at a sheet of paper in his hand. He gave a long, low whistle.

"What is it?" she asked, sensing his excitement.

"This piece of paper grants safe passage through Cuban territorial waters, and ensures permission to dock at the marina in Havana."

"What?"

"And it's signed by Castro himself."

"No way."

Kaiser stood and held the document up to the light. "Not Fidel. His brother, Raúl. The defense minister. And this document isn't made out in Rusk's name, either. It's made out to Eldon Tarver, MD."

Alex took the paper and read it line by line, her pulse beating faster with every word. "This is a photocopy."

"What it is," Kaiser said, "is inarguable proof that Andrew Rusk and Eldon Tarver were working together."

Alex swallowed hard and handed the paper back to Kaiser. Having finally discovered what she had worked so hard to find, she felt oddly disconnected from herself. Then she realized why: she had really been working to prove that Bill Fennell murdered her sister. Until she possessed evidence that proved that, she could not save Jamie from his father, as Grace had charged her to do.

"Why would Raúl Castro give Tarver permission to emigrate to Cuba?" she asked.

Kaiser looked at her as though she were slow. "The Virus Cancer Program. Viral bioweapons. I'll bet the Cuban DGI made an overture to Tarver at some point after the VCP was terminated, offered him money to come work for them. They approached a lot of scientists who were involved in sensitive research. Tarver must have figured Cuba would be a good place to lie low for a while, until it was safe to transfer to Costa Rica under a different name."

"Was he right?"

"Excepting the fact that he couldn't foresee the timing of Cuban political upheaval, yes."

"Rusk sure placed a lot of trust in Tarver."

"Mistakenly, I'd say." Kaiser tilted his head toward Rusk's corpse.

"What do you think happened here?" Alex asked. "Do you think Tarver did this?"

"Had to be him. This is a torture scene. He put them in the most central room in the house. No windows, multiple walls to deaden sound. It must have been awful in here."

"What killed the wife?"

"Medical examiner says shock."

"From a gunshot wound?"

Kaiser shook his head. "Snakebite."

"What?"

"Isn't that something? She was bitten twice. Once on the forearm and once on the chest, just above the heart."

"My God." Alex shuddered at the idea of what must have happened where she now stood.

"An evidence tech bagged two scales off a bookshelf over there," Kaiser added. "Reptilian for sure, he said. Not fish scales."

"What's the difference?"

"Snake scales are the reptile's actual skin. They're dry and have their own color. Fish scales are attached *to* the skin. They're translucent and colorless."

"Did you know that?" Alex asked, impressed.

Kaiser chuckled. "Hell, no."

"What do you think Tarver was after? I mean, he didn't touch the safe, did he?"

"He might have. He could have taken some things but left the rest. But it's well hidden behind a panel under those shelves. He may not have known it was there."

Alex gazed around the room. "You found that legal pad on the desk? The one with the coordinates on it?"

"No. That was found on top of the kitchen refrigerator, underneath a serving tray. Also, Kelly found a hole out back, in the garden. Looks like something had been dug up recently. The hole was twenty inches deep, in a heavily mulched area. Twelve inches by twenty inches, rectangular."

"Cash?" she speculated.

Kaiser looked skeptical. "Burying cash is tricky business. I'm guessing something more durable. Gold, maybe. Or gems."

"Or something we can't even begin to guess at."

He nodded, grave apprehension in his eyes. "They found a hole at Tarver's house, too. Last night."

"Really? Where?"

"Under the floor of a shed attached to the house. Thin aluminum floor with a square cut out. Tarver's hole was twice as big as Rusk's. Freshly turned earth, same as this one."

"These guys were pulling up stakes."

"Sir?" said a tech who had been examining the study with a powerful light.

"Yes?"

"I've got something on the floor here. Looks like the victim tried to write something with his foot. It's here in the blood."

"What is it?"

The man leaned closer to the floor. "It looks like . . . 'A's number twenty-three.' The number sign, I mean, not the word *number.*"

"Like the Oakland A's?" Kaiser asked.

"Guess so. Was this guy from the Bay Area?"

"No," said Alex, searching her memory. "No connection that I know of."

"Make sure you photograph it," Kaiser said.

He took Alex by the arm and led her out of the study.

"May I see Lisa's body?" she asked, as they moved toward the front door.

"They're loading her out now. Nothing to be learned there. I think she was just collateral damage. It's too bad she didn't make it to the hospital."

"Why didn't she just dial 911?"

"Phone was dead. Somebody cut the wires outside."

"With your agents watching the place?"

Kaiser nodded, then paused before the front door.

"This guy slipped right through six FBI agents. They're not wilderness masters or anything, but they're not stupid. They have ears and eyes. But Tarver moved through them like a ghost. In and out without a sound, and he tortured two people in between."

"And he's fifty-nine years old," Alex observed.

"This is a formidable suspect, no doubt. But now I'm thinking he may be getting help from professionals."

"The Cubans?"

"Who knows? Alex, this case just became a matter of national security. If the CIA finds out about that Castro document, they'll want to rip this case right out of our hands."

"Do you have to report it?"

"I should. Hell, Tyler will hand it to them on a silver platter."

Alex cursed in frustration. "Maybe you should kick this up to the new director. Roberts seemed like a decent guy to me. Maybe he's got some balls."

Kaiser didn't look hopeful. He took hold of Alex's shoulders and looked deep into her eyes. "Listen to me. You *have* to stay out of this. At least until we figure out how we're going to handle it. There is no wiggle room in what I'm saying. Do you get that?"

She suppressed the glib retorts that flashed to the surface. "What about those GPS coordinates? What if that's a rendezvous? Tarver himself could be there, for God's sake."

"Do you think Tarver would have left them here, if so?"

"You said the notepad was found hidden on top of the kitchen fridge, right?"

"True. The coordinates could be legit." Kaiser's eyes

pleaded with her. "I'll speak to the director about you,
Alex. I'll make clear to him that you were the one who
first unearthed these connections. But if I go to bat for
you, you have to stand clear while I do it. If Webb Tyler
finds out you were here . . . let's don't even go there.
You're going back to the hospital."

He opened the door and ushered her out.

Alex was the first to see Associate Deputy Director
Mark Dodson walking up the porch steps. Dodson
glared at her, then transferred the glare to Kaiser.

"Agent Kaiser, what is this woman doing here?"

"I invited Agent Morse to the scene, sir."

"She's not Agent Morse any longer. Please take note
of that fact in your discourse."

"He warned me to stay away," Alex said quickly. "I
disobeyed him and came of my own accord. I felt I
might have specialized knowledge that could help
Agent Kaiser understand this scene."

A satisfied look crossed Dodson's face. "I'll bet you do."

"What do you mean by that?"

"I mean I think you were here last night."

Her mouth fell open. "Are you crazy? I was at—"

"Do you deny ever being inside this house?"

She wanted to deny it, but the truth was, she had
been here before, and with damn good reason.
Triumph shone from Dodson's eyes.

"What are you doing here, sir?" Kaiser asked.

"Last night, Webb Tyler informed me that you were taking unauthorized measures in his area of operations. It's a
good thing he did, since you're obviously getting the Bureau
deep into a case that belongs to the Mississippi authorities.
What can you have been thinking, Agent Kaiser?"

"Sir, I had reason to believe that this case involves

deadly biological weapons and, as such, required immediate federal intervention."

This brought Dodson up short. "Biological weapons?"

"Yes, sir. Yesterday we discovered a clandestine primate lab owned by one Noel D. Traver, which is probably an alias of Dr. Eldon Tarver. Under the guise of a dog-breeding facility, Dr. Tarver appears to have been conducting sophisticated genetic experiments on primates, and possibly even on human beings."

Dodson suddenly looked less certain of his position. "I'm aware of yesterday's fire. Do you have proof that such experiments were conducted?"

"We have some escaped animals in captivity. I was waiting for approval to proceed, due to the complexity of the laboratory studies required."

Dodson licked his lips. "I'll give that further consideration. But I want Ms. Morse held at the local field office for questioning."

Kaiser stiffened. "On what grounds, sir?"

"The Bureau received multiple complaints from Mr. Rusk before his death that he was being persecuted by Ms. Morse. We know she blamed Rusk for the death of her sister. I'm going to have to establish beyond doubt that Ms. Morse did not take the law into her own hands last night."

Kaiser stepped toward Dodson. "Agent Morse has a service record—"

"Of losing control of her emotions during stress," finished Dodson. "Don't overstep the mark, Agent Kaiser. You don't want to throw away your career trying to save hers. That's a lost cause."

Kaiser went pale. "Sir, I happen to know that the disposition of her case is not yet final. And—"

Dodson held a piece of paper up to Kaiser's face. "This is an interview with one Neville Byrd of Canton, Mississippi. Byrd was apprehended in a downtown hotel with both laser and optical surveillance equipment in his possession. He had been surveilling the office of Andrew Rusk. When asked who hired him, Byrd stated that one Alexandra Morse had hired him at double his normal rates."

Alex gasped in disbelief.

Kaiser turned and looked at her. Seeing the doubt and pain in his eyes, she shook her head in denial. Kaiser looked around at the audience of field agents, hungry for the denouement of this battle.

"Sir, I want to state for the record that it was Agent Morse who first uncovered a connection between Andrew Rusk and Eldon Tarver. Six weeks ago, she suspected criminal collusion between them, and she proceeded to investigate them despite active resistance by the SAC of the Jackson field office and by yourself."

Dodson laughed scornfully. "You've just defined insubordination. You can testify against Morse at her final hearing."

"I don't think so," Kaiser said in a voice so commanding that a glimmer of fear came into Dodson's face. "I don't think there's going to be any such hearing." He held up a plastic evidence bag that he'd been holding alongside his right leg. "I'd like you to examine this evidence, sir."

A wary look from Dodson. "What is it?"

"A document. It's self-explanatory."

The ADD took the Ziploc bag and tilted back his head so that he could read it through the bottom of his no-line bifocals. His skeptical expression didn't change until he reached the bottom of the document. Then his mouth opened like that of a fish gasping for air.

"You noted the signature, sir?" Kaiser asked.

Dodson's face had gone slack with horror, the horror of a bureaucrat realizing he has backed the wrong horse. "Where was this found?" he asked in a scarcely audible voice.

"In the victim's safe. That document is absolute proof of criminal collusion between Rusk and Tarver and may well prove espionage against the United States."

"Not another word," said Dodson, his eyes blinking. "Agent Kaiser, join me in my car."

Kaiser glanced at Alex, then followed Dodson down to a dark Ford in the driveway. Alex stood on the porch, trying to contain her glee at seeing Dodson taken down a peg, and so publicly. But what truly warmed her heart was the way Kaiser had stood up for her, and at great personal risk. She looked down at the Ford, but its windows were too darkly tinted for her to see what was going on inside.

Two minutes passed before Kaiser and Dodson got out. Dodson's face was red, but Kaiser looked cool and composed. He motioned for Alex to join him. As she walked, she caught encouraging looks from three different FBI agents, two of them women. When she passed Dodson, the deputy director didn't even acknowledge her. Kaiser took her hand and led her to the Suburban he had driven up in.

"What about my car?" she asked quietly.

"Drop your keys on the ground. I'll have one of my guys bring it."

"What?"

"Drop them."

Alex dropped her keys on some pine straw and let herself be pushed into the backseat of the Suburban. She settled into the deep leather while Kaiser climbed behind the wheel.

"What happened in the car?" she asked.

"Nothing's decided yet. You are *so* goddamned lucky that piece of paper was in Rusk's safe."

"And you're not? Thanks, by the way."

Kaiser sighed heavily, then began to laugh. "You don't get many paybacks like that in this life."

"Did you tell Dodson about the GPS coordinates?"

"Had to. There's no holding back anything now. It's all going to be kicked upstairs to Director Roberts. We only won a skirmish, not the war."

"It still felt good."

Kaiser started the engine, backed around, then stopped and waited for a coroner's wagon to come through the long line of law enforcement vehicles.

"Where are we going now?" Alex asked.

"You're going back to the hospital. Don't even think about arguing. I'm putting out a statewide alert for Rusk's powerboat, as soon as I can get a description of it. Then I'm going to see this Neville Byrd character, the one who claims you hired him to watch Rusk." Kaiser cut his eyes at her. "You didn't do that, did you?"

"I've never even heard of the guy. I swear to God."

Kaiser nodded. "I'm hoping Tarver hired him. To make sure his partner wasn't crossing him, you know?"

"Absolutely."

As the coroner's wagon rolled by, something occurred to Alex. "Did you tell Dodson about the writing on the floor? 'A's number twenty-three'?"

Kaiser said nothing.

Alex suppressed her delight. "I thought you weren't holding anything back anymore."

"Screw that precious little bastard."

"Amen."

A young FBI agent rapped on Kaiser's window. Kaiser rolled down the glass. "What is it?"

"They sent me to get you, sir. The AD, I mean. They found something in the garage."

"What?"

"I don't know. But they're pretty freaked out."

Kaiser put the Suburban in park and got out. "Stay here, Alex."

She slammed the dashboard with her hand as Kaiser ran back to the house. Then she counted to five, got out, and sprinted after him.

CHAPTER

51

Alex stood outside Chris's room, wiping her eyes with Kleenex given to her by a nurse. She had been trying for five minutes to summon the courage to walk in and tell Chris that his wife was dead, but for some reason, she couldn't manage it. The irony was unbelievable. She had butted into Chris Shepard's life because she'd believed that his wife was trying to kill him. Now his wife lay on a table with a pathologist cutting a Y-incision into her chest.

When Alex crept into Andrew Rusk's garage behind John Kaiser, she hadn't had the slightest inkling that she would find a body there. Lethal biological agents, maybe, or bags of gold coins—anything but Thora Shepard. The woman Alex had always seen wearing only the finest clothes had been rolled in a paint-stained drop cloth and folded into the rear compartment of an SUV. *At least it was a Porsche,* Alex had thought at the time. But the condition of Thora's corpse banished even black humor from her mind. Thora's silky blond hair had been matted with what looked like pints of blood— a blessing since it covered the shattered skull beneath—

and her once-flawless skin looked like the grayish white underbelly of a frog. When Kaiser saw Alex behind him, he lifted the matted hair and asked her to identify the body. Thora's eyes were open. Those beautiful sea-blue orbs that Alex remembered from the photo in Chris's house were the deadest things she had ever seen—dull, cloudy marbles already shrinking into their sockets.

"May I help you, ma'am?" asked a passing nurse.

"No, thank you." Alex stuffed the Kleenex into her pocket and walked into Chris's room.

When she saw him shivering in the bed, she told herself that this was the wrong time to tell him about Thora. What good could it possibly do? It would surely harm his chances of winning his battle against an unknown illness. Dr. Clarke had warned her that Chris might be suffering. At the suggestion of Peter Connolly, Clarke had administered yet another antiviral drug—this one experimental—and Chris's reaction had been yet another fever.

"Alex?" he whispered. "Come closer. I don't think I'm contagious."

She walked over to his bed, took his shaking hands in hers, and kissed him on the cheek. "I know."

He responded with a weak smile. "Sympathy kiss?"

"Maybe."

He jerked his hands away and hugged himself during a particularly violent bout of shivering. "Sorry."

"You don't have to talk now."

He gritted his teeth, then gave his hands back to her.

She wanted to distract him, but she didn't know how. "So Ben is at Dr. Cage's house?"

"Yeah. Tom's wife is great, but Ben's really scared. I wish I was in good enough shape to have him here."

"What about the chemotherapy option? You still haven't taken any chemo drugs?"

"No. After what I've learned about the Virus Cancer Program—and Tarver's primate lab—I'm more convinced than ever that he injected me with some sort of retrovirus. No virus can induce cancer in a matter of days, so the way to attack it right now is with antiviral drugs." Chris struggled to shift on the bed. "I don't want to risk getting leukemia or lymphoma by taking melphalan or something else just as dangerous."

Alex squeezed his hands. "I think you just don't want to lose your hair."

He closed his eyes, but the ghost of a smile touched his lips.

"Are we friends, Chris?" she asked softly.

His eyes opened, questioning her without words. "Of course we are. I owe you my life. If I live through this, that is."

"I've got to tell you something else about Thora."

"Oh, God," he said wearily. "What has she done?" Sudden fear flashed in his eyes. "She hasn't taken Ben, has she?"

Alex shook her head. "No." *And she never will again.* "Thora's dead, Chris."

He stared up from the pillow without changing expression. His eyes seemed the same, but she knew that inside, the tenuous hold that he had on reality was tearing loose. After studying her face for a few moments, he saw that she had spoken the truth. "How?" he whispered.

"Somebody killed her. We're not sure who yet. Probably Rusk or Tarver."

Chris blinked once. "Killed her how?"

"She was beaten to death with a blunt instrument. Probably a claw hammer."

Alex saw despair in his eyes, and then he rolled over to face the wall.

"I didn't want to tell you," she said helplessly, "but the idea of someone else telling you was worse."

The back of his head was shaking, as though in denial of the news. But she knew he had believed her. "Where's Thora now?" he asked.

"They're doing a postmortem on her."

She heard a sharp exhalation. Chris knew too well what that meant in medical terms.

"Ben doesn't know, does he?"

"No, no."

"Could he hear it on TV or anything like that?"

"No."

"I need to see him."

Alex had already taken care of this. "He's on his way." She glanced at her watch. "He should be here any minute, actually. I called Tom Cage as soon as we—as soon as I knew. Tom went to check Ben out of school, and he promised to have him here as fast as possible."

Chris sighed heavily. "Thank you for doing that. Tom deals with death every day. He'll know how to handle Ben."

"Will you look at me, Chris?"

After nearly a minute, he rolled over and looked at her with red-rimmed eyes. She was about to speak when he said, "Help me up."

"What? You shouldn't—"

"Come on." Pulling against her hands, he managed to bring himself into a sitting position. He was still

shivering and panting, but his eyes held only determination. "You can go now."

"I'm fine right here."

Chris's eyes narrowed. "Fine? Why aren't you out
trying to find Tarver?"

"They won't let me. They've turned me into a goddamn bystander."

"So? You never waited for permission before. And
the only way you're going to save Jamie—or me—is by
nailing Tarver. Only he can convict your brother-in-law
now. And only he can tell the doctors what he shot into
me. Without that knowledge, it won't matter that I have
Ben. I'll die before he grows out of Little League."

Alex was stunned by the anger in Chris's voice and
eyes. She was trying to think of some reassuring reply
when her cell phone vibrated in her pocket. It was
Kaiser. She pressed SEND and held the phone to her ear.

"Tell me something good, John."

"Solve this puzzle, and I'll give you the best news
you ever had."

"What are you talking about?"

"I'm sitting with your alleged friend Neville Byrd.
He's recanted his statements about you and admitted
that he was hired by Eldon Tarver."

Alex closed her eyes in relief. "How did you manage
that?"

While Kaiser answered, Alex clicked her cell phone's
speaker function, so that Chris could listen in.

"When Mr. Byrd and his attorney heard the words
Patriot Act, they became very talkative," Kaiser said.
"But Tarver didn't hire Byrd just to keep tabs on Rusk.
Rusk had set up a digital mechanism that would
destroy Tarver in the event that Tarver killed him.

Insurance, right? Byrd was hired to find out what that mechanism was."

"Did he?" asked Alex.

"Yes. Rusk used a Dutch Internet service called EX NIHILO. Every day he had to log on and enter a series of passwords to verify that he was alive. If he didn't, a digital catalog of every crime Rusk and Tarver had committed would be sent to the Bureau and the Mississippi State Police."

"Dear God. Tell me you have that file, John."

"I'm looking at it right now. But I can't open it."

"Why not?"

"I don't have the final password. Rusk never accessed the file while Byrd was watching him. Neville stole enough passwords for Tarver to log in and pretend he was Rusk, but not to open or delete the confession file. Neville's been trying to hack the password since last night, but he hasn't been able to do it."

Chris was staring at the cell phone with laserlike focus.

"Do you have any idea what it could be?" Alex asked.

"What I'm thinking," said Kaiser, "is that after Dr. Tarver smacked Rusk in the head a few times with that putter, Rusk's last conscious thought was to get revenge on the bastard if he could. He couldn't use the telephone, but he could move his foot enough to write in the blood on the floor."

"A's number twenty-three!" Alex cried.

"Exactly. But Neville and I have googled our way through all the baseball rosters of the Oakland A's for the past hundred and six years. We've tried every player we can find who wore number twenty-three, but no combination of any of their names or birthdays or batting averages or anything else is the password."

Alex thought furiously. "You're making an assumption that *A's* refers to the baseball team. Throw that out and start from zero. *A's number* . . . What else could it mean?"

"The only hits that search engines kick up are baseball-related. I just put in a call to the NSA in Washington. They've put it in the queue for a super-computer."

"It can't be that hard," said Alex. "It's something Rusk thought we could figure out. What were his other passwords?"

"One was pi to the ninth decimal place."

"Pi," Alex echoed.

"A couple were names from classical literature. One was the speed of light."

In a strangely detached voice, Chris said, "How did he write 'miles per second squared'?"

"Who's that talking?" asked Kaiser.

"Chris," Alex replied. "Can you answer his question?"

"Hang on."

Alex looked down. Chris had taken hold of her elbow. "The only *A's number* I know about is Avogadro's number," he said.

"What's that?"

"A constant in chemistry. It has to do with molar concentration. Every high school chemistry student has to memorize it."

"What was that?" asked Kaiser.

"Chris has got a password for you to try. Hold on." She looked at Chris. "What's the number exactly?"

"Six-point-oh-two-two times ten to the twenty-third power."

"The twenty-third power?" Alex echoed.

Chris nodded.

"That's the twenty-three? A's number *twenty-three*."

"How would you type all that out?" asked Kaiser.

Chris looked up at the ceiling. "Six period zero two two X one zero two three."

"I heard him," said Kaiser. "Neville's typing it in."

Alex's ears roared as she waited.

"No dice," said Kaiser, obviously deflated. "That's not it."

Alex closed her eyes.

"Try leaving out the decimal," said Chris.

"All right," said Kaiser. "Byrd's trying it—"

Alex winced as a scream of triumph came through the phone.

"That's it!" shouted Kaiser. "We're in!"

Alex was squeezing the phone so tightly that her hand hurt. "What does it say? What's in the file, John?"

"Hang on. My God . . . it's a confession, all right. There's pages and pages of it."

Alex caught Chris's hand in hers. "Do you see Grace's name? Tell me you see Grace's name."

"I'm looking . . . I see several of the victims you listed for me."

Alex's whole body was shaking. Chris's jaw muscles were working steadily.

"I see it," Kaiser murmured. "Grace Fennell. I'm reading it right off the page."

Alex felt tears streaming down her cheeks. The lump in her throat kept her from speaking until she managed to swallow. "Copy that file *now*, John."

"Neville already copied it," he assured her. "He's printing it out right now."

"What about Thora?" Chris asked. "Or anything about me?"

"It's probably the last entry in the file," Alex said.

"No. The last entry is a guy named Barnett. An oil-man. Rusk thinks Barnett is going to approach him any day about getting a divorce."

"Keep looking."

"I am. Wait . . . here it is, Christopher Shepard, MD. It's all here, Alex. All the proof in the world."

Chris was holding his fist over his mouth, as though he might lose control of himself.

"I've never seen anything like this," Kaiser said in a fascinated voice. "I mean, I've discovered the trophies of serial murderers . . . monsters, aberrations . . . but this is just *business*. Naked fucking greed, by people who knew better."

Alex saw tears in Chris's eyes.

"Listen to this," said Kaiser. "'In November of 1998, I was approached by a law school classmate named Michael Collins, a criminal lawyer who works for Gage, Taft, and LeBlanc. Collins wanted my advice about a client, a physician named Eldon Tarver. Dr. Tarver's wife had recently died of cancer, but his wife's family believed she was the victim of foul play. They were a wealthy family, and Tarver feared they had gotten the police involved. He'd hired Collins because he believed he was in danger of being arrested. I was puzzled that Collins would seek out my help, because I specialize in divorce, but Michael told me that he needed my psychological insight, not legal expertise.

"'Over the course of two interviews with Dr. Tarver,

I realized the nature of Michael's problem. His client was guilty. Tarver didn't come right out and state this fact, but it was plain to me. I had never encountered such arrogant self-assurance in my life, not even from my father, and that's saying a lot. In the end, no charges were brought against Dr. Tarver, mainly because no forensic evidence of murder could be produced, despite two separate autopsies, one by a renowned pathologist. In fact, the second autopsy was what convinced the police that no murder had in fact occurred. But I knew different.'

"Do you want me to go on?" Kaiser asked.

Alex looked at Chris, whose eyes were closed. "Do you want me to turn off the speaker?"

"No."

"Go ahead, John."

" 'I had no further contact with Dr. Tarver until almost two years later, when I encountered him during a weekend hunting trip at the Chickamauga Hunting Camp. During that weekend, I found myself alone with him for an extended period. He asked several forward questions about my divorce practice, questions that I took to be a strange sort of overture. Strangely sure that I could trust Tarver, I decided to step out on a limb. I remarked that, after years of experience in my field, I had come to believe that in certain cases involving wealthy clients, a timely death would be a preferable alternative to divorce. Dr. Tarver's response was instantaneous: "I think you mean an *untimely* death, don't you?"

" 'That was the beginning of our partnership. Under the influence of a moderate amount of alcohol, Dr. Tarver assured me that he could kill anyone without leaving a forensic trace. He looked on this, he said, as a sort of professional challenge and claimed that every pathologist had at some point in his life had thoughts along those lines. It was only natural, he said.

"'Before we left Chickamauga that weekend, the basics of our plan had been worked out. I had wealthy clients coming to my office every week, begging me to spare them a huge settlement and get them more time with their children. I could judge which clients had sufficient hatred and anger to consider actually eliminating their spouses. Dr. Tarver and I would have as little contact as possible. After securing a go-order from a client, I would initiate contact by sending a false spam message to one of his e-mail accounts. The next day I would park my car at the Annandale Golf Club and play eighteen holes of golf. There would be a large packet in my trunk when I arrived. When I left, the packet would be gone. That packet contained everything about the intended victim, and all of it supplied by the victim's spouse: medical history, daily schedule, car keys, house keys, vacation plans, security codes, e-mail passwords, everything. That was the only "contact" Tarver and I ever had, and even that involved no face-to-face interaction. It could never be proved or traced because Dr. Tarver wasn't a member of that club. He had a friend who played golf there almost every day, and Tarver could go as a guest whenever he chose. He opened the trunk with a key I gave him that first weekend at Chickamauga. I have only spoken to Dr. Tarver a few times in the past five years, and those times by pure happenstance. But together, he and I have murdered nineteen people.'"

"Nineteen," Alex breathed. "I knew there were more."

"Wait," said Kaiser, his voice quickening. "While I was reading that, Kelly handed me a note. A deputy sheriff in Forrest County just spotted Andrew Rusk's powerboat. It's being towed on a trailer behind a black Dodge pickup truck on Highway 49."

Chris looked at the cell phone with something like hatred.

"Did he see the driver?" Alex asked.

"A bald man with a gray beard and a bright birth-mark on his left cheek."

Alex's heart began to race. "Jesus God, we've got him."

"No, we don't. We know where he was fifteen min-utes ago."

"The deputy's not trying to stop him, is he?"

"No. Forrest County's on the way to the Gulf Coast, right?"

"Could be. That's near Hattiesburg. It's the back way to the Coast. Did you ever get an exact location on those GPS coordinates?"

"Yes," said Kaiser. "That location is *in* the Gulf of Mexico. Twenty-four miles south of Petit Bois Island."

"Past the reach of the Coast Guard." Alex looked at her watch. "Two p.m. is less than two hours away."

"Don't worry. You're going to be there."

Alex caught her breath. "Seriously?"

"You and me, babe."

She felt as though a steel band had been cut free from her chest.

"I've got a chopper on standby," Kaiser said, panting as though he were running. "You get upstairs to the UMC helipad. We'll take six SWAT guys from Jackson and link up with some of my guys from the New Orleans office."

"I'm hanging up now. Don't you dare leave me

behind, John. I don't care if the director forbids you on pain of termination. You set that chopper down on the UMC roof."

"I'll be there in ten minutes. You be waiting."

"Go," she said, and hung up.

Chris was watching her, his body completely still.

"I need to go with him, Chris. I don't want to leave you alone, but—"

"I'm all right. I have—"

Three soft knocks sounded in the room. Then the door opened a crack and a voice Alex didn't recognize said, "Hello? Chris Shepard?"

"Yes," she called, walking to the door.

It opened before she reached it, revealing a handsome man in his early forties with two children standing in front of him, a boy and a girl.

"I'm Penn Cage," said the man, extending his hand. "Tom Cage's son. Are you Alex Morse?"

She nodded and shook the hand.

"My father was having some angina this morning," Penn said, "so I thought Annie and I should drive Ben up to see his dad. I hope that's all right."

Only then did Alex realize that the boy standing before her in the school uniform was Ben Shepard. "Oh, yes. I really appreciate it." She backed out of the way so that Chris could see his visitors.

"Penn?" Chris said from the bed. "What . . . ?"

Cage walked forward and gently shook Chris's hand. "I thought Ben might like to ride up with Annie and me."

Alex saw Chris wipe his eyes before the children got close enough to see his tears.

Annie Cage was a well-knit girl of about eleven with tawny hair and wise eyes. She took Ben's hand to lead him to his father's bed, and to Alex's surprise, Ben allowed it.

"Hey, buddy," Chris said weakly.

Ben's face was red. He was about to cry. "Are you sick, Dad?"

"Just a little. But I'm going to be fine in a couple of days. How are you doing?"

Ben nodded. "The mayor brought me to see you."

"I see that. Hello, Annie."

"Hi, Dr. Chris," Annie Cage replied.

Penn smiled, then touched Annie's shoulder and pulled her back toward him. "I think we're going to let you two visit for a while."

Chris looked up gratefully.

"Do you need anything?" Penn asked. "A Coke or something?"

"No, thanks."

"We'll see you in a while, then."

With a pointed look at Alex, Penn backed into the hall with Annie in tow.

Chris put his hand on Ben's shoulder, then looked up at Alex and said, "Go get him. And don't come back here until you have. Okay?"

Forcing down a rush of emotion, Alex nodded, then waved good-bye and walked into the hall. Penn Cage was waiting for her. Looking down the corridor, she saw his daughter sitting on a bench by the nurses' station.

"How bad is he?" Penn asked.

"He could die."

Penn blew air from his cheeks. "Is there anything I can do to help you? I'm not just saying that. I used to be a prosecutor in Houston, and I have a lot of contacts in federal law enforcement."

Alex suddenly realized that Penn Cage was the lawyer who had destroyed a former director of the FBI, by implicating him in a civil rights murder cover-up that dated to the 1960s. "I wish you'd made that offer a week ago."

Cage's eyes burned with surprising intensity. "I'm making it now. You tell me what Dr. Shepard needs, I'll do everything in my power to get it or make it happen."

Alex glanced at her watch, her mind on Kaiser's chopper. "Do you know Chris well?"

"Not as well as I'd like. But my father says he's as fine a man as he's ever worked with. That's saying something."

"I think so, too," Alex said, surprising herself.

"Don't let me keep you. Just remember what I said."

"I will."

Alex turned and ran toward the elevators. Ten steps down the hall, she passed her mother's door. Margaret Morse would never know whether her daughter had stopped, and Alex almost kept running. But halfway to the elevators, she slid to a stop, then ran back and darted into her mother's room. As she had done with Chris, she squeezed her mother's hand and bent low beside her face.

"Mom?" she whispered. "It's Alexandra. Jamie's going to be all right. You can go now."

She prayed for a sign, a blinking eye or moving finger—but there was nothing. She kissed her mother's cheek, then fled the room.

CHAPTER

52

The helicopter that touched down on the roof of the University Medical Center was a sleek, white Bell 430, capable of carrying eight passengers plus crew at 140 knots for nearly four hours. Alex had flown into many hostage situations, but rarely in a chopper as powerful as this. A 430 would deliver them to the Gulf of Mexico with time to spare. She bent almost double as she ran beneath the whirling rotors. The familiar *whup-whup-whup* set her heart racing. She leapt through the open door, took a quick look at the six black-clad SWAT agents behind Kaiser, then strapped herself in beside him.

"Ready?" Kaiser shouted.

She gave him a thumbs-up.

Kaiser smiled as the whine of the engine rose. "These things always remind me of Vietnam."

"Is that good or bad?"

"Good question." He squeezed her shoulder in reassurance. "The trick now is taking Tarver alive."

Alex nodded.

"That's where you come in. That's how I sold the director on you being here."

"So I'm a hostage negotiator again?"

"In a manner of speaking. You're going to negotiate, only there won't be any hostages. Or so we hope, anyway."

"Amen."

"I'm going up front for a second. I need to speak to the pilot before we lift off."

Kaiser went forward and leaned down beside the pilot's helmet. Alex looked out at the sky, gray overhead and piled with black clouds to the east. Feeling a vibration against her thigh, she took out her cell phone and looked at the LCD window. It read: 1 NEW MESSAGE. When she opened the phone, she saw that the message was from Jamie. Finally! She hit READ. The message read, *Dad's packing our stuff! Says we're moving. 2DAY! Heard him talking 2 HER about Mexico. Can he take me 2 Mexico? He seems scared. I'm scared. Can u come get me? On computer. Dad wont let me call u.*

Alex slammed the phone against her leg. Bill's timing was perfect, as usual. She wanted to tell Kaiser to order the chopper to the Ross Barnett Reservoir to pick up Jamie, but of course she couldn't. Andrew Rusk's written confession would soon nail Bill Fennell's hide to the wall, but right this minute, Bill had legal custody of the boy.

Alex had thought this chopper was taking her to the man who'd murdered Grace, but now she realized that Eldon Tarver hadn't really murdered her sister. He was just the weapon. Bill Fennell was the real killer. And now, like Tarver, Bill was planning to flee the country—with Jamie in tow. That left Alex no choice about what to do. But she couldn't tell Kaiser why she had to get out of the helicopter. She might just have to commit a felony herself in the next half hour—a kidnapping. And Kaiser couldn't be party to that.

She lifted the cell phone to her ear and began simulating a conversation with one of her mother's nurses. "*What?*" she yelled. "I can't hear you!"

Kaiser turned and watched her from the cockpit.

"When?" she shouted. "What does that mean? . . . Her *kidneys*? Now? Or in the next couple of hours? . . . Jesus, all right. I'm on my way. . . . Probably ten minutes."

Kaiser walked back and knelt beside her. "What is it?"

"My mother's crashing. All systems. She signed a DNR, so she's probably going to die in the next few minutes. Do you believe this shit?"

Kaiser looked at his watch, then the metal deck, then back up at Alex. "It's your call. We can't wait for you if you go back down. Is she conscious?"

"In and out. Mostly out. But still . . . it's my mother, you know?"

"I know." He looked at his watch again, silently calculating. "I wish you could be there. You know it's going to come down to a standoff, and you could be the one holding the bullhorn."

"Don't make it worse, okay?" She forced a smile. "I appreciate you getting me the chance. Just go. Nailing Tarver is the thing."

Alex unstrapped her harness and climbed back down to the roof. Kaiser knelt in the big sliding door, watching her with compassion. Under the roaring blades he shouted, "I'm sorry about your mom!"

Alex waved and sprinted toward the breezeway at the edge of the helipad.

The 430 lifted into the darkening sky before she reached the door, then swooped off in a wide arc to the south.

She took out her cell phone and dialed Will Kilmer.

The FBI helicopter was thirty miles south of Jackson when the doubt gnawing in Kaiser's gut became intolerable. He took out his cell phone, dialed directory assistance, and got the number for the University Medical Center. When UMC's switchboard operator came on the line, he identified himself as an FBI agent in an emergency and demanded to speak to the chief nurse on the Oncology floor. While he waited, one of the agents behind him moved forward and said, "What's going on, John? Something new?"

Kaiser shook his head. "I don't buy Morse's story about her mother."

"Why not?"

"No way would that girl miss a chance to take down the guy who killed her sister. I don't care if her mother *is* dying. Morse almost ruined her career over this, and there's no way she'd miss the final act."

"Hello?" said an irritated female voice. "Who is this?"

"Special Agent John Kaiser of the FBI. We have a life-or-death emergency in progress, and it involves the daughter of one of your patients, Margaret Morse. Her daughter is Special Agent Alex Morse."

"I . . . her."

"Could you speak up please? I'm in a helicopter."

"*I know her!*"

"I read you loud and clear now. Is she in the hospital now? Alex Morse, I mean."

"I haven't seen her since she ran out twenty minutes ago."

"I see. Can you tell me about her mother? Has her condition suddenly worsened?"

"I don't think it could get much worse."

"What I mean is, has she crashed? Have you called Agent Morse in the last few minutes and told her that her mother was dying?"

"Oh, I don't think so. Not that I'm aware of. Let me check."

Kaiser looked at his pilot, pointed at the airspeed indicator, and signaled that they should slow down. After nearly a minute, the nurse came back on the line.

"No, sir. No call like that went out from here. In fact, Mrs. Morse's kidneys seemed to be a little better this morning. Putting out more urine."

Kaiser hung up, leaned over the pilot's helmet, and spun his forefinger in a circle. "Turn around!"

As the 430 banked over I-55, Kaiser dialed the Jackson field office and demanded to speak to a technical specialist.

"Yes, sir?" said an even younger voice than he'd expected.

"I need GPS coordinates on a cell phone. As fast as you can get them. Call the cell company and tell them lives depend on it." Kaiser read off Alex's cell number, then said, "I think it's a Cingular phone. Call me back the instant you have the coordinates."

"Will do, sir."

As soon as he hung up, the pilot leaned over and said, "Where are we going?"

Where the hell *was* Alex going? Kaiser wondered. Did she not believe that the man towing Rusk's boat toward the Gulf Coast was Tarver? Could someone have called and told her that? He didn't think so. Chris Shepard certainly had no way of knowing that. Was Will Kilmer still working the case? Could the old ex-cop have discovered something at the last minute? Possibly. But then again, Alex's reason for bailing might be something completely unrelated to Tarver—something that overrode her concern for the murder case. What could possibly be that important?

"Hover!" he said to the pilot. "Keep us where we are!"

As the 430 slowed to a hover, Kaiser sensed that desperation was blocking efficient thought. He'd seen the phenomenon many times: people in emergencies couldn't make the simplest logical connections. No one was immune, not combat veterans, not astronauts, not— His phone was ringing.

"Hello? Hello!"

"I've got the coordinates, sir. That phone is at thirty-two degrees, twenty-five minutes and some-odd north; and ninety degrees, four minutes—"

"Just tell me where they are, son! Lay a map over those numbers!"

"We already did. It's Coachman's Road, near the Jackson Yacht Club. Right on the edge of the reservoir."

"The Ross Barnett Reservoir?"

"Yes, sir."

"Would Rose's Bluff Drive be near there?"

"Yes, sir. Right there. And whoever has that phone is even closer to there now."

"Damn it! That's her brother-in-law's house."

"Sir?"

The pilot looked over at Kaiser, his eyes questioning behind his faceplate.

Her nephew, Kaiser thought angrily. *Is this some kind of custody crap?* Jamie Fennell was the reason Alex had worked this case so hard and so recklessly. But . . . what if it was something else? What if the kid meant something to Tarver, too? Was that possible? Could Bill Fennell somehow be helping Tarver to escape? Not if the pathologist was driving down to the Gulf, he couldn't. But what if he wasn't? What if someone else was driving that truck?

CHAPTER

53

Bill Fennell lived on the southwestern bank of the Ross Barnett Reservoir, fifty square miles of water that could kick up ocean-sized whitecaps in a storm like the one that was on its way. Despite their proximity to the Jackson Yacht Club, most houses here were older than the McMansions on the eastern shore. Bill had solved that problem by buying four contiguous lots just north of the yacht club, then tearing down the houses on them and building his vision of nouveau riche paradise.

Alex and Will were less than five minutes away from the result, roaring along Coachman's Road in the blue Nissan Titan Will had substituted for his Explorer, which was recovering from the explosion at the primate lab. Will's .357 magnum lay on the seat between them, and a 12-gauge shotgun was lying on the backseat. Alex's borrowed Sig was in the glove box, and she had a Smith & Wesson .38 strapped to her left ankle.

"You get any more text messages?" Will asked.

"No. I just hope they haven't left yet. They've got to come out this way, right?"

"Not necessarily. There's half a dozen ways out of that old neighborhood."

"Great."

The turbulent waters of the reservoir came into sight. Will turned south, heading along the spit of land that held the yacht club and the Fennell home. "How do you want to play it?" he asked.

"We're going to ask nicely for Jamie," said Alex. "Then we're going to take him out of there. Bill should be arrested for murder before the day is out."

"Bill can be a cranky son of a bitch," Will said. "He almost went to jail for beating up a guy on the side of the road one time. Road rage."

"I didn't know that." Alex let her left hand fall on the magnum. "But I'd say we're prepared to deal with that." She pointed to a tall, wrought-iron gate fifty meters ahead. "Slow down."

Will pulled up to the gate and stopped.

"Chained shut," Alex said, pointing at a heavy padlock.

Will got out, climbed into the bed of his truck, opened the shining toolbox, and removed a long pair of bolt cutters. He cut the chain easily, then tossed the cutters into the truck bed and climbed back behind the wheel.

"You're handy to have around," said Alex.

Will looked hard into her eyes. "Before we go in, let me ask you one thing. What's the chance that we're walking into some kind of trap?"

She had tried not to focus on this possibility, but rather to prepare herself for whatever might happen. But now Will had given voice to her fear.

"That's why you're here," she said softly. "If I knew

for sure it was just Bill, I wouldn't need anybody to help me deal with him."

Will sighed like an old man in need of a nap. "That's what I figured."

"I can go without you," Alex said, meaning it. "You can wait right here."

The detective cocked his head and looked over at her, his watery eyes like those of an old hound dog. "Honey, your daddy pulled me out of so many tight spots I couldn't begin to count 'em. I'm here now because he can't be. And I'm gonna do exactly what I know he'd do." Will put the truck into gear and rolled forward. "Let's go get that boy."

He drove through the gate and around the long, sweeping drive that led to the rear of the Fennell mansion, an oversize copy of a Louisiana plantation house, with tall, white columns and a wraparound porch. He stopped when they were still a hundred meters away and parked behind a thick stand of trees.

"This is far enough," he said.

As he switched off the engine, the rain that had been threatening for hours finally swept over the property like advancing waves of gray-clad soldiers. The first drops hit the truck like shots from a pellet gun, and then the aggregate blotted out the mansion. Through the gaps in the trees, Alex could just make out the leaden surface of the reservoir. She opened the glove box and took out the Sig-Sauer Will had given her two days ago, then got out and walked up to an oak tree. Will carried the shotgun loosely along his left leg, his pistol gripped in his right hand. When he drew up beside her, they turned together and surveyed the house and grounds while the rain soaked their clothes.

The mansion had been built facing the reservoir. Hundreds of trees and shrubs dotted the twelve-acre lot, with gardens and ponds placed throughout in the English style. The landscaping alone had cost more than the houses around it. To their left stood a tennis court, to their right an infinity pool with a serpentine slide for Jamie.

In front of the house, Alex knew, a broad pier ran far out over the reservoir. A boathouse stood at the end of it, and it held twice the boat that Andrew Rusk owned. A Carrera bowrider, she remembered, with twin outboards that could push it to ninety knots, which was almost flying.

"Me and Jim did this many a time," Will said. "Thousands of times, I bet, if you count domestic calls."

Alex's abraded elbows stung as though the rain were acid. "That's Bill's Hummer," she said, pointing to a splash of yellow sticking out of the distant garage. "He's got a pair of them. H1s."

"I know," said Will. "I used to see them when he'd drop off Jamie to go fishing with Jim."

"I forgot you used to go with them sometimes."

Will nodded, then started marching across the open ground. "Jamie's a good boy. Never liked his daddy much, though. Loudmouthed prick, you ask me."

"You know what I think," said Alex, following closely.

As the house grew larger, a low growl crossed the space between them. It was Will's voice, she realized, speaking in an entirely different register.

"If Bill tries to stop us taking Jamie out of there," he said, "you go outside and wait for me."

"Uncle Will, you—"

"Hush, girl." The detective turned toward her as he walked, his eyes flat and hard. "None of that hostage-negotiator bullshit. You get out of there and let me do what needs to be done."

Alex had never heard Will speak this way. He was talking to her across a generation. But she understood. Will Kilmer had worked homicide for two decades, and he knew that a murder trial was a notoriously unreliable business, especially if the defendant could afford top criminal lawyers. But if Bill Fennell perished in the confusion of a domestic disturbance, there would be no custody battle over Jamie. It was an inhuman train of thought, she knew—or was it *essentially* human? Either way, Will had a point. All that mattered now was Jamie.

They moved like shadows through the rain. Will walked faster, breathing hard but showing no sign of slowing. When the house was twenty meters away, they halted behind some tall evergreen shrubs.

"Up the porch steps?" Alex asked.

Will shook his head. "Circle the house and try to get a look inside."

"Split up?"

"Normally, I'd say yes. Today? No. When we reach the right corner of the house, we'll climb onto the porch so we can see through the windows."

They moved out from behind the shrubs and started toward the right side of the house. Will pushed through the thick hedge below the porch, then climbed over the rail at the corner and waited for Alex. He moved with surprising grace, she noted, clambering over behind him.

Through the first window they saw only an empty

room. They moved lightly along the wall to the next window. Again, she saw no people.

"Put your hands in the air," said a commanding voice from behind them. "I'm pointing a sawed-off twelve-gauge shotgun at your backs."

Utter blackness descended in Alex's soul.

"Keep facing the wall, but toss your weapons back over the rail. All of them."

"Where did he come from?" Will whispered from her left.

The hedge, she realized. *He was waiting behind the hedge.*

Will half-turned and in a tough voice said, "Listen to me, Bill Fennell. You're already in a bucketful of shit. You don't want to—"

"That's not Bill," Alex told him.

Will looked over his shoulder, then closed his eyes and shook his head.

Alex had to admire Dr. Tarver's strategy. He had sent the "message from Jamie," then waited behind the porch hedge to assess the response. Simple but brilliant, since it would have prevented him from being trapped in the house had an army of SWAT agents descended on it. But no such army was coming. The question was, why was Tarver here at all?

"Don't try to play hero, partner," said the doctor. "Chivalry is expensive, and you're past the age for it." Tarver took a step to his right. "I have a picture of you in my cell phone, Pop. You're sleeping soundly after a few beers."

Will muttered something unintelligible.

"And you, Agent Alex. You remember what it feels like to be hit with buckshot, don't you?"

The right side of her face tingled. She could feel Will tensing beside her, like a cat preparing to spring. She closed her eyes and tried to reach him by force of will. *Don't try it . . . you can't beat a bullet, not even buckshot—*

"Get those guns over the rail!" Tarver snapped again. *"Now!"*

"Where's Jamie?" Alex asked, tossing the Sig over her shoulder.

"You'll see."

Dear Lord, let him be alive . . .

"I love you, baby girl," said the faintest whisper beside her.

Baby girl? That was what Will had called his daughter, before she died in the—

In the same motion that Will tossed his shotgun over his shoulder, he whirled away from Alex with all the speed that a seventy-year-old man could muster. He fired his pistol as he spun, trying to disorient Tarver as much as possible while he bought Alex one chance. Her hand was almost to the .38 in her ankle holster when the artillery-like boom of the shotgun blotted out the reports of Will's pistol. The sound hurled her back to the Federal Reserve bank, when a desperate man had shattered her closest friend and half her face in a matter of seconds. When she came up with her .38, the smoking mouth of Dr. Tarver's shotgun was only two feet from her eyes.

"It would be a shame to ruin the other half," he said.

Moving only her eyes, Alex glanced down to her right.

Will lay on his stomach, a dark pool spreading

beneath him. Several ragged exit wounds revealed splintered white bone from his scapula. One hole was almost directly over his spine.

"Aaahhhh," Alex moaned, her eyes stinging. "You son of a bitch!"

"He chose his fate," Dr. Tarver said. "A brave man."

He died like my daddy did, said the voice of the little girl inside her.

"What?" asked Tarver, snatching the .38 from her hand.

Had she spoken aloud?

"Into the house," Tarver ordered. "Go."

Alex started to step over Will, but Tarver shook his head and pointed to the front of the house—the reservoir side. As she walked, she stared along the pier, wondering if the Carrera was in the boathouse. Bill often left the key out there. If she could get Jamie out of the house . . . then get him to the boathouse—

The front section of the wraparound porch was screened. She opened the door to the protected area, walked in, then stopped before the stained cypress door that led to the main house. What nightmare lay on the other side of it?

"Go in," Dr. Tarver said.

She turned the knob and pushed open the door.

Bill Fennell lay sprawled at the foot of the main staircase. His long legs were bent at odd angles, and his mouth appeared to be frozen open. As Alex swept her eyes across the room, frantically searching for Jamie, the shotgun barrel prodded her between the shoulder blades, driving her forward.

"Why did you kill him?"

"He's not dead," said Dr. Tarver. "I sedated him."

True or false? "Where's Jamie?"

Tarver pointed the shotgun across the room to a hall that led to the rear of the house. "That way."

A paralyzing numbness made itself known in her lower trunk. It was spreading upward fast. She looked back at the doctor. "Are you taking me to Jamie?"

A chiding smile in the gray beard. "You're not here for a reunion."

Her palms tingled.

"Open the laundry room."

She braced herself for unendurable horror, then opened the slatted door.

Jamie was perched atop the washing machine, staring down at two black coils on the floor. It took Alex a moment to absorb the reality. The snakes were thick and short, with big triangular heads and pointed snouts. *Water moccasins—*

"Aunt Alex!" Jamie cried, his eyes flashing. "You came!"

She forced herself to grin as though everything were fine now. "I sure did, buddy." She turned back to Dr. Tarver and hissed, *"You sadist."*

Tarver chuckled. "The boy's fine. See those cases?"

He'd gestured at two large waterproof cases on the safe side of the snakes. Pelicans, Alex thought. The kind of cases engineers used to haul expensive gear around the world. The larger case was bright yellow, the other white.

"I want you to carry them to the front of the house," Tarver said. "Move it."

"I'll be back, Jamie," she promised.

Jamie nodded with complete faith, but his eyes

quickly returned to the snakes on the floor. The cases were almost too heavy for Alex to lift. As she backed out with them, she saw Dr. Tarver pick up a white croker sack with a drawstring and open it wide. Maybe he was going to bag the damned snakes for a while.

Realizing that Tarver had not followed her to the front room, she dropped the cases and rushed to Bill's gun cabinet. Behind those doors lay a wealth of firearms, but they were locked tight. She was trying to break them open when Tarver walked back into the room, dragging Jamie by one arm. Jamie screamed blue murder as he came, in the furious high-pitched voice of a ten-year-old boy. "My aunt Alex is going to blow your goddamn head off, you big ape!"

Tarver smacked the boy on the side of his head, dropping him to the floor. Jamie's screaming ceased.

Where's the shotgun? Alex wondered.

Tarver walked over to a bookshelf, reached up to a high one, and brought down an automatic pistol that Alex recognized as a Beretta from Bill's collection. Then he drew Alex's borrowed Sig-Sauer from the small of his back.

"Why are you doing this?" she asked. "Why didn't you just take off when you had the chance?"

Tarver gave her a tight smile. "I'm entering a new life today. Vanishing into another identity. And I would gladly have let you live to old age. But I'm afraid you have a clue to the road I'm taking to my new life. You may not know you have it, but you do. And if I let you live, you'll eventually remember."

With the most casual of motions, Dr. Tarver half turned and shot Bill Fennell in the head with Alex's Sig.

She jumped back in shock, but she had no time to

worry about Bill. Jamie was stirring on the floor. If he raised his head, he would see his father's ruined face. She lunged across the space between them and covered Jamie with her body.

"Perfect," said Tarver. "How's this sound? You couldn't live another minute with the idea that your nephew was under the power of your brother-in-law. You came to rescue him. Fennell resisted, so you shot him. Sadly, the boy was killed in the crossfire. I think the Bureau will want the investigation closed as quickly as possible."

"Please," Alex said to the emotionless face. "Kill me, just let him live."

Tarver shook his head. "He can't survive to tell your friends at the Bureau that he had two strangers as overnight guests last night."

She blinked in bewilderment. "Two?"

"My brother Judah."

Alex pondered this. "Is that who's driving the truck? With the boat?"

Tarver smiled. "A little makeup can do wonders. Good-bye, Alexandra. You led a merry chase."

He switched the Beretta to his right hand, then stepped back, moving the gun left and right as though selecting a target appropriate to the intended fiction. An almost irresistible rush of instinct told Alex to lift Jamie as best she could and run. She knew she would accomplish nothing, but wasn't it better to die trying? The Beretta stabilized as Tarver settled on his final target. At least Jamie was unconscious for the end. Forcing her arms under him, she struggled to lift his sagging weight. No shot came. *Why hasn't he fired?* she wondered.

Dr. Tarver had cocked his head as though straining to hear something above the sound of the storm outside. Alex found herself listening, too, first in vain, but then . . . the relentless slapping of rotor blades separated from the rain, and she knew that John Kaiser's glorious Bell 430 was dropping down over the house like the Air Cav descending on a besieged hamlet in Vietnam.

"Your plan won't work now, Doctor," she said, summoning the calm equanimity of a hostage negotiator who has nothing personal at stake in a confrontation. "You'll never sell that story now, no matter what you do. Your being here screws it all up."

Tarver stepped forward and laid the pistol barrel against her forehead. Clearly, he was not convinced. If he shot her now, Alex realized, then somehow slipped away in the storm, his tale of domestic tragedy might still play at FBI headquarters. But time was his enemy, time and the men gathering outside.

The Beretta slammed into her face with blinding force. She collapsed onto Jamie. Pounding footsteps receded, then returned. Dr. Tarver jerked her to her feet. As her vision returned, she saw he was carrying a coil of rope and a roll of duct tape. His backpack lay at his feet.

"That's FBI SWAT out there," Alex said. "You don't have a prayer of getting away."

Tarver cut a length of rope, bound Jamie's legs together, then tied him to the heavy leg of the nearby sofa. "Tell me who's in charge."

"I'm the negotiator. You talk to me."

He hit her again, this time on the bridge of the nose. A river of blood gushed over her lips and chin. Coughing blood, she dug her cell phone from her pocket and handed it over. "Speed dial four. John Kaiser."

Dr. Tarver ripped off some duct tape and bound her wrists as though he did this every day. Then he put her phone in his pocket and pulled his own cell out of the other. He pressed one button and waited. Alex knelt and hugged Jamie as best she could. The slap of beating rotors had diminished, but she could still hear them from the rear of the house. Had Kaiser landed between the tennis courts and the infinity pool? She prayed that the SWAT agents were already dispersing across the grounds.

"Edward?" Tarver said into the phone. "How close are you? . . . Ten minutes or less. Stay at altitude until I give you the final position. . . . Right."

Altitude? Alex thought. *Does Tarver have an aircraft nearby?*

Now the doctor took out Alex's cell phone, opened the clamshell, and pressed a button. "Is this Agent Kaiser? . . . Good. These are my demands. I want an FBI Suburban with its windows spray-painted black driven to the rear door of this house and left there. That's the side where your helicopter is. I want a Cessna Citation fully fueled and waiting at the Madison County Airport with one pilot and its engines running. An FBI pilot is acceptable. Don't attempt to block the driveway when we leave. Don't ask to exchange FBI agents for my hostages. The Suburban should be here in twenty minutes or less— Stop talking, Agent Kaiser, you have nothing to tell me. . . . No, I'm not going to make any threats. Listen very closely, and you'll see why. When the back door opens, do not fire. The Fennell boy will be in front of me. Remember, twenty minutes for the Suburban."

Tarver hung up the phone and shoved it deep in his pocket. Then he picked up Bill Fennell's shotgun from behind the sofa and fired it into the floor.

Jamie cringed into Alex's chest when the weapon roared.

Tarver took hold of Bill's corpse by the ankles and dragged it toward the back of the house. Alex crawled to the sofa, shoved her bound hands under it, and lifted with all her strength. She heard the back door open, then a massive grunt, which told her that Tarver was trying to lift Bill Fennell's corpse, a nearly impossible feat with dead weight. "Yank the rope loose!" she told Jamie. "Hurry."

She heard another grunt, this one like the sound of a shot-putter making a heroic heave, and then the back door slammed. Jamie had almost gotten the rope loose from the sofa leg when Tarver marched back into the room. Alex shook her head, and Jamie lay back down.

"You see why I don't make threats?" Tarver said into her cell phone. "The boy's next, Kaiser. You have nineteen minutes."

Alex saw that he'd brought a bedsheet from the laundry room, one of Grace's five-hundred-thread-count Egyptians. Tarver shook it open, then took a pair of scissors from his back pocket and cut two holes like ghost's eyes near the center of the cream-colored sheet.

"What are you doing?" Jamie asked from the floor. "Making a Halloween costume?"

Tarver laughed. "That's right, boy. And it's going to scare the hell out of some people."

He bent and cut the rope that bound Jamie to the sofa leg, then cut a longer piece and tied Jamie to his own body by tying them both around their waists. He left less than three feet of slack between them.

"Please don't do this, Doctor," Alex begged. "Send Jamie outside. I'll go with you anywhere you want to go. I'll shield you all the way out."

She might as well have been talking to a statue.

"Put on my backpack," Tarver said to Alex, pointing at the blue Kelty on the floor.

"That's where the snakes are," Jamie said quietly.

"There's more than snakes in there," Tarver said, cutting the duct tape from Alex's wrists.

She hesitated, making sure the pack was fastened shut, then carefully shouldered it. The pack was heavy, but to her relief she felt no movement inside.

"Get ready to carry those cases," Tarver said, his eyes on the front door. "Both of them."

Alex suddenly realized that Tarver had made his demands only to put Kaiser and his men at the maximum tactical disadvantage. At this moment, they would be setting up interlocking fields of fire to cover the few feet of porch space between the back door and the spot where the FBI Suburban would pull up in fifteen minutes. They were rehearsing for a scene that would never be played. And they were doing it on the wrong side of the house.

Dr. Tarver picked up Jamie as easily as he would a sack of groceries, then pulled the king-size bedsheet over both of them. Alex could no longer tell where Dr. Tarver stopped and Jamie began.

"We're going to the boathouse," Tarver said in a slightly muffled voice. "Listen to me, Alex. If you drop those cases, I'll shoot him in the head. Tell her where the gun is, Jamie."

Alex saw a jerk under the sheet.

"Under my chin," answered the small voice.

"You walk ahead of us all the way. If you jump off the pier, I'll shoot him. I know there's damn little chance of you abandoning him, but people do crazy things under stress. Remember your gray-haired friend on the porch."

Alex would never forget him. She picked up the heavy cases.

As Dr. Tarver reached for the doorknob, Alex's cell phone rang beneath the sheet. She saw movement, then Tarver said, "I assume you're calling to tell me that everything I asked for is being done, so you don't need to talk. I'm watching the clock. Good-bye." He opened the door and gestured for Alex to exit first. "Straight to the boathouse. If you slow down, Jamie's gone."

Alex set off across the grass, marching into the teeth of the rain. She tried to make out SWAT agents among the shrubs and trees, but she saw none. She started to look back, but Dr. Tarver shouted, *"Faster!"*

She was almost jogging now. Kaiser had to be panicking; Eldon Tarver had turned the tactical situation inside out. Reinforcements could not have arrived yet, so Kaiser was limited to the agents he'd brought in the chopper. He'd probably posted one or two on this side of the house, no more. Right now, they would be describing the strange parade: a baggage-laden woman leading a ghost toward the lake.

She was on the pier now. The impact of her feet echoed up from the whitecaps beneath the wood, despite the hissing patter of the rain. Barring a mistake by a nervous sniper, they would all reach the boathouse alive. Dr. Tarver had already proved that he would kill without hesitation, and even if Kaiser believed one of his men had a decent shot, he wouldn't give the fire order. From his point of view, Dr. Tarver had nowhere to run. Fifty square miles of water might seem like a lot of running room to a man with a speedboat, but when you had a Bell 430 full of SWAT agents at your command, it was nothing.

"Move your ass!" Tarver shouted from behind her.

Alex heard her cell phone ringing faintly as she ran, but Dr. Tarver didn't answer. One of his earlier phrases replayed constantly in her mind: *Stay at altitude until I give you the final position.* Who could be coming to rescue Tarver by air? A foreign intelligence service? That would be an act of war.

"Open the door!" shouted Tarver.

She'd reached the boathouse. Alex pushed through the door into fetid darkness. The gleaming white Carrera had already been lowered into the water. It rolled on the waves that crashed under the mildewed walls.

"Load the cases into the stern!" shouted Tarver. "Go!"

Alex set down the larger Pelican and climbed carefully into the pitching speedboat. She stowed the white case back near the huge twin outboard motors.

"Now the other one!"

She climbed out and retrieved the yellow case. As she stowed it, she reflected on how well-planned this escape had been. They had ordered these watertight cases long ago, preparing for an eventuality just like this one. Even if the heavily laden Pelicans went into the water, they would float, and in yellow and white, they would be highly visible from the air.

"Move up into the bow," Dr. Tarver ordered, still under the sheet with Jamie.

Alex unslung the Kelty, then walked forward to the

cushioned area where people usually sat to drink beer or sunbathe while others water-skied. A big hand shot out from beneath the sheet and jerked one of her wrists over the other.

"Hold them together!" Tarver shouted.

Two seconds later, he whipped a long strip of duct tape around her wrists. Once they were restrained, he used both hands and wrapped them so tightly that she feared they would go numb.

Her cell phone was ringing again.

This time Tarver answered. "Change of plan, Kaiser. I'm going for a cruise. If your chopper moves within three hundred meters of my boat, I'll kill the boy without hesitation."

Still under the bedsheet, Dr. Tarver got behind the wheel and cranked the Carrera's massive engines. The entire craft shook with their power. The bedsheet covered the throttle, and then the boat was moving forward, steadily gaining way as it moved out of the boathouse into the slashing rain.

The boat shuddered from the impact of waves against the bow, but as the engines gained power, the sharp craft began to leap from crest to crest. Alex tried to think clearly, but no hope came to her. Kaiser probably thought Tarver was making a fatal mistake. Alex knew better. There was a helicopter out here somewhere, waiting to swoop down and carry the doctor to freedom. She wanted to signal Kaiser—there had to be a sniper watching her through a scope—but Tarver was looking right past her through the eyeholes of his ghost costume.

As naturally as she could, she faced the windshield and hunched over as though shielding herself from the rain. She saw the Bell 430 rise above the Fennell house. It climbed and climbed, then banked and arrowed out over the lake, tracking them steadily from six hundred meters out.

When Dr. Tarver turned to look at the pursuing chopper, Alex pointed at him, then stabbed her hand skyward and twirled her finger in a wide arc to indicate the motion of a rotor. She prayed that a sniper was watching her through a scope, but even if one was, what were the chances that he'd read her signal correctly? He'd probably think she was asking for aerial rescue by the FBI chopper.

Dr. Tarver was bearing for a small island that lay a few hundred meters offshore. Only about forty meters long, it was heavily wooded. Alex remembered fishing from it once, with Jamie and her father. Could it conceal a helicopter?

Tarver gunned the throttles, and the boat began to spend more time in the air than on the water. When the little island was dead ahead, he swerved to starboard, circled to the far side, and pulled underneath some overhanging trees.

"Hit the deck!" he shouted, throwing off the bedsheet and pointing his pistol at Alex. "Do it!"

She did. Soon she heard the *whup-whup-whup* of the FBI helicopter over the Carrera's idling engines. Kaiser was moving closer. She knew he was torn between hanging back for safety's sake and fear that Dr. Tarver would execute his hostages while Kaiser stood helplessly by. The rotor noise increased. Alex couldn't make out anything through the limbs above her, but she knew Kaiser was easing still closer. Her cell phone began to ring.

"Stay down!" Tarver shouted.

Alex flattened herself between the boat seats. A

moment later, two gunshots crashed against her ears. Terrified for Jamie, she looked up and saw Dr. Tarver fire a third shot into the choppy water beside the boat.

What the hell is he doing?

Dr. Tarver crouched and opened a long, narrow compartment in the deck of the boat. It had been put there to stow skis, but Tarver pulled a high-powered rifle out of it. From the ornate engraving on the stock, Alex recognized it as another weapon from her dead brother-in-law's collection.

What happened next occurred with the terrible inevitability of nightmares. The FBI chopper dropped into sight a hundred meters from the boat. Dr. Tarver smiled, then jumped up like a hunter coming out of a duck blind and fired five shots in quick succession.

Black smoke billowed from the Bell's turbines even before the final shot struck home. The ship began to yaw wildly in the air. Alex heard an explosion, and then the chopper began dropping toward the water. Its rotors were still spinning; the pilot was using their stored energy to try to reach the surface without shattering the spines of the agents seated behind him.

"It's too fast," Alex murmured, picturing Kaiser bracing himself in the doomed craft. "Oh, God—"

The chopper slammed nose-first into the whitecaps, sending a column of spray high into the air. Mercifully, there were no more explosions. Alex stood up to look for survivors in the water, but she was thrown to the deck when the Carrera sped from beneath the trees. Tarver had his cell phone in his hand, and he was yelling over the roar of the engines.

"There's an island just east of the rendezvous! It's small and oblong. There's a downed chopper on one side. I'll be on the other. Stay clear of that chopper!"

Tarver hugged the perimeter of the island, and soon they were idling in its lee. The island shielded them from the wind, but the rain still stung Alex's face as she searched the dark sky. Jamie crouched on the deck, holding his hands over his ears as though afraid that the madman he was tied to might start firing the rifle again. Alex hunted for something she could use to cut the rope that bound them together. Jamie was an excellent swimmer, and she wouldn't hesitate to throw him overboard if she could. But there was no blade in sight.

The *whup-whup* of rotors reached her again. She froze. Was this Tarver's accomplice? Or had Kaiser summoned aerial reinforcements? The Highway Patrol and the DEA almost certainly had helicopters based in Jackson, not to mention the sheriff's departments of the surrounding counties.

She could hear the chopper descending through the black sky, but no matter how hard she tried, she couldn't see it. The rotor noise grew to a roar, and then a group of lights flashed on fifty meters above the boat. No wonder she hadn't seen the damned thing! It was dark gray, almost indistinguishable from the sky. As she watched the chopper descend, hope died within her. Dr. Tarver was talking to the pilot on his cell phone, carefully guiding him in.

The rotor blast drove her to the deck, and static electricity crackled around the boat. As Dr. Tarver shouted above the thunder, she suddenly realized why he hadn't cut the rope binding him to Jamie. With the FBI so close, simply escaping was not enough. Tarver needed insurance to guarantee his survival.

Jamie was it.

CHAPTER

54

The gray helicopter hovered next to the speedboat in the rain, so low that whitecaps were washing over its skids. A huge door slid back, opening a space big enough for a squad of marines to rappel through. At Dr. Tarver's signal a black man leaped from the helicopter into the speedboat.

"Load those cases!" the doctor shouted, pointing to the Pelicans in the stern.

While the newcomer hustled to the back of the boat, Tarver slashed the rope binding him to Jamie, then wrapped the end still tied to Jamie's waist twice around his hand like a leash. Alex got to her feet, waiting for a chance to do something, anything. Tarver jammed his pistol into his waistband, then pulled the high-powered rifle out of the ski locker and tossed it into the hovering chopper.

The black man had already loaded one case and was going back for the other. Dr. Tarver lifted Jamie into the crook of his arm, then planted his right foot on the gunwale of the boat and prepared to toss Jamie into the rocking chopper.

"Aunt Alex!" Jamie screamed, his face white with terror. "Don't let them take me!"

As Jamie flailed against Tarver, Alex lunged forward and grabbed for the pistol at the small of Tarver's back. Her fingers closed around the butt—

Then she was gazing up from the deck, the left side of her face numb. She saw a blurry image of a black man staring down at her with a gun in his hand. Sure that she was down for the count, the man made two more trips to the stern of the boat. As he stepped over Alex for the last time, the Kelty pack in his hand, she struggled onto one elbow, then to her knees. Looking over the pitching gunwale, she saw Tarver grinning from the chopper door while the black man secured the cases inside.

Jamie was nowhere in sight.

When Dr. Tarver turned away to help the loader, Alex saw the chopper pilot, and her breath caught in her throat. It was the gray-haired man who had visited Tarver's clinic yesterday. In that frozen moment, she realized he was also the army officer standing with Tarver and the blonde in the VCP photograph in Tarver's office. Then she saw Jamie strapped into a seat behind the pilot, his face a mask of fear. Alex saw the terrified eyes of Grace on her deathbed, dying with the awful knowledge that she was leaving her son in the care of a monster.

Alex looked frantically around the boat, but Dr. Tarver had left her nothing: not a flare gun, not an ax. He had even taken the key with him. When the helicopter lifted into the sky, she would be left alone in the roaring storm, and Jamie would be gone forever. She screamed from the depths of her being, a cry of utter failure and desolation.

As if on cue, the chopper dipped its nose and began to rise. Twenty feet, forty, sixty. As it rose, the pilot kept the open door facing the boat, and Alex soon saw why. Dr. Tarver had picked up the rifle and was now kneeling in the door, aiming at her chest. Some distant part of her brain screamed, *Drop!* Yet her body remained frozen. If she could not fulfill her promise to Grace, what did her own fate matter? She would watch Jamie until he disappeared, no matter what the cost. If Grace called her to account in some other world, she could at least say she had done that.

Waiting for the muzzle flash, she saw a blur of white descend in front of Dr. Tarver's face. *The bedsheet?* No, that lay discarded on the deck behind her. Then she saw Jamie, his face beside the flapping whiteness. He'd thrown his little arms around Dr. Tarver's neck. As the black man appeared in the door and grabbed for Jamie, one of those little arms jerked something tight.

A drawstring, Alex realized. *The croker sack!*

Tarver began flailing his arms, and the rifle flew out of the door. The doctor looked like a scarecrow being jerked around by a mad puppeteer. He swung back into the cabin, lurching into the pilot. The helicopter stopped ascending and began to pitch wildly in the air. Seventy feet above the lake, the chopper spun through 360 degrees. As the door came around, the yellow Pelican case flew out, followed by the black man. He turned two long somersaults in the air, then smacked the choppy surface of the lake.

When the helicopter came around the second time, Alex saw Dr. Tarver in the door again. He seized the white sack with both hands and tore it violently from his neck. A thick black rope hung from one of his cheeks. She shuddered as she realized it was one of the cottonmouths, attached to the doctor by its two-inch fangs. Tarver ripped the snake away from his face and flung it into space. The black serpent seemed to hang in the air, twisting wildly, then it fell.

As Dr. Tarver turned back to the interior, the chopper dipped fifteen feet, and Jamie shot from the open door like a cannonball. Alex screamed in horror, but as Jamie fell, she realized that his was a controlled fall. He wasn't flipping like the man who had gone before him. He was dropping straight down, feetfirst, like a schoolboy showing off at a swimming hole. He landed seventy yards from the boat, and Alex lost him in the chop.

She jumped behind the wheel, then remembered that Dr. Tarver had taken the key. Slamming her bound hands against the gunwale, she ran to the stern. Hope flooded through her. On the port side of the Carrera was an emergency trolling motor. Bill had used it to quietly propel the boat around fishing holes. A bracket allowed the electric motor to be lifted out of the water when not in use. Two cables connected it to a battery on the stern deck. Alex looked back toward the spot where Jamie had fallen. The helicopter was descending over it. Her first thought was Jamie, but then she realized they were after the fallen case.

She ran her hands along the head of the trolling motor until she found the power switch. Then she lifted the bracket so that the propeller emerged from the water and protruded just above the gunwale. She knew she could steer the boat with bound hands, but she would be useless once she reached Jamie. When she hit the start switch, the prop instantly spun into a black blur. She held her taped wrists over the whirring prop and yanked her forearms as far apart as they would go, slightly stretching the duct tape. With every molecule of her instinct rebelling, she lowered the tape onto the edge of the prop.

The ripping whine of a Weed Eater assaulted her eardrums, and a red mist filled the air. She tumbled onto the deck. The force of the prop had kicked her hands into her face, knocking her backward. But when she looked down at her bloody wrists, only a shred of tape remained intact. Yanking her arms apart, she got to her feet and thrust the spinning prop down into the water.

The speedboat slowly moved forward. Alex jumped behind the wheel and aimed the bow toward the spot where she believed Jamie had landed. Her left hand was covered with blood. The prop had gouged deep into that wrist, chewing up veins and exposing a radiant white carpal bone. She forced herself to look away. She didn't care how much blood she lost, so long as she had the strength to pull Jamie out of the water when she reached him.

Ahead and to her right, the gray helicopter had settled just above the surface of the lake. Dr. Tarver was straddling its left skid, trying desperately to pluck the heavy yellow case from the waves. Alex had reached the spot where she thought Jamie had fallen, but she saw no sign of him. Twenty meters away, Dr. Tarver heaved the yellow case into the belly of the chopper. As he did, a big wave sloshed inside the machine. Almost instantly, the chopper bellied, and another wave flung itself inside. Obviously panicked, the pilot dipped his rotors to the right, venting the water from the door and lifting the chopper six feet above the waves. This maneuver dumped Dr. Tarver into the lake.

The pilot ascended another ten feet and hovered there, as though uncertain what to do. He had Tarver's bag and cases. Did he really need the man?

Apparently so.

As Alex slowly circled in search of Jamie, the chopper settled back to the surface, low enough for Dr. Tarver to climb onto the skid and into the cabin. This time the nose tilted forward, and the chopper beat its way powerfully into the air. Fifty feet. A hundred. Higher. Alex was searching for Jamie again when the crack of rifle fire echoed over the water. Two shots . . . five. An explosion reverberated off the shore behind her. The helicopter had risen high enough for Kaiser's snipers to get an angle on it! Alex glanced up only a moment, but it was enough to see the chopper plummeting toward the lake, black smoke pouring from its engine.

Afraid that it might crash on top of her, she steered away. At the last moment the pilot flared, and the chopper hit the waves with a strange whump, not twenty-five meters from her.

She steered in ever-wider circles, trying to control her fear. What part of Jamie might she see first? A tangle of reddish hair? A silver tennis shoe?

"Jamie!" she shouted, astonished that she hadn't called out until now. *Maybe I'm in shock,* she thought, looking down at the growing pool of blood around her feet. *"Jamie! Jamie! It's Aunt Alex!"*

Nothing.

The trolling motor was maddeningly slow. She glanced to her right. Tarver's helicopter had already sunk to its engine cowling.

"Jamie!" she screamed. "Answer me!"

"Here!" shouted a weak voice. "Over here."

That wasn't Jamie. It was either Tarver or his pilot. Then she saw the doctor's bald head moving through the water with surprising speed. He disappeared behind a wave, then shouted again.

"I have him, Alex! Jamie's over here. Help us!"

She knew it was probably a trick, that Dr. Tarver might still have a gun, but she had to be sure that he hadn't found Jamie. Ducking behind the gunwale, she slowly turned the blood-slickened wheel, taking the Carrera in a wide circle that would carry her nearer the doctor. Seconds later, her heart thumped her sternum, and her pulse began to race. Jamie was floating faceup in the heaving waves, and Tarver was swimming toward him. He would reach Jamie long before Alex could get there with the boat.

Instead of veering toward them, Alex continued her circle, which carried her out of Dr. Tarver's line of sight. A rush of instinct so powerful that she could not ignore it told her that Eldon Tarver was about to enter her element. For six weeks she had been playing catch-up, following cold clues that led nowhere. Even after she'd gotten the doctor in her sights, he had always been three steps ahead. But this would be different.

This was a negotiation.

As the boat circled, she ran to the stern and searched for the fuel line. *There.* A transparent hose no bigger than her little finger. The aorta of a human was hardly bigger, and this was the main artery of the boat. She yanked it loose, and gasoline began running onto the stern deck. She went back to the wheel and steered toward Dr. Tarver, who was now holding Jamie in a lifeguard's cross-chest carry. The boy appeared to be unconscious. When Alex was thirty feet away, she ran back to the stern and switched off the trolling motor.

"Let's talk!" shouted Tarver. "We don't have much time."

As she moved back to the bow, a memory flashed into Alex's head. She saw Bill Fennell on the Fourth of July, yanking up a seat cushion to get at some tools. She stopped, tucked her fingers under that same seat, and pulled. The seat cushion popped free. In the small compartment below, she saw a screwdriver, a roll of electrical tape, a set of Allen wrenches, and some copper wire. No knife. No flare gun. *Shit*—

"What are you doing?" shouted Tarver. "I want to make a deal."

"I'm hurt!" Alex yelled back. "Bleeding bad . . . hang on."

She pulled off her soaked shirt and wrapped it tightly around her mangled wrist. Then she took the screwdriver from the compartment and slid it underneath the makeshift bandage.

"I want the boat!" Tarver shouted.

Alex looked up. The boat had drifted closer to the doctor. She ducked below the gunwale. "I want Jamie!"

Tarver stroked nearer, holding Jamie's head above the water. "Then I'd say we have a deal."

She shook her head. "You have a gun. I know you do."

"I lost it in the crash."

Alex shook her head again. "No gun, no boat!"

Dr. Tarver's right hand stopped treading water, dipped under the surface, then reappeared holding an automatic.

"Throw it away!" Alex yelled.

She saw rage in his eyes, but he threw the gun into the waves.

"Get out of the boat!" he bellowed. "I have the key. When you're out, I'll swim to the transom and get in."

"No!" cried Alex. "Swim away from Jamie first."

"He'll sink."

She turned and snatched up a life ring, one of the few things Tarver had left in the boat. She tossed it to him. "Put that under his arms, then swim away."

Seeing no alternative, Dr. Tarver struggled to push Jamie's body into the life ring. As he worked, Alex saw that the dark purple mark on the left side of his face was not his deformity as she had thought, but the livid swelling of a snakebite.

"All right!" Dr. Tarver shouted.

"Swim away!"

Obviously reluctant to give up his leverage, Dr. Tarver released Jamie and swam quickly toward the stern of the boat.

"Jump out!" he shouted.

Still suspicious, Alex pulled off her shoes and stripped off her jeans. Wet jeans could quickly drown you in water like this. She climbed onto the gunwale and dropped into the cold water. As she breaststroked toward Jamie, she sensed movement to her left. Dr. Tarver had not climbed into the boat. He was kicking toward Jamie again. She started to swim freestyle, but Tarver still got there first. As Alex stared in disbelief, he put his big hand on top of Jamie's head and shoved him right through the life ring, deep under the water.

"Save him now," he snarled.

Alex couldn't see Jamie, but he didn't appear to be

struggling. Dr. Tarver held him under as easily as he might an infant. She thought of pulling out the screwdriver, but that was no solution. She'd never overpower Tarver face-to-face.

The answer struck her with the force of revelation. As she dove beneath the waves, her father's voice echoed in her head: *When your back's against the wall, do the unexpected. That's how you stay alive.* She kicked deeper, deeper, until she was fifteen feet below the surface. Then she opened her eyes and looked up. All she could make out was a dark blur against the gray surface. As she floated slowly upward, a tentacle of darkness swept past her eyes. She grabbed it.

It was an ankle—the smooth ankle of a boy.

Knowing that Tarver was braced for a fight, she expelled all the air from her lungs and jerked the ankle straight down, then swam toward the bottom with all her strength. With a rush of joy, she felt Jamie's body come with her. After a few seconds of kicking, she started trying to tow him laterally, but her oxygen was disappearing fast. She had to surface.

As she kicked upward, she saw a splash above, then a black shape sweeping down toward her, trailing bubbles. Switching Jamie's ankle to her left hand, she drew the screwdriver from her "bandage" and waited. When the shadow reached for her, she kicked upward and stabbed with savage force.

The tool struck something, but the shadow didn't stop. A powerful hand seized her throat. Alex flung her arm wide and stabbed from the side. An explosion of bubbles enveloped her. Tarver's big body thrashed like a wounded shark's, and then his hand let go. Hope surged through her, urging her to a final blow. She yanked back on the handle of her weapon, but the screwdriver wouldn't pull free.

Terrified that she'd lose Jamie, she released the tool and tried to swim clear, but now her air was truly gone. Lungs burning, she grabbed Jamie beneath both arms and kicked for the gray light above.

She broke through the waves and saw the boat bobbing fifteen meters away. She was shifting Jamie to a lifeguard's carry when Dr. Tarver surfaced directly in front of her. His eyes shone like those of a man in the grip of a religious vision, but something about his mouth was wrong. It sagged the way Grace's had after her stroke. Alex had no idea how to keep hold of Jamie and fight Tarver in the waves, nor had she the strength to do it. But when Tarver's hand rose from the water, it did not reach for her. The hand was open, and it moved to the side of his head, as though searching for a wound. Alex and the doctor understood the horror of his plight at the same moment: the handle of the screwdriver protruded from Tarver's left ear, where the metal shaft had been buried to the hilt.

Tarver's eyes widened as his hand closed around the handle. He seemed about to jerk the screwdriver free, but then some flicker of knowledge overrode his instinct. His hand dropped into the water, and he looked over his shoulder. With a last wild look into Alex's eyes, he turned and began swimming awkwardly toward the boat.

Alex turned in the water and started kicking toward the island. It appeared to be fifty or sixty meters away, not a difficult swim under normal conditions, but now potentially lethal. Her burning lungs and blurred vision told her she'd lost more blood than she knew. Still, she kicked on through the battering waves. Forty meters. Thirty. Her leaden limbs began to sink. Jamie's face was blue, but she could no longer kick. She knew then that they might die within a few meters of the shore.

An image of Grace rose into her mind, and then her father. Then her mother lying unconscious in the hospital. *We're the last,* she thought helplessly. *Jamie and me.* She tried to kick, but there was nothing left. She kissed Jamie's cheek and prayed for the strength to hold his head above the surface while she drowned.

Her mouth was full of water when she heard a male voice barking orders. *Kaiser?* She shoved Jamie higher, trying to kick with dead legs. Then a powerful arm swept around her, propelling them both toward shore. Someone dragged Jamie from her arms. She was dimly aware of someone counting chest compressions. A blessedly warm hand touched her face, and she opened her eyes. John Kaiser knelt above her, looking anxiously into her face.

"Can you hear me, Alex?"

She nodded.

"Is there anyone else in the boat?"

She shook her head. "Jamie," she gasped. "Is he alive?"

As if in answer, there was a fit of coughing beside her, then the sound of a boy crying.

"Disable the boat!" shouted Kaiser, getting to his feet. "Fire at the engine!"

"No," Alex cried, remembering the disconnected fuel line, which from the roar of the engines, Tarver must have reconnected.

Her cry was drowned by the crack of rifle fire.

She rose onto her elbow and tried to shout. "Stop . . . the fuel—"

"What?" called Kaiser, moving back to her.

But the rifle cracked again, and the stern of the fleeing Carrera erupted into flame. A figure leaped onto the starboard gunwale, but before it could jump clear, the speedboat blew apart.

Alex collapsed in the mud, rain falling steadily on her face. She tried to explain about the Pelican cases, but her voice was lost in the squawk of radios, Kaiser's barked orders, and shouts about a man in the water. The pilot of the doctor's helicopter? None of it mattered now. She rolled onto her side and saw Jamie lying beside her, staring at her with wide eyes. But it was Grace looking out through those eyes—and no longer with despair. When Jamie held out a shivering hand, Alex pulled him to her, burying his face in her chest.

She had kept her promise at last.

EPILOGUE

Two Weeks Later

Alex slowed the Corolla and told Jamie to watch for a gravel road on the left. They were driving down a deserted gray road through an endless tunnel of oak trees.

"Are you sure you know where you're going?" asked Jamie.

"I think so. It wasn't that long ago that I was here. I stood with him on that big bridge we just went over."

Jamie took off his seat belt, got onto his knees on the seat, and propped his elbow on the terra-cotta jar between them.

"Careful," said Alex.

"Sorry." Jamie leaned forward and pressed his forehead against the windshield. "I think I see it. Is that a road?"

"It is. Eagle eyes."

Jamie was staring anxiously at the narrow gap in the trees. "Man, it's dark in there."

Alex slowed to a stop, then turned left onto deeply rutted gravel. "Chris told me that bad outlaws used to hide out on this road."

"When?" asked Jamie. "A long time ago? Or like now?"

The car jounced so hard that his head hit the roof. "Ow!"

"Sorry," said Alex. "Like two hundred years ago."

"Oh." Jamie had lost all interest.

Alex almost regretted coming. The washed-out road was virtually impassable without a four-wheel drive. After fifty yards, she had to give up and park, unsure how she would ever get back to the Trace proper.

"Come on," she said. "From here we walk."

Jamie looked surprised, but he got out. Alex lifted the clay jar off the seat, locked the door, and led Jamie along the gravel road that quickly turned to sand. The air was close and muggy, and horseflies dived around their faces, thirsty for blood.

"This sucks," said Jamie. "I don't think there's anything down here."

"Have a little faith, huh? You're a tough guy."

She walked a few more yards, then stopped, listening. "Do you hear that?"

Jamie stopped, too. "What's that sound?"

Alex smiled. "Water."

She broke into a trot, and Jamie ran alongside her. A moment later they broke out of the trees into bright sunlight that flashed like diamonds from the surface of a broad, clear stream.

"Hey!" called a male voice. "We thought you'd given up."

Alex shielded her eyes against the sun and looked

down the course of the stream. A hundred feet away, Chris and Ben Shepard sat on a fallen log facing a small campfire. The smell of cooking meat drifted on the wind. Jamie yelped and started sprinting across the sand. Alex followed more slowly.

By the time she reached the fire, Ben and Jamie had charged into the creek and were splashing fifty yards downstream, searching for arrowheads and dinosaur bones. Chris got up and gave her a welcoming hug.

"What's in the jar?" he asked, smiling.

She pulled off the clay lid and lifted out a bottle of chilled white wine. "My contribution," she said. "Raising the tone a little bit."

Chris laughed and took the bottle. "I hope you brought a corkscrew."

She smiled. "Screw-off cap."

He did the honors, then filled two styrofoam cups. They sat on the log a few feet apart and sipped slowly.

"How's Ben doing?" she asked at length.

Chris looked down the creek. "He has some bad nights. He's sleeping with me for now. But overall, he's doing really well."

"I'm glad."

Chris looked at her. "I think Ben knew Thora better than I did."

Alex had suspected this from the start. "Children see what's there, not what we pretend to be."

"What about Jamie?"

She smiled. "He's much better. I think he misses Will Kilmer more than he misses his father. Will makes him think of his grandfather. My dad."

Chris picked up a stick and poked the fire.

"How are *you* doing?" Alex asked.

"Physically? Or otherwise?"

"Both."

"Not too bad, physically. I'm still having some strange symptoms, but Pete Connolly thinks it's a reaction to the antidote drug. Dr. Tarver's notes mention similar reactions in some of the patients at his free clinic."

Alex had not been made privy to all the details of Dr. Tarver's work. Chris had been treated by an army doctor authorized to administer injections taken from one of the vials in Dr. Tarver's captured Pelican cases. That vial represented Chris's only hope for neutralizing the cancer-causing virus that Tarver had injected into him. FBI director Roberts had repeatedly assured her that Dr. Tarver's notes had been studied intensively by some of the best virologists in the country, and that they felt confident Chris would recover without a trace of the virus in his system. That was easy for Director Roberts to say, of course; he wasn't the one who had been injected. But Chris had been given more technical information than she, and he seemed confident that he would recover his health in time.

Alex held up her glass in a silent toast. He touched hers, and they drank.

"What about otherwise?" Alex asked softly.

"Day by day. Penn Cage has helped me a lot."

"How so?"

"He lost his wife to cancer when he was thirty-seven. Ben and Annie have become good friends. I think she helps him a lot with his 'Why me?' issues."

"I could use some help with those sometimes," Alex confessed.

"Yeah." Chris leaned over and refilled her cup. "How's the custody thing coming?"

"Jamie's mine, no doubt. The judge upheld the clause in the original will. I'm Jamie's godmother, and the will made it clear that if both Grace and Bill died, I should raise Jamie. So that's that."

"Have you thought any more about where you're going to go?"

"The director offered me Washington again."

"As a hostage negotiator?"

Alex nodded. "My old job back."

"That's what you wanted, isn't it?"

"I thought it was. But a couple of days ago, I got another offer."

Chris's eyes narrowed. "What?"

"The SAC in New Orleans asked if I could be assigned to his office in the same capacity."

Chris raised his eyebrows. "Is John Kaiser behind that?"

She nodded. "I think Kaiser has a lot of influence down there. Anyway, there's a lot happening in New Orleans now. Crime is really out of hand."

"Sounds like a great place to raise a kid."

Alex smiled ruefully. "I know. Kaiser and Jordan live across Lake Pontchartrain, though. It's really nice over there. And it's the South, you know? I think it's time for me to come back home."

Chris was looking steadily at her. "I think you're right."

She looked back at him for a while, then reached into her pocket and brought out a small plastic case.

"What's that?" he asked.

"It's the original MiniDV of Thora and Lansing on the balcony."

Chris scowled and shook his head. "Why'd you bring it here?"

"Not to upset you. It was in Will's things, but I figure it's yours."

Chris was staring into the fire again.

"I thought you might want to pay Shane Lansing back."

Chris reached out for the tape. She handed it to him.

"Lansing's a bastard," he said. "But he's got four kids. If he makes a hell of his own life, so be it. I won't be the one to break up his family."

Chris dropped the tape into the fire. As the plastic melted, a harsh toxic odor rose from the flames. They stood and moved a few steps away.

"Leave the past in the past?" Alex asked.

He nodded, his eyes on hers. "You could try that, too, you know?"

Without warning, he raised his fingers to her face and touched the cluster of scars around her right eye. Alex flinched and started to pull back, but something steadied her, and she endured it.

"You hated Thora's beauty, didn't you?" he said softly, his fingers exploring the discolored flesh.

Shivering within, she nodded without speaking.

"Thora was perfect on the outside," Chris said. "But inside . . . she was ugly. Selfish and cruel."

"That doesn't make this easier."

He looked down into her face. "You must know those scars don't matter."

She smiled wistfully. "But they do. I know, because there was a time when I didn't have them. And people treated me differently."

He leaned forward and pressed his lips to the worst scar, a purplish ridge of tissue beneath her temple. "Like this?"

So deeply was Alex moved that she felt driven to turn away, but Chris held her in place. "I asked you a question," he said.

"Maybe," she whispered, covering her mouth with a shaking hand. "Something like that."

A high-pitched scream echoed over the water. They both looked downstream. Ben and Jamie were racing up the creek, splashing water high above their heads as they drew near. Jamie's right arm was held high, and Ben was pointing at it as they ran.

"I think they've found something," Chris said.

"Looks like it."

Chris let his hand fall, then took her hand in his and led her across the warm sand. "Let's go see what it is."

Alex wiped her eyes with her free hand and followed him into the cool, clear water.

ACKNOWLEDGMENTS

As always, I am indebted to many individuals for their help in the writing of this novel. I am constantly amazed and gratified to see how generous people are with their time when they know they are contributing to a creative enterprise

First and foremost, I thank the physicians who gave of their time: Joe Files, MD, Rod Givens, MD, Tom Carey, MD, Jerry Iles, MD.

No reader should infer that the Medical Center in the novel is based on the University of Mississippi Medical Center. I did not visit the actual Cancer Institute there until my first draft was completed, specifically to minimize any accidental similarities that might occur. Anyone familiar with the real UMC will see that I have created a fictional hospital with a fictional staff. That said, I want all readers to know that Dr. Files and his colleagues have built a world-class facility in Jackson, especially as regards their bone marrow transplant unit. I urge all Mississippians, and all Americans concerned with providing healthcare to some of our nation's most disadvantaged citizens, to support the UMC Cancer Institute with their dollars. You could not find a worthier cause.

Second, many friends have supplied expertise that helped a great deal with this book. Mike MacInnis, a fine lawyer and great friend from my college days, helped in a pinch. Also Lee Jones, Clinton Heard, Kent Hudson, Betty Iles, Nancy Hungerford, and Curtis Moroney.

For his help in all stages of the process, my good friend and former editor, Ed Stackler.

My appreciation also to the professionals in the chain, primarily for seeing my books as more than business: Aaron Priest, Susan Moldow, and Louise Burke. Special thanks to my editor, Colin Harrison, for knowing what a writer needs, being one himself. Also to Karen Thompson, who brought equanimity to the job of interfacing with my frantic working habits. Finally, my deep appreciation to artist and designer John Fulbrook, who worked heroically through many jacket ideas, for actually giving a damn and being willing to go the extra mile for something good. Thanks also to Eileen Hutton at Brilliance Audio for her generous support of Trinity Episcopal Day School.

For their help with the remarkable and exciting cover shoot of a rather irritated cottonmouth water moccasin: Ben Hillyer (photographer), Keith Benoist (snake wrangler), Terry Vandeventer (herpetologist), Amanda Hargrove (bed provider), Melissa Morrison (decor), Jane Hargrove (beer and food and reminding us that "YOU'RE TOO CLOSE TO THE SNAKE!").

At least one mistake of fact finds its way into each of my books, and some have more. The above experts are absolved of everything. All mistakes are mine.